Nora Roberts is the number one *New York Times* bestseller of more than 200 novels. With over 500 million copies of her books in print, she is indisputably one of the most celebrated and popular writers in the world. She is both a *Sunday Times* bestseller in the UK and a number one bestseller in Australia.

D0543523

By Nora Roberts

Many of Nora Roberts' other titles are now available in eBook and she is also the author of the In Death series using the pseudonym J.D. Robb.

NORA ROBERTS

Honest Illusions

piatkus

PIATKUS

First published in Great Britain in 2016 by Piatkus
First published in the United States by G. P. Putnam and Sons in 1992
Mass-market edition published in the United States by Jove in 1993
Trade paperback edition published in the United States by Berkley in 2002
French flap edition published in the United States by Berkley in 2010
This edition published in 2020 by Piatkus

1 3 5 7 9 10 8 6 4 2

Copyright © 1992 by Nora Roberts

The moral right of the author has been asserted.

*All characters and events in this publication, other than those
clearly in the public domain, are fictitious and any resemblance
to real persons, living or dead, is purely coincidental.*

All rights reserved.
No part of this publication may be reproduced, stored in a
retrieval system, or transmitted, in any form, or by any means, without
the prior permission in writing of the publisher, nor be otherwise circulated
in any form of binding or cover other than that in which it is published
and without a similar condition including this condition being
imposed on the subsequent purchaser.

A CIP catalogue record for this book
is available from the British Library.

ISBN 978-0-349-40808-8

Printed and bound in Great Britain by Clays Ltd, Elcograf S.p.A.

Papers used by Piatkus are from well-managed forests
and other responsible sources.

MIX
Paper from
responsible sources
FSC
www.fsc.org   FSC® C104740

Piatkus
An imprint of
Little, Brown Book Group
Carmelite House
50 Victoria Embankment
London EC4Y 0DZ

An Hachette UK Company
www.hachette.co.uk

www.littlebrown.co.uk

To Bruce, Dan and Jason,
the magic in my life

PART ONE

O brave new world,
That has such people in't!

—William Shakespeare

Prologue

THE LADY VANISHES. IT WAS AN OLD ILLUSION, GIVEN A modern twist, and never failed to leave the audience gasping. The glittery crowd at Radio City was as eager to be duped as a group of slack-jawed rubes at a dog and pony show.

Even as Roxanne stepped onto the glass pedestal she could feel their anticipation—the silvery edge of it that was a merging of hope and doubt glued together with wonder. Those inching forward in their seats ranged from president to peon.

Magic made equals of them all.

Max had said that, she recalled. Many, many times.

Amid the swirl of mist and the flash of light, the pedestal slowly ascended, circling majestically to the tune of Gershwin's *Rhapsody in Blue*. The gentle three-hundred-and-sixty-degree revolution showed the crowd all sides of the ice-clear pedestal and the slender woman atop it—and distracted them from the trickery at hand.

Presentation, she'd been taught, was often the slim difference between a charlatan and an artist.

In keeping with the theme of the music, Roxanne wore a sparkling gown of midnight blue that clung to her long, willowy

3

form—clung so closely that no one studying her would believe there was anything under the spangled silk but her own flesh. Her hair, a waterfall of flame curling to her waist, twinkled with thousands of tiny iridescent stars.

Fire and ice. More than one man had wondered how one woman could be both at the same time.

As in sleep or a trance, her eyes were closed—or seemed to be—and her elegant face was lifted toward the star-pricked ceiling of the stage.

As she rose, she let her arms sway to the music, then held them high above her head, for showmanship and for the practical necessity that underscores all magic.

It was a beautiful illusion, she knew. The mist, the lights, the music, the woman. She enjoyed the sheer drama of it, and was not above being amused by the irony of using the age-old symbol of the lone, lovely woman placed on a pedestal, above the common worry and toils of man.

It was also a miserably complex bit of business, requiring a great deal of physical control and split-second timing. But not even those fortunate enough to be seated in the first row could detect the intense concentration in her serene face. None of them could know how many tedious hours she had put in, perfecting every aspect of the act on paper, then in practice. Unrelenting practice.

Slowly, again to Gershwin's rhythm, her body began to turn, dip, sway. A partnerless dance ten feet above stage, all color and fluid movement. There were murmurs from the audience, scattered applause.

They could see her—yes, they could see her through the blue-tinted mist and spinning lights. The glitter of the dark gown, the flow of flame-colored hair, the gleam of that alabaster skin.

Then, in a breath, in a gasp, they could not. In less time than it takes to blink an eye, she was gone. In her place was a sleek Bengal tiger who reared on his hind legs to paw the air and roar.

There was a pause, that most satisfying of pauses to an

4

entertainer where an audience held its stunned collective breath before the applause thundered, echoing as the pedestal descended once more. The big cat leaped down to stalk stage right. He stopped by an ebony box, sent up another roar that had a woman in the front row giggling nervously. As one, the four sides of the box collapsed.

And there was Roxanne, dressed not in shimmery blue but in a silver cat suit. She took her bows as she'd been taught almost from birth. With a flourish.

As the sound of success continued to pound in her ears, she mounted the tiger and rode the beast offstage.

"Nice work, Oscar." With a little sigh, she bent forward to scratch the cat between the ears.

"You looked real pretty, Roxy." Her big, burly assistant clipped a leash to Oscar's spangled collar.

"Thanks, Mouse." Dismounting, she tossed her hair back. The backstage area was already hopping. Those trusted to do so would secure her equipment and guard it from prying eyes. Since she'd scheduled a press conference for the following day, she would see no reporters now. Roxanne had high hopes for a bottle of iced champagne and a stingingly hot whirlpool bath.

Alone.

Absently she rubbed her hands together—an old habit Mouse could have told her she'd picked up from her father.

"I've got the fidgets," she said with a half laugh. "Had them all damn night. It feels like someone's breathing down my neck."

"Well, ah ... " Mouse stood where he was, letting Oscar rub against his knees. Never articulate under the best of circumstances, Mouse fumbled for the best way to phrase the news. "You got company, Roxy. In the dressing room."

"Oh?" Her brows drew together, forming the faint line of impatience between them. "Who?"

"Take another bow, honey." Lily, Roxanne's onstage assistant and surrogate mother, swept over to grab her arm. "You brought down the house." Lily dabbed a handkerchief around the false eyelashes she wore onstage and off. "Max would be so proud."

The quick twist in Roxanne's gut had her willing away her own tears. They didn't show. They were never permitted to show in public. She started forward, moving into the swell of applause. "Who's waiting for me?" she called over her shoulder, but Mouse was already leading the big cat away.

He'd been taught by the master that discretion was the better part of survival.

Ten minutes later, flushed with success, Roxanne opened the door of her dressing room. The scent hit her first—roses and greasepaint. That mix of fragrances had become so familiar she breathed it in like fresh air. But there was another scent here—the sting of rich tobacco. Elegant, exotic, French. Her hand trembled once on the knob as she pushed the door fully open.

There was one man she would forever associate with that aroma. One man she knew who habitually smoked slim French cigars.

She said nothing when she saw him. Could say nothing as he rose from a chair where he'd been enjoying his cigar and her champagne. Oh, God, it was thrilling and horrible to watch that wonderful mouth quirk in that very familiar grin, to meet those impossibly blue eyes with her own.

His hair was still long, a mane of ebony waving back from his face. Even as a child he'd been gorgeous, an elegant gypsy with eyes that could freeze or burn. Age had only enhanced his looks, fining down that compelling face, the long bones and shadowy hollows, the faint cleft in the chin. Beyond the physical, there was a drama that shivered around him like an aura.

He was a man women shuddered over and wanted.

She had. Oh, she had.

Five years had passed since she'd seen that smile, since she'd run her hands through that thick hair or felt the searing pressure of that clever mouth. Five years to mourn, to weep and to hate.

Why wasn't he dead? she wondered as she forced herself to close the door at her back. Why hadn't he had the decency to succumb to any of the varied and gruesome tragedies she'd imagined for him?

And what in God's name was she going to do with this terrible yearning she felt just looking at him again?

"Roxanne." Training kept Luke's voice steady as he said her name. He'd watched her over the years. Tonight he'd studied her every move from the shadows of the wings. Judging, weighing. Wanting. But here, now, face-to-face, she was almost too beautiful to bear. "It was a good show. The finale was spectacular."

"Thank you."

His hand was steady as he poured her a flute of champagne, as hers was when she accepted it. They were, after all, showmen, cast in an odd way from the same mold. Max's mold.

"I'm sorry about Max."

Her eyes went flat. "Are you?"

Because Luke felt he deserved more than the slash of sarcasm, he merely nodded, then glanced down at his bubbling wine, remembering. His mouth curved when he looked back at her. "The Calais job, the rubies. Was that yours?"

She sipped, the silver sparkling on her shoulders as she moved them in a careless shrug. "Of course."

"Ah." He nodded again, pleased. He had to be sure she hadn't lost her touch—for magic or for larceny. "I heard rumors that a first edition of Poe's *House of Usher* was lifted from a vault in London."

"Your hearing was always good, Callahan."

He continued to smile, wondering when she'd learned to exude sex like breath. He remembered the clever child, the coltish adolescent, the irresistible bloom of the young woman. The bloom had blossomed seductively. And he could feel the pull that had always been between them. He would use it now, with regret, but he would use it to gain his own ends.

The end justifies everything. Another of Maximillian Nouvelle's maxims.

7

"I have a proposition for you, Rox."

"Really?" She took a last sip before setting her glass aside. The bubbles were bitter on her tongue.

"Business," he said lightly, tapping out the stub of his cigar. Taking her hand, he brought her fingers to his lips. "And personal. I've missed you, Roxanne." It was the truest statement he could make. One flash of sterling honesty in years of tricks, illusions and pretense. Caught up in his own feelings, he missed the warning flash in her eyes.

"Have you, Luke? Have you really?"

"More than I can tell you." Swamped by memories and needs, he drew her closer, felt his blood begin to pump as her body brushed his. She'd always been the one. No matter how many escapes he'd accomplished, he'd never freed himself from the trap in which Roxanne Nouvelle had caught him. "Come back to my hotel." His breath whispered over her face as she went fluidly into his arms. "We'll have a late supper. Talk."

"Talk?" Her arms wound sinuously around him. Her rings flashed as she dipped her fingers into his hair. Beside them the makeup mirror over her dressing table reflected them in triplicate. As if showing them past, present, future. When she spoke, her voice was like the mist she'd vanished into. Dark and rich and mysterious. "Is that what you want to do with me, Luke?"

He forgot the importance of control, forgot everything but the fact that her mouth was an inch from his. The taste he'd once gorged on was a wish away. "No."

He dropped his head toward hers. Then his breath exploded as her knee shot up between his legs. Even as he was doubling over, she slammed her fist onto his chin.

His grunt of surprise, and the splintering of wood from the table he smashed on his way down gave Roxanne enormous satisfaction. Roses flew, water splashed. A few slender buds drifted over him as he lay on the dampening carpet.

"You . . . " Scowling, he dragged a rose from his hair. The brat had always been sneaky, he remembered. "You're quicker than you used to be, Rox."

Hands on her hips, she stood over him, a slim, silver warrior who'd never learned to sample her revenge cold. "I'm a lot of things I didn't used to be." Her knuckles hurt like fire, but she used that pain to block another, deeper ache. "Now, you lying Irish bastard, crawl back into whatever hole you dug for yourself five years ago. Come near me again, and I swear, I'll make you disappear for good."

Delighted with her exit line, she turned on her heel, then let out a shriek when Luke snagged her ankle. She went down hard on her rump and before she could put nails and teeth to use, he had her pinned. She'd forgotten how strong and how quick he was.

A miscalculation, Max would have said. And miscalculations were the root of all failures.

"Okay, Rox, we can talk here." Though he was breathless and still in pain, he grinned. "Your choice."

"I'll see you in hell—"

"Very likely." His grin faded. "Damn it, Roxy, I never could resist you." When he crushed his mouth to hers, he tossed them both back into the past.

Chapter One

1973, Near Portland, Maine

"HUR-RY, HUR-RY, STEP RIGHT UP. BE AMAZED, BE ASTOUNDED. Watch the Great Nouvelle defy the laws of nature. For one small dollar, see him make cards dance in midair. Before your eyes, right before your astonished eyes, see a beautiful woman sawed in two."

While the barker ran through his spiel, Luke Callahan slithered through the carnival crowd, busily picking pockets. He had quick hands, agile fingers and that most important asset of a successful thief, a complete lack of conscience.

He was twelve.

For nearly six weeks he'd been on the road, on the run. Luke had big plans to head south before the steamy New England summer became a frigid New England winter.

He wasn't going to get very far with pickings like this, he thought and nipped a billfold from the sagging overalls pocket. There weren't many of those who had come to ride the Tilt-a-Whirl or challenge the Wheel of Fortune who had more than a few creased dollars on them.

Now, when he got to Miami, things would be different. In the shadows behind the milk bottle toss, he discarded the imitation leather wallet and counted his take for the evening.

Twenty-eight dollars. Pathetic.

But in Miami, that land of sun, fun and high rollers, he'd clean house. All he had to do was get there first, and so far he'd managed to squirrel away nearly two hundred dollars. A little more and he'd be able to afford to take the bus at least part of the way. A Greyhound, he thought with a quick grin. He'd leave the driving to them, all right, and take a break from hitching rides with stoned-out hippies and fat-fingered perverts.

A runaway couldn't be choosy about his mode of transportation. Luke was already aware that a ride from an upstanding citizen could lead to a police report or—nearly as bad—a lecture on the dangers of a young boy leaving home.

It was no use telling anyone that home was much more dangerous than the perils of the road.

After flipping off two singles, Luke tucked the rest of his take into his battered chukkas. He needed food. The smell of hot grease had been tantalizing his stomach for nearly an hour. He'd reward himself with an overcooked burger and fries, and wash it all down with some fresh lemonade.

Like most twelve-year-old boys, Luke would have enjoyed a ride on the Whip, but if there was a longing in him toward the spinning lights, he covered it with a sneer. Jerks thought they were having an adventure, he mused while sour grapes stuck in his throat. They'd be tucked in their beds tonight while he slept under the stars and when they woke up Mommy and Daddy would tell them what to do and how to do it.

No one would tell him any of those things ever again.

Feeling superior in every way, he tucked his thumbs in the front pockets of his jeans and strutted toward the concession stands.

He passed the poster again—the larger-than-life-sized picture of the magician. The Great Nouvelle, with his sweep of black hair, flowing moustache, his hypnotic dark eyes. Every time Luke looked at the poster he felt himself being pulled toward something he couldn't understand.

The eyes in the picture seemed to look right into him, as if they could see and understand much too much about Luke Callahan, late of Bangor, Maine, by way of Burlington and Utica and Christ knew where because Luke had forgotten.

He almost expected the painted mouth to speak and the hand that held the fan of cards to shoot out, snatch him by the throat and pull him right inside that poster. He'd be trapped there forever, beating on the other side of that pasteboard the way he'd beat on so many of the locked doors of his childhood.

Because the idea gave him the willies, Luke curled his lip. "Magic's bunk," he said, but he said it in a whisper. And his heart pounded hard as he dared the painted face to challenge him. "Big deal," he went on, gaining confidence. "Pulling stupid rabbits out of stupid hats and doing a few dumbass card tricks."

He wanted to see those dumbass tricks more than he wanted to ride on the Whip. More even than he wanted to stuff his mouth with ketchup-dripping fries. Luke wavered, fingering one of the dollars in his pocket.

It would be worth a buck, he decided, just to prove to himself that the magician was no big deal. It would be worth a buck to sit down. In the dark, he mused as he drew out the crumpled bill and paid the price. There were bound to be a few pockets he could slip his nimble fingers into.

The heavy canvas flap swung shut behind him and blocked out most of the light and air from the midway. Noise battered against it like rainfall. People were already crowded on the low wooden seats, murmuring among themselves, shifting and waving paper fans against the stifling heat.

He stood in the back a moment, scanning. With an instinct that had been honed sharp as a switchblade over the past six weeks, he skipped over a huddle of kids, crossed off a few couples as being too poor to net him anything but his admission price and cagily chose his marks. The situation called for him to look to women, as most of the men would be sitting on their money.

"Excuse me," he said, polite as a Boy Scout, as he squeezed in behind a grandmotherly type who seemed distracted by the antics of the boy and girl on either side of her.

The moment he was settled, the Great Nouvelle took the stage. He was dressed in full formal gear. The black tux and starched white shirt looked exotic in the heat-drenched tent. His shoes gleamed with polish. On the pinkie of his left hand he wore a gold ring with a black center stone that winked in the stage lights.

The impression of greatness was set the moment he faced his audience.

The magician said nothing, yet the tent filled with his presence, swelled with it. He was every bit as dramatic as his poster, though the black hair was shot with glints of silver. The Great Nouvelle lifted his hands, held them palm out toward the audience. With a flick of his wrist, his spread, empty fingers held a coin. Another flick, another coin, and another, until the wide vee's of his fingers were filled with the gleam of gold.

Luke's attention was snagged enough for him to lean forward, eyes narrowed. He wanted to know how it was done. It was a trick, of course. He was all too aware the world was full of them. He'd already stopped wondering why, but he hadn't stopped wondering how.

The coins became colored balls that changed size and hue. They multiplied, subtracted, appeared and vanished while the audience applauded.

Pulling his eyes from the show was difficult. Lifting six dollars from Grandma's purse was easy. After tucking his take away, Luke slid out of his seat to move into position behind a blonde whose straw purse was sitting carelessly on the floor beside her.

As the sleight of hand warmed up the audience, Luke pocketed another four dollars. But he kept losing his concentration. Telling himself he'd wait before hitting the fat lady to his right, he settled down to watch.

For the next few moments, Luke was only a child, his eyes wide with amazement as the magician fanned the cards, passed his hand over their tops and his other hand over the bottoms so that the spread deck hung suspended in the air. At a stylish movement of his hands, the cards swayed, dipped, turned. The audience cheered, wholly intent on the show. And Luke missed his chance to clean house.

"You there." Nouvelle's voice resounded. Luke froze as he felt those dark eyes pin him. "You're a likely-looking boy. I need a smart . . . " The eyes twinkled. "An honest boy to help me with my next trick. Up here." Nouvelle scooped up the hanging cards and gestured.

"Go ahead, kid. Go on." An elbow rammed into Luke's ribs.

Flushing to his toes, Luke rose. He knew it was dangerous when people noticed you. They would notice him all the more if he refused.

"Pick a card," Nouvelle invited as Luke climbed onstage. "Any card."

He fanned them again, outward to the audience so that they could see it was an ordinary deck. Quick and deft, Nouvelle shuffled them, then spread them on a small table.

"Any card," he repeated, and Luke frowned in concentration as he slid one from the pile. "Turn toward our gracious audience," Nouvelle instructed. "Hold the card facing out so all can see. Good, excellent. You're a natural."

Chuckling to himself, Nouvelle picked up the discarded pack, manipulating it again with his long, clever fingers. "Now . . . " His eyes on Luke, he held out the deck. "Slip your card in anywhere. Anywhere at all. Excellent." His lips were curved as he offered the deck to the boy. "Shuffle them as you please." Nouvelle's gaze remained on Luke as the boy mixed the cards. "Now." Nouvelle laid a hand on Luke's shoulder. "On the table, if you please. Would you like to cut them, or shall I?"

"I'll do it." Luke laid his hands over the cards, certain he couldn't be tricked. Not when he was so close.

"Is your card the top one?"

Luke flipped it up, grinned. "No."

Nouvelle looked amazed as the audience tittered. "No? The bottom one, perhaps?"

Getting into the spirit, Luke turned the deck over and held the card out. "No. Guess you screwed up, mister."

"Odd, odd indeed," Nouvelle murmured, tapping a finger to his moustache. "You're a more clever boy than I imagined. It seems you've tricked me. The card you chose isn't in that deck at all. Because it's ... " He snapped his fingers, turned his wrist, and plucked the eight of hearts out of thin air. "Here."

While Luke goggled, the audience broke into appreciative applause. Under the cover of the sound, Nouvelle spoke quietly.

"Come backstage after the show."

And that was all. Giving Luke a nudge, Nouvelle sent him back to his seat.

For the next twenty minutes, Luke forgot everything but the magic. He watched the little redheaded girl dance out on the stage in spangled tights. Grinned when she stepped into an oversized top hat and changed into a white rabbit. He felt adult and amused when the girl and the magician staged a mock argument over her bedtime. The girl tossed her curling red hair and stomped her feet. With a sigh, Nouvelle whipped a black cape over her, tapped three times with his magic wand. The cape slithered to the floor, and the child was gone.

"A parent," Nouvelle said soberly, "must be firm."

For a finale, Nouvelle sawed a curvy blonde in a skimpy leotard in half. The curves and the costume had elicited a great deal of whistling and cheers.

One enthusiastic man in a paisley shirt and starched bell-bottom jeans leaped up, shouting, "Hey, Nouvelle, if you're done with the lady, I'll take either half!"

The divided lady was pushed apart. At Nouvelle's command, she wriggled her fingers and toes. Once the box was pushed back together, Nouvelle removed the steel dividers, waved his wand and threw open the lid.

Magically reassembled, the lady stepped out to a round of applause.

Luke had forgotten all about the fat woman's purse, but decided he'd gotten his money's worth.

As the audience filed out to take a ride on the Loop De Loop or gawk at Sahib the Snake Charmer, Luke sidled toward the stage. He thought maybe, since he'd been a kind of assistant for the card trick, that Nouvelle would show him how it was done.

"Kid."

Luke looked up. From his vantage point, the man looked like a giant. Six feet five inches and two hundred and sixty pounds of solid muscle. The smooth-shaven face was as wide as a dinner plate, the eyes like two raisins stuck slightly off center. There was an unfiltered cigarette dangling from the mouth.

As ugly went, Herbert Mouse Patrinski had all the bases covered.

Luke instinctively struck a pose, chin jutted forward, shoulders hunched, legs spread and braced. "Yeah?"

For an answer, Mouse jerked his head and lumbered away. Luke debated for less than ten seconds, then followed.

Most of the tawdry glamour of the carnival faded to gray as they crossed the yellowed and trampled grass toward the huddle of trailers and trucks.

Nouvelle's trailer looked like a thoroughbred in a field of hacks. It was long and sleek, its black paint gleaming in the shadowy moonlight. A flourish of silver scrolled on the side proclaimed THE GREAT NOUVELLE, CONJURER EXTRAORDINAIRE.

Mouse rapped once on the door before pushing it open. Luke caught a scent that reminded him oddly and comfortingly of church as he stepped inside behind Mouse.

The Great Nouvelle had already changed out of his stage tux and was lounging on the narrow built-in sofa in a black silk dressing gown. Thin plumes of smoke curled lazily upward from a half a dozen incense cones. Sitar music played in the background while Nouvelle swirled two inches of brandy.

Luke tucked his suddenly nervous hands in his pockets and gauged his surroundings. He knew he'd just walked into a trailer but there was a strong illusion of some exotic den. The scents, of course, and the colors from the plush, vivid pillows heaped here and there, the small richly woven mats tossed helter-skelter over the floor, the draping silks over the windows, the mysterious dip and sway of candlelight.

And, of course, Maximillian Nouvelle himself.

"Ah." His amused smile half hidden by his moustache, Max toasted the boy. "So glad you could join me."

To show he was unimpressed, Luke shrugged his bony shoulders. "It was a pretty decent show."

"I blush at the compliment," Max said dryly and waved with the back of his hand for Luke to sit. "Do you have an interest in magic, Mr...?"

"I'm Luke Callahan. I figured it was worth a buck to see some tricks."

"A princely sum, I agree." Slowly, his eyes on Luke, Max sipped his brandy. "But a good investment for you, I trust?"

"Investment?" Uneasy, Luke slid his eyes toward Mouse, who seemed to be hulking around, blocking the door.

"You took several more dollars out with you than you came in with. In finance we would call it a quick upward turn on your money."

Luke resisted, barely, the urge to squirm, and met Max's eyes levelly. Well done, Max thought to himself. Quite well done.

"I don't know what you're talking about. I gotta take off."

"Sit." All Max did was utter the single syllable and raise one finger. Luke tensed, but sat. "You see, Mr. Callahan—or may I call you Luke? A good name that. From Lucius, the Latin for *light*." He chuckled, sipped again. "But I digress. You see, Luke, while you were watching me, I was watching you. It wouldn't be sporting of me to ask how much you got, but an educated guess would put it at eight to ten dollars." He smiled charmingly. "Not at all a bad turn, you see, on a single."

Luke narrowed his eyes to slits. A thin trail of sweat dribbled down his back. "Are you calling me a thief?"

"Not if it offends you. After all, you're my guest. And I'm being a remiss host. What can I offer you as refreshment?"

"What's the deal here, mister?"

"Oh, we'll get to that. Indeed, we'll get to that. But first things first, I always say. I know a young boy's appetite, having been one myself." And this young boy was so thin Max could all but count the ribs beneath the grubby T-shirt. "Mouse, I believe our guest would enjoy a hamburger or two, with all the accompaniments."

"'Kay."

Max rose as Mouse slipped out the door. "A cold drink?" he offered, opening the small refrigerator. He didn't have to see to know the boy's eyes cut to the door. "You can run, of course," he said casually as he took out a bottle of Pepsi. "I doubt the money you have tucked in your right shoe would slow you down very much. Or you can relax, enjoy a civilized meal and some conversation."

Luke considered bolting. His stomach rumbled. Compromising, he slid an inch closer to the door. "What do you want?"

"Why, your company," Max said as he poured Pepsi over ice. His brow lifted a fraction at the quickly smothered flash in Luke's eyes. So, he thought as his own mouth grimaced. It had been that bad. Hoping to signal the boy that he would be safe from that sort of advance, Max called for Lily.

She stepped through a curtain of crimson silk. Like Max, she was also in a robe. Hers was pale pink and trimmed with fuchsia feathers, as were the high-heeled slippers on her feet. She tapped over the scattered rugs in a wave of Chanel.

"We have company." She had a pippy voice that seemed to be stuck in perpetual giggle.

"Yes. Lily, my dear." Max took her hand and brought it to his lips, lingered over it. "Meet Luke Callahan. Luke, my invaluable assistant and adored companion, Lily Bates."

Luke swallowed a hard knot in his throat. He'd never seen anything like her. She was all curves and scent, her eyes and mouth exotically painted. She smiled, batting incredibly long lashes. "Pleased to meet you," she said, and snuggled closer to Max when he slipped an arm around her waist.

"Ma'am."

"Luke and I have some things to discuss. I didn't want you to wait up for me."

"I don't mind."

He kissed her lightly, but with such tenderness, Luke's cheeks went hot before he looked away. "*Je t'aime, ma belle.*"

"Oh, Max." That French business always made Lily's toes curl.

"Get some sleep," he murmured.

"Okay." But her eyes told him, quite clearly, that she would wait. "Nice meeting you, Luke."

"Ma'am," he managed again as she swayed back through the red curtain.

"A wonderful woman," Max commented as he offered Luke the glass of Pepsi. "Roxanne and I would be quite lost without her. Wouldn't we, *ma petite*?"

"Daddy." On a little huff of breath, Roxanne crawled under the curtain then popped to her feet. "I was so quiet, even Lily didn't see me."

"Ah, but I sensed you." Smiling at her, he tapped a finger to his nose. "Your shampoo. Your soap. The crayons you've been drawing with."

Roxanne made a face and shuffled forward in her bare feet. "You always know."

"And I always will know when my little girl is close." He lifted her up and settled her on his hip.

Luke recognized the kid from the act, though she was dressed for bed now in a long ruffled nightgown. Bright, fiery red hair curled halfway down her back. While Luke sipped his drink, she twined an arm around her father's neck and studied their guest with wide, sea-green eyes.

"He looks mean," Roxanne decided, and her father chuckled and kissed her temple.

"I'm sure you're mistaken."

Roxanne debated, then temporized. "He looks like he could be mean."

"Much more accurate." He set her down and ran a hand over her hair. "Now say a polite hello."

She tilted her head, then inclined it like a little queen granting audience. "Hello."

"Yeah. Hi." Snotty little brat, Luke thought, then flushed again as his stomach growled.

"I guess you have to feed him," Roxanne said, very much as though Luke were a stray dog found rooting through the garbage. "But I don't know if you should keep him."

Torn between exasperation and amusement, Max gave her bottom a light swat. "Go to bed, old woman."

"One more hour, please, Daddy."

He shook his head and bent to kiss her. "*Bon nuit, bambine.*"

Her brows drew together, forming a faint verticle crease between them. "When I grow up, I'll stay up all night when I want."

"I'm sure you will, more than once. Until then . . . " He pointed toward the curtain.

Roxanne's bottom lip poked out, but she obeyed. She parted the silk, then shot a look back over her shoulder. "I love you anyway."

"And I you." Max felt that old, always deep warmth flutter into him. His child. The one thing he had made without tricks or illusions. "She's growing up," Max said to himself.

"Shit." Luke snorted into his Pepsi. "She's just a kid."

"So it seems, I'm sure, to one of your vast years and experience." The sarcasm was so pleasant, Luke missed it.

"Kids're a pain in the butt."

"In the heart, quite often," Max corrected, sitting again. "But I've never found one that gave me any discomfort in another part of the anatomy."

"They cost money, don't they?" A trickle of old anger worked its way into the words. "And they get in the way all the time. People have them mostly because they get too hot to think about the consequences when they screw around."

Max stroked a finger over his moustache as he picked up his brandy. "An interesting philosophy. One we'll have to discuss in depth sometime. But for tonight ... Ah, your meal."

Confused, Luke looked at the door. It was still closed. He heard nothing. Only seconds later there was the scrape of feet and the single quick rap. Mouse entered carrying a brown bag already spotted with grease. The smell had saliva pooling in Luke's mouth.

"Thank you, Mouse." Out of the corner of his eye, Max noted Luke restraining himself from snatching the bag.

"You want me to hang around?" Mouse asked and set the food on the small round table that fronted the sofa.

"Not necessary. I'm sure you're tired."

"'Kay. Good night then."

"Good night. Please," Max continued as Mouse closed the door behind him. "Help yourself."

Luke shot a hand into the bag and pulled out a burger. Striving for nonchalance, he took the first bite slowly, then, before he could stop himself, he bolted the rest. Max settled back, swirling brandy, his eyes half closed.

The boy ate like a young wolf, Max thought as Luke plowed his way through the second burger and a pile of fries. Starved, Max imagined, for a great many things. He knew perfectly well what it was to starve—for a great many things. Because he trusted his instincts, and what he believed he saw behind the sly defiance in the boy's eyes, he would offer a chance for a feast.

"I occasionally do a mentalist act," Max said quietly. "You may not be aware of that."

Because his mouth was full, Luke only managed to grunt.

"I thought not. A demonstration then, if you will. You've left home and have been traveling for some time now."

Luke swallowed, belched. "Got that one wrong. My folks have a farm a couple miles from here. I just came for the rides."

Max opened his eyes. There was power in them and something that made the power more acute. Simple kindness. "Don't lie to me. To others if you must, but not to me. You've run away." He moved so quickly, Luke had no chance to avoid the hand that clamped like steel over his wrist. "Tell me this, have you left behind a mother, a father, an aged grandparent with a broken heart?"

"I told you . . ." The clever lies, the ones that he'd learned to tell so easily, withered on his tongue. It was the eyes, he thought on a flutter of panic. Just like the eyes in the poster, which seemed to look into him and see everything. "I don't know who my father is." He spat it out as his body began to vibrate with shame and fury. "I don't figure she knows either. She sure as hell don't care. Maybe she's sorry I'm gone 'cause there's no one around to fetch her a bottle, or steal one for her if she ain't got the money. And maybe that bastard she's living with is sorry because he doesn't have any-body to knock around anymore." Tears he wasn't even aware of burned in his eyes. But he was aware of the panic that had leaped like a dragon to claw at his throat. "I won't go back. I swear to God I'll kill you before you make me go back to that."

Max gentled his hand on Luke's wrist. He felt that pain, so much like his own at that age. "The man beat you."

"When he could catch me." There was defiance even in that. The tears shimmered briefly, then dried up.

"The authorities."

Luke curled his lip. "Shit."

23

"Yes." Max indulged in a sigh. "You have no one?"

The chin with its faint cleft firmed. "I got myself."

An excellent answer, Max reflected. "And your plans?"

"I'm heading south, Miami."

"Mmmm." Max took Luke's other wrist and turned his hands up. When he felt the boy tense, he showed his first sign of impatience. "I'm not interested in men sexually," he snapped. "And if I were, I wouldn't lower myself to pawing a boy." Luke lifted his eyes, and Max saw something there, something no twelve-year-old should know existed. "Did this man abuse you in other ways?"

Luke shook his head quickly, too humiliated to speak.

But someone had, Max concluded. Or someone had tried. That would wait, until there was trust. "You have good hands, quick agile fingers. Your timing is also quite keen for one so young. I could make use of those qualities, perhaps help you refine them, if you choose to work for me."

"Work?" Luke didn't quite recognize the emotion working through him. A child's memory is often short, and it had already been a long time since he'd known hope. "What kind of work?"

"This and that." Max sat back again, smiled. "You might like to learn a few tricks, young Luke. It happens we'll be heading south in another few weeks. You can work off your room and board, and earn a small salary if you deserve it. I'd have to ask that you refrain from lifting wallets for a time, of course. But I doubt if anything else I'd ask would cramp your style."

His chest hurt. It wasn't until he'd let out a breath that he realized he'd been holding it until his lungs burned. "I'd, like, be in the magic show?"

Max smiled again. "You would not. You would, however, assist in the setting up and breaking down. And you would learn, if you have any affinity for such things. Eventually, you may learn enough."

There had to be a catch. There was always a catch. Luke circled around the offer as a man might circle a sleeping snake. "I guess I could think about it."

"That's always wise." Max rose, setting his empty snifter aside. "Why don't you sleep here? We'll see where we stand in the morning. I'll get you some linens," Max offered, and walked out without waiting for a response.

Maybe it was a scam, Luke thought, gnawing on his knuckles. But he couldn't see the trap, not yet. And it would be good, so good, to sleep inside for once, with a full stomach. He stretched out, telling himself he was just testing his ground. But his eyelids drooped. The candlelight played hypnotically over them.

Because his back still troubled him, he shifted to his side. Before he let his eyes close again, he judged the distance to the door in case he had to get out quickly.

He could always take off in the morning, he told himself. No one could make him stay. No one could make him do anything anymore.

That was his last thought as he tumbled into sleep. He didn't hear Max come back with a clean sheet and the pillow. He didn't feel the slight tug as his shoes were removed and placed beside the sofa. He didn't even murmur or shift as his head was lifted and laid, quite gently, on the linen-cased pillow that smelled faintly of lilacs.

"I know where you've been," Max murmured. "I wonder where you'll go."

For another moment he studied the sleeping boy, noting the strong facial bones, the hand that was clutched in a defensive fist, the deep rise and fall of the frail chest that spoke of utter exhaustion.

He left Luke to sleep and went to Lily's soft, waiting arms.

Chapter Two

LUKE AWOKE IN STAGES. HE HEARD THE BIRDS CHATTERING outside first, then felt the sun warm on his face. In his mind he imagined it to be gold and liquid with a taste like sweet honey. He caught the scent of coffee next and wondered where he was.

Then he opened his eyes, saw the girl and remembered.

She was standing between the round table and the sofa where he was sprawled, her lips pursed, her head tilted as she stared at him. Her eyes were bright and curious—a not entirely friendly curiosity.

He noted there was a faint dusting of freckles over the bridge of her nose that he hadn't seen when she'd been onstage or in the candleglow.

As wary as she, Luke stared back, slowly running his tongue over his teeth. His toothbrush was in the denim knapsack he'd stolen from a Kmart and hidden in some bushes nearby. He was fastidious about brushing his teeth, a habit which grew directly out of his paralyzing fear of the dentist. Particularly the one his mother had dragged him to nearly three years before. The one with breath fouled by gin and knuckles covered with coarse black hair.

He wanted to brush his teeth, to gulp down some of that hot coffee and to be alone.

"What the hell are you looking at?"

"You." She'd been thinking about poking him and was a little disappointed that he'd awakened before she'd had the chance. "You're skinny. Lily said you have a beautiful face, but it just looks mean to me."

He felt a wave of disgust, and of confusion at being called beautiful by the curvy Lily. Luke had no such twisted feelings about Roxanne. She was what his stepfather called a class-A bitch. Of course, Luke couldn't remember any woman Al Cobb hadn't considered one kind of bitch or another.

"You're skinny *and* ugly. Now, beat it."

"I live here," she pointed out grandly. "And if I don't like you I can make my daddy send you away."

"Big freaking deal."

"That's bad language." She gave a prim, ladylike sniff. At least she thought it was.

"No." Maybe if he shocked her angelic ears, she'd take off. "Big fucking deal is bad language."

"It is?" Interested now, she leaned closer. "What does fucking mean?"

"Christ." He rubbed the heels of his hands over his eyes as he sat up. "Get out of my face, will you?"

"*I* know how to be polite." And if she was, Roxanne thought she might get him to tell her what the new word meant. "Because I'm the hostess, I'll get you a cup of coffee. I already made it."

"You?" It bothered him that he hadn't heard her rattling around.

"It's my job." She strutted importantly to the stove. "Because Daddy and Lily sleep late in the mornings, and I don't like to. I hardly ever need any sleep. I didn't even when I was a baby. It's metabolism," she told him, pleased with the word her father had taught her.

"Yeah. Right." He watched her pour the coffee into a china cup.

Probably tasted like mud, Luke thought, and looked forward to telling her so.

"Cream and sugar?" She chanted the words, like a peppy flight attendant.

"Lots of both."

She took him at his word, then, with her tongue caught between her teeth, brought the brimming cup to the table. "You can have orange juice, too, with breakfast." Though she didn't particularly like him, Roxanne enjoyed the idea of playing the gracious hostess, and imagined herself wearing one of Lily's long silk gowns and teetering on high heels. "I'll make my special one."

"Great." Luke braced to wince at the taste of the coffee and was surprised when it went down smoothly. It was a bit sweet, even for his taste, but he'd never had better. "It's pretty good," he muttered, and Roxanne granted him a quick smile that was innately female.

"I have a magic touch with coffee. Everyone says so." Enthusiastic now, she popped slices of bread into the toaster, then opened the fridge. "How come you don't live with your mother and father?"

"Because I don't want to."

"But you have to," she pointed out. "Even if you don't want to."

"The hell I do. Besides, I don't have a father."

"Oh." She pressed her lips together. Though she was only eight, she knew such things happened. She herself had lost a mother, one she had no memory of. Since Lily had slid so seamlessly into the gap, it wasn't a loss that jarred her. But the idea of being without a father always made her sad—and scared. "Did he get sick, or have a terrible accident?"

"I don't know or give a good damn. Drop it."

Under any other circumstances, the sharp tone would have loosened her temper. Instead, it sparked her sympathies. "What part of the show did you like best?"

"I don't know. The card tricks were pretty cool."

"I know one. I can show you." Carefully, she poured juice into crystal glasses. "After breakfast I will. You can use the bathroom back there to wash your hands 'cause it's almost ready."

He was a lot more interested in emptying his straining bladder and, following the direction of her hand, found the closet-sized bathroom behind the red curtain. It smelled of woman—not the heavy, cloying scent that often trailed around his mother, but sweet, luxurious femininity.

There were stockings draped over the rung of the narrow shower stall, and a floral box of dusting powder and a big pink puff sat on a crocheted doily on the back of the toilet. In the corner was a small wedge of counter space that was crowded from edge to edge with bottles and pots and tubes.

Whore's tools, Cobb would have called them, but Luke thought they looked kind of nice and pretty jumbled there, like a garden he'd seen on his travels, where flowers and weeds had run wild together.

Despite the clutter, the room was scrupulously clean. A far cry, he realized as he scrubbed hot water over his face, from the filthy bathroom in the filthy apartment he'd escaped from.

Unable to resist, he peeked into the medicine cabinet. There were men's things in there. A razor, shaving cream, aftershave. There was also a spare toothbrush still in its box. The terror of cavities overpowered any sense of guilt he might have had as he made use of it.

It wasn't until he was back in the hall, wondering if he could take a chance and poke around a bit that he remembered his shoes.

He was back in the living area like a shot, diving under the table and checking his stash.

As calm as a queen on her throne, Roxanne sat on a satin pillow and sipped her juice. "How come you keep your money in your shoe when you've got pockets?"

"Because it's safer there." And it had been, he noted with relief. Every last dollar. He slid up into his seat and looked at his plate.

There was a piece of toast in the center of it. It had been mounded with chunky peanut butter, drizzled with what looked like honey, sprinkled with cinnamon and sugar, then cut into two neat triangles.

"It's very good," Roxanne assured him, taking dainty bites of her own.

Luke bit a triangle in two, and was forced to agree. She smiled again when he'd finished the last crumb.

"I'll make more."

An hour later, when Max pushed through the curtain, he saw them sitting hip to hip on the sofa. His little girl had a short pile of bills at her elbow and was expertly shifting three cards over the table.

"Okay, where's the queen?"

Luke blew the hair out of his eyes, hesitated, then tapped the center card. "I know it's there this time, damn it."

Smug, Roxanne flipped over the card, then giggled when he swore again.

"Roxy," Max said as he crossed to them. "It's quite rude to fleece a guest."

"I told him Three Card Monte was a sucker's game, Daddy." All innocence, she beamed up at her father. "He didn't listen."

He chuckled and clucked her on the chin. "My little swindler. How did you sleep, Luke?"

"Okay." He'd lost five bucks to the little cheat. It was mortifying.

"And I see you've eaten. If you've decided to stay, I'll give you over to Mouse shortly. He'll put you to work."

"That'd be good." But he knew better than to sound anxious. When you sounded anxious, that was when they pulled the rug out from under you. "For a couple days, anyhow."

"Splendid. A free lesson before we begin." He paused to pour coffee, sniff appreciatively, then sip. "Never bet on the house game unless losing is to your advantage. Will you need clothes?"

Though he couldn't see how losing could ever be an advantage, Luke didn't comment. "I've got some stuff."

"All right then, you can go retrieve it. Then we'll get started."

ONE OF THE ADVANTAGES of being a boy like Luke was that he had no expectations. Another might have anticipated touches of glamour, or adventure, perhaps a bit of jolly camaraderie of carny life. But in Luke's philosophy, people generally got less than they paid for of the good things, and more than they could handle of the bad.

So when he was put to work by the taciturn Mouse lifting, hauling, cleaning, painting and fetching, he followed orders without complaint or conversation. Since Mouse had little to say for himself, Luke was able to keep his own counsel and observe.

Life in a carnival wasn't glamorous, he noted. It was sweaty, and dirty. The air snapped with the scents of frying food, cheap cologne and unwashed bodies. Colors that looked so bright at night were dingy in the light of day. And the rides that seemed so fast and fearsome under a starry sky appeared tired, and more than a little unsafe under a hard summer sun.

As for adventure, there was nothing exciting about scrubbing down the long black trailer, or helping Mouse change the spark plugs in the Chevy pickup that hauled it.

Mouse had head and shoulders under the hood, and his tiny eyes were slitted nearly closed as he listened to the idling engine. Occasionally he would hum a little tune, or grunt and make a few more adjustments.

Luke shifted from foot to foot. The heat was terrible. Sweat was beginning to seep through the faded bandanna he'd tied around his head. He didn't know a damn thing about cars, and didn't see why he needed to when he wouldn't be able to drive one for years and years. The way Mouse was humming and fiddling was getting on his nerves.

"It sounds okay to me."

Mouse blinked his eyes open. There was grease on his hands, streaked on his moon pie face, smeared on his baggy white T-shirt. He was quite simply in Mouse heaven.

"Missing," he corrected, then closed his eyes again. He made minute adjustments, as gently as a man in love would initiate a virgin. The engine purred for him. "Sweet baby," he said under his breath.

There was nothing in Mouse's world more fascinating, or seductive, than a well-oiled machine.

"Jesus, it's just a stupid truck."

Mouse opened his eyes again, and there was a smile in them. He was barely twenty, and because of his size and plodding manner, had been considered a freak by the other children in the state home where he'd grown up. He neither trusted nor liked a great many people, but he'd already developed a tolerant affection for Luke.

There was something about his smile—it was slow and pure as a baby's—that made Luke grin back. "You done yet or what?"

"Done." To prove it Mouse closed the hood, then rounded it to take the keys from the ignition and pocket them. He'd never forgotten the surge of pride he'd felt when Max had trusted him with the keys for the first time. "She'll run fine tonight when we head to Manchester."

"How long are we there?"

"Three days." Mouse took a pack of Pall Malls from his rolled sleeve, shook the pack and nipped one out with his teeth before offering the pack to Luke. Luke accepted it as casually as possible. "Hard work tonight. Loading up."

Luke let the cigarette dangle from the corner of his mouth and waited for Mouse to light a match. "How come somebody like Mr. Nouvelle's in a cheap carny like this?"

The match flared as Mouse touched it to the end of his cigarette. "Got his reasons." He held the match to the tip of Luke's, then leaned back on the truck and began to daydream about the long, quiet drive.

Luke took an experimental puff, choked back a hacking cough

and made the mistake of inhaling. He coughed hard enough to make his eyes water, but when Mouse glanced his way, he struggled for dignity.

"Not my usual brand." His voice was a thin squeak before he took another determined drag. This time he swallowed the smoke, gagged and fought a sweaty battle to keep from losing his lunch. It felt as though his eyes were rolling back in his head to meet his rising stomach.

"Hey. Hey, kid." Concern at the green tinge of Luke's skin had Mouse slapping a fist to his back hard enough to take Luke to his knees. When he vomited weakly, Mouse patted his head with a greasy hand. "Holy cow. You sick or something?"

"Do we have a problem here?" Max crossed to them. Lily broke from his side to crouch beside Luke.

"Oh, honey. You poor thing," she crooned, rubbing a hand up and down Luke's back. "Just stay down there, sweetie, till it passes." She spotted the smoldering cigarette that had dropped from Luke's hand and clucked her tongue. "What in the world was this child doing with one of those awful things?"

"My fault." Mouse stared miserably at his own feet. "I wasn't thinking when I gave him a cigarette, Max. It's my fault."

"He didn't have to take it." Max shook his head as Luke braced himself on his hands and knees and struggled with the nausea. "And he's certainly paying for it. Another free lesson. Don't take what you can't hold."

"Oh, leave the child be." Her mothering instinct on overdrive, Lily pressed Luke's clammy face to her breast, where he breathed in a heady mixture of Chanel and sweat. Holding Luke close, Lily glared at Max. "Just because you've never been sick a day in your life is no reason to be unsympathetic."

"Quite right," Max agreed and hid a smile. "Mouse and I will leave him to your tender care."

"We'll fix you up," she murmured to Luke. "You just come with Lily, honey. Come on now, lean on me."

"I'm okay." But as he dragged himself to his feet, his head spun in counterpoint to his roiling stomach. The sickness spread its slippery fingers through him so expertly, he had no room for embarrassment as Lily half carried him back to the trailer.

"Don't you worry about a thing, baby doll. You just need to lie down awhile, that's all."

"Yes, ma'am." He wanted to lie down. It would be easier to die that way.

"Now, you don't have to ma'am me, honey. You call me Lily just like everybody." She had him tucked under one arm as she opened the trailer door. "You lie right on down on the sofa and I'll get you a nice, cold cloth."

Groaning, he collapsed facedown and began to pray with a fervor he'd just discovered that he wouldn't throw up again.

"Here you go, baby." Armed with a damp cloth and a basin—just in case—Lily knelt beside him. After slipping the sweaty bandanna from his head, she laid the cloth over his brow. "You'll feel better soon, I promise. I had a brother who got sick the first time he smoked." She spoke quietly, in that soothing sickroom voice some women assume so naturally. "But he got over it in no time."

The best Luke could manage was a moan. Lily continued to talk as she turned the cloth over and stroked his face and neck with it. "You just rest." Her lips curved as she felt him drifting off. "That's the way, honey pie. You sleep it out."

Indulging herself, she brushed her fingers through his hair. It was long and thick, and smooth as silk. If she and Max had been able to make a child together, he might have had hair like that, she thought, wistful. But as fertile as her heart was to love a brood of children, her womb was sterile.

The boy did have a beautiful face, she mused. His skin gold from the sun and smooth as a girl's. Good strong bones beneath it. And those lashes. She let out another sigh. Still, as appealing as the boy was, and as much as her soul ached to fill her life with children, she wasn't certain Max had done the right thing by taking him in.

He wasn't an orphan like Mouse. The child had a mother, after all. As hard as her own life had been, Lily found it next to impossible to believe that a mother wouldn't do all in her power to protect, to shelter, to love her child.

"I bet she's frantic for you, baby doll," Lily murmured. She clucked her tongue. "You're hardly more than skin and bones. And look here, you've sweated right through this shirt. All right then, we'll slip you out of it and get it washed up for you."

Gently, she tugged it up his back. Her fingers froze on the damp cloth. Her quick, involuntary cry had him moaning in his sleep. As tears of grief and rage sprang hot to her eyes, she slid the shirt back down.

MAX STOOD IN FRONT of the mirror he'd set on stage and rehearsed his sleight-of-hand routine. He watched as the audience would watch as coins slipped in and out of his fingers. Max had performed his version of the Sympathetic Coins countless times, enhancing it, refining it as he did with every trick and illusion he'd learned or invented since he'd first stood on the corner of Bourbon and St. Louis in New Orleans, with his folding table, his cardboard box salted with coins, and the Cups and Balls.

He didn't often think of those early days now, not now that he was a successful man, past forty. But the bitter, desperate child he had been could sneak back to haunt him. As it had now, in the guise of Luke Callahan.

The boy had potential, Max mused as he split a gold coin into two, then three.

With a little time, care and direction, Luke would make something of himself. What that something might be, Max left up to the gods. If the boy was still with them when they reached New Orleans, they would see.

Max lifted his hands, clapped them together, and all coins save the one he'd started with vanished.

"Nothing up my sleeve," he murmured and wondered why it was that people always believed it.

"Max!" A little out of breath from her dash across the fairgrounds, Lily hurried toward the stage.

For Max it was, always was, a pleasure to watch her. Lily in snug shorts, snug T-shirt, with her painted toes peeking out of dusty sandals was a sight to behold. But when he caught her hand to help her onto the stage and saw her face, his smile faded.

"What's happened? Roxanne?"

"No, no." Shaken, she threw her arms around him and held tight. "Roxy's fine. She talked one of the roustabouts into giving her a ride on the carousel. But that boy, Max, that poor little boy."

He laughed then and gave her a quick, affectionate hug. "Lily, my love, he'll be queasy for a while, and perfectly miserable with embarrassment for a great deal longer, but it'll pass."

"No, it's not that." Tears already rolling, she pressed her face into his neck. "I had him lie down on the sofa, and when he fell asleep I was going to take off his shirt. It was all sweaty, and I wanted him to be comfortable." She paused and took a deep, steadying breath. "His back, Max, his poor little back. The scars, old scars and new welts that have barely healed. From a strap, or a belt, or God knows." She rubbed tears away with the heels of her hands. "Someone must have beaten that boy horribly."

"His stepfather." Max's voice was flat. The emotions pumping through him required the most finite control. Memories, however vicious, he could battle back. But the rage for the boy all but defeated him. "I'm afraid I didn't believe it was that serious. Do you think he should see a doctor?"

"No." With her lips pressed tight, she shook her head. "It's mostly scars, awful scars. I don't understand how anyone could do that to a child." She sniffled, accepted the handkerchief Max offered. "I wasn't sure you'd done the right thing by taking him in.

36

I thought his mother must be desperate for news of him." Her soft eyes hardened like glass. "His mother," she spat out. "I'd like to get my hands on that bitch. Even if she didn't use the strap herself, she allowed this to happen to her own little boy. Well, she ought to be beaten. I'd do it myself if I had the chance."

"So fierce." Gently Max cupped her face in his hands and kissed her. "By God, I love you, Lily. For so many reasons. Now go fix your face, make yourself a nice cup of tea so you'll be calm. No one will hurt the boy again."

"No, no one will hurt him again." She curled her fingers around Max's wrists. Her eyes were hot with passion now, and her voice amazingly steady. "He's ours now."

MOST OF LUKE'S NAUSEA FADED, but his embarrassment peaked as he awakened to find Lily sitting beside him, drinking tea. He tried to make some excuse, but she spoke cheerfully over his stammerings and made him a bowl of soup.

She continued to talk as he ate, bright, sunny conversation that nearly convinced him no one had noticed that he'd disgraced himself.

Then Roxanne burst in.

She was dusty from head to toe, the hair Lily had braided so neatly that morning in wild disarray. There was a fresh scrape on her knee, and a long jagged tear in her shorts. The ripe scent of animal followed her into the trailer. She'd just finished playing with the trio of terriers from the dog show.

Lily gave the grubby girl an indulgent smile. Next to seeing a child eat, Lily loved to see them covered with dirt as evidence that they had played hard and well.

"Is that my Roxy under there?"

Roxanne grinned, then reached into the refrigerator for a cold drink. "I rode on the carousel forever, and Big Jim let me toss the rings as long as I wanted." She glugged down grape Nehi, adding a rakish purple moustache to the dirt. "Then played with the dogs." She turned her gaze on Luke. "Did you really smoke a cigarette and get sick all over?"

Luke bared his teeth, but didn't speak.

"What'd you want to do that for, anyway?" she went on, bright as a magpie. "Kids aren't supposed to smoke."

"Roxy." Her voice a trill of cheer, Lily hopped up and began to nudge the girl toward the curtain. "You have to get cleaned up."

"But I just want to know—"

"Hurry up now. It'll be time for the first show before you know it."

"I only wondered—"

"You wonder too much. Now scoot."

Annoyed with the dismissal, Roxanne shot a look of dislike at Luke, and met one equally unfriendly. Doing what came naturally, she stuck out her tongue before flipping the curtain behind her.

Torn between laughter and sympathy, Lily turned back. "Well now." Luke's anger and humiliation were so clear on his face. "I guess we'd better get busy." She was too wise to ask him if he felt up to the night's work. "Why don't you run over and tell one of the boys to give you some flyers to pass out once people start dribbling in?"

He shrugged his shoulders by way of agreement, then jerked back as Lily's hand shot toward him. He'd expected a blow. She could see that by the dark, fixed look in his eyes. Just as she could see that look turn to blank confusion when what she gave him was a fast, affectionate ruffling of his hair.

No one had ever touched him like that. While he stared up at her, stunned, a knot formed in his throat, making speech of any kind impossible.

"You don't have to be afraid." She said it quietly, as though it were a secret between only them. "I won't hurt you." She slid her hand down to cup his cheek. "Not now. Not ever." She would have liked to have held him then, but judged it too soon. He couldn't know, as she did, that he was her son now. And what belonged to Lily Bates, she protected. "If you need anything," she said briskly, "you come to me. Understand?"

He could do no more than nod as he scrambled to his feet. There was a pressure in his chest, a dryness to his throat. Knowing he was perilously close to tears, he darted outside.

He'd learned three things that day. He supposed Max would call them free lessons, and they were three he would never forget. First, he would never again smoke an unfiltered cigarette. Second, he detested the little snot-nosed Roxanne. And third, most important, he had fallen in love with Lily Bates.

Chapter Three

Summer heated up as they traveled south. Portland to Manchester, on to Albany, and then Poughkeepsie, where it rained hard for two miserable days. Wilkes-Barre, then west to Allentown, where Roxanne had the time of her life palling around with twin girls named Tessie and Trudie. When they parted two days later, amid tears and solemn vows of eternal friendship, Roxanne had her first taste of the disadvantages of life on the road.

She pouted for a week, driving Luke crazy with praise for her lost friends. He avoided her whenever possible but it was difficult, as they were all but living under the same roof.

He bunked with Mouse under the capped bed of the truck, but a good many of his meals were taken in the trailer. And more than once, he found her waiting to spring out at him when he stepped out of the bathroom.

It wasn't that she liked him. In fact, she had developed the bone-deep disgust that neither yet recognized as natural sibling rivalry. But since her experience with Tessie and Trudie, Roxanne had come to crave companionship of her own age.

40

Even if he was a boy.

She did what little sisters have been doing to big brothers since time began. She made his life hell.

From Hagerstown to Winchester, from there to Roanoke and on to Winston-Salem, she nagged him unmercifully, dogged his footsteps and pestered relentlessly. If it hadn't been for Lily, Luke might have fought back. But for reasons that eluded him, Lily was crazy about the little brat.

Proof of that affection was obvious during a run-through of the performance in Winston-Salem.

Roxanne's messing up the timing, Luke thought smugly as he watched the rehearsal while loitering in the tent. Skinny twerp couldn't get anything right today. And she was whining.

The poor rehearsal gave him hope. He could do the trick a lot better than she could. If Max would give him the chance. If Max would just teach him a little. Luke had already practiced some of the flourishes and stage moves in front of the tiny bathroom mirror.

All he needed was for prune-faced Rox to get some incurable disease, or have a tragic accident. If she was out of the picture, he could slip right in and take her place.

"Roxanne," Max said patiently, interrupting Luke's thoughts. "You're not paying attention."

"I am too." Her lip poked out; her eyes filled. She hated being cooped up in this hot old tent.

"Max," said Lily, coming up to the stage. "Maybe we should give her a break."

"Lily." Max was struggling to keep his temper.

"I'm tired of rehearsing," Roxanne continued, lifting her flushed, miserable face. "I'm tired of the trailer, and the show and everything. I want to go back to Allentown and see Tessie and Trudie."

"I'm afraid that's impossible." Her words had wounded Max's pride and opened up a hole for guilt to seep into. "If you don't want to perform, that will be your choice. But if I can't depend on you, I'll have to replace you."

"Max!" Appalled, Lily took a step forward, only to freeze in place when Max held up a hand.

"As my daughter," he continued while a single tear trickled down Roxanne's cheek, "you're entitled to as many temper tantrums as you like. But as my employee, you will rehearse when rehearsals are called. Is that understood?"

Roxanne's head dropped. "Yes, Daddy."

"All right then. Now, why don't we take a moment to regroup. Dry your face," he began and tucked a hand under her chin. "I want you to . . ." He trailed off and pressed his palm to her brow. His stomach took a nosedive to his knees and froze there. "She's burning up," he said in an odd voice. "Lily." And the Great Nouvelle, Conjurer Extraordinaire, looked toward his lover help-lessly. "She's ill."

"Oh, little lamb." Instantly, Lily was on her knees, checking for fever herself. Roxanne's brow was hot and clammy under her hand. "Baby, does your head hurt? Your stomach?"

Two big tears plopped on the stage floor. "I'm okay. It's just hot in here. I'm not sick, I want to rehearse. Don't let Daddy replace me."

"Oh, that's nonsense." Lily's busy fingers were checking for swollen glands. "No one could replace you." Tucking Roxanne's head on her shoulder, Lily looked up at Max. He was white as a sheet. "I think we should go into town and find a doctor."

Speechless, Luke watched Max carry a weeping Roxanne away. His fondest wish had come true, he realized. The brat was sick. Maybe she even had the plague. Heart thumping, he raced out of the tent and watched the plume of dust as the truck raced off.

She might die before they even got into town. That thought brought on a shiver of panic that was followed hard on the heels by a hideous guilt. She'd looked awfully small when Max had car-ried her out.

"Where'd they go?" Mouse demanded, puffing a bit as he'd raced over when he'd heard his beloved engine start.

"Doctor." Luke bit down hard on his lip. "Roxanne's sick."

Before Mouse could ask any more questions, Luke dashed away. He hoped if there really was a God He'd believe he hadn't really meant it.

It was two terrifying hours later before the truck returned from town. As it pulled in, Luke started toward it, but his heart stopped when he saw Max take a limp Roxanne from Lily's arms and walk with her toward the trailer.

"Is she . . . " His throat closed on the "D" word.

"Sleeping." Lily gave him a distracted smile. "I'm sorry, Luke, you better run along now. We'll be busy for a while."

"But—but—" He got his feet moving and dogged Lily to the trailer. "Is she, I mean . . . "

"It'll be rough for a few days, but once the crisis passes, she'll do."

"Crisis?" His voice was a croak. Jesus please us, it *was* the plague.

"It's so miserably hot, too," she murmured. "Well, we'll make her as comfortable as we can while it lasts."

"I didn't mean it," Luke blurted out. "I swear I didn't mean to make her sick."

Though her mind was elsewhere, Lily paused at the door. "You didn't, honey. Actually, I suspect Roxy got more from Trudie and Tessie than a vow of endless friendship." She smiled as she stepped inside. "Looks like she got a bonus of the chicken pox."

Luke's mouth dropped open as Lily closed the door in his face.

Chicken pox? He'd practically died of fright, and all the little brat had was the damn chicken pox?

*

43

"I CAN DO IT." Luke stood stubbornly in center stage, scowling as Max continued to manipulate the cards. "I can do anything she can do."

"You're far from ready to perform." Max set the cards on the folding table, did a flashy turnover.

It had been three days since Roxanne had been put to bed, hot, itchy and miserable. And at every opportunity during that time span, Luke had been singing the same tune.

"You just have to show me what to do." He'd badgered Mouse to teach him the oversized-hat trick, and had run headlong into a wall of insurmountable loyalty. "I heard you tell Lily that there's a hole in the act with Roxanne sick. And she won't be able to be in the show for at least ten more days."

Toying with the idea of adding a bit of close-up conjuring to offset Roxanne's absence, Max began to set up a variation of Aces High. "Your concern for her health is touching, Luke."

His color rose as he jammed his hands in his pockets. "I didn't make her sick." He was almost sure of that now. "And it's just the chicken pox."

Dissatisfied with the sleight of hand, Max set the cards aside. The boy had a sturdy mind, Max mused, and could be trusted with something as basic as the oversized hat.

"Come here." Luke took a step forward; when his gaze clashed with Max's, something in the man's eyes made Luke suppress a shudder. "Swear," Max said, his voice deep and commanding in the dusty tent. "Swear by all you are and all you will be that you will never reveal any of the secrets of the art that are shown to you."

Luke wanted to grin, to remind Max that it was only a trick after all. But he couldn't. There was something here bigger than he could imagine. When he could speak, his voice was a whisper. "I swear."

Max took another moment to study Luke's face, then nodded. "Very well. This is what I want you to do."

It was so simple really. When Luke discovered how remarkably simple it all was he was amazed that he, or anyone else, could have been duped. He hated to admit it to himself, and refused to admit it to Max, but now that he knew how Roxanne had become the rabbit, how she had disappeared from under the cape, he was a little sorry.

Max gave him no time to grieve over the loss of innocence. They worked, repeating the sequence for more than an hour. Perfecting the timing, choreographing each move, removing bits of business that had suited Roxanne and replacing them with some that fit Luke.

It was tiring work, unbelievably monotonous, but Max refused to accept anything less than perfection.

"How come you go through all this for a bunch of hicks? For a lousy buck they'd be satisfied with a couple of card tricks and a rabbit in a hat."

"I wouldn't. Perform for yourself first, and you will always do your best work."

"But you, with the stuff you can do, you don't have to be in a two-bit carnival."

Max's lips curved under his finger as he smoothed his moustache. "Your compliment, however ill phrased, is appreciated. It's a mistake to believe anyone has to be anywhere they don't choose to be. I find a certain pleasure in the gypsy's life. And, as you are obviously unaware, I own this two-bit carnival."

He swung his cape over Luke, snapped his fingers twice, then chuckled when the shape under the black material stayed in place. "A good magician's assistant never misses a cue, however distracted he might be."

There was a quick huff of breath from under the cape, and the shape dissolved. Far from displeased with Luke's progress, Max thought the boy would do. He would use Luke's cockiness, his hunger and defiance, along with that underlying vulnerability. He would use all that Luke was, and in turn he would give the boy a home, and a chance to choose.

A fair bargain, Max considered. "Again," he said simply as Luke stepped onto the stage from the wings.

After another hour, Luke wondered why he'd wanted to be a part of the act in the first place. When Lily walked into the tent he was on the verge of telling Max exactly what he could do with his magic wand.

"I know I'm late," she began as she hurried forward. "Everything's running behind today."

"Roxanne?"

"Hot and cranky, but bearing up." Worry creased Lily's brow as she looked over her shoulder. "I hate leaving her alone. Everyone's tied up right now, so I . . . Luke." Instantly Lily's brow cleared. "Honey, you'd be doing me such a huge favor if you'd go sit with her for an hour or so."

"Me?" She might as well have asked him to eat toads.

"She could really use the company. It takes her mind off the itching."

"Well, yeah, but . . . " Inspiration hit. "I'd like to, but Max needs me to rehearse."

"Rehearse?"

No mentalist could have read Luke's mind more clearly. Max smiled, setting a friendly hand on the boy's shoulder. Progress, he thought briefly. Luke had tensed at the touch only for a moment. "Meet the newest member of our happy crew," he said to Lily. "Luke's going to fill in tonight."

"Tonight?" Alerted, Luke swung about so he faced Max. "Just tonight? I haven't been sweating through all this practice for one night."

"That remains to be seen. If you do well tonight, there'll be tomorrow night. It's what we call a probationary period. In any case, we've rehearsed enough for the moment, so you're quite free to entertain Roxanne." There was a twinkle in his eye as he leaned toward the boy. "You gambled against the house again, Luke. You lose."

"I don't know what the hell I'm supposed to do with her," Luke muttered as he clumped offstage. Lily sighed at his language.

"Play a game with her," she suggested. "And, honey, I really wish you wouldn't swear around Roxy."

Fine, he thought and continued out of the shadowy tent into the white flash of sunlight. He wouldn't swear around her. He'd swear at her.

He tugged open the trailer door and headed straight for the refrigerator. The impulse to check over his shoulder as he reached for a cold drink was still strong. Luke always expected someone to leap out and smack him for taking food.

No one did. But he was still faintly embarrassed by his actions during the first week with Max. He'd come into the trailer alone and found a big bowl of leftover spaghetti. He'd wolfed it down cold, stuffing himself, the memory of so many hungry days clawing at him.

He'd waited to be punished. Waited to be told he could have nothing more for a day, or even two. As his mother had done to him so many times. Preparing for it, he'd secreted candy bars and sandwiches into his knapsack.

But he hadn't been punished. No one had mentioned it.

Not one to press his luck, Luke wrapped a piece of bread around some lunch meat and gulped down the makeshift sandwich before going back to Roxanne.

He moved quietly, another habit he'd developed out of necessity. As he started down the narrow hallway, he could hear Jim Croce's sly ballad of Leroy Brown. Roxanne sang along with the radio, adding a warbling soprano.

Amused, Luke peeked in the doorway. She was lying flat on her back, staring up at the ceiling as the radio played beside her. A small round table beside the bed held a pitcher of juice and a glass along with some bottles of medication and a deck of cards.

Someone had tacked posters to the walls. Most were magic-related, but the glossy one of David Cassidy made Luke want to puke. It only proved girls were hopeless.

"Man, that's gross."

Roxanne shifted her eyes and spotted him. She nearly smiled, that desperate was she for diversion. "What's gross?"

"That." He gestured toward the poster with his Coke. "Hanging that pussy teenybopper star on your wall."

Satisfied with the jibe, Luke gulped down Coke as he studied her. Her white skin was blotchy, spotted with ugly red sores. They were all over her face, too, which Luke thought was *really* gross. He wondered how Lily and Max could stand to look at her.

"Boy oh boy, you got that shit all over, don't you? Makes you look like something out of 'Creature Feature.' "

"Lily says they'll go away soon and I'll be beautiful."

"They'll *probably* go away," he said, tingeing his voice with enough doubt to make Roxanne's brow crease with worry. "But you'll still be ugly."

She forgot all about the horrible itching on her stomach and pushed herself to a sitting position. "I hope I give you the chicken pox. I hope you get spots all over—even on your weenie."

Luke choked on his drink, then grinned. "Tough break. I had them already. Chicken pox is for babies."

"I'm not a baby." Nothing could have infuriated her more. Before Luke could dodge, she leaped up and launched herself at him, fists hammering. His Coke bottle flew, hitting the wall and spraying Coke everywhere. It would have been funny; in fact he let out one bray of laughter before it struck him how frail she was. Her arms were like little burning sticks.

"Okay, okay." Because he figured he'd had one close call with wishing her dead, he didn't want to take a chance on giving her some kind of seizure. "You're not a baby. Now get back into bed."

"I'm tired of bed." But she stumbled back into it, prompted by his not-so-gentle shove.

"Well, tough. Shit, look at this mess. I guess I have to clean it up."

"Your fault," she said and, prim-mouthed, looked determinedly out of the window, an old woman's pose in a child's body. Grumbling all the way, Luke went off to find a rag.

After he'd mopped up the spill she continued to ignore him. As strategies went, it was inspired.

He shifted from foot to foot. "Look, I took it back, didn't I?"

Her face turned a fraction in his direction, but the ice didn't thaw. "Are you sorry you said I was ugly?"

"I guess I could be."

Silence.

"Okay, okay. Jeez. I'm sorry I said you were ugly."

The faintest hint of a smile. "And you're sorry you said David Cassidy was gross."

Now he grinned. "No way."

Her lips curved in response. "I guess that's okay, since you're just a boy." The small taste of power had been pleasant. Hoping to milk it, Roxanne widened the smile. Even at eight, there was power in it. She was, after all, her father's daughter. "Would you pour me some juice?"

"I guess."

He poured some from pitcher to glass and handed it to her.

"You don't talk very much," she said after a bit.

"You talk too much."

"I have lots to say. Everyone says I'm very bright." She was also horribly bored. "We could play a game, if you'd like."

"I'm too old for games."

"No, you're not. Daddy says no one ever is. That's why people get suckered into Three Card Monte or the Cups and Balls on street corners and lose their money." She caught the brief flicker of interest on his face and pounced. "If you play Go Fish with me, I'll teach you a card trick."

Luke hadn't survived to the age of twelve without knowing how to bargain. "Teach me the card trick, and then I'll play."

"Nuh-uh." Her smile was smug, a younger, only slightly more innocent version of a woman's who knew she'd trapped her man.

"I'll *show* you the trick, then we'll play. Then I'll teach you how to do it."

She picked up her rubber-band-bound deck from the table, riffled it with considerable skill. Caught, Luke sat on the edge of the bed and watched her hands.

"Now this is called Lost and Found. You pick any card you see, and name the card out loud."

"Big-deal trick if I'm telling you the card," Luke muttered. But when she riffled the deck again, he chose the king of spades.

"Oh, you can't have that card," Roxanne told him.

"Why the hell not? You said any card I saw."

"But you couldn't see the king of spades. It's not there." Smiling, she flipped the cards again, and Luke's mouth fell open. Damn it, he'd just seen that king. How had she gotten rid of it?

"You palmed it."

Her grin was wide and pleased. "Nothing up my sleeve," she said and, setting the pack down on her lap, held up both hands to show them empty. "You can pick another one."

This time, eyes sharp, Luke picked the three of clubs. With a showy sigh, Roxanne shook her head.

"You keep picking missing cards." A slow flip, and Luke saw that not only was the three missing, but the king was back. Frustrated, he made a grab for the pack, but Roxanne swung them up over her head.

"I don't believe it's a regular deck."

"Not believing is what makes magic magic." Roxanne quoted her father with great seriousness. She gave the pack a sharp riffle, then spread it faceup on the sheets. A wave of her hand to point out both cards Luke had chosen were among the fifty-two.

He huffed out a breath, defeated. "Okay, how'd you do it?"

Grinning again, she executed a nearly successful turnover. "First, Go Fish."

He would have told her to go to hell. But more than the satisfaction of telling her off he wanted to know how the trick was done.

After two games of fish, he unbent enough to get them both a snack of cold drinks and cookies.

"I'll show you now," Roxanne offered, pleased that he hadn't nagged. "But you have to swear never to tell the secret."

"I already took the oath."

Her eyes narrowed. "When? How come?"

He could have bitten off his tongue. "At rehearsal, a little while ago," he said reluctantly. "I'm filling in until you're not full of spots."

Her lip poked out. Slowly, she picked up the cards and began to shuffle them. It always helped her to think if she did something with her hands. "You're taking my place."

"Max said there was a hole in the act without you. I'm filling it." Then with a diplomacy he hadn't been aware of possessing, he added, "Temporarily. That's what Max said. Maybe just tonight."

After another moment of consideration, she nodded. "If Daddy said so, it's okay. He said he was sorry about telling me he'd replace me. That nobody ever would."

Luke had no idea what it would be like to be loved that way or to have that much trust. Envy was a fist punching his heart.

"Here's what you have to do," Roxanne began, drawing his attention back to her. "First you have to set the cards up in a riffle pack." She dealt out two heaps and began to teach him with all the patience of a first-grade teacher instructing a student on how to print his name.

She ran through the trick twice, step by step, then handed him the pack. "You try."

As Max had said, the boy had good hands.

"This is cool," he murmured.

"Magic's the coolest."

When she smiled, he smiled back. For a moment, at least, they were simply two children with a good secret between them.

Chapter Four

STAGE FRIGHT WAS A NEW AND HUMBLING EXPERIENCE FOR Luke. He was set, cocky, even eager as he waited in the wings. His secondhand tuxedo, hastily altered by Mama Franconi's nimble fingers, made him feel like a star. Over and over in his head he ran through the blocking, his moves, his patter while Max warmed up the crowd with some sleight of hand.

There was nothing to it, he thought. It would be a grade-A cinch that would earn him an extra ten bucks a night as long as Roxanne remained covered with those little red welts. If the doctor's prognosis ran true, that would mean a hundred dollars for Luke's Miami fund.

He was congratulating himself on his good fortune and sneering at the pop-eyed group of rubes in the front row when Mouse tapped him on the shoulder.

"Cue's coming up."

"Huh?"

"Your cue." Mouse jerked his head toward the stage where Lily was flouncing in her spangled tights, adding a little hip motion for the men in the audience.

"My cue," Luke said as his bowels turned to ice water and his heart became a hot little ball in his throat.

Having been prepared for this possibility by Max, Mouse gave a grunt of assent and shoved Luke onstage.

There was a titter of laughter as the thin boy in the baggy tux stumbled on. In contrast to his shiny black lapels, Luke's face was sheet white. He missed his mark, and his first line. The best he could manage as his back ran with what any pro could have told him was flop sweat was to stand rock still while his eyes darted wildly over the grinning faces of his first audience.

"Ah." Smooth as the silk he'd caused to appear and vanish, Max strode to him. "My young friend seems to be lost." To the audience it appeared that Max stroked a friendly hand over Luke's hair. They didn't see the agile fingers pinch hard at the back of the boy's neck to shock him out of opening-night jitters.

Luke jerked, blinked and swallowed. "I, ah . . . " Shit, what was he supposed to say? "Lost my hat," he finished in a rush, then went from white to red as the chuckles bounced toward the stage. The hell with them, he told himself and straightened his shoulders. In that moment, he was transformed from a frightened little boy to an arrogant young man. "I got a date with Lily. Can't take a beautiful woman dancing without my hat."

"A date with Lily?" As rehearsed, Max looked surprised, then annoyed, then sly. "I'm afraid you must be mistaken, the lovely Lily is engaged for the evening with me."

"Guess she changed her mind." Luke grinned, and hooked his fingers around his lapels. "She's waiting for me. We're going . . . " A little flourish, and a big red rose popped out on his lapel. "Out on the town."

The scattering of applause for his first public magic trick beckoned like a seductive woman.

Luke Callahan had found his calling.

"I see." Max shot a sideways glance at the audience. "Aren't you a little young for a woman of Lily's charms?"

He was rolling now. "What I lack in years I make up for in energy."

This remark, delivered with a sneer, brought a loud guffaw from the audience. Luke felt something shift inside him at the sound. As it settled comfortably into place, the sneer turned to a grin.

"But of course, a gentleman can't escort a lady out on the town without his hat." Max rubbed his hands together and glanced stage left. "I'm afraid that's the only hat I've seen tonight." The key light swung on the oversized top hat. "It seems a little large, even for one with your swelled head."

Rocking back on his heels, Luke tucked his thumbs in his waist-band. "I'm on to your tricks, old man. It'll go easier on you if you change my hat back the way it was."

"I?" Eyebrows lifting, Max placed a hand to his breast. "Are you accusing me of sorcery in order to spoil your evening with Lily?"

"Damn right." It wasn't precisely the line as rehearsed, but Luke delivered it with relish as he stalked over and tapped the rim of the hat. "Just get on with it."

"Very well then." With a sigh for the boy's obvious lack of man-ners, Max gestured. "If you'd be so kind as to step into the hat." He smiled as Luke eyed him owlishly.

"Okay, but no funny business." Agile and quick, Luke hopped inside. "Remember, I'm on to you."

The moment Luke's head disappeared below the rim, Max whipped out his magic wand. "And presto! Suitable magic." He reached in the hat and pulled out a white rabbit. As the audience roared their approval, Max tipped the hat toward them so they could see for themselves that it was quite empty. "I doubt Lily will be interested in a night on the town with him now."

Responding to cue, Lily sauntered out. One look at the wrig-gling rabbit in Max's hand made her shriek. "Not again!" Exasperation clear on her face, she turned to the audience. "That's the fourth rabbit this month. Let me tell you, ladies, don't get yourself hung up on a jealous magician." Amid the laughter, she turned to Max. "Change him back."

"But, Lily—"

"Change him back right this minute." She fisted her hands on her glitter-slicked hips. "Or we're through."

"Very well." With exaggerated reluctance, Max slipped the rabbit back into the hat, sighed, then tapped the rim twice with his wand. Luke popped up, fury on every feature.

The audience was still applauding as Luke scrambled clear of the hat, fists raised. Then there were gales of laughter as they spotted the white cottontail strategically placed on the back of his tux.

It hadn't taken Luke long to learn how to milk a bit. His head craned, he turned three circles, struggling to get a look at his own rear.

"A slight miscalculation," Max apologized when things quieted. "To prove no hard feelings, I'll make it disappear."

Lily pouted prettily. "You promise?"

"On my honor," Max swore, placing a hand over his heart. He whipped off his cape, swirled it over Luke, then passed his wand over the silk-shrouded form. Even as the cape began to drift toward the floor, Max took up a corner and swung the silk high.

"Max!" Lily gasped out his name, horrified.

"I kept my word." He took a deep bow toward her, then the cheering audience. "The tail's gone. And so is the presumptuous brat."

As Lily and Max segued into the finale, Luke stood in the wings. Transfixed. They were applauding. They were cheering. For him. Luke leaned forward in the wings, staring at Max as he prepared to saw Lily in half.

It was only for the barest of instants that their eyes met, held. But in that instant there was such a wealth of understanding, and joy, that Luke felt his throat burn.

For the first time in his life he began to love another man. And there was no shame in it.

*

LUKE HAUNTED THE MIDWAY. It was long after the last show, but he still carried the sound of applause and laughter inside his head, like an old song that kept repeating its melody over and over.

He'd been somebody. For a few brief moments, he'd been someone who'd mattered. Before the baffled eyes of dozens of people, he'd vanished.

And they'd believed.

That was the secret, Luke thought to himself as he strutted along past the tired carnies who were still rambling out their spiel to the dwindling crowd. Making people believe an illusion was reality, if only for a split second. That was power, true power that went beyond fists and fury. He wondered if he would be able to explain to anyone that it was all in the mind. And his mind was now so full of that power it felt as though it might split apart, and light would spill out, hot and white.

He knew Max would understand the sensation, but he wasn't ready to share what was inside him with anyone. For tonight, this first night, it was his alone.

The ten dollars Max had given him after the last show crinkled against his fingers when he slipped a hand into his pocket. The urge to spend it was amazingly strong—stronger than the hunger he'd learned to ignore. He stared at the blur of lights from the Ferris wheel, heard the rumble of cars whirling on the Crack the Whip. Tonight he could ride them all.

The little figure in jeans and a baggy shirt darted across his vision, made him stop, then frown, then swear.

"Roxanne! Hey, hey, Rox!" He scrambled after her, grabbing her arm. "What the hell do you think you are doing out?"

She'd thought about it all right. She'd thought about being cooped up in bed feeling miserable while Luke took her place onstage. She'd thought about how endless the days had become, and how itchy the nights. And she'd thought about the fact that they would be in New Orleans, the summer season behind them, before she was clear of spots.

"I'm going for a ride."

"Like hell."

Her pale face flushed with angry color. "You can't tell me what to do, Luke Callahan. Not now, not ever. I'm going for a ride on the Ferris wheel, right now."

"Look, little miss shit for brains." But before he could finish the thought, she'd rapped him hard in the stomach with her elbow. She was off and running before he caught his breath. "Goddammit, Roxy." He snagged her again only because she got stuck in line. He started to tug her out, but this time she rounded on him with teeth.

"You crazy or what?"

"I'm going for a ride." She folded her arms over her thin chest. The colored lights played over her face, making her blotches eerily festive.

He could walk away. She certainly would tell no one he'd seen her. After all, she wasn't his responsibility. But for reasons he couldn't begin to fathom he stuck by her side. He'd even reached for his money to pay their fares when the operator, who knew Roxy well, waved them both on.

Like a princess granting an audience, Roxanne nodded to Luke. "You can ride with me if you want."

"Thanks loads." He dropped down beside her and waited for the clang of the safety bar.

Roxanne didn't squeal or gasp as the wheel started its backward ascent. She merely sat back, closed her eyes and let a small, satisfied smile play around her lips. Years later, Luke would look back on that moment and realize that she had looked like a satisfied woman relaxing in an easy chair after a long day.

She didn't speak until the wheel had completed a full revolution. When she did, her voice was oddly adult.

"I'm tired of being inside. I can't see the lights, I can't see the people."

"It's the same every night."

"It's different every night." She opened her eyes then, emeralds in which all the colors around them flashed. She leaned forward against the bar, and the wind rippled her hair back witchlike into the sky. "See that skinny man down there, the one with the straw hat? I've never seen him before. And that girl in the shorts carrying the stuffed poodle? I don't know her either. So it's different." As they climbed again, she threw her face back to the stars. "I used to think that we'd go right up through the sky. That I could touch it and bring it back down with me." She smiled a little, just old enough to be amused at the childishness of the thought—and child enough to wish it could be true. "I wanted to do it. Just once."

"A lot of good it would do you down here." But he smiled as well. It had been a long time since he'd ridden a Ferris wheel. So long he could barely remember the sensation of having his stomach drop away and his body circling fast to catch up.

"You did a good job tonight, with the act," Roxanne said suddenly. "I heard Daddy say so when he was talking to Lily. They thought I was asleep."

"Yeah?" He struggled to feign indifference.

"He said that he'd seen something in you, and you didn't disappoint him." Roxanne lifted her arms straight up. The rush of air felt glorious on her itchy skin. "I guess you're going to be part of the act."

The ripple of excitement Luke felt had nothing to do with the quick downward drop. "It's something to do." He shrugged to show insouciance. "As long as I'm hanging around." When he glanced over she was watching him, measuring.

"He says you've done things, seen things you shouldn't have. What things?"

Humiliation, anger and a sick sense of horror collided inside of him. Max knew, Luke thought. Somehow he knew. He felt his skin heat up, but his voice was cool. "I don't know what you're talking about."

"Yes, you do."

"If I do, it's none of your business."

"If you stay with us, it is. I know all about Mouse and Lily and LeClerc."

"Who the hell's LeClerc?"

"He cooks for us in New Orleans and helps Daddy with the cabaret act. He robbed banks."

"No shit?"

Pleased that she'd snagged his full attention, Roxanne nodded. "He's been to prison and everything 'cause he got caught. He taught Daddy how to open any lock there is." Because she felt like pulling away from him, she rounded back. "So, I should know all about you, too. That's the way it works."

"I haven't said I'm staying yet. I got plans of my own."

"You'll stay," Roxanne said half to herself. "Daddy wants you to. And Lily. Daddy will teach you magic if you want to learn. Like he teaches me. Only I'll be better." Her lashes didn't even flutter at his snort of derision. "I'm going to be the best."

"We'll see about that," he murmured as they wheeled into the sky. He turned his face to the wind. When he did, he almost believed that what he had done was nothing, nothing compared to what he could do.

Chapter Five

LUKE'S FIRST IMPRESSION OF NEW ORLEANS WAS A JUMBLED whirl of sounds and scents. While Max, Lily and Roxanne bedded down in the trailer, he'd been curled in the cab of the truck, bored into patchy sleep by the sound of Mouse's tuneless humming. They'd argued about the radio since Shreveport, but Mouse stood firm. He refused to have any noise that would interfere with the pleasure of listening to his engine.

Now other sounds had begun to drift into Luke's logy brain. Voices pitched high and shrieking laughter, the clashes of sax and drum and trumpet. As he floated awake, he thought they were back at the carnival. He could smell food, a spice on the air and the underlying reek of garbage gone ripe in the heat.

Yawning, he opened his eyes and blinked out his open window.

People, masses of people, streamed past in the streets. He saw a juggler who looked like Jesus tossing bright orange balls that glowed in the dark. An enormously fat woman in a flowered muumuu was doing a solo boogie to the backwash of Dixieland that poured through an open doorway. He smelled hot dogs.

The circus is in town, he thought as he struggled to sit up.

And he saw they had left the traveling carnival behind to join a more massive and more permanent one.

"Where are we?"

Mouse negotiated the truck and trailer through the narrow streets. "Home," he said simply as he drove past Bourbon Street toward Chartres.

Luke couldn't have said why the word made him grin.

He could still hear the music, but it was fainter now. There were fewer people walking along these quieter streets. Some were heading to the action, some away. In the flickering lights of the streetlamps, he caught glimpses of old brick buildings, of flower-drenched balconies, of cabs hurrying by with fares and of figures curled up to sleep in doorways.

He didn't see how anyone could sleep with the music, the smells, the unbelievable heat. His own fatigue had vanished, to be replaced by a clenching impatience with the way Mouse was creeping along.

Luke wanted to get where they were going. Wherever it was.

"Jesus, Mouse, you go any slower, we'll be backing up."

"No hurry," Mouse said, then stunned Luke by stopping completely in the middle of the street and getting out.

"What the hell are you doing?" Luke scrambled out himself to see Mouse standing by an open iron gate. "You can't leave that thing sitting in the middle of the road. You'll bring the cops."

"Just refreshing my memory." Mouse stood, stroking his chin. "Gotta back her in."

"Back *what?*" Luke's eyes popped wide. He did a quick dance of disbelief toward the gate and back to the truck. "Back that thing in here?" Luke scanned the opening between two unforgiving brick walls, then turned to judge the width of the trailer. "No way in hell."

Mouse smiled. His eyes glowed like a sinner's who'd just found religion. "You just stand out here, in case I need you." He sauntered back to the truck.

"Can't be done," Luke called after him.

But Mouse was humming again as he began to maneuver the truck and trailer across the narrow street.

"You're going to hit. Jesus, Mouse." Luke braced for the sound of scraping metal. His mouth dropped open when the big black trailer slid into the opening as easily as a hand into a glove. As the truck backed in behind it, Mouse glanced over at Luke. And winked.

It was a fine thing. For some reason the parking of the truck and trailer struck Luke as an event as fine as Christmas, or the opening day of a new baseball season. His own laughter rocked him back on his heels while he stood blinded by the headlights.

"Man, you are number one," Luke shouted as Mouse climbed out of the truck. Then he whirled like a boxer at the ready when a light flashed on in the house beside them. "Who's that?" he demanded of Mouse as he spotted a figure in the doorway.

"LeClerc." Jiggling the keys in his pocket, Mouse moved forward to shut the iron gates to the courtyard.

"So, you've returned." LeClerc stepped down, and in the backwash of light Luke saw a small man with gray hair and a full beard. He wore a snowy white athletic T-shirt and baggy gray trousers held up with a hunk of rope. His voice was touched with a slight accent, not the fluid drawl of Max's, but something sharper that seemed to add syllables to words. "And you're hungry, yes?"

"Didn't stop to eat," Mouse called out.

"Good you didn't." LeClerc came forward, his gait stiff and uneven. Luke saw that he was old, older than Max by a decade or more. The boy's impression was of an ancient face, a tattered leather map scored with hundreds of deeply traveled roads. The brown eyes were wide-set and shrewd under wiry brows.

LeClerc saw a slim young boy with a beautiful face dominated by wary eyes. A boy who was poised on the balls of his feet as if to run, or to fight.

"And who would this be?"

"This is Luke," Max said as he stepped out of the trailer with a dozing Roxanne in his arms. "He's with us now."

Something passed between the two men that seemed all the more intimate with being left unsaid.

"Another one, eh?" LeClerc's lips curved briefly around the stem of the pipe he kept clenched permanently between his teeth. "We'll see. And how is my *bébé*?"

Heavy-eyed, Roxanne held out her arms and was gathered up to LeClerc. She settled against the bone and sinew as though he were a feather pillow. "Can I have a beignet?"

"I make just for you, don't I?" LeClerc pulled the pipe out of his mouth to kiss her cheek. "You are better, *oui*?"

"I had the chicken pox forever. I'm never, never getting sick again."

"I make you a gris-gris for good health." He settled her comfortably on his hip as Lily stepped out. She carried a heavy makeup bag over one arm of her flowing negligee. "Ah, Mademoiselle Lily." LeClerc managed to bow despite the child on his hip. "More beautiful than ever."

She giggled and held out a hand for him to kiss, which he did with smooth aplomb. "It's good to be home, Jean."

"Come in, come in. Enjoy the midnight supper I make for you."

At the mention of dinner, Max stepped over from the trailer and greeted LeClerc as he led the way across the courtyard, where roses and lilies and begonias bloomed in profusion, up a short flight of steps and through a door that opened into the kitchen. There a light was burning to shine on the polished surfaces of white tile and dark wood.

There was a small hearth of bricks that had been smoked from red to a comfortable rose gray. Atop it stood a plastic glow-in-the-dark statue of the Blessed Virgin, and what looked like an Indian rattle dressed with beads and feathers.

Though it was too miraculously cool inside for Luke to believe the bricked oven had been used, he would have sworn he caught the tantalizing odor of bread just baked.

Dried bouquets of spices and herbs hung from the ceiling, along with dangling ropes of onion and garlic. Gleaming copper pots were suspended from iron hooks above the stove. Another pot, with steam puffing out, sat on the back burner. Whatever was simmering inside smelled like paradise.

A long butcher-block table had already been set with bowls and plates and brightly checked linen napkins. Still carrying Roxanne, LeClerc reached inside a cupboard for another place setting.

"Gumbo." Lily sighed as she slipped an arm around Luke's shoulders. She wanted badly to welcome him home. "No one cooks like Jean, honey. Just wait until you taste. If I don't watch myself, I'll be popping right out of my costume within a week."

"Tonight you don't worry, you just eat." LeClerc set Roxanne down in a chair, then picking up two thick cloths, hefted the pot from the stove.

Luke watched, fascinated, as the tattoo which wound from bony wrist to bony shoulder rippled and danced. They were snakes, Luke realized. A nest of vipers in faded blue and red that twisted and twined over the leathered skin.

They all but hissed.

"You like?" LeClerc's eyes were merry as he studied Luke. "Snakes, they are quick, and cunning. Good luck for me." He made a sibilant sound as he darted his arm toward Luke. "Snakes won't do for you, boy." He chuckled to himself as he dished up the thick, spicy gumbo. "You bring me a young wolf, Max. He'll bite first."

"A wolf needs a pack." Casually, Max lifted a basket from the table and uncovered a golden loaf of bread. He offered the basket to Lily.

"What am I, LeClerc?" Wide awake now, Roxanne was spooning up her gumbo.

"You." The leathery, lined face softened as he passed his wide, gnarled hand over her hair. "My little kitten."

"Just a kitten?"

"Ah, but kittens are clever and brave and wise, and some grow to be tigers."

That brightened her look. She slanted her eyes toward Luke. "Tigers can eat wolves."

WHEN THE MOON HAD BEGUN to set, and even the echoes of music from Bourbon Street had faded, LeClerc sat on a marble bench in the courtyard, surrounded by the flowers he loved.

It was Max who owned the house, but it was Jean LeClerc who had made it a home. He'd taken long-ago memories of a cabin in the bayou, and flowers that had run wild, blossoms his mother had tamed in plastic pots, the smells of potpourri and spice, of colored cloths and polished woods, and had mixed them together with Max's need for elegance.

LeClerc would have been happy back in the swamp, but he wouldn't have been happy without Max, and the family Max had given him.

He smoked his pipe and listened to the night. The faintest breeze rustled the magnolia leaves, stirring the heat and promising rain much as a teasing woman might promise a kiss. The dampness that was gradually wearing away the brick and stone of the French Quarter hung like a mist in the air.

He didn't see Max approach, nor did he hear him, though his hearing was keen. He felt him.

"So." He puffed on his pipe and studied the stars. "What will you do with the boy?"

"Give him a chance," Max said. "The same as you gave me a lifetime ago."

"His eyes want to swallow everything he sees. Such appetites can be difficult."

"So I'll feed him." There was a hint of impatience in Max's voice as he joined LeClerc on the bench. "Would you have me send him away?"

"It's too late to be practical now that your heart's involved."

"Lily's attached," Max began and was cut off by LeClerc's rumbling laugh.

"Only Lily, *mon ami*?"

Max took time to light a cigar, draw in smoke. "I'm fond of the boy."

"You love the boy," LeClerc corrected. "And how could it be otherwise, when you look and see yourself? He makes you remember."

It was difficult to admit it. Max knew when you loved you could also hurt and be hurt. "He makes me remember not to forget. If you forget all the pain, the loneliness, the despair, you forget to be grateful for the lack of it. You taught me that, Jean."

"So good, my student is now the master. This contents me." LeClerc turned his head and his dark eyes gleamed through the shadows. "Will it content you when he outreaches what you are?"

"I don't know." Max looked down at his hands. They were good ones, agile, quick and clever. He was afraid what it would do to his heart when they slowed. "I've begun to teach him magic. I haven't decided if I'll teach him the rest."

"You won't keep secrets from those eyes for long. What was he doing when you found him?"

Max had to smile. "Picking pockets."

"Ah." LeClerc chuckled over his pipe. "So, he is already one of us. Is he as good as you were?"

"Every bit as good," Max admitted. "Perhaps better than I at that age. Less fear of reprisal, more ruthless. But there is a long leap between lifting wallets at a carnival and picking locks at grand houses and fine hotels."

"A leap you made gracefully. Regrets, *mon ami*?"

"None." Max laughed again. "What's wrong with me?"

"You were born to steal," LeClerc said with a shrug. "Just as you were to pull rabbits out of hats. And, apparently, as you were to take in strays. It's good to have you home."

"It's good to be home."

For a moment they sat in silence, enjoying the night. Then LeClerc got down to business.

"The diamonds you sent from Boston were exceptional."

"I preferred the pearls from Charleston."

"Ah, yes." LeClerc sighed out smoke. "They were elegant, but the diamonds had such fire. It pained me to take money for them."

"And you got ...?"

"Ten thousand, only five for the pearls, despite their elegance."

"The pleasure of holding them outweighs the profit." He remembered, with pleasure, how they had looked against Lily's skin for one glorious evening. "And the painting?"

"Twenty-two thousand. Me, I thought it a clumsy work. Those English painters had no passion," he added, dismissing the Turner landscape with a shrug. "The Chinese vase I hold awhile longer. Did you bring the coin collection with you?"

"No, I didn't get it. When Roxanne took sick, I canceled that engagement."

"Best." LeClerc nodded and smoked. "Worry for her would have distracted you."

"I would hardly have been at my best. So, until the vase is placed, that makes the tithe ... thirty-seven hundred." A glance at LeClerc's scowl made Max smile. "So little to resent so much."

"By the end of the year, you'll have thrown fifteen thousand away at least. Add this to each year you've been taking ten percent to ease your conscience—"

"A gift to charity," Max interrupted, amused. "I don't do it to ease my conscience, but to appease my soul. I'm a thief, Jean, an excellent one who thinks nothing of the people from whom I steal, but quite a bit about those I see who have nothing worth stealing."

He studied the glowing tip of his cigar. "I may not be able to live with the morality of others, but I must live with my own."

"The churches you give your tithe to would damn you to hell."

"I've escaped from worse places than the hell priests imagine for us."

"It's not a joke."

Max smothered a smile as he rose. He knew that LeClerc's religion ran the gamut from Catholicism to voodoo, and any handy superstition in between. "Then think of it as insurance. Perhaps my foolish generosity will ensure us both a cooler place in the hereafter. Let's get some sleep." He laid a hand on LeClerc's shoulder. "Tomorrow I'll tell you what I've planned for the next few months."

LUKE KNEW HE'D FOUND HEAVEN. There was no list of chores the next day so he was free to wander the house, which he did gobbling beignets he'd snatched from the kitchen. The trail of powdered sugar in his wake dribbled through the first floor, up the stairs, onto one of the long flower-twined balconies and back again.

He couldn't believe his good fortune.

He'd been given a room of his own, and had spent a great deal of a wakeful night looking, touching. The high, carved headboard had fascinated him, as had the soft sheen of the wallpaper and the muted pattern of the rug. There was a huge cupboard that Max had called an armoire. Luke figured it would hold more clothes than any one person would need in a lifetime.

And there were flowers. A tall blue vase was filled with them. He'd never had flowers in his room before, and though he knew he should dismiss them as sissy, their fragrance brought him a deep and secret pleasure.

Luke drifted through the house as soundlessly as smoke. He wasn't sure of LeClerc as yet and easily avoided the man while he made his explorations.

The furnishings reflected Max's elegance. It gave Luke a sense of his mentor, though he didn't recognize the French and British antiques. What he saw were graceful gleaming tables, curvy sofas, pretty china lamps and peaceful landscapes.

As much as he liked the house, Luke found his favorite spot on the balcony outside his room. From there he could smell the heat of the flowers and the street. He could watch people snapping pictures and searching for souvenirs.

He couldn't help but notice how careless people were with their wallets. Women with their shoulder bags dangling, men with their cash tucked into the back pocket of their bell-bottoms. A pickpocket's paradise. If Miami didn't pan out, Luke decided he could do very well here, supplementing his salary as a sorcerer's apprentice.

"You got sugar all over," Roxanne said from behind him.

Luke tensed. He snuck a look down at his hands and saw with disgust that the evidence was all over his fingers. Hastily, he wiped them on his jeans. "So?"

"LeClerc'll get mad. Sugar draws bugs."

He wiped his hands again, because they'd grown damp. "I'll clean it up."

She joined him at the rail, looking pretty and prim in a yellow shorts set. "What're you doing?"

"Just looking."

"Daddy says we can take the whole day off. Tomorrow we have to start rehearsing the new cabaret act for the club."

"What club?"

"The Magic Door. We work there." She began to play with the flowers that twined along the rail. "We can do bigger illusions there than at the carnival, and sometimes Daddy goes over during the day and does close-up work for some of the customers."

LeClerc's annoyance and any possible reprisals shifted to the back of Luke's mind. He didn't know what his place would be in a cabaret act, but he was going to make sure he had one. "How many shows a night?"

"Two." After plucking a clematis bloom, she tried to wind the slim stem around her ear. "Eight, and eleven. We're the headliners." She wrinkled her nose. "I have to take a nap after school every day. Like a baby."

Luke wasn't the least bit concerned about Roxanne's problems. "Does he keep in the card tricks?"

She patted the flower as she wandered back into Luke's bedroom to study the result in the mirror. "Oh, he'll make up other ones."

Luke nodded and began to plan. He was getting pretty good at the tricks he'd wheedled Roxanne into showing him. And he'd been practicing at least an hour a day with the Cups and Balls. He just needed to show Max. He couldn't bear it if they cut him out of the act now.

"Daddy gave me money for ice cream." She poked her head back out the French doors. "You want to go get some?"

"No." Luke was much too busy to be distracted by a treat and an eight-year-old's company. "Take off, will you? I have to think."

"More for me," Roxanne shot back, barely controlling a pout.

The minute he was alone, Luke dug out his cards and began to practice. He'd hardly begun to set up Aces High when he was distracted again.

It was the voice. He'd never heard anything like it. He tried to brush it out of his mind, but it kept flowing back. A rich, heartbreaking alto that seemed to be singing just for him. Unable to resist, he walked back out on the balcony.

He spotted her instantly. A woman in a flowing flowered dress, a red turban over her head, her skin gleaming like ebony. She stood on the corner, a cardboard box at her feet as she sang swaying gospel a cappella.

He couldn't turn away, the sound all but hypnotizing him. This was true beauty. Even as he realized it, it reached deep inside him to a place he didn't know existed.

That voice rang out over the Quarter. It never paused or hesitated when she drew a small crowd. She never glanced down when coins thudded into the box.

It made his skin prickle and his throat ache.

On impulse he dashed back inside and dug out the bag he'd secreted under his pillow. From it he took a crumpled dollar. His heart was still soaring to the music as he raced out of the room and down the stairs.

He saw Roxanne in the hallway, sweeping up powdered sugar while LeClerc stood behind her, lecturing.

"You eat in the kitchen, not all over the house. You be sure you get all those crumbs, you hear?"

"I'm getting them." She lifted her head to stick her tongue out at Luke.

His heart was so full of the music, his brain so dazzled by the idea that Roxanne was taking the blame for him, he missed the last step. On a muffled cry, he threw out a hand to save himself.

For Luke it happened in slow motion. He saw the vase, the faceted crystal alive with sunlight, filled with bloodred roses. In horror, he saw his own hand sweep at it, watched it teeter even as he scrambled for balance.

His fingers brushed it. He felt the cool glass on his skin and let out a groan of despair as it slipped away.

The sound of the vase shattering on the hardwood was like a volley of pistol shots. Luke stood frozen, the glistening shards at his feet, and the smell of roses heavy in the air.

LeClerc was swearing. Luke didn't have to understand French to know the oaths were strong and furious. He didn't move, didn't bother to run. He was braced for a blow, had already taken that part of himself that felt pain and humiliation away. What stood there was a silent shell that would refuse to care.

"You run through my house like a wild Indian. Now you break

the Waterford, you bruise the roses and you have water all over my floor. *Imbécile!* Look what you've done to my beauties."

"Jean." Max's voice was hardly more than a whisper, but it cut through the old man's tantrum.

"The Waterford, Max." LeClerc crouched down to save his roses. "The boy was running like hounds of hell were after him. I tell you he needs to be—"

"Jean," Max said again. "Enough. Look at his face."

With roses dripping from his hands, LeClerc glanced up. The boy was ghost white, his eyes dark and glazed over with something too deep to be termed fear. With a sigh, he straightened. "I'll get another vase," he said quietly and walked away.

"Daddy." Shaken, Roxanne gripped her father's hand. "Why does he look that way?"

"It's all right, Roxy. Run along."

"But, Daddy—"

"Run along," he repeated, and gave her a nudge.

She stepped back into the parlor, but she didn't go far. For once her father was too intent on someone else to notice.

"You disappoint me, Luke," Max said quietly.

Something flickered in Luke's belly, and showed briefly in his eyes. An oath, a blow, wouldn't have touched him, but the simple sadness in Max's voice cut deep.

"I'm sorry." The words burned like acid in his icy throat. "I can pay for it. I have money."

Don't send me away, his heart begged. God, please don't send me away.

"What are you sorry for?"

"I wasn't looking where I was going. I'm clumsy. Stupid." And all the rest he'd been accused of during his twelve short years. "I'm sorry," he said again, becoming more desperate as he waited for the blow. Or worse, so much worse, a shove out the door. "I was hurrying because I thought she might go away."

"Who?"

"The woman. Singing on the corner. I wanted to . . . " Realizing the absurdity of it, Luke looked helplessly at the bill still crumpled in his hand.

"I see." And because he did, Max's heart all but broke. "She often sings there. You'll hear her again."

Fresh terror swam into his eyes as he looked back at Max. It was so much more frightening to hope. "I can—I can stay?"

On a long breath, Max bent down and picked up a piece of shattered crystal. "What do you see here?"

"It's broken. I broke it. I never think about anyone else but myself, and I—"

"Stop it."

The sharp order had Luke's head snapping up. Somewhere inside he began to tremble as he realized he couldn't hide from this. When Max hit him it wouldn't just be the physical pain, it would shatter his hopes as completely as he'd shattered the vase.

"It's broken," Max said, struggling for calm. "And it's quite true you broke it. Did you mean to?"

"No, but I—"

"Look at this." He held the piece of glass toward Luke. "It's a thing. An object. Something anyone with the price can own. Do you think you mean less to me than this?" When he tossed it aside, Luke couldn't hold the trembling inside any longer. "Do you think so little of me that you believe I'd strike you for breaking a glass?"

"I don't . . . " Luke's breath began to hitch as the pressure in his chest spread like brushfire. He couldn't stop the hot, hateful tears from spilling out. "Please. Don't make me go."

"My dear child, can you have been with me all these weeks and not know I'm different from them? Did they scar you that badly?"

Beyond words now, Luke only shook his head.

"I've been where you've been," Max murmured, and took the next step by gathering Luke against him. The boy stiffened, the primitive fear running deep. Then even the fear crumbled as Max eased him down on the steps and rocked him. "No one can make you go back. You're safe here."

He knew he should be humiliated, blubbering like a baby against Max's shirt. But the arms around him were strong, solid, real.

What kind of a boy is it, Max wondered, who can be so moved by a song that he would part with one of his precious dollars to pay for it? How deeply could such a boy be hurt by casual cruelty, and the lack of choice?

"Can you tell me what they did to you?"

Shame welled up, and the need—oh the need for someone to understand. "I couldn't do anything. I couldn't make it stop."

"I know."

The old angers simmered out even as the tears fell. "They beat me all the time. If I did something, if I didn't do it. If they were drunk, if they were sober." His fists clenched against Max's shirt like small balls of iron. "Sometimes they'd lock me up, and I'd beat on the closet door and beg them to let me out. I couldn't get out. I could never get out."

It was hideous to remember that, weeping hysterically in the dark coffin of the closet, with no hope, no help, no escape.

"The social workers would come, and if I didn't say the right thing, he'd take after me with the belt. The last time, that last time before I left, I thought he was going to kill me. He wanted to. I know he wanted to—you can tell when it's in their eyes, but I don't know why. I don't know why."

"It wasn't your fault. None of it was your fault." Max stroked the boy's head and fought back his own demons. "People tell their children there are no monsters in the world. They tell them that because they believe it, or they want the child to feel safe. But there are monsters, Luke, all the more frightening because they look like people." He drew the boy back to study his wet, ravaged face. "You're free of them now."

"I hate him."

"You're entitled to that."

There was more. He wasn't certain he dared speak of it. The shame was black and oily. But with Max's eyes so quiet and intense on his, Luke stumbled through it. "He—he brought a man one night. It was late and they were drunk. Al went out and locked the door. And the man—he tried—"

"It's all right." He tried to gather Luke close again, but the horror had the boy scrambling back.

"He put his fat hands on me, and his mouth." Luke wiped his own with the back of his hand. "He said how he'd paid Al, and I was supposed to do things to him, and let him do them to me. And I was stupid, 'cause I didn't know what he meant."

There were no tears now, but a rage, burning dry. "I didn't know until he got on top of me. I thought he was going to smother me until ... " The sheer terror of it boomeranged back. The sweaty skin and the stink of gin, the greedy hands groping.

"Then I knew, all right. I knew." His hands clenched and unclenched, leaving deep crescents in his palms. "I hit him, and I hit him, but he wouldn't stop. So I bit and I scratched. I had his blood all over my hands, and he was holding his face and screaming. Then Al came in, and he beat me for a long time. And I don't remember—I don't know if ... " That was the worst, the not knowing. It was a shame he couldn't speak out loud. "That's the night he wanted to kill me. That's the night I left."

Max was silent for a long time, so long Luke was afraid he'd said too much, much too much to ever be forgiven.

"You did everything right." There was a heaviness in Max's voice that had tears stinging Luke's eyes again. "And I can promise you this. No one will ever touch you in that way again, while you're with me. And I'll teach you the way out of the closet." Max's eyes came back to Luke's and held. "They may lock you in, but they won't keep you there."

Luke tried to speak, but the words caught in his throat before he forced them out. His life depended on the answer. "I can stay?"

"Until you want to go."

His gratitude was so huge, he thought it might burst from him like light. Like love. "I'll pay for the vase," he managed. "I promise."

"You already have. Now, run wash your face. We'd best clean this up before LeClerc has another tantrum."

Max sat on the steps as Luke bounded up them. From her hiding place in the parlor, Roxanne heard her father sigh. And she wept.

Chapter Six

Over the next few days, Luke felt his way carefully. He was unsure of LeClerc, and knew only that the Cajun was in charge of the house. Luke did his best to keep out of the way. He never made the mistake of dropping crumbs through the house again.

He went shopping with Lily, carrying boxes and bags for her up and down the steamy streets. He sat patiently in boutiques as she picked over new clothes, stood by while she oohed and aahed over trinkets in windows.

His love for her was deep enough to have him tolerating her choosing outfits for him. So deep that he hardly winced at the paisley shirts she bought him. If he had free time, he haunted the Quarter, content to explore, to listen to the street musicians, to watch the artists work around Jackson Square.

But the best time for Luke was when they rehearsed.

The Magic Door was a cramped, dim club that smelled of the whiskey fumes and smoke that had soaked into the walls for decades. On those hot afternoons, the shades would be drawn against the sun and the tourists. The air conditioner made grinding sounds that were more industrious than the resulting puff of tepid air it produced. The ceiling fan did a bit more, but with the stage lights lit, the club was like a small furnace.

The walls were papered in red and gold velvet, the wall behind the bar mirrored to give the illusion of space. It was like being a bug inside a decorated box, and the forgetful child who'd captured you had neglected to punch holes in the top.

Luke loved it.

Every afternoon, Lester Friedmont, the manager, would sit at the front table, nursing a beer and the short stub of a lit cigar. He was a tall man who carried all of his extra weight in his belly. Invariably he wore a white short-sleeved shirt, with a tie and matching suspenders. His black laced shoes were always shined. His thinning hair was slicked back and gleamed wetly under the lights. He looked at his world through the smudged lenses of heavy black glasses perched on the end of his angular nose.

A fat calico cat he called Fifi would prowl around his legs, waddle off to nibble from the dish set under the bar, then prowl back again.

Friedmont kept a phone on the table. He had the ability to watch the rehearsal and add his comments, harass whoever was cleaning the club and talk on the phone simultaneously.

It took Luke several afternoons to realize that Friedmont was a bookie.

No matter how often they would run through a bit, Lester would hoot and shake his head. "Jesus please us, that was a good one. You going to tell me how you did that one, Max?"

"Sorry, Lester. Trade secret."

So Lester would go back to taking bets and scratching his belly.

Max planned to start off the act with sleight of hand, and some colored scarf tricks, similar to what he'd done in the carnival. Then he wanted to add his own version of the Floating Ball before bringing Roxanne out for his new Levitating Girl. He'd added a spin to sawing a woman in half by using a vertical box and cutting Lily into three parts. It was nearly perfected.

He was trying Luke out in bits and pieces. He had no doubts about the boy's quick mind and quick hands. Now he was testing Luke's heart. "Watch," he said to Luke. "Learn."

Standing center stage, Max pulled silks out of his pocket; color after vivid color poured out. Luke's lips began to twitch. He didn't understand that what he was seeing was pure timing. The longer the bit lasted, the longer the audience would laugh—and be misdirected.

"Hold out your arms," Max ordered, then draped the scarves over Luke's arms seemingly at random. "We'll have music to go with this. Lily?"

She turned on the tape recorder. "The Blue Danube."

"The waltz is slow, lovely," Max said. "The gestures mirror it." His hands flowed over the scarves, lifted, fell as he walked around Luke. "And, of course, if I've chosen a beautiful woman from the audience to stand in your place, this adds to the showmanship, and the beauty of the illusion. And her reaction will cue the audience to theirs." A snap of the wrist and Max plucked the end of a scarf; as he whipped it back, the others followed, all neatly tied together, scarlet to yellow, yellow to sapphire, sapphire to emerald.

Luke's eyes popped wide an instant before his grin spread.

"Excellent." Max scooped up the scarves, balled them into a colorful orb as he spoke. "So you see, even in such a small trick, showmanship, stage presence, is every bit as important as dexterity. To do a trick well is never enough. But to do it with a flourish . . ." He tossed the ball into the air, and the scarves, no longer joined, floated down.

Nearby Roxanne giggled and clapped her hands. "I like that one, Daddy."

"My best audience." He bent down to pick up the silks. "Show me."

Roxanne rubbed her hands together, gnawed on her lip. "I can't do as many yet."

"What you can, then."

Nerves and pride jangled together as she chose six of the scarves. Turning to the imaginary audience, she tugged each between her hands, then waving each in the air, draped them on Luke's arms. There was an undeniably feminine touch to her gestures that made Max smile as she turned her hands over and under the silks. Though she moved to the music as she executed a series of slow pirouettes around Luke, her concentration was total. There was no such thing as a small trick in Roxanne's world. They were all huge.

Facing Luke again, she smiled, skimmed her hands over the scarves once more, as a woman might stroke a cat, then taking the end, she whirled them over her head. She laughed in triumph as she wound the tied scarves around her shoulders.

"Well done." Max scooped her up to kiss her. "Quite well done."

"She's a pistol, Max," Lester called out. "You ought to let her try it out in front of a crowd."

"What do you say, Roxanne?" Max stroked a hand over her hair as he set her down. "Ready to try a solo?"

"Can I?" Her heart leaped into her eyes. "Daddy, please, can I?"

"We'll try it out in the first show, then we'll see."

She let out a shriek and raced to Lily. "Can I wear earrings? Real ones? Can I?"

She smiled at Max over Roxanne's head. "You can pick out the ones you like best."

"The ones in the window down the street. The blue ones."

"Take twenty minutes, Lily," Max suggested. "A woman needs at least that much time to choose accessories for her costume." And he wanted a moment alone with Luke.

"So." As Roxanne dragged Lily out, Max picked up a deck of cards. He began to do one-handed cuts. "You're wondering why a little girl can do something you can't."

Luke flushed, but his chin stayed up. "I can learn anything she can."

"Possibly." To entertain himself, Max fanned the cards. "I could tell you it's a mistake to use her, or anyone, as a yardstick for yourself. But you wouldn't listen."

"You could teach me."

"I could," Max agreed.

"I already know some. I've been practicing."

"Indeed." Raising a brow, Max offered the cards. "Show me."

Nerves dampened his fingertips as Luke shuffled the cards. "It won't be as good, because you know how I'll do it."

"Ah, there you're wrong. A magician's best audience is another magician. Because they understand the purpose. Do you?"

"To do a trick," Luke responded, struggling to concentrate on the cards.

"As simple as that? Sit," Max suggested. Once they were seated at one of the tables, he chose a card from the pack Luke held out. "Anyone can learn to do a trick. It only takes an understanding of how it works, and a basic skill that can be refined with practice. But magic." He glanced at the card, then slipped it back into the pack. "Magic is taking what's real and what's not, and blending them into one, for a short period. It's causing someone who doesn't believe to blink in amazement. It's giving people what they want."

"What do they want?" Luke shuffled the cards, tapped the top, then turned over Max's card. His heart swelled at Max's nod of approval.

"Excellent. Do another." He sat back as Luke fumbled through a one-handed cut. "What do they want? To be duped, to be fooled, and amazed. To watch the astounding happen under their nose." Max opened his hand and showed Luke a small red ball. "Right before their eyes." He slapped the ball on the table, then took his other hand from under the wood. The ball was there, his other hand empty. Luke grinned and set the cards for Aces High.

"You palmed it," Luke said. "I know you did, but I didn't see."

"Because I looked at you, in your eyes. So you looked in mine. Always look them in the eye. Innocently, smugly, however you choose. But look them in the eye. This makes an illusion honest."

"A trick's a cheat, isn't it?"

"Only if you can't make them enjoy the deception." He nodded again when Luke drew the four aces from the top of the shuffled deck. "Your mechanics are good, but where is your flair? Where is that drama that tells the audience it's not simply a well-practiced trick, but magic? Again," he said, shoving the cards toward Luke. "Astound me."

Max watched the concentration come into Luke's eyes, heard the two deep indrawn breaths as he prepared.

"I want to do the first one again."

"All right. Let me hear your patter."

Luke's color came up, but he cleared his throat and dived in. He'd been practicing for weeks. "I'd like to show you a few card tricks." He did a fair Russian shuffle, and a snappy turnover. "Now, not many magicians will tell you what they're going to do beforehand. But I'm just a kid. I don't know any better." He fanned the cards face out toward his imaginary audience so they could identify it as an ordinary deck. "I'm going to ask this gentleman here to pick a card, any card at all." Luke spread the cards facedown on the table, waited a beat while Max reached for one. "That one?" he said and looked uneasy. "You sure you want that one?"

Playing along, Max inclined his head. "Indeed I do."

"You sure you wouldn't rather take this one?" Luke tapped the end card. "No?" He swallowed audibly when Max held firm. "Okay. Remember, I'm just a kid. If you'd show the card to the audience. Make sure I don't see it," Luke added as he tried to crane his neck to get a glimpse of the card. "Good." His voice shook. "I guess you can put it back in, anywhere, anywhere at all. Then you can shuffle them—unless you want me to," he asked hopefully as he gathered the cards.

"No, I believe I'll do it myself."

"Terrific." He heaved a sigh. "Once they're shuffled, I'll cut the cards and magically reveal the one this fine gentleman chose." He reached in his pocket, pulled out an invisible handkerchief and wiped his brow. "I think that's enough. Really, really, you've done enough." Luke snatched the deck back. After setting it on the table, he waved his hands over it and mumbled. "Almost got it. And!" He cut the cards and held one up in triumph. At the gentle shake of Max's head, he looked crestfallen. "That's not it? I was sure I did this right. Hold on a minute." He set the cards back, mumbled over them again, and again chose incorrectly.

"Something must be wrong with this deck. I don't think your card's there at all. I think you cheated." He rose, incensed, and stalked toward the audience. "And someone out here must be working with you. You there." He pointed a finger at Lester, who was busily taking bets. "Come on, give it up."

"Give what up, kid?"

"The card. I know you've got it."

"Hey." Lester cocked the phone on his shoulder and held up both hands. "I ain't got no card, kid."

"Oh no?" Luke reached down past Lester's bulging belly under the waistband of his slacks and pulled out a nine of diamonds. "Guess you were just on your way to a poker game."

While Lester howled with laughter, Luke held the card overhead for the audience to identify. "Thank you. Thank you. Hey, you've been a good sport," he said to Lester. "Why don't you stand up and take a bow."

"Sure, kid, sure." Amused, Lester rose. "You got an up-and-comer here, Max. You sure as hell do."

The compliment had Luke beaming. But it was nothing, nothing compared to hearing Max laugh.

"Now." Max rose to drop a hand on Luke's shoulder. "That's showmanship. Let's see if we can work it into the act."

Luke's jaw dropped to his knees. "No shit?"

Max ruffled Luke's hair, pleased that the boy didn't stiffen at the touch. "No shit."

IT WASN'T A LONG TRIP from New Orleans to Lafayette. With Mouse at the wheel of the dark sedan, Max could sit back, close his eyes and prepare. Stealing wasn't so different from performing. Or it had never been for him. When he had first begun, so many years ago, he'd blended the two skills. That had been a matter of survival.

Now, older, more mature, he separated his performances from his thievery. That, too, was survival. As his name became more well known, it would have been reckless to steal from his audience.

Max was not a reckless man.

Some might have pointed out that he no longer had to steal to keep food in his belly or a roof over his head. Max would have agreed. He also would have added that not only was it difficult to break a habit of such long standing, particularly when he was so skilled, but he enjoyed stealing.

As a child who had been abused, abandoned and unloved, stealing had been a matter of control, and of defiance.

Now, it was a matter of pride.

He was, quite simply, one of the best. And he considered himself gracious enough to choose his marks carefully, taking only from those who could afford to lose.

It was rare for him to work this close to home. Max considered it not only risky but messy. Still, rules were made to be broken.

With his eyes shut, he could conjure the flash and beauty of the aquamarine and diamond necklace. All that icy blue and white. For himself, he preferred hot gems. Rubies, sapphires, deep, rich colors that held passion as well as glory. But personal taste often had to be set aside for practicality. If his information was correct, those emerald-cut aquamarines would bring a hefty sum once they were popped free of their setting.

LeClerc already had a buyer.

EVEN AFTER THE TITHE, and expenses, Max calculated there would be a nice chunk left over for Roxanne's college fund, and for the one he'd recently started for Luke.

He smiled to himself. Irony rarely escaped him. He was a thief who worried about interest rates and mutual funds.

Too many hungry years had taught him the value of investments. His children wouldn't go hungry, and they would have a choice over which path they took.

"This is the corner, Max."

Max opened his eyes and noted that Mouse had the car idling at the curb. It was a quiet neighborhood, tree-lined, with big, elegant houses shielded by leaves and flowering shrubs.

"Ah, yes. The time?"

Mouse checked his watch as Max did. "Two-ten."

"Good."

"The alarm system's really basic. You just snip both red wires. But if you're not sure, I can come do it for you."

"Thank you, Mouse." Max pulled on thin black gloves. "I believe I can handle it. If the safe is as LeClerc led me to believe, I'll need only seven or eight minutes to open it. Meet me back here at precisely two-thirty. If I'm more than five minutes late, you leave." When Mouse only grumbled, Max tapped his shoulder. "I have to be able to count on you for that."

"You'll be back," Mouse said and hunched down in the seat.

"And we'll be several thousand dollars richer." Max slipped from the car and faded into the shadows.

Half a block down, he vaulted over a low stone wall. There were no lights on in the three-story brick house, but he made a circuit just to be sure before locating the alarm box. Once the red wires were snipped, he didn't hesitate. Mouse was never wrong.

He took his glass cutter and suction cup from the soft leather pouch at his waist. Clouds dancing over the moon kept the light shifting, but he needed none at all. If he'd been struck blind, Max could have found his way in or out of a locked door.

There was a quiet click as he reached in and undid the latch. Then silence. As always, he listened to it, let it cloak him before he stepped inside.

He could never describe to anyone the feeling that rose inside him each and every time he stepped into a dark, quiet house. It was a kind of power, he supposed, in being where you weren't supposed to be, and going undiscovered.

Silent as a shadow, he slipped through the kitchen, into the dining room and into the hall.

His heart beat fast. A pleasant feeling, one he knew was similar to the anticipation of good sex.

He found the library exactly where LeClerc had told him it would be, and the safe, hidden behind a false door.

With a penlight clamped between his teeth and a stethoscope pressed near the lock, Max went to work.

He was enjoying the job. The library smelled faintly of overblown roses and cherry tobacco. A light breeze was tapping the branches of a chestnut against the window. He imagined, if he had the time, he'd find a brandy decanter close by and could indulge in a sip or two before going on his way.

The third of the four tumblers fell into place, with eight minutes to spare. Then he heard the whimpering.

Braced to run, he turned slowly. Using the penlight, he scanned toward the sound. A puppy, no more than a few weeks old, stood watching him. With another whimper, he squatted and piddled on the Turkish carpet.

"A little too late to ask me to let you out," Max murmured. "And I'm sorry, but I can't afford the time to clean up after you. You'll just have to take your lumps in the morning."

Max worked on the fourth tumbler as the pup waddled over to sniff his shoes. With a satisfied sigh, he opened the safe.

"Fortunately for me, I didn't plan this job a year from now, when you'd be big enough to take a bite out of me. Though I do have a scar on my rump from a poodle not much bigger than you."

He bypassed stock certificates and opened a velvet box. The aquamarines gleamed up at him. Using the penlight and a jeweler's loupe, he checked the stones, gave a satisfied sigh.

"Lovely, aren't they?" He slid them out of the box and into his pouch.

As he bent to give the puppy a farewell pat on the head, he heard the rustle on the stairs. "Frisky?" It was a female voice, pitched to a stage whisper. "Frisky, are you down here?"

"Frisky?" Max said under his breath, giving the dog a sympathetic stroke. "Some of us are forced to rise above our names." He clicked the safe shut, then faded back into the shadows.

A middle-aged woman with her hair in a sleep net and her face gleaming with night cream tiptoed into the room. The puppy whined, slapped his tail on the rug, then started in Max's direction.

"There you are! Mama's baby!" Less than a foot away from Max, she scooped the dog up. "What have you been up to? You naughty dog." She gave him loud kisses as the pup tried to wriggle away. "Are you hungry? Are you hungry, honey bunny? Let's give you a nice bowl of milk."

Max closed his eyes, wholeheartedly on the side of the dog, who yipped and tried to gain his freedom. But the woman clung tight, bundling Frisky to her breast as she started out toward the kitchen.

Since that meant Max couldn't get out the way he'd come in, he eased up a window. If his luck held, she would be too involved with the pup to notice the nice, neat hole in the beveled glass kitchen door.

If it didn't, Max mused as he tossed a leg out the window, he'd still have a head start.

He closed the window after him and did his best not to trample the pansies.

LUKE COULDN'T SLEEP. The idea of performing the next night had him tied up in knots of exhilaration and terror. The what-ifs plagued him.

What if he fumbled. What if he forgot the trick. What if the audience thought he was just a dumb kid.

He could be good. He knew that inside him was the potential to be really good. But so many years of being told he was stupid, worthless, good for nothing, had left their mark.

For Luke there was only one way to deal with insomnia. That was food. He still believed the best time to feast was when no one was around to tell him not to.

He pulled on a pair of cutoffs and moved silently downstairs. Images of LeClerc's barbecued pork and pecan pie waltzed through his head.

The sound of LeClerc's voice made him stop, and swear. He was far from sure of the old man. But when he heard Max's laugh, he crept closer.

"Your information is always reliable, Jean. The blueprints, the safe, the gems." Max cupped a brandy in one hand, the jewels in the other. "I can't complain overmuch about one small dog."

"They didn't have a dog last week. Not even five days ago."

"They have one now." Max laughed and drank more brandy. "Who hasn't been housebroken."

"Thank the Virgin he didn't bark." LeClerc added bourbon to his coffee. "I don't like surprises."

"There we part ways. I like them very much." And the light of success glowed in Max's eyes, even as the necklace shimmered in the overhead light. "Otherwise, a job would become routine. And routine too easily becomes a rut. So, will they miss them by morning, do you think?" He held the necklace up, letting gems drip through his fingers. "And will the fact that these were payment for a gambling debt prevent them from reporting the loss?"

"Reported or not, they won't be traced here." LeClerc started to raise his coffee cup in toast, then stopped. His eyes narrowed as he set it on the table. "I'm afraid the walls have at least two ears tonight."

Alerted, Max glanced up, then sighed. "Luke." He said the name, and gestured toward the shadows. "Come into the light." He waited, gauging the boy's face as Luke walked into the kitchen. "You're up late."

"I couldn't sleep." Despite his attempt not to, Luke couldn't stop himself from staring at the necklace. It was a matter of trust, pure trust, that allowed him to look back at Max and speak. "You stole them."

"Yes."

With a tentative finger, Luke reached out to touch one pale blue gem. "Why?"

Max leaned back, sipping brandy and considering. "Why not?"

Luke's lips twitched at that. It was a good answer. One that satisfied him more than a dozen heartfelt justifications. "Then you're a thief."

"Among other things." Max leaned forward then, but resisted the urge to lay a hand over Luke's. "Do I disappoint you?"

Luke's eyes filled with a love he had no words to express. "You couldn't." He shook his head in frantic denial. "Ever."

"Don't be sure of that." Max touched his hand briefly, then picked up the necklace. "The vase you broke that day was a thing— so is this. Things are worth only as much or as little as people believe." He closed his hand over it, bumped his fists together, then opened both hands. Empty. "One more illusion. My reasons for taking what others value are mine. One day I may share them with you. Until then, I'll ask you not to speak of it."

"I won't tell anyone." He'd have died first. "I can help you. I can," he repeated, furious with LeClerc's derisive snort. "I can make good money picking pockets."

"Luke, there's no such thing as bad money. But I'd prefer you didn't pick pockets unless it's part of a performance."

"But why—"

"I'll tell you." He gestured for Luke to sit, and the gems were back in his hand. "If you'd continued at the carnival, you might very well have been caught. That would have been untidy, and unfortunate."

"I'm careful."

"You're young," Max corrected. "I doubt if it occurred to you to wonder if the people you took from could afford to lose what you slipped from their wallets." He shook his head before Luke could speak. "And your need was great at the time. It isn't great now."

"But you steal."

"Because I choose to. Because, quite simply, I enjoy it. And for complex reasons you—" He broke off and chuckled softly. "I started to say that you wouldn't understand. But you would." His eyes darkened. "I was hardly older than you when LeClerc found me. I was hustling nickels and dimes with the Cups and Balls, card tricks. Lifting wallets. I, too, had escaped from the kind of nightmare no child should experience. Magic sustained me. So did stealing. I had a choice, and I chose to hone my craft on both paths. I don't apologize for being a thief. Every time I steal, I take back something that was stolen from me."

He laughed and sipped. "Oh, what a psychiatrist would make of that. No, I don't apologize, but neither will I play modern-day Fagin with you. I'll give you magic, Luke. And when you're older, you'll make your own choices."

Luke thought it over. "Does Roxanne know?"

For the first time a flicker of doubt showed on Max's face. "I see no reason why she should."

That made it better. For Luke, knowing something Roxanne didn't made all the difference. "I'll wait. I'll learn."

"I'm sure you will. And speaking of that, we should begin to see to your education."

Luke's enthusiasm suffered a direct hit. "Education? I'm not going to school."

"Oh, but you are." Casually, Max handed the necklace to LeClerc. "The paperwork should be simple enough. I think he should be my cousin's boy, recently orphaned."

"It'll take me a week," LeClerc stated. "Maybe two."

"Excellent. Then we'll be set for fall classes."

"I'm not going to school," Luke repeated. "I don't need school. You can't make me go."

"On the contrary," Max said mildly. "You will go to school, you certainly need it and I most assuredly can make you go."

Luke was prepared to die for him, would have been delighted with the opportunity to try. But he was not willing to suffer through several hours of boredom five days a week. "I won't go."

Max only smiled.

Chapter Seven

LUKE WENT TO SCHOOL. PLEAS AND BARGAINS AND THREATS fell on deaf ears. When he discovered even the softhearted Lily was against him, Luke surrendered.

Or pretended to.

They could make him go. At least they could make him get dressed, heft a bunch of stupid books and head toward school under LeClerc's eagle eye.

But they couldn't make him learn anything.

The smirky way Roxanne showed off her A's and gold stars began to tick him off. It really got his goat when she'd smile at him as Max or Lily voiced their approval. And each night the little brat would sit backstage, industriously doing her homework between acts.

Max had expanded her bit with the scarves.

Luke knew he could get A's. If he felt like it.

It wasn't any big deal—just numbers on a paper—but to prove that he couldn't be bested by some snotty, monkey-faced girl, he studied for a geography test.

It wasn't so bad, really, studying about the states and capitals.

Especially when he started counting up how many of those states he'd visited.

Afterward he couldn't wait to show off. But he made himself stay cool. If his geography test with the bright red A on it happened to slip out of his notebook backstage, it wasn't his fault.

He nearly exploded with impatience until Lily spotted it and scooped it up.

"What's this?" He saw Lily's eyes go wide and bright with an emotion he'd seen so rarely he blushed to his toes. It was pride. "Luke! This is great! Why didn't you tell us?"

"What?" The foolish grin that spread over his face ruined his show of indifference, but he shrugged anyway. "Oh, that. No big deal."

"No big deal?" Laughing, she squeezed him against her. "It's a huge deal. You didn't miss one. Not even one." With one arm still slung around him she called Max away from a discussion with Lester. "Max, Max, honey, come see this."

"What do I have to see?"

"This." Triumphant, Lily waved the test in front of him. "Look what our Luke did, and never said a word to anyone."

"I'd be glad to look, if you'd hold it still." His brow lifted as he glanced down at Luke. "Well, well. You've decided to apply your brain after all. And with excellent results."

"It's no big thing." He hadn't known it could be. "It's just memorizing."

"My dear boy." Max reached out and flicked a finger down Luke's cheek. "Life is just memorizing. Once you learn the trick, there's very little you can't do. You've done well. Quite well."

As they moved off to prepare for the next act, Luke stood still, absorbing all the pleasure. It dimmed only a little when he turned and saw Roxanne studying him with wise eyes.

"What the hell are you looking at?"

"You," she said simply.

"Well, cut it out."

But even when he stalked away, she continued to look after him. As she would with anything that puzzled her.

SCHOOL WASN'T SO BAD. Luke discovered he could tolerate it, and rarely hooked more than one or two days a month. His grades were good. He might not have gotten consistent A's like Roxanne, but he copped his share.

Luke wasn't a quick study in all things. It took a black eye and a bloodied lip before that last revelation came to him.

Walking home bruised, disgusted and minus three dollars and twenty-seven cents spending money, he plotted revenge. He'd have taken them, he thought. He'd have taken all three of the bastard creeps if the principal, Mr. Limp Dick, hadn't come along and broken things up.

Actually, if Mr. Rampwick hadn't spotted the tussle, Luke would have been sporting two black eyes at the very least, but adolescent pride colored the event differently. He just hoped he could get cleaned up at home before anyone saw him. He wondered if he could cover the worst of the damage with greasepaint.

"What did you do?"

Luke cursed himself for scowling down at the sidewalk instead of keeping a lookout. Now he'd all but run into Roxanne.

"None of your goddamn business."

"You've been fighting." Roxanne swung her pink book-bag over her shoulder and planted her fists on her hips. "Daddy won't like it."

"That's tough shit." But it worried him. Was Max going to punish him? Max wouldn't hit him—he'd promised he wouldn't. As much as Luke longed to believe that, a part of him still doubted. And feared.

"Your lip's bleeding." Sighing, Roxanne dug into the pocket of her blue skirt for a tissue. "Here. No, don't wipe it with your hand, you'll just smear it." Patient as an old woman, she dabbed at the cut herself. "You'd better sit down. You're too tall for me to reach."

Grumbling, Luke dropped down on the steps of a shop. He wanted a minute anyway, to prepare for Max and Lily. "I can do it myself."

She didn't complain when he snatched the tissue. Roxanne was too interested in studying his eye, where a bruise was already blooming. "Did you make somebody mad?"

"Yeah. They were mad because I wanted to keep my money. Now shut up."

Her eyes narrowed. "They? They beat you up and took your money?"

The humiliation of that stung more than his eye. "That creep Alex Custer sucker-punched me. I'd have held my own if he hadn't had two of his slimy pals holding me down."

"Where'd they go?" She was revved now, and surprised Luke by bounding up from the stoop. "We'll go get Mouse and take care of them."

"We, shit." He grinned and turned his split lip into fire. "You're just a kid—a girl kid. Hey!" He grabbed at the shin she kicked. "What the hell?"

"I can take care of myself," she pointed out grandly. "You're the one with the smashed-up face."

"And the broken leg," he said, amused despite himself. She looked hot and ready and oddly dangerous. "And I can take care of myself, too. I don't need help."

"Yeah, right," she shot back, mimicking him. But she took a deep breath, letting the autumn breeze cool her heated cheeks. "Anyway it's better not to fight. It's more fun to be smarter."

"Smarter than Alex?" Luke hooted. "A head of cabbage is smarter than him."

"Then be a head of cabbage." She sat again, devious rather than angry. "We'll scam him," she said, with quiet relish.

"What's this 'we' shit again?" But he was interested.

"You don't have enough experience to do it on your own. You've got to do the con so he doesn't know he's been conned." She brushed her skirt smooth and put her flexible mind to work. "I know his little brother, Bobby. He's always pinching girls and stealing food." Roxanne smiled slowly. "Well, I was thinking about doing this job on Bobby, but I guess you could have it for Alex."

"What?"

"I'll show you later. We have to get home. They'll start to worry."

He didn't nag her only because he didn't want to seem too interested. And secondly, he was worried about the reaction when he walked in the kitchen door. He'd probably get yelled at, he decided, dragging his feet. Or worse, infinitely worse, Max would give him that long, slow look and say those awful words.

You disappoint me, Luke.

They did yell when he followed Roxanne in the kitchen door. All of them at once, but it was hardly what Luke had expected.

"Happy birthday!"

He jumped back as though he'd been struck. They stood around the kitchen table, Max, Lily, Mouse, LeClerc, with a big lushly iced cake lit with candles. As he gaped, dumbfounded, Lily's beaming smile turned to an O of dismay.

"Baby! What happened?" Max halted Lily's forward rush by snagging her wrist. His eyes stayed on Luke's, and while there was a flicker of anger, his voice was calm.

"Had a tussle, did you?"

Luke only shrugged, but Roxanne picked up his banner. "There were three of them, Daddy. That makes them cowards, doesn't it?"

"Indeed." He leaned forward, gently cupping Luke's chin in his hand. "Choose your odds more carefully next time."

"Try this." LeClerc chose a bottle from a shelf and shook some of the contents on a clean cloth. When he pressed it to Luke's swollen eye the worst of the ache faded. "Three?" he said and winked. "This is some of their blood on your shirt, *oui?*"

It was the first time he'd ever felt LeClerc's approval. Luke risked opening his lip again and sneered. "Damn right."

"Well," said Lily, "you've just given us as big a surprise as we planned to give you. I hope ours is better. Happy birthday, baby."

"Better blow out the candles," Max suggested when Luke merely stood, staring. "Before we burn down the house."

"Don't forget to make a wish." This from Roxanne, who was angling herself into the frame as Mouse focused a camera.

He only had one, and that was to belong. It seemed that had already been granted.

THE DAZZLING EXCITEMENT of his first birthday cake, of opening presents that had been bought just for him, wiped all thoughts of Alex and revenge out of his mind.

Roxanne was more single-minded.

Two days later, Luke found himself in the middle of a sting that could bring him great satisfaction, or a broken face.

He had to admit it was clever. Even—to borrow one of Roxanne's ten-dollar words—diabolical. Following Roxanne's advice, Luke made certain Alex and his two juvenile henchmen saw him saunter into a market on the corner a block from school. He paid for the bottle of grape Nehi—Alex's personal favorite— popped the cap and took a long swig as he stepped back out.

Then he pretended to spot Alex for the first time, forced himself to appear afraid. Like a shark scenting blood, Alex needed no more than that to pursue.

Little peabrain had it right, Luke thought as he darted down an alleyway, uncapping the vial that held one of LeClerc's home remedies.

With quick hands, Luke dumped the strong laxative into the Nehi. He trusted Roxanne knew what she was doing, and that he wasn't about to kill anyone. Though his conscience wouldn't have suffered overmuch.

Stuffing the empty vial back in his pocket, he whirled, as if in panic. He'd chosen the blind alley cold-bloodedly. They might pound on him again, but at least one of them would pay for it later.

"What's the matter, fart breath?" Seeing his quarry pinned, Alex puffed out his chest and grinned. "Lost?"

"I don't want any trouble." Luke buried pride under vengeance and made his voice and hands shake. "I ain't got no money left. I spent it on this."

"No money?" Alex grabbed the bottle before shoving Luke back against the wall. "See if he's lying, Jerry." Alex took a long pull on the spiked soft drink and grinned under a purple moustache.

Luke whimpered, allowing the other boy to poke and prod through his pockets. He wanted to make sure Alex emptied the bottle.

"He's got nothing," Jerry announced. "Give me a sip, Alex."

"Get your own." Alex tilted the bottle back and drained it. "Now." He tossed the bottle aside. "Let's kick ass."

But this time Luke was ready for them. When you couldn't fight, you ran. He ducked his head and plowed into Alex's gut, knocking one boy into the other until the three of them wobbled like a house of cards. He dashed to the mouth of the alley. He was faster, he knew, and could have gotten away before they'd sorted themselves out to come after him. But he wanted them to chase him. A little exercise, he thought, should get things moving through Alex's system.

He led them on a chase, toward Jackson Square and down Royal, skidding around the corner at St. Ann and hotfooting it over to Decatur. A glance back showed him Alex's face was sheet white and running with sweat. Luke made it to his own courtyard and was debating whether to race out and continue, when Alex groaned and clutched his belly.

"Hey, what's the matter?" Jerry pulled at him. "Come on, man. He's getting away."

"My gut! My gut!" Alex dashed toward some rhododendrons and squatted.

"Je-sus!" Jerry shouted in disgust. "That is gr-oss."

"Can't, can't," was all Alex could say as LeClerc's laxative purged him pitilessly.

"Oh, look!" Roxanne popped out of nowhere to point. "There's a boy in the bushes doing number two. Mommy!" She squealed in a baby-doll voice. "Mommy, come quick."

"Come on, Alex, *jeez*, come on." After a quick look around, both Jerry and his companion left the groaning Alex and took off for safer ground as several adults began to hurry over.

With a careless smile on her face, Roxanne strolled into the courtyard. "That's better than punching him," she said to Luke. "He'd forget about that, but he won't ever forget about this."

He had to grin. "And you said I was mean."

From the balcony Max had seen most of the little drama, and had heard all he needed to hear. His children, he thought with a warm glow of pride, were coming along nicely, very nicely indeed. How pleased Moira would have been with her girl.

It wasn't often he thought of his wife, that redheaded firebrand who'd zoomed so quickly in and out of his life. He'd loved her—oh yes, he'd loved her with a kind of greedy wonder. How could he have done otherwise when she'd been beautiful and fearless?

Even after all the years that had passed he found it difficult to believe that all that flash and dash had been snuffed out. So quickly. So uselessly.

A burst appendix. She'd been too impatient to complain about the pain—and then it had been too late. A frantic rush to the hospital, the emergency surgery hadn't saved her. She'd streamed out of his life, leaving him with the most precious thing they'd made together.

Yes, he was certain Moira would be proud of her daughter.

Turning back into the bedroom, he watched Lily slip an extra pair of his argyle socks into his overnight bag.

Lily. Even her name made him smile. Sweet, lovely Lily. A man could hardly curse God when he'd been given two such glorious women to love in one lifetime.

"You don't have to do that for me."

"I don't mind." She checked his shaving kit to be certain it contained fresh razors before packing it. "I'm going to miss you."

"I'll be back before you know I'm gone. Houston's practically next door."

"I know." She sighed and snuggled against him. "I'd just feel better if I were going with you."

"Mouse and LeClerc are quite enough protection, don't you think?" He kissed her again, one temple, then the other. His Lily had skin as smooth as the petals of her namesake.

"I suppose." She tilted her head, letting her eyes close when he skimmed his lips down her throat. "And someone has to stay with the children. Do you really think the job will be worth a quarter of a million?"

"Oh, at a minimum. These oil men like to put their spare change into art and jewelry."

The idea of that much money excited her, but not nearly as much as what Max's clever tongue was currently doing to her ear. "I locked the door."

Max chuckled as he pressed her down on the bed. "I know."

THERE WAS PLENTY OF TIME during the short flight from New Orleans to Houston, with Mouse at the controls of the Cessna, to go over the blueprints again. The house they would hit a few hours later was huge, a sprawling fifty-five hundred square feet.

The blueprints Max was currently poring over had cost a little more than five thousand in bribes. It was an investment Max calculated well worth the ultimate payoff.

The Crooked R Ranch, as it was overcutely named, was loaded with nineteenth- and twentieth-century art, heavy on the American and Oriental, all of which had been chosen for the owners by agents. It had been purchased not for its aesthetic value or simple beauty but as an investment.

A good one, Max had no doubt. It was about to make him a great deal of money.

There was jewelry, too. The list Max had obtained—from a file drawer in Security Insurance, Inc.'s home base in Atlanta—contained enough baubles and beads to stock a modest jewelry store.

Since his marks were heavily insured, Max figured Security's loss would be his gain. And after all, insurance was a bet, between insurer and insuree. Eventually someone had to lose.

Max glanced up and grinned at LeClerc. The Cajun's knuckles were white as he gripped his armrest. Around his neck were a silver cross, a gold ankh, a crystal talisman and an eagle feather. There were rosary beads, a black rabbit's foot and a pouch full of colored stones in his lap.

LeClerc covered all the bases when he flew.

Because LeClerc's eyes were tightly closed, and his mouth moving in silent prayer, Max said nothing as he rose to pour a small brandy for both of them.

LeClerc downed the brandy. "It's unnatural for a man to be in the air. He dares the gods."

"He dares them every time he takes a breath. I'm sorry to subject you to something you dislike, but my absence in New Orleans couldn't possibly go unnoticed if we'd taken the time to drive."

"Your magic makes you too famous."

"I'm nothing without it. And there are advantages to fame. It's becoming quite the thing for the more important hostesses to invite me to dinner parties, as a guest." He pulled a coin out of the air and began to manipulate it through his fingers. "With the hopes that I'll entertain her, and her party, in the parlor."

"Like a juggler," LeClerc said in disgust, but Max only shrugged.

"If you like. I'm always willing to pay for a well-presented meal. And I'm more than paid back in kind with the contacts I've made. Our friends in Houston were delighted with my impromptu performance at a soiree in Washington last year. How fortunate for us that they'd decided to visit their cousin the senator."

"More fortunate for us that they're in Europe now."

"Much more. Though it's not much of a challenge to steal from an uninhabited house." He moved his shoulders again and turned one coin into two.

They picked up a limo at Hobby, and Mouse donned his chauffeur's cap and jacket for the drive. The long stretch limousine would be less conspicuous in the rich neighborhood than an unmarked sedan.

And Max preferred to travel well whenever possible.

In the backseat, to the strains of a Mozart cantata, he checked his tools one last time.

"Two hours," he announced. "No more."

LeClerc was already slipping on his gloves—an old firehorse who hears the alarm bells and quivers for the harness.

It had been months since he had heard the tumblers click and fall, months since he had had the pleasure of opening the door of a safe and reaching into the darkness beyond. For the long summer, he had been celibate—at least figuratively—and was anxious for the romance of theft.

Without Max, he knew this pleasure would be lost to him by now. Though they never spoke of it, they both knew that LeClerc was slowing down. A younger man would have fit the triangle made up of himself, Mouse and Max more practically. And that day would come. Already he accompanied Max only on less arduous jobs. If the oil man's house hadn't been empty, LeClerc knew he would be at home waiting, as Lily was waiting.

But he wasn't bitter. He was grateful for the opportunity of one more chance at the thrill.

They purred up the sweeping drive, past a statue of a nude boy holding a carp. When the Texans were in residence, Max imagined the carp would vomit water into the birdbath.

"A lesson for you, Mouse. Money can't buy taste."

When they parked in front of the house, the men moved in silence. Max and LeClerc walked to the trunk, Mouse lumbered off to deal with the security system. It was pitch dark, without even a hint of moon.

"Lots of land," LeClerc murmured, pleased. "Lots of big trees. The neighbors must need binoculars to peek in each other's windows."

"Let's hope no one's playing Peeping Tom tonight." Max took a large velvet-lined box from the trunk, and a roll of soundproofing often used in theaters.

And they waited.

Ten minutes later, Mouse hurried back. "Sorry. Was a pretty good system. Took some time."

"No apologies necessary." Max felt the familiar tingling in his fingertips as he approached the front door. Taking out his packet of picks, he went to work.

"Why fool with that? Have Mouse break it in. The alarm's down."

"Lacks finesse," Max muttered, his eyes half closed, his mind inside the tumblers. "There . . . only a moment more."

He was as good as his word. Minutes later they stood inside a dazzling three-story black-and-white marble foyer, facing a reproduction of Venus and an indoor goldfish pond.

"Jeez," was all Mouse could think of to say.

"Indeed. It nearly makes one want to pause and reflect." Max glanced toward an enormous coatrack made of steer horns. "Nearly."

They separated, LeClerc going up the wide curving stairs toward the bedroom safe and milady's jewels, Mouse and Max covering the first floor.

They worked smoothly, cutting paintings from what Max considered overly ornate frames and rolling them inside the velvet box. Sculptures of bronze and marble and stone were wrapped in the thick soundproofing.

"A Rodin." Max paused a moment to teach. "A truly remarkable piece. See the movement, Mouse? The fluidity, the emotion of the artist for his subject."

Mouse saw a funny-looking glob of stone. "Ah, sure, Max. It's neat."

Max could only sigh as he tucked the Rodin reverently between folds of the heavy cloth. "No, not that one," he said when he noted the bronze work Mouse was holding.

"It's real heavy," Mouse told him. "Solid. Must be worth a lot."

"Undoubtedly, or it wouldn't be in this collection. But it lacks style, Mouse, and beauty. It's much more important to steal the beautiful than the valuable. Otherwise, we'd be robbing banks, wouldn't we?"

"I guess." He moved to the next room and came back hefting a Remington piece of a cowboy astride a bucking horse. "How about this one, Max?"

Max eyed it. A good piece and probably as heavy as a truck. Though it wasn't to his personal taste, he could see Mouse was drawn to it. "Excellent choice. Best take it out to the limo as it is. We're nearly done here."

"We're well done," LeClerc stated, striding downstairs and tapping his bulging pouch. "I don't know what Madame and Monsieur took to Europe, but they left behind plenty of baubles for us." It had been difficult to ignore the negotiable bonds and cold cash he'd found in the twin safes, but Max was superstitious about stealing money. LeClerc never sneezed on anyone's superstitions. "Look at this one."

He pulled out a blinding array of diamonds and rubies worked into a three-tiered necklace. With a grunt Max took it and held it up to the light. "How can one take such beautiful stones and make something so hideous from them? The lady should thank us for never having to wear this again."

"Must be worth fifty thousand, at least."

"Hmmm." Possibly, Max thought and wished for his loupe. He

would choose a few of the choicer stones and have a more suitable necklace made for Lily. A check of his watch, and a nod. "I believe our shopping spree is over. Shall we load up? I believe we can be back home in time for brunch."

PART TWO

A devil, a born devil, on whose nature
Nurture can never stick; on whom my pains,
Humanely taken, all, all lost, quite lost . . .

—William Shakespeare

Chapter Eight

When Luke was sixteen, Mouse taught him to drive. They did a lot of bumping and grinding on the back roads, and once, when Luke attempted to shift, steer and brake at the same time, nearly ended up in a swamp. But Mouse had an endless store of patience.

Getting his driver's license was a momentous occasion for Luke, that giant step toward reaching the manhood he was beginning to crave. But even that paled against another momentous occasion. His date with Annabelle Walker that included the fantasy roller coaster of *Star Wars*, two giant tubes of popcorn and an evening ending in sex in the backseat of the secondhand Nova he'd bought with his savings.

Neither Annabelle nor the Nova were strangers to the backseat boogie. But it was Luke's first time, and for him, the dark road, the music of the cicadas in counterpoint to all the gasps and grunts, the miraculous feel of Annabelle's braless breasts in his hands were as romantic and majestic as the Taj Mahal.

Annabelle might have been considered easy, but she only crawled into the backseat with a boy if he was cute, if he treated her well and if he was a good kisser.

Luke qualified on all counts.

When she let him under her T-shirt to sample those generous, milk-white globes, he thought he'd found heaven. But when she tugged down the zipper on his Levi's and took hold, he understood the gates of paradise were swinging open.

"Christ, Annabelle." He fumbled with her jeans while she jack-hammered him toward delirium. He'd hoped she'd let him touch, but he'd had no idea a handful of dates and an evening watching worlds being saved would convince her to let him do the big IT.

Still he wasn't one to miss an opportunity once it was presented. Max had taught him that much.

"Let me . . ." Let him what he wasn't precisely sure, but he got his hand inside her lacy red panties.

Wet, hot, slippery. His blood swam wildly downstream from his head to his crotch, throbbing there in a jungle drumbeat that set the rhythm for his seeking fingers. Annabelle's pleasure sounded in a low hum that became quick greedy moans, desperate pants, delightful little whimpers. Her generous hips arched and fell, slapping against the tattered seat of the Nova. The windows Luke had rolled up against the chill of oncoming winter fogged up, turning the car into a steamy sauna that smelled of sex.

He could feel, actually feel, her muscles contract around him as she pitched higher and happily came in his hand.

His breath hitched in and out as he struggled toward something that had been only a dark dream punctuated by locker-room talk.

With his face pillowed between her breasts, one hand busily working her, he tugged his hips free of the Levi's. The sensation of being inside of a woman this way was nearly enough to shatter his control. Yet a part of him, some small corner of his brain, remained cool, oddly detached, even amused.

Here was Luke Callahan, bare-assed in his '72 Nova, with the Bee Gees warbling on the radio—Christ, did it have to be the Bee Gees?—and Annabelle spreading her legs in her best cheerleader style beneath him.

110

His cock felt like a rocket, huge and hot, vibrating on the launching pad of his arousal. He could only hope lift-off didn't occur prematurely.

It wasn't skill that had him giving her more than the other boys she'd dated. It was pure inexperience mixed with healthy curiosity and a love of beautiful things. Feeling all that hot moisture, feeling a female form tremble and buck beneath him was one of the most beautiful things Luke had ever experienced.

"Oh, baby." A veteran of close-quarters sex, Annabelle wriggled and shifted and locked her legs around his hips. "I can't wait. I just can't."

Neither could he. Blind instinct had him driving himself into her. Control that was as much instinct as the tutelage of four years had him holding back that need for instant release. He worked them both into a delirious sweat before letting go. The last thing he heard was her calling out his name. She all but sang it.

Courtesy of Annabelle, he would return to school Monday with a reputation a growing boy could be proud of.

THE HOUSE WAS DARK but for a light left burning in the kitchen when he arrived home, smelling of sex and sweat and Annabelle's Charlie cologne. He was grateful no one was up to greet him. Even more was he grateful that he'd been given every other weekend off from the club to, as Max put it, develop a well-rounded social life.

He sure as hell was feeling well rounded tonight.

He opened the fridge and drained a pint of orange juice straight from the bottle. He was grinning still, and humming the Eagles' "Witchy Woman" under his breath, when he turned and spotted Roxanne in the doorway.

"That's disgusting." She inclined her head toward the bottle he held.

She'd sprung up over the years, as he had. But while Luke skimmed under six foot yet, and was no more than average height for his age, Roxanne was the tallest girl in her class—taller, in fact, than most of the boys. Most of it was leg, as showed now in the short nightshirt she wore. Since her hair was neatly brushed, something Luke knew she did every night before bed, he assumed she'd yet to go to sleep.

"Stuff it." He smiled and set the bottle on the counter.

"Maybe someone else wanted some." Though she wasn't in the least thirsty, she marched to the refrigerator and searched. As she chose a Dr Pepper, she wrinkled her nose at Luke. "You smell." Sniffing the air she caught, among other things, the fading hint of Annabelle's cologne. "You went out with *her* again."

Roxanne hated Annabelle Walker on principle. The principle being that she was petite and blond and pretty, and that Luke spent time with her.

"What's it to you?"

"She bleaches her hair and wears her clothes too tight."

"She wears sexy clothes," Luke corrected, feeling an expert on the subject. "You're just jealous because she's got tits and you don't."

"I'll get them." On the cusp of thirteen, Roxanne was mortified by the snail's pace of her feminine development. Almost all the girls in her class had at least the buds of breasts, and she was still as flat as LeClerc's breadboard. "When I do, they'll be better than hers."

"Right." The idea of Roxanne with breasts amused him. Initially. When he began to think about it, it became uncomfortably warm. "Beat it."

"I'm getting a drink." She poured Dr Pepper into a glass to prove it. "I don't have a bedtime on Saturday nights."

"Then I'm going." How was a guy supposed to float around on a cloud of lust with that little whiner around? he wondered as he strode out and up the stairs. Not wanting to miss a moment of the indulgent dream he had planned, Luke stripped and plopped naked onto the bed.

He'd gotten used to the scent and feel of clean sheets, though he'd yet to take them for granted. It was a rare thing for him to go to bed hungry, and for long periods of time he'd forgotten what real fear was.

In the past four years, he'd traveled over most of the eastern United States, had performed in fallow fields, in dingy clubs and on polished stages. The previous summer after Max—with some regret—had sold the carnival, they'd traveled to Europe, where Max had added to his reputation as a master magician.

He could speak French, haltingly, and had learned to make the cards dance. As far as he could see, he had it all. Life was perfect, Luke thought as he drifted to sleep.

So he was stunned when he woke in a cold sweat an hour later with a whimper in his throat.

He'd been back, all the way back to that cramped two-room apartment. Al's belt had whipped like a razor across his skin, and there'd been nowhere to run, nowhere to hide.

Sitting up, Luke gulped in huge breaths of the heavy, autumn air and waited for the shaking to pass. It hadn't happened in months, he told himself as he rested his head on his knees. Months and months without his subconscious zapping him back there. He'd thought he'd beaten it. Each time weeks or months passed without one of those hideous dreams, he was sure it was behind him.

Then it would pop back, like a cackling gremlin out of a closet, to taunt and torture.

He wasn't a kid anymore, Luke reminded himself and stumbled from the bed. He wasn't supposed to have nightmares and wake up shaking and wanting Lily or Max to come and make it all go away again.

So he'd walk it off. Luke pulled on pants and told himself he'd walk over to Bourbon and back and shake off the sticky dregs of the nightmare.

When he reached the bottom of the steps he heard the high-pitched scream and the muffled mutter of voices. Glancing into the den, he spotted Roxanne seated crosslegged on the floor, a bowl of popcorn on her lap.

"What're you doing?"

She jolted, but didn't take her eyes off the screen. "I'm watching 'Terror Theater.' *Castle of the Walking Dead*. This count guy's embalming people. It's neat."

"Gross." But he was caught, at least enough to sit on the end of the couch and dip a hand into Roxanne's popcorn. He was still feeling shaky, but before Christopher Lee got what was coming to him, he had fallen asleep.

Roxanne waited until she was sure he had, then, leaning her cheek against the cushion on the couch, reached up to stroke his hair.

"THEY'RE GROWING UP on us, Lily."

"I know, honey." She sighed as she settled into the brightly painted horizontal box. They were rehearsing alone in the club, a new bit Max called the Divided Woman.

"Roxy's going to be a teenager." Max clamped the locks into place while doing a stylish turn around the box for the benefit of the potential audience. "How much longer are the boys going to stay away?"

Lily smiled and wriggled the feet and hands that stuck out of the holes in the box. "Not much longer. Don't worry, Max, she's too smart to settle for anything less than exactly what she wants."

"I hope you're right."

"She's her father's daughter." Lily made the appropriate whimpers and moans while Max demonstrated the keenness of the blade of a jewel-encrusted scimitar.

"By that you mean she's stubborn, ambitious and one-track-minded."

Lily was silent as Max went through the routine of cutting the box apart and then joining the halves together. Then she asked, "You're not sad the kids are growing up, are you, sweetie?"

"Maybe a little. It reminds me I'm getting older. Luke driving a car and chasing girls."

"He doesn't have to chase them." Lily's brow creased in annoyance. "They throw themselves at him. Anyway," she sighed, "they're good kids, Max. A terrific pair."

HALF OF THAT TERRIFIC PAIR was two blocks away, running a brisk game of Three Card Monte. A flood of conventioneers had poured into town. Roxanne simply didn't have the willpower to resist.

She was neatly dressed in pink jeans and matching jacket, a flowered shirt and snow-white sneakers. Her hair was pulled back in a bouncy ponytail, and her face was scrubbed clean of everything but freckles.

She looked like a sweet, wholesome, all-American girl. Which was precisely her intention. Roxanne knew the value of illusion and imagery.

She'd already taken in over two hundred, though she made certain to hit no one mark too hard. She wasn't doing it for the money—though she was every bit as fond of what money could buy as her father. She was doing it because it was fun.

Once again she slapped three cards on the little folding table. She took the five-dollar bet from her current mark—a portly man in an aloha shirt—flipped the cards facedown and began to manipulate them. And the rest of the crowd.

"Keep your eye on the black queen. Don't blink. Don't sneeze. Keep watching her. Keep watching." Her small, long-fingered hands moved like lightning. And, of course, the queen was already palmed.

She took in another fifty, paid out twenty of it to maintain good community relations. Somewhere close by a street-corner musician blew a lonely trumpet. Roxanne decided it was time to close down and move on.

"That's all for today. Thank you, ladies and gentlemen. Enjoy your stay in New Orleans." She started to scoop up the cards when a hand clamped over her wrist.

"One more game. I didn't get to try my luck."

It was a boy of eighteen or nineteen. Under his faded jeans and Grateful Dead T-shirt was a wiry build—all lean muscle. His shaggy hair was a golden blond, a scruffy halo around a narrow face of sharp angles. His eyes, a deep, dark brown, were locked on Roxanne's.

He reminded her of Luke—not in looks but in that inner wildness and potential for mean. His voice didn't sound like New Orleans. It didn't sound like anywhere at all.

"You're too late," she told him.

His hand remained firmly locked around her wrist. When he smiled, showing perfect, even white teeth, her nerves jangled. "One game," he said. "I've been watching you."

It was nearly impossible for Roxanne to resist a direct challenge. Instinct told her to, but pride was stronger.

"I've got time, for one. The bet's five dollars."

With a nod, he pulled a folded bill from his back pocket and laid it on the table.

Roxanne laid the cards down, two red queens with the black in the center. "Watch the black lady," she began as she flipped the cards over. In a split-second decision she opted not to palm it, but to face the challenger even up. She shifted the cards in an ever-increasing rhythm, and kept her eye on the boy.

He wasn't new to the game. She'd been in it herself too long not to recognize a pro. Roxanne bet her ego against the five-dollar bill.

Though she hadn't looked at the cards since she'd begun, she knew exactly where the black queen hid. "Where is she?"

He didn't hesitate, but tapped a finger against the left-hand card. Before she could turn it up herself, he snagged her wrist again. "I'll do it." He flipped up the queen of hearts.

"Looks like my hand's quicker than your eye."

Still holding her hand aloft, he turned up the other cards. He blinked once when he saw the black queen was exactly where she'd begun. In the center.

"Looks like," he murmured. His eyes narrowed as he watched her slip his five and the cards into a bag she'd put under the table.

"Better luck next time." She folded the table, hitched it under her arm and started toward the Magic Door.

He didn't give up that easily. "Hey, kid. What's your name?"

She slanted him a look as he fell into step beside her. "Roxanne. Why?"

"Just like to know. I'm Sam. Sam Wyatt. You're good. Real good."

"I know."

He chuckled, but his mind was working on the possibilities. If he could lure her into a less crowded area, he could get his five back, and the rest of her take as well. "You took them smooth. What are you, twelve, thirteen?"

"So?"

"Hey, that's a compliment, sweetheart."

He saw her preen, just a little. Whether it was in response to the compliment, or to the fact that a boy his age would call a twelve-year-old "sweetheart," he wasn't sure. Either way, it was working.

"I was in New York a few months ago. There was a guy working a corner there, taking in five, six hundred a day. He wasn't any better than you. How long you been on the grift?"

"I'm not a grifter." The idea that she could be mistaken for a common con artist had Roxanne bristling. "I'm a magician," she informed him. "Working that crowd was a kind of rehearsal." She smiled to herself. "A paying rehearsal."

"A magician." Sam noted that the pedestrian traffic was thinner here. He could see no one who would give him any real trouble when he snatched the kid's bag and ran. "Why don't you show me a trick?" He put a hand on her arm and prepared to shove her to the ground.

117

"Roxanne." Scowling, Luke loped across the street. "What the hell are you doing? You're supposed to be at rehearsal."

"I'm going." She scowled right back, furious that he'd come along just when she was going to try her hand at flirting. "You're not there either."

"That's beside the point." He'd noted the table and bag and guessed what she'd been up to. It annoyed the hell out of him that she hadn't cut him in. Pushing that aside for now, he sized up Sam. In the way of the male animal, his hackles rose.

"Who's this?"

"A friend of mine," Roxanne decided on the spot. "Sam, this is Luke."

Sam flashed an easygoing smile. "How's it going?"

"Okay. You're not from around here."

"Just got into town a couple days ago. I'm traveling around, you know?"

"Right." Luke didn't like him. The greedy look in Sam's eyes didn't match the generous smile. "We're late, Roxy. Let's go."

"In a minute." If Luke was going to treat her like a baby, she'd damn well show him she was her own woman. "Maybe you'd like to hang out, Sam. Watch the rehearsal. We're right down there at the Magic Door."

It didn't look like he was going to get his hand on the bag, but Sam wasn't one to give up. The encounter with Roxanne had to be worth something. "That'd be great. If you're sure it's okay."

"It's fine." She took his hand and led him to her father.

SAM KNEW HOW TO BE CHARMING. The veneer of affability, manners and deprecating good humor was as much a part of the game as a marked deck. Sam sat in the Magic Door and applauded, expressed astonished disbelief and laughed at all the right places.

When Lily extended an invitation to dinner, he accepted with shy gratitude.

He found LeClerc old and stupid, Mouse slow and stupid, and went out of his way to make a good impression on both.

Afterward, he made himself scarce for a day so as not to seem too forward. When he showed up at the Magic Door to watch a show, he was greeted warmly. He made certain Lily saw him carefully counting out enough change to buy a soft drink.

"Max." She tugged on his arm when he came backstage, leaving Luke in front to do his five-minute sleight of hand. "That boy's in trouble."

"Luke?"

"No, no. Sam."

"He's hardly a boy, Lily. He's nearly a man."

"He's barely older than Luke." She peeked out, spotted Sam at the bar and noted that he was nursing the same watered-down Coke. "I don't think he has any money, and anywhere to go."

"He doesn't seem to be looking for work." Max knew he was being harsh, and had no real clue as to why he felt so reluctant to offer this helping hand.

"Honey, you know how hard it is to find any. Couldn't you find something for him?"

"Perhaps. Give me a day or two."

A day or two was all Sam needed. To cap his image, he curled up to sleep in the Nouvelle courtyard one night, making sure he was discovered in the morning.

Fully awake, he kept his eyes closed, watching under his lashes as Roxanne darted out of the kitchen door. He groaned, shifted, then blinked his eyes open on a muffled cry of alarm when she spotted him.

"What're you doing?"

"Nothing." He rolled up a tattered blanket and scrambled to his feet. "I wasn't doing anything."

Brow puckered, she came closer. "Were you sleeping out here?"

Sam moistened his lips. "Listen, it's no big deal, okay. Don't say anything."

"Don't you have a room?"

"I lost it." He shrugged, managing to look brave and hopeless at the same time. "Hey, something'll turn up. I just didn't want to be out on the street all night. I didn't figure I'd bother anybody here."

She had her father's heart. "Come on in." She held out a hand. "LeClerc's fixing breakfast."

"I don't need a handout."

Because she understood pride, she softened further. "Daddy can give you a job. I'll ask him."

"You would?" He slipped a hand into hers. "Man, I'd really owe you, Rox. I'd owe you big."

Chapter Nine

THERE WAS VERY LITTLE MAX DENIED ROXANNE. IT WAS because of her that he hired Sam Wyatt, despite an odd reluctance to add the boy to his entourage. He gave Sam a job hauling props, an occupation Sam knew was beneath his dignity and abilities.

But Sam had instincts as well. His told him that joining the Nouvelle troupe could be the gateway to much bigger and much better things. They were saps, all of them. Even as he derided them he detested them for taking him in off the street like some lost mongrel dog. But for Sam the long con had more appeal than the short shuffle. He could be patient.

He spent hours loading and unloading equipment, polishing the boxes and hinges Max used for various routines. He vowed to pay the old man back one day for offering him such demeaning work but he was unflaggingly kind and attentive to Roxanne and shyly flattering to Lily. Sam had long ago decided that the real power in any group was held by the women.

He didn't make the mistake of competing with Luke. He doubted it would be wise to openly antagonize the person Max considered a son, but the enmity Sam nursed for Luke saw him through the menial, boring days. The fact that the antagonism was shared made it all the better. Neither could have said why, but they had detested each other on sight. One let his feelings bubble to the surface, the other secreted his away, hoarding hate like a miser hoards gold.

Sam looked for the day when he made that gold pay.

In the meantime he was satisfied with his toehold, and with the fact that they were about to spend a week in L.A.

Max was pleased with the upcoming trip as well. They would have the opportunity to perform at the Magic Castle, attend a dinner party hosted by Brent Taylor, movie star and amateur magician, and Max would have the pleasure of showing his family some of the glitter of Hollywood.

He also intended to take some of the more expensive glitter back east with him. Beverly Hills, and its mansions filled with treasures, was going to add to an already lucrative gig.

He had two houses targeted, and would choose between them after he had arrived in Los Angeles and had cased the areas firsthand.

They took over several rooms at the Beverly Hills Hotel. It amused Max to watch Luke charm the bellman and the chambermaid with a few pocket tricks. The boy had learned, he thought. And learned well.

He arranged an elaborate lunch at Maxim's, treating his family and all the members of his troupe down to the lowliest back-door boy. Afterward he sent Lily and Roxanne shopping.

"Now then." Max lit a post-meal cigar. "Mouse and I have some business to attend to, but the rest of you have the day free to explore, sightsee, whatever strikes your fancy. I'll need everyone bright-eyed for rehearsals at nine A.M. tomorrow."

While the others left, Luke shifted chairs to sit next to Max. "I need to talk to you."

"Of course." Recognizing both nerves and determination, Max lifted a brow. "Is there a problem?"

"I don't think it's a problem." Luke took a deep breath and dived. "I want to go with you." He shook his head before Max could speak. He'd been preparing this speech for days. "I know the routine, Max. You and Mouse are going out to case a couple of houses. You'll already have most of the important stuff. A copy of the insurance lists, blueprints, the schematics of the security systems, an idea of the basic household routine. Now you'll do some checking firsthand and decide when and where to hit."

Max brushed at his moustache. He wasn't certain if he was annoyed or impressed. "You've been keeping up."

"I've had four years to study the routine while I've waited for you to let me in."

Max tapped away cigar ash before taking a considering drag. "My dear boy—"

"I'm not a boy anymore." Luke's eyes flashed as he leaned closer. "You either trust me or you don't. I have to know."

Max puffed out a breath and held his silence while the waiter cleared the dishes. "It's not a matter of trust, Luke, but of timing."

"You're not going to tell me you're trying to save me from a life of crime."

Max's lips twitched. "Certainly not. I've never been a hypocrite, and I'm as egocentric as any father, hoping his son will follow in his footsteps. But . . . "

Luke laid a hand on Max's wrist. "But?"

"You are still young. I'm not sure you're ready. To be a successful thief takes maturity, experience."

"It takes balls," Luke put in and made Max throw back his head and laugh.

"Oh, indeed it does. But besides that, a certain amount of skill, finesse, coolheadedness. In a few more years you may ripen, but for now—"

"What time is it?"

Distracted, Max blinked, then glanced down at his watch. Or where his watch should have been. "I always said you had good hands," he murmured.

"Don't have the time?" Luke turned his wrist. The sunlight

glinted off the gold of Max's Rolex. "It's nearly three. I guess you'd better pay the check and get going." Luke signaled for the waiter himself. Absently, Max reached inside his jacket for his wallet. And came up empty.

"A little short?" Luke smiled and took Max's wallet out of his own pocket. "This one's on me. I happen to have come into some money recently."

Point taken, Max thought and smiled at Mouse. "Why don't you take the afternoon off as well? Luke can drive me."

"Sure, Max. I can go over and see those footprints at the Chinese place."

"Enjoy yourself." With a sigh, Max held out his hand for his wallet. "Ready to go?" he asked Luke.

"I've been ready for years."

BEVERLY HILLS appealed to Luke. Not like New Orleans with its party streets and decaying glamour. That was the only place he would ever consider home. But the wide, palm-lined avenues and fantasy aura of houses tucked onto hilltops in the smog-misted distance was like a movie. He supposed that was why so many movie stars chose that section of real estate to live.

He tooled along, following Max's directions. He noted the occasional police cruiser. No scratched and dusty cars for the cops here. Each one was glittering clean in the afternoon sun.

Most of the estates were tucked behind high walls and hedges. Twice as they circled around they passed one of the buses that toured movie stars' homes. Luke wondered why anyone would pay for the ride when all they would really see would be stone walls and the tops of trees.

"Why," Max asked as he opened his briefcase, "do you want to steal?"

"Because it's fun," Luke answered without thinking. "And I'm good at it."

"Mmmm." Max could only agree that it was best to spend your life doing something you enjoyed and were skilled at. "The bellman who brought up our bags and was so entertained by your pocket tricks. He had a watch and a wallet. Did you take them?"

"No." Surprised, Luke turned his head to stare. "Why would I?"

"Why wouldn't you is more to the point." Max loosened his tie and folded it inside the case.

"Well, hell, it's no fun if it's that easy. Besides he was just some guy trying to make a living."

"One could argue that a thief is also just some guy trying to make a living."

"If that's all I wanted, I could knock over some convenience store."

"Ah, so you'd consider such an enterprise out of the question."

"It's low-class."

"Luke." Max sighed as he folded his crisp white shirt into the case. "You do make me proud."

"It's like magic," Luke said after a moment. "You want to do the best you're capable of. If you're going to dupe somebody, then you ought to do it with some flair. Right?"

"Precisely right." Max slipped into a short-sleeved polyester shirt in screaming checks of green and orange.

"What are you doing?"

"Just donning the appropriate costume." Max added a Phillies baseball cap and a pair of mirrored sunglasses. "I do hope I look like a tourist."

Luke pulled up at a stop sign and took the time to study Max. "You look like an idiot."

"Close enough. See the tour bus halfway down the block? Pull up behind it."

Obeying orders, Luke parked the car, but he scowled down at the fielder's cap Max held out to him. "Pittsburgh. You know I'm not a National League fan."

"Tough it out." Max wound binocular and camera straps

around his neck. "This here's Elsa Langtree's house," Max said in a thick Midwestern twang as he pushed out of the car. He added a whistle before jockeying with the other tourists for a peek through the wrought-iron gate. "Man oh man, is she something!"

Luke picked up on the tone and craned his neck. "Hell, Daddy, she's old."

"She can retire in my neck of the woods anytime."

This brought a few chuckles from the rest of the crowd before the tour guide began his routine. Stepping back, Max circled the bus and climbed nimbly on its roof while the rest of the tour listened and snapped pictures. Max used the telescopic lens on his camera to take shots of the wall, the three-story colonial house, its outbuildings, the outdoor lighting.

"Hey, buddy." The bus driver squinted up from under the bill of his cap. "Get the hell down from there, will ya? Christ, there's one in every crowd."

"I just wanted to see if I could catch a look at Elsa."

"Come on, Daddy. Jeez, you're embarrassing me."

"Okay, okay. Oh, wait! I think I see her. Elsa!" he shouted, using the confusion as people scrabbled back to the gate to take the last of his pictures.

While the driver cursed and threatened, Max climbed down. He offered a sheepish grin and an apology. "I've been a fan for twenty years. Even named my parakeet after her."

"Yeah, she'd be thrilled."

With obvious reluctance, Max let Luke drag him back to the car. "Wait till I tell the boys back in Omaha. Just wait."

"Did you get what you needed?" Luke asked.

"Oh, I imagine so. We'll take a look at one more. Lawrence Trent's home isn't on the tour, but he's reputed to have an excellent collection of nineteenth-century snuffboxes."

"What does Elsa have?"

"Besides the obvious feminine charms?" Max adjusted the radio and found some Chopin. "Emeralds, my dear boy. The lady is particularly fond of emeralds. They match her eyes."

MAX WAS FOND OF EMERALDS as well. Once LeClerc had arranged for the pictures to be developed, it was obvious that Trent's estate would be the easier mark. Max needed little else to decide him. He'd go for the stones.

"HEELS, ROXANNE?"

Roxanne stood proudly in the wings, teetering a bit on her new inch-high pumps. "I'm practically a teenager," she told her father.

"I believe we have several months yet before that momentous occasion."

"That's hardly any time. And besides, they punch up the costume." She turned, carefully, in her blue spangled leotard. "And the extra inch gives me more stage presence." If her breasts were going to take forever to develop, at least she'd take advantage of her height. "Making a good impression here at the Magic Castle's important, isn't it?" She smiled winningly.

"Naturally." And they had thirty seconds to cue. "I don't suppose you brought along any spare shoes."

Her smile widened before she kissed his cheek. "We're going to knock them dead."

Perhaps it was a trick of those lights, or his own thoughts, but for a moment when the curtain went up he saw her as a woman grown, slim and lovely, glowing with confidence, her eyes glinting with secrets only the female heart ever truly understands.

Then she was just his little girl again, wearing grown-up shoes and charming the audience with her skill with the silks. Moments later the silks were pooled at her feet, and she turned to her father, prepared to be put into a trance for his new levitation routine, a combination of the old broomstick illusion and the floating girl.

The music cued. "Für Elise." Slowly, gracefully, Max passed his hands in front of her face. Her head swayed. Her eyes drooped closed.

He used brooms with sparkling brushes, wanting beauty as well as drama. The first he placed between her shoulder blades, then taking a step stage left, held out his arms, gesturing. As if weightless, her legs began to rise, straight and extended, until her body was parallel to the stage. He used the other broomstick to sweep, over and under. Her long, already dramatic mane of red hair tumbled downward. When he removed the only brace, passing both brooms to a waiting Lily, the crowd was already applauding.

To the liquid strains of Beethoven, Roxanne began to revolve. The light changed to gold as her body turned, tilted, became vertical a foot above the stage. He brought her down gently, inch by inch, until her feet touched the stage.

And he awakened her.

Roxanne opened her eyes to a thunder of applause. Already in her mind, there was no sweeter sound.

"Told you, Daddy," she said under her breath.

"So you did, my sweet."

Sam watched from backstage and shook his head. It was all a scam, he thought. What pissed him off the most was that no one would let him in on the secret of how it was done. It was just one more thing the Nouvelles would have to pay for eventually.

All he needed was a couple of the steps, then he imagined he could duplicate it, or any of the other tricks, if he chose to. It amazed him, and appealed to his sense of greed, that people would actually pay good money to watch someone pretend he could do what couldn't be done.

There had to be a way to cash in on it, he considered. He lit a cigarette and watched Luke make his entrance. Big fucking deal, he thought. The bastard thought he was hot shit, standing out there in the spotlight, getting the applause and the attention.

The day would come, Sam told himself, when he would have all the attention. Because when you had that, you had power. And that was what Sam wanted most.

"Mr. Nouvelle." The moment the performance was over Brent Taylor, the actor with matinee-idol looks and a cream-rich baritone voice, sought Max out in his dressing room. "I have never, never seen better." Taylor pumped Max's hand enthusiastically.

"You flatter me, Mr. Taylor."

"Brent, please."

"Brent, then, and you'll call me Max. It's a bit cramped in here, but I'd be honored if you'd join me in a brandy."

"My pleasure. The transformation routine," Taylor continued while Max poured. "Simply marvelous. And the levitation was spectacular. I'm anxious for my dinner party so that we'll have more time to discuss magic."

"I'm always happy to discuss magic." He offered a snifter full of Napoleon.

"And perhaps we could also discuss the magic of the small screen. Television," Taylor said when Max merely smiled politely.

"Yes, I'm afraid I have little opportunity to watch it. My children now, they're experts."

"And impressive magicians in their own right. I imagine they'd be delighted to try their luck in a television special."

Max gestured for Taylor to sit on the small settee and took his own seat in front of the makeup table. "Magic loses power on film."

"It can, of course. But with your sense of theater, it could be marvelous. I'll be frank, Max. I've been given an opportunity by one of the networks to produce a series of variety specials. I'd like very much to produce an hour of 'The Amazing Nouvelle.'"

"Max." Luke paused, one hand on the door. "I'm sorry. There's a reporter from the *LA Times*."

"I'll speak with him in a moment. Brent Taylor, Luke Callahan."

"A pleasure to meet you." Taylor rose to shake Luke's hand. "You have a lot of talent—it's not surprising when you've been taught by the best."

"Thanks. I like your movies." Luke glanced from Taylor to Max. "I'll ask him to wait at the bar."

"That's fine."

"An amazingly good-looking boy," Taylor commented when Luke left them alone. "If he decides not to follow in your footsteps, I could get him six roles tomorrow."

Max smiled and studied his nails. "I'm afraid he's quite determined to follow in mine. Now, as to your offer . . . "

LUKE COULD HARDLY BEAR to wait. There was no time to speak to Max privately until after the second show. The moment Max slipped into his dressing room, Luke pounced.

"When are we going to do it?"

"Do?" Max sat at the makeup table and dipped his fingers into cold cream. "Do what?"

"The television thing." Excitement shimmered around him as he stared at Max's reflection. "The special Taylor wants to produce. Would we do it here, in L.A.?"

With deliberate strokes, Max creamed off greasepaint. "No."

"We could do it on location in New Orleans." He could already see it—the lights, the cameras, the fame.

Max tossed aside used tissues. "We're not doing it, Luke."

"We should probably cut out any close-up work, but we could fill in . . . " He trailed off, excitement fading into astonishment. "What? What do you mean we're not doing it?"

"Just that." Max loosened the tie of his tux before rising to change. "I turned it down."

"But why? We'd reach millions of people in one evening."

"Magic loses impact on film." Max hung up his jacket and went to work on the studs of his shirt.

"It doesn't have to. We could do it live. Lots of times they have a studio audience."

"Our schedule wouldn't permit it in any case." Max placed the studs in a small gold box. A movement of *Swan Lake* wafted out when he opened the lid.

"That's bull." Luke's voice quieted as something other than confusion worked into him. Max hadn't met his eyes once, not once since they'd come into the room. "It's all bull. You're not doing it because of me."

Deliberately, Max closed the lid on the music. "That's a remarkably foolish idea."

"No, it's not. You don't want that kind of exposure, not with me along. Just like you turned down the Carson show last year. You don't want to do TV because you think that son of a bitch might see me, him or my mother, and make trouble. So you're saying no to the kind of stuff that would put you over the top."

Max stripped off his tuxedo shirt and stood in a white undershirt and dress pants. Out of habit, he hung the shirt on a padded hanger, brushed a finger down the pleats. "I make my own choices, Luke, for my own reasons."

"Because of me," Luke murmured. It hurt, this pressure in the chest, this twisting in the gut. "It's not right."

"It's right for me. Luke." Max reached out to touch his shoulder, but Luke jerked away. It was the first time in years the boy had made that sharp, defensive movement. That, too, hurt. "There's no need to take it this way."

"How am I supposed to take it?" Luke demanded. He wanted to smash something, anything, but managed to clench his fists at his sides. "It's my fault."

"Blame doesn't enter into it. Priorities do. You may not be quite old enough yet to understand that, or that time passes. In another two years, you'll be eighteen. If I choose to accept an offer to do television at that time, I'll do so."

"I don't want you to wait. Not for me." His eyes were bright and furious. "If there's trouble, I'll handle it. I'm not a kid anymore. And for all we know, she's dead. I hope to God she's dead."

"Don't." Max's voice was sharp as a sword. "Whatever she did or didn't do, she remains your mother, and gave you life. Don't wish for death, Luke. It comes to all of us soon enough."

"Do you expect me not to hate her?"

"Your feelings are your responsibility. Just as my decisions are mine." Suddenly tired, Max scrubbed his hands over his face. He'd known the time would come to speak of it. The time always came for what you dreaded most. "She isn't dead."

Luke's body coiled like a whip. "How do you know?"

"Do you think I would take chances with you?" Furious at having to explain himself, Max snatched a clean shirt from the hanger. "I've kept track of where she is, how she is, what she's doing. One move toward you, one, and I'd have taken you where she couldn't find you."

All of the anger drained out of Luke, leaving him empty and miserable. "I don't know what I'm supposed to say to you."

"There's nothing you have to say. I did what I did, and will continue to do, because I love you. If I have to ask anything of you in return, I'll ask you to be patient for two short years."

Shoulders slumped, Luke poked at the pots on Max's dressing table. "I'll never be able to pay you back."

"Don't insult me by trying."

"You and Lily . . . " He picked up a jar, set it down again. Some emotions were too huge for words. "I'd do anything for you."

"Then put this out of your mind for now. Go and change. I have work to do yet tonight."

Luke looked up again. Max wondered how it could be that the boy could turn into a man in the short time they'd stood inside that cramped room. But it was a man who turned to him now, his shoulders broad and erect, his eyes no longer bright, but dark and direct.

"You're going to do the Langtree job tonight. I want to go with you."

Max sighed and sat to remove his stage shoes. "You're making things difficult this evening, Luke. I indulged you before, but there's a big step between casing a job and executing one."

"I'm going with you, Max." Luke stepped forward so that Max was forced to tilt back his head to meet Luke's eyes. "You're always talking about choices. Isn't it time you let me start making some of my own?"

There was a long pause before Max spoke again. "We leave in an hour. You'll need dark clothes."

MAX WAS GRATEFUL that Elsa Langtree didn't collect the small fru-fru dogs many actresses found fashionable. Elsa's eccentricities ran toward collecting men—younger and brawnier as the years passed. She was currently between husbands number seven and eight, having recently divorced a professional linebacker. Wedding plans were under way with her current amour, a twenty-eight-year-old bodybuilder.

Elsa was forty-nine and counting.

While her taste was admittedly poor in men, it was otherwise flawless. A fact that Max pointed out to Luke as they climbed over her eight-foot security wall.

"The wealthy often lose perspective," Max said softly as they hurried across the trim lawn. "But as you'll see, the house Elsa had built about ten years ago is simply lovely. She hired decorators, of course. Baxter and Fitch, quite good. But she inspected and approved every swatch, every piece, every detail personally."

"How do you know all this?"

"When one prepares to break into a home, it's imperative to know all about the inhabitants, as well as the structural layout." He paused in the shelter of some mimosa trees. "There, as you see, is an excellent example of Colonial architecture. Very traditional lines, slightly fluid and feminine and perfectly suited to Elsa."

"It's big," Luke remarked.

"Naturally, but not ostentatious. Once we're inside, you will speak only when absolutely necessary, stay beside me at all times and follow my instructions to the letter, and without hesitation."

133

Luke nodded. Anticipation was bubbling in his blood. "I'm ready."

Max found the alarm system camouflaged by the window boxes off the rear patio. Following Mouse's instructions, he unscrewed the shield and snipped the proper wires. Fighting impatience, Luke waited while Max replaced the screws and moved to the terrace door.

"Etched glass, cut and designed by an artist in New Hampshire," Max murmured. "A crime to damage it." Instead of using his cutter, he took out his picks and went to work on the two locks.

It took time. As the minutes clicked by, Luke heard every sound in the air. The faint hum from the pool filter, the rustle of night birds in the trees, the quiet click of metal on metal as Max finessed the locks. Then the whisper of success as Max slid the door open.

Now, for the first time, he felt what Max always experienced. That thrumming excitement of walking inside a locked house, that eerie pleasure of knowing people slept inside, the itchy power of moving through the darkness to take the prize.

They walked silently, single file through the spacious drawing room. A light scent of mums, a whisper of female perfume lingering. With the blueprints clear in his mind, Max headed for the kitchen, and the door that led to the basement.

"Why—"

Max shook his head for silence and moved downstairs. The walls were paneled in dark pine. A pool table stood in the center of the main room and was surrounded by weight equipment. An oak bar dominated one wall.

"Play room," Max said quietly. "To keep her men happy."

"She keeps her jewelry down here?"

"No." Max chuckled at the thought. "But the breaker box is. The safe is a time release. Quite sophisticated and difficult to crack. Of course, if the power's off . . ."

"The safe will open."

"Bingo." Max creaked open the door of the utility room. "Isn't

134

this handy?" he said to Luke. "All neatly labeled. Library." He flipped the breaker. "That should do it." He turned to Luke with a smile. "People so often hide their safe among their books. It's interesting, don't you think?"

"Yeah." Inside his gloves, his hands were sweating.

"How do you feel?"

"Like I did the first time I climbed into the backseat with Annabelle," Luke heard himself say, then flushed.

Max pressed a hand to his heart but couldn't hold back the quick chuckle. "Oh yes," he managed after a moment. "A very apt analogy." Turning, he led the way back up the stairs.

They found the safe in the library, behind a gorgeous O'Keeffe. With the time release negated, it was as simple to open as a child's puzzle box. Max stepped back and gestured to Luke.

From father to son, he thought proudly while Luke removed the jeweler's boxes from the safe. The narrow beam of his penlight shone on the gems when Luke opened the tops.

They were beautiful. That was all Luke could think as he stared down at the sparkle of stones, magnificently set in gold and platinum. That he didn't think at all of their monetary value in that first instant would have pleased Max enormously.

"Not yet," Max said with his mouth close to Luke's ear. "What shimmers is often paste." He removed a loupe from his pouch and, handing the light for Luke to hold over the gems, examined them. "Gorgeous," he murmured, sighing. "Simply gorgeous. As I said, Elsa has exquisite taste." He closed the safe and levered the painting back over it. "It's a shame to leave the O'Keeffe behind. But it seems only fair, don't you think?"

Luke stood with thousands of dollars in emeralds in his hands. And grinned.

Chapter Ten

THE TRICK OF PULLING OFF A CLEAN SCAM, AS FAR AS SAM was concerned, was to exploit the weakest link. In the short time he'd been with the Nouvelle troupe, he had made himself available for all and any jobs, kept an eager smile on his face and a word of flattery ready on his tongue. He had listened sympathetically when Lily told him about Luke's past and won her heart by inventing a story of a dead mother and a brutal father—which would have surprised his parents, who lived in a modest home in Bloomfield, New Jersey, and who had never in the sixteen years he'd lived under their roof raised an angry hand to him.

He'd hated the suburbs, and for reasons that had baffled both of his quiet, hardworking parents, had despised them, their lifestyle and their modest ambitions.

Throughout his teenage years, he had broken their hearts with defiance and rebellion. He'd stolen the family car for the first time at fourteen and had headed for Manhattan. He might have made it, if he'd bothered to pay the toll at the tunnel. The cops brought him back to Bloomfield, surly and unrepentant.

He became adept at shoplifting, stealing watches, costume

jewelry, department store makeup. He'd box the merchandise neatly in a leather suitcase he'd lifted, then sell it all at a discount to schoolmates.

Twice he broke into school and vandalized it, for the pleasure of breaking windows or busting water pipes. He was clever enough not to brag about his exploits, and was so charming to his teachers, they never glanced in his direction.

At home he was a hellion, driving his mother to tears on a regular basis. His parents knew he stole from them; a twenty would be missing from a wallet, knickknacks would disappear, a piece of jewelry would vanish. They couldn't understand why he felt compelled to take when they provided well for him. They didn't understand that their son didn't particularly like to steal. But he liked, very much, to hurt people.

He refused to go to counseling sessions, or if they did manage to drag him to the therapist, he would sit sullenly and speak not at all. When at sixteen his mother had refused to allow him the use of her car, he had responded by striking her, splitting her lip and bruising her eye. Then he had calmly taken up the keys, walked out the door and driven away.

He'd ditched the car near the Pennsylvania border, and he'd never gone back.

He never thought about his parents. No memories played through his mind of Christmases or birthdays, trips to the shore. For Sam, they meant less than nothing, and therefore didn't exist.

The Nouvelles were providing him with some pocket change, an excellent front and the time to plan another score. Because he was able to use them, he despised them as much as he had despised the quiet couple who'd given him life.

For reasons he didn't understand, or try to explore, he hated Luke the most. Because he sensed that Roxanne had developed a childish crush on Luke, Sam set about wooing her away.

He also considered her the weakest link.

He gave her time and attention, listened to her ideas, complimented her magic skills. He flattered her into showing him a few tricks and gradually built up her trust and affection for him.

He was dead sure of her loyalty, and toward the end of his second month in New Orleans, he decided to put it to use.

He'd often walk out to meet her on her way home from school, a habit that had endeared him to both Max and Lily. It was a chill, damp winter, and people hurried along the streets, seeking the comfort of home. It was easy to spot Roxanne, strolling slowly along the sidewalk, keeping out of the thin rain by walking under the overhanging terracing while she looked in shop windows. Many of the shopkeepers knew her well and would welcome her in if she came to browse.

She handled what she touched with respect and admiration, often asking questions and storing the knowledge away.

She was still two blocks away when he saw her, the bright hair and deep blue jacket shining out of the gloom. He'd already chosen his mark and, as he walked to meet her, was in the best of moods.

"Hey, Rox, how was school?"

"It was okay." She smiled up at him, just old enough, and certainly female enough, to be flattered by the attentions of a nineteen-year-old man. The heart inside her stubbornly undeveloped breast picked up its rhythm.

One of the shops along Royal was stocked with more junk than treasure. There were some interesting pieces, most of them inexpensive. The woman who ran the shop took merchandise on consignment, and supplemented her income by reading tarot cards and palms. Sam had chosen the shop because the proprietor usually worked alone, and because Roxanne often stopped in for a reading.

"Want to get your cards read?" He grinned at her. "Maybe you can find out how you did on that test?"

"I never ask dumb stuff like that."

"You could ask her about a boyfriend." He sent her a look that had her pulse jittering, and opened the door before she had a chance to move on. "Maybe she'll tell you when you're going to get married."

Roxanne stared down at her shoes. "You don't really believe in the cards."

"Let's see what she tells you. Maybe I will."

Madame D'Amour sat behind the counter. She had an angular, heavily rouged face dominated by dark brown eyes. Today she wore one of her many turbans, a purple one that covered all but a few wisps of her mercilessly dyed ebony hair. She added heavy rhinestone earrings that fell nearly to the shoulders of her purple caftan. Around her neck were several silver chains. Bracelets jangled on both wrists.

She was somewhere in her sixties and claimed to be descended from Gypsies. It might have been true, but regardless of her heritage, Roxanne was fascinated by her.

As the bells on the door jingled, she glanced up and smiled. Colorfully illustrated tarot cards were on the counter before her, arranged in a Celtic cross.

"I thought my little friend would visit me today."

Roxanne moved closer so that she could study the cards. It was overly warm in the shop, but she never minded. It always smelled wonderful from the incense Madame burned and the woman's generous use of perfume.

"Did you come to shop," Madame asked her, "or to seek?"

"Do you have time for a reading?"

"For you, my love, always. Perhaps we can share some hot chocolate, *oui?*" She glanced over at Sam, and her smile dimmed a bit. There was something about the boy she couldn't like, despite his open, friendly smile and pretty eyes. "And you? You have a question for the cards?"

"That's okay." He made his smile sheepish. "I guess it spooks me a little. Go ahead, Rox, take your time. I've got to go pick up some stuff at the drugstore. I'll meet you back home."

"Okay." As Madame scooped up the cards and rose, Roxanne moved toward the curtain that separated the shop from the back room. "Tell Daddy I'm coming."

"Sure. See you." He started toward the door, stopping when he heard the curtain whisk closed. His smile was no longer friendly as he deliberately opened the outside door, letting the bells jangle, then shut it again. Moving quickly, he skirted the tables loaded with trash and treasures and headed for the counter. Beneath it was a painted cigar box where Madame kept the day's receipts. The haul wasn't huge—business was slow on rainy winter days, but Sam scooped out everything, down to the last penny. He stuffed bills and change into his pocket, glanced quickly around to see if anything else was worth his time. He would have preferred smashing some of the glass and china. That made a statement. Instead, he filled his jacket pockets with some of the smaller knickknacks. Carefully holding the bells still, he eased the door open, slipped out and closed it slowly, quietly behind him.

OVER THE NEXT WEEK, Sam hit four more shops in the Quarter. When it was to his advantage, he enlisted Roxanne's help, wandering into stores with her and waiting while she, a familiar face in the district, caught the clerk's attention. He'd stuff whatever was handy into his pockets, whether it was a valuable Limoges box or a cheap souvenir ashtray. Once he was lucky enough to clean out another cash drawer when Roxanne was taken in the back to be shown a porcelain doll that had just been shipped in from Paris.

It didn't matter to Sam how much his loot was worth. What he enjoyed most was knowing that the wide-eyed, trusting Roxanne was his unwitting partner. No one would accuse Maximillian Nouvelle's little darling of lifting trinkets. As long as he was with her, he could line his pockets to his frigid heart's content.

But the best part of that New Orleans winter was seducing Annabelle away from the lovesick Luke.

It was easy, as easy as his compulsive and mean-spirited shoplifting. All he had to do was watch, listen and take advantage of opportunities offered.

Like most young lovers, Luke and Annabelle had their share of spats. Most of them revolved around the limited amount of time Luke had to entertain her, and her increasing demand for every moment of his day. She nagged at him to skip rehearsals, to bow out of performances so that he could take her to a party, to a dance, for a ride. Maybe he was being led around by his hormones, but Luke was too professional an entertainer—and too dedicated a thief—to cancel a performance or a heist, even for Annabelle.

"Listen, I can't." Luke blew out an impatient breath and shifted the phone to his other ear. "Annabelle, I explained all this days ago."

"You're just being stubborn." Through the receiver the tears in her voice came clearly. And made Luke feel like sludge. "You know Mr. Nouvelle would understand."

"No, I don't," Luke responded—because he hadn't asked Max to understand, and had no intention of doing so. "It's not my weekend off, Annabelle. I have a commitment to the act."

"I guess it means more to you than I do."

Naturally it did, but Luke doubted it would be wise to say so. "It's something I have to do."

"Lucy's party's going to be the biggest one of the year. Everybody's going to be there. Her dad even hired a live band. I'll just die if I miss it."

"Then go," Luke said between his teeth. "I told you it was okay with me. I don't expect you to sit home alone."

"Oh, sure." Derision, on the shrill side, joined the tears. "Go to the biggest party of the year without my boyfriend." She sniffled, then put all the wheedling at her disposal into her voice. "Oh, please, honey, couldn't you just get out of the first show? It wouldn't be so bad if we went to it together, then you had to leave."

It was tempting, as the Crack the Whip had once been tempting not so many years ago. It promised excitement, a fast, breathless ride. Luke hadn't changed so much in the last years that he didn't know when to resist the offer of pleasure.

"I'm sorry, Annabelle. I can't."

"Won't." The single word was ice.

"Listen," he began, then winced as the crash of the receiver echoed in his ear. "Christ," he muttered and dropped the phone on the hook.

"Women trouble?" It appeared as though Sam was just wandering in from the kitchen, an apple in one hand. In truth, he'd eavesdropped on the entire conversation, and was already formulating plans.

"They don't understand anything." It wasn't usual for Luke to confide in Sam, but he was just angry and frustrated enough to dump on the first available ear. "How the hell am I supposed to screw around with everyone's schedule just because Lucy Harbecker's having some party?"

Sam nodded in sympathy and bit into his apple. "Hey, she'll get over it." He gave Luke a friendly punch in the arm. "And if she doesn't, there are plenty of babes in the woods. Right?" He winked and started upstairs. It looked as though he needed to shake loose from tonight's show. Sam had a party to go to.

A faked fever and sick headache were all he needed. While Luke was preparing to warm up the audience at the Magic Door, Sam knocked on Annabelle's door. She answered it herself, her eyes puffy from weeping and bad temper.

"Oh, hi, Sam." She sniffled and smoothed at her hair. "What're you doing around here?"

"Luke sent me." With an apologetic smile, he brought his hand from behind his back and offered a clutch of painted daisies.

"Oh." She took the flowers and sniffed at them. They were nice, but they didn't make up for missing the biggest night of the year. "I guess he's trying to make up."

"He's really sorry, Annabelle. He felt bad about your missing the party."

"Me too." Her eyes hardened, then she sighed and shrugged. Her parents were out for the evening, her own night was ruined and all she had to show for it was a bunch of stupid flowers. "Well, thanks for bringing them by."

"My pleasure. It's not exactly a hardship to bring flowers to a beautiful woman." Admiration, with a touch of lust, showed in his eyes before he looked hurriedly away. "I guess I should take off. You've got things to do."

"No, not really." She was flattered by the look, touched by the fact that he'd tried to conceal it. With the long, dull night stretched in front of her, it seemed foolish to shut the door on an attractive male. "Maybe you'd like to come in for a Coke or something. Unless you've got plans."

"That'd be nice, if you're sure it's okay with your folks."

"Oh, they're out, won't be back for hours." She batted her eyes at him. "I'd really like some company."

"Me too." He closed the door behind him.

He played shy at first, keeping plenty of distance between them on the couch while they drank Cokes and listened to records. Gradually, he moved to sympathetic confidant. He was careful to stop just short of criticizing Luke, aware of how easily Annabelle could turn on him. Under the guise of making up to her the missed party, he invited her—with just a touch of awkwardness—to dance.

She found his shy admiration sweet and snuggled her head against his shoulder as she swayed over the rug. When his hand began to move rhythmically up and down her spine, she only sighed.

"I'm so glad you came by," she murmured. "I feel so much better."

"I hated to think about you being alone and upset. Luke's so lucky to have a girl like you." He swallowed, making sure it was audible. When he spoke again, his voice was unsteady. "I, ah, I think about you all the time, Annabelle. I know I shouldn't, but I can't help it."

"Really?" Her eyes were shining as she tilted back her head to look at his face. "What do you think about me?"

"About how beautiful you are." He brought his mouth close to hers, felt her shudder. It amused him how easy women were. Tell them they were beautiful, and they believed anything you said. "When you come over to the house, or to the club, I can't keep my eyes off you." He touched his lips to hers, just a whisper, then, as if coming to his senses, jerked back. "I'm sorry." He dragged a trembling hand through his hair. "I should go."

But he didn't move, only stood, staring at her. In a moment it was she, as he had hoped, as he had planned, who stepped to him, who wrapped her arms around his neck. "Don't go, Sam."

He was cute, he was nice to her and he was a good kisser. Annabelle's requirements had just been met.

When he had lowered her to the couch and had her, his body shuddered from the climax. But it shuddered more from the pleasure of knowing he had taken something that had been Luke's.

WHILE SAM WAS making Annabelle moan on the faded cabbage roses of her mother's couch, Madame walked backstage of the Magic Door. It disturbed her to be the bearer of bad tidings. It was something she did not so much for the other merchants in the Quarter, not so much even for herself, but for Roxanne.

"Monsieur Nouvelle."

Max glanced up from the sketches he was making and saw Madame in his dressing room door. Real pleasure brightened his eyes as he rose, taking her hand to kiss. "Ah, Madame, *bonsoir, bienvenu.* It's a delight to see you again."

"I wish I could say I had come to watch the performance, *mon ami*, but I have not." She saw the smile in his eyes fade to concern.

"There's a problem."

"*Oui*, one I must pass to you, with regret. We may speak?"

"Of course." He closed the door, ushered her to a chair.

"Early this week, my store was robbed."

Perhaps it was ironic that anger should fill him at the idea, when he himself was a thief. Max didn't consider it so. Madame was a friend, and a friend who could ill afford a robbery. "What did you lose?"

"A hundred dollars, more or less, and several trinkets. It is an inconvenience, monsieur, not quite a tragedy. I reported it, of course, and of course, there was little to be done. When one is in business, one learns to accept losses. I would have thought little more about it, but a day or two later, I heard that two more shops—the New Orleans Boutique on Bourbon and Rendezvous on Conti—had also been robbed, of small amounts to be sure. One day later, the shop next to mine took a loss—not quite so small. Several valuable porcelain pieces were taken, as well as several hundred in cash."

Max brushed a finger over his moustache. "Did anyone see the robber?"

"Perhaps." Madame toyed with the amulet that rested on the red silk bodice of her flowing caftan. "Perhaps not. As we merchants conferred to complain about our troubles, it came out that someone we knew had been in the shop each time the losses occurred. Coincidence, perhaps."

"Coincidence?" Max arched a brow. "An unlikely one to be sure. Why do you come to me with this, Madame?"

"Because the visitor to each of the shops was Roxanne."

Madame pressed her lips tight as she saw Max's face change. Gone, vanished was the concern, the interest, the obvious desire to help. In its place was a dangerous rage that burned out of his eyes. "Madame," he said in a voice no louder than a whisper and as frightening as a sword. "You dare?"

"I dare, monsieur, because I love the child."

"Yet you accuse her of sneaking into your shop, stealing from those who love and trust her?"

"No." Madame's shoulders lifted. "I do not accuse her. She would not take what was mine when in her heart she knows she had only to ask to be given. She was not alone on these visits, monsieur."

Battling rage, Max shifted to pour brandies for both of them. He waited to speak until he had offered a snifter to Madame and had taken his own first sip. "And who was she with?"

"Samuel Wyatt."

Max digested the information and nodded. He only wished he could say he was surprised. Only wished he didn't feel the inevitability of it. He had taken the boy in, done his best by him, but he had known, somehow he had known, that it would not be repaid in kind.

"You will give me a moment?" He moved to the door and called for Roxanne. Still in costume, she came to her father's dressing room. Her smile blossomed when she spotted Madame.

"You came!" She scooted over to kiss the woman's cheek. "I'm so glad you did. You can see the new illusion. Luke and I did it for the first time to an audience in the early show. We did it well, didn't we, Daddy?"

"Yes." He shut the door, then crouched down to lay his hand on her shoulders. "I have something to ask you, Roxanne. Something important. You must tell me the truth, no matter what."

The smile died out of her eyes, turning them solemn and a little frightened. "I wouldn't lie to you, Daddy. Not ever."

"You were in Madame's shop early this week?"

"On Monday after school. Madame read the cards for me."

"You were alone?"

"Yes—when she read the cards, I mean. Sam went with me, but he left."

"Did you take anything from Madame's shop?"

"No. I think I might buy the little blue bottle, the one with the peacock on it?" She looked at Madame for confirmation. "For Lily's birthday, but I didn't have my money with me."

"Not buy, Roxanne. Take."

"I ..." Her mouth quivered open as she understood. "I wouldn't take from Madame, Daddy. How could I? She's my friend."

"Did you see Sam take anything, from Madame, or any of the other shops he visited with you this week?"

"Oh, Daddy, no." The idea had tears swimming in her eyes. "He couldn't."

"We'll see." He kissed her cheek. "I'm sorry, Roxanne. You have to put it out of your mind until after the show, and be prepared to accept the truth, whatever it is."

"He's my friend."

"I hope so."

IT WAS AFTER ONE WHEN MAX opened the door of Sam's room. He saw the figure under the covers and moved quietly to the side of the bed. Wide awake, Sam shifted, blinked his eyes sleepily open. Moonlight slanted over his face.

"Feeling better?" Max asked.

"I think so." Sam offered a weak smile. "I'm sorry I let you down tonight."

"That's a small thing." Max switched on the light, ignoring Sam's grunt of surprise. "I'll apologize in advance for this intrusion. It's quite necessary." He walked to the closet.

"What's going on?"

"There are two ways to look at it." Max pushed aside hanging clothes. "Either I'm defending my home, or I'm doing you a grave disservice. I sincerely hope it's the latter."

"You've no right to pry into my personal things." Sam leaped out of bed in his underwear and grabbed at Max's arm.

"By doing so I may save your reputation."

"Come on, Sam." Embarrassment evident by the redness in his cheeks, Mouse stepped into the room to pull Sam aside.

"You fucking creep, take your hands off me." Sam jerked and bucked, and Mouse held firm. The fury that always bubbled beneath the surface burst out of Sam when he saw Max reach for a box on the closet shelf. "You goddamn bastard, I'll kill you for this."

Calmly, Max took the lid off the box and studied the contents. Cash was neatly stacked and bound with rubber bands. Some of the trinkets on the list Madame had given him were there as well. Others had probably been sold, Max assumed. There was a heaviness around his heart as he looked over at Sam.

"I took you into my home," Max said slowly. "I don't expect gratitude for that since you worked for your room and board. But I trusted you with my child, and she trusted you as her friend. You used her, and in such a way that you've stolen a piece of her childhood along with these. If I were a man of violence, I would kill you for that alone."

"She knew what I was doing," Sam spat out. "She was part of it. She—"

He broke off as Max struck him hard across the face with the back of his hand. "Perhaps I'm a man of violence after all." He stepped forward so that his eyes were close to Sam's. "You'll take your clothes and leave tonight. I'll give you what pay you have owed to you. You'll not only leave this house, but the Quarter. Understand me, I know every inch of the Vieux Carré. If you're still in it by dawn, I'll know. And I'll find you."

He turned and, taking the box, started out. "Let him go, Mouse. See that he packs his things and his things only."

"You'll pay, you bastard." Sam wiped at the blood on his lip. "I swear to Christ, you'll pay."

"I have," Max said over his shoulder. "By subjecting my family to you."

Sam grabbed a pair of jeans off the back of a chair. He sneered at Mouse while he tugged them on. "Get your rocks off watching me dress, faggot?"

Mouse flushed a little, but said nothing.

"I'll be glad to get the hell out of here anyway." He pulled out a shirt. "The past couple of months I've been bored out of my gourd."

"Then get moving." Luke stood in the doorway. His eyes glittered. "It'll give us time to fumigate the stink in here from a creep that uses a little kid to cover his ass."

"Don't you think she liked to be used?" Grinning a challenge, Sam stuffed his remaining clothes in a denim laundry bag. "That's what females like best, asshole. Just ask Annabelle."

"What the hell does that mean?"

"Well now." Sam shrugged into the jacket Lily had bought for him. It would keep him warm through the winter. "Since you ask, maybe you'd be interested to know that while you were being the good little trouper tonight, I was busy fucking your girl's brains out." He saw the fury on Luke's face, and the disbelief. His lips spread over his teeth. "Right on that ugly flowered couch in the living room." Sam's grin was hard and cold as ice. "I had her out of those red lace panties in five minutes. She likes to be on top best, doesn't she? So you can give it to her real deep. That mole under her left tit's sexy as hell, don't you think?"

He braced, eager for a fight, as Luke leaped at him. But Mouse moved fast, grabbing Luke and dragging him toward the door. "It's not worth it," Mouse kept saying. "Come on, Luke, let it go. It's not worth it." Sam's laugh echoed after them as Mouse shoved Luke toward the stairs. "Go out and cool off."

"Get the hell out of my way."

"Max wants him to go." Mouse stood firm at the top of the stairs. He would, if he had to, knock Luke down them. "That's all he wants. You go outside, take a walk. I gotta make sure he goes."

Fine, Luke thought. Dandy. He'd go out all right. And he'd wait for Sam. He stormed down the steps and out into the courtyard.

His blood was up, boiling Irish in his veins. His fists were already curled and ready. He planned to wait on the street, follow Sam for a block or two, then beat the shit out of him.

But he heard her crying. He was turned toward the street, his body braced, his mind full of violence. She was crying as if her heart were broken, curled up on a stone bench by the dormant azaleas.

Perhaps if she'd been given to tears, Luke could have ignored it and gone about his business. But in all the years he'd lived with the Nouvelles, he'd never once heard Roxanne cry since her bout with chicken pox. The sound of it reached inside and took him by the heart.

"Come on, Roxy." Awkward and out of his depth, Luke walked to the bench and patted her head. "Don't do that."

She kept her face pressed against her knees and sobbed.

"Jesus." However reluctant he was, Luke found himself sitting beside her and drawing her into his arms. "Come on, baby, don't let him make you cry like this. He's a bastard, a freaking creep." He sighed and rocked and found himself gradually calming. "He's not worth it," he said half to himself, realizing Mouse's words had been right on target.

"He used me," Roxanne murmured against Luke's chest. She had control of the sobbing now, and nearly felt strong enough to stop the tears. "He pretended to be my friend, but he never was. He used me to take things from people I cared about. I heard what he said to Daddy. It was like he hated us, like he'd hated us all along."

"Maybe he did. What do we care?"

"I brought him home." She pressed her lips together. She wasn't sure she could forgive herself for that. "Did he—did he really do that with Annabelle?"

Luke let out a breath and settled his cheek against Roxanne's hair. "I guess he probably did."

"I'm sorry."

"If she'd let him, just like that, I don't think she was really mine anyway."

"He wanted to hurt you." She stroked her finger down Luke's arm, comforted. "He wanted to hurt everybody, I guess. That's why he took things. It's not like what Daddy does."

"Uh-uh," Luke said absently, then froze. "What?"

"You know, stealing. Daddy wouldn't steal from a friend, or from somebody who'd get hurt because of what he took." She yawned. The crying jag had tired her out. "He takes jewels and stuff like that. It's always insured."

"Jesus Christ." He pushed her off his lap so that she landed hard on her rump on the bench. "How long have you known about all that? How long have you known what we're doing?"

She smiled indulgently, her swollen eyes sparkled with moonlight. "Always," she said simply. "I've always known."

SAM LEFT THE HOUSE, but he didn't leave the Quarter. Not when he had a score to settle. There was only one way he could have been found out so completely. Roxanne had ratted on him.

It was easy to convince himself that she'd known what he was doing from the beginning. She'd waltzed into those shops, and had waltzed out again, making it all so slick. And then, she'd turned on him, so that he'd been kicked out of a warm bed, humiliated. She'd have to pay for that.

He waited for her. He knew the route she took to school. He'd even walked her there himself from time to time, trying to be nice to her. Trying to be nice, Sam thought, grinding a fist into his open palm. Look how she'd paid him back.

He spent several cold hours huddled in an alley trying to keep out of a thin, chill drizzle. He hated being cold.

It was one more thing she'd pay for.

He spotted her and drew back a little. There was no need for the precaution, he noted. She was dragging along, her knapsack over her back, her eyes cast down. He waited, and when she was close enough, pounced.

Roxanne didn't even get out a scream when she was grabbed from behind and yanked into the alley. Her fists came up—she was a natural fighter—but they lowered again when she saw Sam.

Her eyes were still puffy. She resented that. Resented that he'd driven her to tears. But they were all used up. Her chin leveled, and her eyes, perfectly dry, gleamed dangerously up at his.

"What do you want?"

"A nice little talk. Just you and me."

There was something in his face that made her want to run, something she hadn't seen in it before. There was hate, yes, but there was a dullness about it. Like a rusty razor that would infect as well as slice.

"Daddy told you to leave."

"You think that old man scares me?" He shoved her, surprising more than hurting her as she slammed back into the wall. "I do what I want, and what I want right now is to settle up with you. You owe me, Rox."

"Owe you?" Forgetting surprise, forgetting the ache where her shoulder had bumped stone, she pushed herself away from the wall. "I brought you home. I asked Daddy to give you a job. I helped you, and then you stole from my friends. I don't owe you jack."

"Where are you going?" He shoved her back into place when she tried to stalk past him. "Off to school? I don't think so. I think you should spend some time with me." He slid a hand around her throat. She would have screamed then, loud and long, but she couldn't draw enough air. "You ratted on me, Rox."

"I didn't," she managed to whisper. "But I would have if I'd known."

"Same thing, isn't it?" He shoved her again so that her head knocked painfully into the wall.

Fear had her reaching up, without thought, without warning

and raking her nails down his face. He howled, his grip loosened. She nearly made the mouth of the alley before he caught her.

"You little bitch." He was breathing hard as he sent her sprawling. There was anger, there was pain, but there was also excitement. He could do whatever he wanted with her, anything, everything, and no one would stop him.

Her head was swimming. She saw him coming as she pushed herself up on her hands and knees. He was going to hurt her, she knew, and it was going to be really bad. Aim low, she told herself, and hit him hard.

She didn't have to. Even as she was bracing for the attack, Luke flew into the alley. He made a sound in his throat as he leaped on Sam. A sound Roxanne could only describe as wolfish.

Then there was the thud of fists against flesh. She managed to gain her feet, though her legs wobbled. She looked first for a weapon, a plank, a rock, a piece of metal. In the end she settled for the lid of a garbage can and, hefting it, advanced on the fight.

It took her only a moment to see that Luke didn't need her help. He was straddling Sam now and methodically, mercilessly, pounding his fists into Sam's face.

"That's enough now." She tossed the lid aside to use both hands on Luke's pumping arms. "You've got to stop. We'll get in trouble if you kill him." She had to get down so that Luke's fierce eyes could meet hers. "Luke, Daddy wouldn't want you to hurt your hands."

Something about the cool, logical tone had him looking down. His knuckles were bruised and raw and bloody. He had to laugh. "Right." But he touched one of those bleeding hands to her face. He'd been furious about Annabelle, but that was nothing, nothing compared with what he'd felt when he'd seen Roxanne on the ground and Sam looming over her. "Are you okay?"

"Yeah. I was going to go for his balls, but thanks for beating him up for me."

"No problem, I enjoyed it. Go pick up your bookbag. Wait for me on the sidewalk."

"You're not going to hit him again, are you?" She glanced down dispassionately into Sam's battered face. Unless she missed her guess, his nose was broken, and he'd lose a couple of teeth.

"No." He jerked his head toward the mouth of the alley. "Go on, Rox. Wait for me."

With one last glance at Sam, she turned and walked away.

"I could kill you for touching her." Luke leaned down close. "You come near her or any of my family again, and I will kill you."

Sam struggled onto his elbows when Luke rose. His face was on fire, his body felt as though it had been hit by a truck. No one, no one, had ever hurt him before.

"I'll pay you back." His voice was a croak that made Luke's brow lift in derision.

"You can try. Free lesson, Wyatt, quit while you're able to walk away. Next time I'll break more than your nose."

When Luke left him, Sam curled up in a ball to try to stop the pain. But it ate through him, tangling with the hate. One day, he promised himself as he wept and dragged himself to his feet. One day, they'd all pay for hurting him.

Chapter Eleven

Paris, 1982

"I'm not a child anymore." Roxanne's temper was up. It snapped in her voice, sizzled in her eyes as she whirled from her view of Paris in the spring.

"I'm aware of that." In deliberate contrast, Max's tone was mild. He seemed completely unaffected by his daughter's fury as he added a dash of cream to his strong French coffee. The years had turned his hair to a gleaming pewter.

"I have a right to go with you, a right to be a part of it."

Max spread butter generously on his croissant, nibbled, then dabbed his lips with a linen napkin. "No," he said, smiled sweetly and continued to eat.

She could have screamed. God knew she wanted to—scream and rant and rave. And that sort of behavior would hardly convince her father that she was a competent adult, ready to assume her place in his business.

The parlor of their suite at the Ritz was beautifully appointed, sumptuous in comfort. In her flowing silk robe splashed with vivid flowers, the discreet emeralds winking at her ears, the intricate French braid spilling down her back, she looked as though she belonged there.

But Roxanne's heart and soul longed for dark alleys, sooty rooftops. The blood that pumped through her veins under that lily-soft skin was the blood of a thief. She only needed to convince her father it was time for her debut.

"Daddy ... " She topped off his coffee, giving him another engaging smile. "I understand you only want to protect me."

"A parent's most important job."

"And I love you for it. But you have to let me grow up."

He looked at her then. Though his lips remained curved, his eyes were unbearably sad. "All the magic at my disposal couldn't have stopped you from that."

"I'm ready." She took advantage of his long sigh, cupping his hand in hers, leaning forward. Her eyes were soft again, her smile persuasive. "I've been ready. I'm every bit as good as Luke—"

"You have no idea how good Luke is." Max patted her hand and went back to his breakfast. How often had they had this discussion? he wondered, since she had announced at the tender age of fourteen that she was ready to join his after-hours show? He'd had no idea she'd even known what he did when the spotlights dimmed and the crowds went home.

Roxanne's eyes iced over. Max nearly chuckled. Such was a woman's magic, he thought. "However good he is," she said, "I can be better."

"It's not a competition, my love."

He was wrong there, Roxanne mused as she sprang up to pace the room again. It had been a competition, a fierce one, for years. "It's because I'm not a man." There was bitterness in every syllable.

"That has nothing to do with it. I take some pride in considering myself a feminist." Max sighed again, pushing his plate aside. "You're too young, Roxy."

That was the wrong button to push. Outraged, she spun

around. "I'm nearly eighteen. How old was he when you took him with you the first time?"

"Years older," Max murmured. "Inside. Roxanne, I want you to go to college, learn the things I can't teach you. Discover yourself."

"I know who I am." Her head came up, her shoulders straightened. Max saw a glimpse of the woman she would be. The pride burned so hot and fast it caused his eyes to swim. "You've taught me everything I need to know."

"Not nearly enough," Max said quietly. "Lily and I have kept you close, perhaps too close, because we couldn't bear to do otherwise. We only want you to take a step away, on your own. If you come back, I'll be content it's right for you."

"What about what I want?" she demanded. "I want to be there when you go to Chaumet, when you open the safe. I want to know what it feels like to stand in the dark and hold the Azzedine diamonds in my hands."

Max understood, only too well. He could regret that he'd told her about the jewels, their history, their spectacular beauty and the mystique that went along with the glittery stones. But there was little room for regret in his life.

"Your day will come, if it's meant to. But not this time."

"Damn it, I want—"

"Your wants have to wait." His tone was flat and final. Only he knew how relieved he was when the knock on the door interrupted them. He gestured for Roxanne to answer it and went back to his coffee.

She managed to fight her fury back, to open the door with a pleasant smile on her face. It faded immediately when she saw Luke. The look she aimed at him was sharp enough to cut bone.

"Got turned down, did you?" He grinned, tucked his hands in his pockets and strolled past her. The teasing, feminine scent of her perfume kindled an instant fire in his blood. He'd learned he couldn't ignore it, but he could keep her from seeing his reaction to her, and making him pay for it.

"Max." He poked through the silver basket of pastries and helped himself. "I thought you'd want to know, the rest of the equipment finally arrived."

"Ah, at last." With a nod he gestured for Luke to sit. "Have some coffee. I'll go check it myself. You can keep Roxanne company."

Damned if he wanted to be alone with her, It was hard enough in the day-to-day order of things. But he knew, he damn well knew, she was wearing nothing under that robe. "I'll go with you."

He was half out of his chair when Max stood and pushed him down again. "No need. Mouse and I can make sure everything's in order. We should be able to rehearse this afternoon." He moved to the mirror to straighten his tie and brush at his moustache.

Didn't they realize the sparks they set off each other? Max wondered. An innocent bystander could go up in flames. Youth, he thought with a sigh and a smile. In the mirror, he could see their reflections, both of them tensed as alley cats with most of the room between them.

"If Lily wakes soon, tell her to enjoy her morning. We'll meet at La Palace at two." He crossed over to kiss his daughter's cheek. "*Au revoir, ma belle.*"

"We're not finished with this."

"Two o'clock," he said. "Meanwhile you two should go out, take a walk in the Paris sunshine."

The minute the door closed behind her father, Roxanne rounded on Luke. "I'm not going to be left behind this time."

"It's not up to me."

She marched to the table where he sat, slapped her palms down on the linen cloth hard enough to make the china rattle. "And if it were?"

He looked her square in the eyes. He could have strangled her for becoming so beautiful. And she'd done it slowly, insidiously, over the last few years, sneaking up on him like a thief to steal his breath away with a look. "I'd do exactly what Max is doing."

That hurt. She sucked in her breath on the sharp pain of betrayal. "Why?"

"Because you're not ready yet."

"How do you know?" She tossed her head back. The light through the windows shivered over her hair and turned it to flame. Luke was afraid she'd read the passion in his eyes. "How do you know what I'm ready for?"

It was a direct challenge. Much too direct. His palms dampened. "Heisting jewels from the Trimalda villa's a far cry from scamming tourists with the Cups and Balls, Rox." Needing a prop, he picked up his coffee. Years of training kept his hand steady. He could make her angry, he knew. It was best. As long as she was angry he could keep his hands off her. He hoped.

"I'm every bit as good as you, Callahan. You didn't even know how to riffle a deck until I taught you."

"It must be tough to know you've been outreached."

Her skin went ice-white then flushed deeper than the roses on the table between them. She straightened, and to his misery, Luke saw every curve of her body beneath the robe. "You witless bastard. You couldn't outreach me if you were standing on stilts."

He only smiled. "Who got the most press the last gig in New York?"

"An idiot who has himself chained in a trunk and gets tossed in the East River is bound to get press." How she hated the fact that the escapes he'd gravitated to were spectacular. Every time he'd lock himself into another box, she was torn in two parts—one thrilled by his skill and his daring, the other disgusted by it.

"I got the press for getting out," he reminded her, and took out one of the French cigars he'd developed a fondness for. "For being the best." He flicked on his lighter and puffed smoke from the cigar. "You should be content with your pretty illusions, Rox, your pretty boyfriends—" All of which he'd like to murder. "Leave the dangerous work to those of us who can handle it."

She was quick. He'd always admired that in her. He barely had time to shoot up a hand and catch her fist before it plowed into his nose. Still gripping her curled fingers, he rose. They were face-to-face now, bodies almost brushing.

She felt a tingle skitter along her spine. A yearning bloomed inside like a flame she'd never been able to stamp out. She wanted to hate him for it.

"Watch your step." The warning was quiet, telling her she'd managed to fan the fires of his temper if nothing else.

"If you think I'm afraid you'll hit me back—"

He shocked them both by catching her chin in tensed fingers, holding her face close. Her lips parted as much in surprise as anticipation. Her mind went blessedly blank.

"I could do worse." He ground the words out. They tasted like glass in his throat. "And we'd both pay for it."

He shoved her away before he did something he'd never forgive himself for. As he strode to the door, he tossed back a clipped order. "Two o'clock. In costume." And slammed the door behind him.

When she realized her knees were shaking, Roxanne lowered herself into a chair. After several deep breaths, she rubbed a hand along her throat until she could swallow over the obstruction lodged there. For an instant, just a flashing instant, he'd looked at her as though he realized she was a woman. A woman he could want. A woman he did want.

On another shaky breath, she shook her head. That was ridiculous. He'd never thought of her as anything but a necessary nuisance. And she didn't care. She'd long ago gotten over that silly childish crush.

She wasn't interested in men anyway. She had bigger plans.

Damn if she was going to wait through four years of college before she implemented them. Her lips firmed. Damn if she was going to wait another week.

It was time to flesh out the idea that had been brewing in her mind. Past time. Smiling to herself, she brought her long legs up, crossed them and casually reached for the cigar Luke had left burning. She sat back, blowing smoke rings at the ceiling. And plotted.

LUKE COULD ONLY THANK GOD he had so much on his mind. Between preparing for the gig at La Palace and the job at Chaumet, he didn't have time to dwell on Roxanne.

Except at three A.M., when he'd awaken in the cold sweat of frustration from dreams of her. Incredibly clear, incredibly provocative dreams of that long, white body wrapped around his. Of that glorious hair spread over a patch of dewy green grass in some secluded glade. Of those witchy eyes, clouded with passion.

If there was a hell, Luke was certain he would burn for those dreams alone. He'd been raised with her, for Christ's sake, and was the closest thing to a brother she had. The only thing keeping her safe from him was the idea he'd fixed in his head that doing what he wanted to do would be a kind of spiritual incest.

And the certainty that she would laugh at him, that the laugh would rake him clean to the bone, if he let his feelings show.

He had to get out, he realized when he'd paced the length and width of the room a dozen times. A nice long walk before dinner, a stroll in the Parisian twilight. He grabbed his black leather bomber jacket and paused in front of the mirror long enough to run fingers through his hair.

He didn't notice the changes in himself over the years. So much was the same. His hair was still dark, still thick, still worn dramatically long to curl over his collar, or to be caught in a queue. His eyes were still blue, and the length of his sooty lashes had ceased to embarrass him. He'd learned that his poetically good looks could charm women who put stock in such things. His skin remained smooth, with long bones pressed taut against it. Once in his teens he'd grown a moustache, but it hadn't suited him. Now his mouth was unadorned.

He'd broken his nose once in an escape, but it had healed straight. That was a slight disappointment.

At twenty-one he'd grown into his full height of six-one, and his body was rangy. The haunted look that had come over him so often during childhood came only rarely now. The years with Max had taught him control: physical, mental, emotional. He was, and always would be, grateful for that.

And given time, given will, he would break clear of the shackles his feelings for Roxanne had clamped on him.

Turning away from the mirror, he went out, started down the long, carpeted hallway toward the elevators. He glanced briefly at the pretty blond maid pushing her cart.

Time for a check for extra towels, mints on the pillow. The child who'd once slept in ditches had become so used to such luxuries he barely noted them.

"*Bon soir*," he murmured with a casual smile as he passed her.

"*Bon soir, monsieur*." Her smile was shy and swift before she knocked on a door across the hall.

Luke was nearly to the elevators when he stopped dead. That scent. Roxanne's scent. Damn her, was he so bedazzled he could smell her everywhere? He shook himself loose, took another step and stopped again. His eyes narrowed as he turned around and studied the maid, who was fitting her master key into the lock.

Those legs. His teeth set as he studied the long slim legs beneath the discreet black skirt of the uniform.

Roxanne's legs.

She was easing the door shut behind her when he slapped a hand against it. "What the hell do you think you're doing?"

She blinked up at him. "*Pardon?*"

"Cut the crap, Roxanne. What's the deal?"

"Shut up." She hissed the words as she grabbed his arm and pulled him inside. She was furious, but that could wait. First she wanted answers. "How did you know it was me?"

He could hardly tell her he'd have recognized her legs anywhere.

So he lied. "Give me a break. Who do you think you're fooling with that getup?"

The fact was, it was perfect. The short sassy blond wig changed her looks dramatically. Even her eye color was different. Colored contacts, he imagined, that turned emerald into smoky brown. She was skilled enough with makeup to subtly change the tone of her skin, the shape of her face. She'd added a bit of padding to her hips and, Luke was certain, was wearing one of those clever bras that should have been illegal.

They pushed up and padded and made a man's mouth water for what was essentially a mirage.

"Bull." Her voice was still an incensed whisper. "I spent ten minutes in Lily's room and she didn't recognize me."

Because she hasn't been drooling over your legs for the past two years.

"I did," he said and left it at that. "Now, what the hell are you doing in here?"

"I'm stealing Mrs. Melville's jewelry."

"Like hell."

Her eyes flared. They might have been brown, Luke thought, but they were Roxanne's. "Leave me alone. I got in here, and I'm not walking out empty-handed. I planned it out down to the last detail, and you're not spoiling it for me."

"And what are you going to do when Mrs. Melville screams down the gendarmes?"

"Look shocked and appalled and outraged, of course. Like every other guest in the hotel." Turning away, she went directly to the dresser. She took a hankie from her pocket, using it to ensure against fingerprints as she opened drawers.

He made a sound in his throat that was equal parts amusement and disgust. "You think you're going to find her stuff just lying around in a drawer? The Ritz has a safe downstairs for that."

Roxanne sent him a withering look. "She doesn't keep it

163

downstairs. I overheard her arguing with her husband the other night. She likes to keep it close so she can pick through it when she's dressing each evening."

It was good, Luke mused. Very good. He searched around for another flaw. "What are you going to do if one of them walks in while you're pawing around?"

"I won't be pawing around." Moving quickly, competently, she closed a drawer. "I'm here to turn down the bed. What's your excuse?"

"Okay, Rox, enough's enough." He grabbed her arm. "We've planned out the Chaumet job for months. I'm not having one of your two-bit games spoil it."

"One has nothing to do with the other." She jerked away from him. "And it's not two-bit. Have you seen the rocks that woman wears?"

"Could be paste."

"That's for me to find out." With one brow arched, she took a jeweler's loupe from her pocket. "I've been around Max nearly eighteen years," she said as she slipped it back in place. "I know what I'm doing."

"What you're doing is getting the hell out—" He broke off when he heard a key rattle in the lock. "Oh, shit."

"I could scream," she said pleasantly. "Claim you'd pushed your way in and attacked me."

There wasn't time for rebuttal. He shot her one fulminating look, then took his only option. He dived under the bed.

With her tongue tucked in her cheek, Roxanne began to turn down the bedclothes. She straightened when the door opened, and blushed prettily.

"Oh, Monsieur Melville," she said in heavily accented English. "I should . . . come back?"

"No need, honey." He was a big, brawny Texan in his fifties, and the damn French food gave him indigestion. "You just keep on with what you're doing."

"*Merci*." Roxanne smoothed the spread and fluffed pillows, well aware Melville's eyes were riveted to her posterior.

"Don't recall seeing you in here before."

"This is not . . . " She leaned over the bed a little further. Might as well give the randy old guy his money's worth, she thought. "My floor usual." Enjoying her character, she turned, slanting him a look from under her lashes. "You would like more towels, monsieur? I can get you something?"

"Well now." He leaned down to tickle her chin. There was a whiff of bourbon on his breath, not entirely unpleasant. "What you got in mind, sugar cakes?"

She giggled and fluttered her lashes again. "Oh, *monsieur*. You tease me, *oui?*"

He'd sure as hell like to, he thought. Unwrapping a pretty little package like this would be a hell of a lot more fun than the opera his wife was dragging him to. But it would also take time. Indigestion forgotten, he decided he could make time for a little slap and tickle.

"I've had this hankering for French pastries." Melville patted her bottom, and when she tittered, gave her breast a light squeeze. From under the bed, Luke was sure he was growing fangs.

Blushing and breathy, Roxanne stared up at Melville with big, brown eyes. "Oh, *monsieur*. You Americans."

"I'm not just American, sweetie. I'm a Texan."

"Ah." She let him nibble at her neck while Luke lay helpless, his fists clenched. "Is it true what they say about Texans, *monsieur?* That everything is . . . bigger?"

Melville let out a hoot and kissed her hard on the mouth. "Damn straight, sugar. Why don't I let you find out?" He forgot about his wife as well as his stomach and started pushing her down on the bed. Luke braced, ready to pounce.

"But, *monsieur*, I'm on duty." Roxanne struggled away, still giggling. "I will be discharged."

"How about when you're not on duty?"

165

Playing the Texan's image of French tart to the hilt, she flushed again, and caught her bottom lip flirtatiously between her teeth. "Perhaps at midnight we could meet." Her lashes fluttered. "There is a little cafe close—Robert's?"

"Well now, I think I could manage that." He pulled her close again to give her padded hips a squeeze. "You keep an eye out for me—what's your name, darling?"

"It's Monique." She trailed her fingers over his cheek. "I will wait for midnight."

He gave her another pinch and a wink before strolling out dreaming of young French sex.

Roxanne plopped onto the bed and howled with laughter.

"Oh yeah, it's a riot," Luke muttered as he crawled out. "You let that sleazeball paw all over you, practically crawl on top of you, and it's a laugh a minute. I should spank you."

Still holding her sides, she let out a last sighing laugh. "Oh, grow up." Then she sucked in her breath when Luke snagged her arm and hauled her to her feet. She recognized real fury when she saw it, and bit off any protest.

"You seem to have done enough growing up for both of us. Damn good at that, weren't you, Rox? How many of those smart college guys you date have you let put their sweaty hands all over you?"

This time her blush was genuine. "That's none of your business."

"The hell it's not. I'm—" Crazy about you. The words nearly tumbled out before he choked them off. "Somebody has to look out for you."

"I can do that fine for myself." She elbowed him away, horrified that her spine was tingling. "And for your information, flea brain, he didn't have his hands on *me*. I've got enough padding where he was groping to stuff a mattress."

"That's beside the point." He grabbed for her hand, but she shoved him away. "Roxanne, we're getting out of here. Now."

"You go. I'm getting what I came for." Prepared to take her

stand, she tossed her head back. "I want it more than ever. That cheating bastard is going to buy his wife a whole new basket of jewelry. Serves him right—going off to meet some little French tootsie at a cheap café."

Despite himself, Luke chuckled and ran a hand through his hair. "You're the French tootsie, Rox."

"And I'm the one who's going to make him pay for adultery." Her gaze sharpened. There was enough deviousness in the look to elicit Luke's reluctant admiration. "And what's he going to say about me? He'll talk about walking in on a maid, describe me— but not in too much detail, because he'll be guilty and scared. It's better this way than if he'd never seen me at all." She marched to the closet and, scanning the top shelf, grinned. "*Et, voilà.*"

She had to stretch to reach the three-tiered jewelry box.

"God, Luke, it must weigh twenty pounds." Before he could assist her, she set it on the floor and crouched beside it. "Mine," she said in a warning hiss, slapping his hand away. She took a set of picks from her pocket, chose one and went to work on the lock.

It took her forty-three seconds—Luke timed her. And he was forced to admit that she was better, much better, than he had imagined.

"Oh, my." Her heart did a quick jig as she opened the top. Sparkles, gleams, shines. She felt like Aladdin exploring his cave. No, no, she thought, like one of the forty thieves. "Aren't they gorgeous?" Indulging herself, she dipped her hand in.

"If they're real." It wasn't possible to completely staunch the familiar tingle, but he kept his voice brisk. "And a pro doesn't drool over the goods."

"I'm not drooling." Then she laughed again, turned that glowing smile on him. "Maybe a little. Luke, isn't it fabulous?"

"If . . . " His voice cracked. He had to clear his throat. "If they're real," he repeated.

Roxanne only sighed at his lack of vision and pulled out the loupe. After examining a chain of sapphires and diamonds, she sat

167

back on her heels. "They're real, Callahan." Moving briskly now, she examined piece after piece before wrapping them in towels. "I wouldn't say the diamonds are better than second water—probably third, but that'll do. I make it to be oh, a hundred and sixty, hundred and seventy thousand net?"

He'd figured the same himself, but didn't want to tell her how closely their thoughts had meshed. Instead, he hauled her to her feet. He wiped the box clean, then using a towel, set it back in place.

"Let's go."

"Come on, Luke." She blocked the door, and her eyes were laughing. "At least you can say I did good."

"Beginner's luck." But he grinned back at her.

"Luck had nothing to do with it." She stabbed a finger at his chest. "Like it or not, Callahan, you've got a new partner."

Chapter Twelve

"YOU'RE NOT BEING FAIR."

Roxanne stood in her father's dressing room in full costume. The spangles and beads on her strapless emerald gown shivered from the lights, and her indignation.

"I proved myself," she insisted.

"You proved you're impulsive, reckless and stubborn." After adjusting the cuff of his tuxedo shirt to his liking, Max met her furious face in his mirror. "And you are not, I repeat not, going on the Chaumet job. Now, I have ten minutes to cue, young lady. Is there anything else?"

In that moment she was plunged back into childhood. Her bottom lip quivered as she dropped into a chair. "Daddy, why don't you trust me?"

"On the contrary, I trust you implicitly. You must trust me, however, when I tell you you're not ready."

"But the Melvilles—"

"Were a risk you should never have taken." He shook his head as he crossed over to take her drooping chin in his hand. He knew—who better?—what it was like to covet those shiny toys, to crave the excitement of stealing in the dark. How could he expect a child of his blood to be any different?

And, truthfully, he was enormously proud of her. Warped, he supposed with a half smile. But a father's pride was a father's pride.

"*Ma belle*, I will tell you this. Never, never muddy your own pond."

Roxanne arched a brow. "I don't recall you putting the jewels back, Daddy."

Caught, he ran his tongue around his teeth. "No," he agreed, drawing the word out. "One shouldn't look a gift diamond in the mouth—so to speak. Still, what you acquired is a fraction of what we hope to acquire tonight. It's been months in the planning, Roxanne. The timing is calculated to the instant. Even if I wanted to add you, or anyone, on at this point, it would tilt those very delicately balanced scales."

"It's an excuse," she tossed back, feeling like a little girl forbidden to attend a party. "Next time you'll have another."

"It's the truth. Next time there'll be another truth. When have I ever lied to you?"

She opened her mouth, closed it again. He'd evaded, avoided and toyed with veracity. But lied to her? No, never. "I'm as good as Luke."

"He used to say the same thing about you, onstage. Speaking of which . . . " He took her hand, lifting her before kissing it lightly. "We have a show to do."

"All right." She opened the door, then glanced over her shoulder. "Daddy, I want my share of the hundred and sixty."

He grinned, ear to ear. Had a father ever had so perfect a child? "That's my girl."

THE AUDIENCE AT LA PALACE was studded with film stars, Paris models and those rich and glamorous enough to rub elbows with them. Max had created a show sophisticated and complicated enough to entertain the discriminating. It wasn't possible for Roxanne to walk through the act with her mind on something else.

As she had been trained, she put everything aside but the magic. It was she who performed the Floating Balls illusion now, a slim woman in shimmering emerald. Watching her, Luke realized she looked like a long-stemmed rose—that sinuous green, the fiery hair. The audience was as captivated by her beauty as by the silvery balls that swayed and danced inches above her graceful hands.

He liked to tease her, of course, that her illusions were all glitz and no meat. But the truth was she was extraordinary. Even knowing what went on behind the trick, he was caught.

She lifted her arms. Three balls shimmered along each arm, from shoulder to wrist. While Debussy played, Lily draped emerald silk over them, stepped back out of the light. By turning her arms over, palms up, Roxanne had the silk drifting to the floor. And there, where the shining globes had been, white doves perched.

The audience exploded as she took her bows and exited. Luke was there in the wings, grinning at Roxanne as Mouse coaxed the doves into their cage. "Birds are okay, Rox, but if you worked with a tiger ... "

"Kiss my—" She broke off only because Lily had followed her off and was already clucking her tongue.

"Don't start." She gave them both affectionate pats on the cheek. "Mouse, honey, you keep these two in line. I've got to go back for this set." She gave an exaggerated sigh. "I swear, Max never stops thinking of ways to cut me into pieces." After a last lingering look at Luke, she walked on, into Max's applause.

"You know what's wrong with her, don't you?" Roxanne said under her breath.

"Nothing's wrong with Lily." Luke's lips curved as he watched Max roll into a flashy routine that began with shooting fire from

171

his fingertips and would end with his cutting Lily into thirds with laser beams.

"She worries about you, God knows why."

That got under his skin, touched on the guilt that always hovered there. "She's got nothing to worry about. I know what I'm doing."

She whirled on him then, struggling back her own needs. Show business was too much a part of what she was to allow her a tantrum in the wings. She spoke her mind, but in whispers. "You always know, don't you, Luke? You've been doing what the hell you pleased since Max and Lily took you in. Damn you, they love you, and it's eating Lily up that you keep pushing."

He shut down his emotions. It was the only way to survive. "It's what I do. You make pretty balls float in the air. I break out of chains. And all of us steal." His eyes flashed down to hers. "It's what we do. It's what we are."

"It wouldn't cost you anything to cut that part of the act."

The look held, a moment, two. She thought she saw something there, just behind his eyes, that she would never understand. "You're wrong," he said simply and walked away.

Roxanne turned quickly to the stage. Because she wanted so badly to go after him, to beg. She knew it would do no good, nor did she expect it to. Luke was right. They did what they did. Lily was able to understand and appreciate the thievery. She would have to learn to do the same with Luke's escapes.

He would always be the lone wolf LeClerc had called him all those years ago. He would go his way when he chose. Always with something to prove, she thought now.

And the truth was, the truth she hated to admit, was that the finale of tonight's show worried her nearly as much as it worried Lily.

She fixed a smile on her face so that neither Max nor Lily could see she was upset. She could control the outward signs of agitation. That was simple mind over matter. But she couldn't stop the image that was running over and over in her brain.

Luke's version of Houdini's Water Torture Escape. Only in that endless loop in her brain, he didn't break free.

IT ALWAYS BROUGHT DOWN the house, Max thought as he turned the spotlight over to Luke. No one, not even Lily, knew what it had cost him to hand Luke the finale. But it had been time, Max mused, flexing his still nimble fingers, for youth to take center stage.

And the boy was so talented. So driven. So ... magical.

The idea made Max smile as the curtain was lifted to reveal the glass water chamber. The boy had designed it himself, painstakingly. The dimensions, the thickness of the glass, even the brass fittings shaped like wizards and sorceresses. Luke knew to the pint how much water it contained to allow for displacement when his body was lowered, chained, into it.

He knew to the second how much time it required for him to free himself from the chains, from the handcuffs, from the manacles that secured him to the bolts at the chamber's sides.

And he knew how much of a grace period his lungs would allow him if something went wrong.

In her costume change of sheer draping white, Roxanne stood beside the water chamber. Despite her thundering heart her face was serene. It was she who slipped Luke's wide-sleeved shirt away so that he stood stripped to the waist.

She didn't look at the scars that crisscrossed white over his tanned back. Not once in all the years they'd been together had she mentioned them. Whatever locks she could open, she wouldn't touch the bolt on his pride.

It was she who stood calmly by as two volunteers from the audience locked the heavy chains around him. When his arms were crossed over his chest and bound there, the steel cuffs fastened over his wrists, his bare feet were attached by the ankles with manacles to a slab of smooth wood.

173

There were cellos playing, low, ominous, as the platform Luke stood on was lifted into the air.

"It's been said," he began in a voice that floated over the heads of the audience, "that the Great Houdini lost his life due to the injuries incurred in this escape. Since his death, it has been a challenge to every magician, every escape artist, to duplicate the escape, and make it his own by triumphing over it."

He glanced down and there was Mouse, embarrassed as hell in his *Arabian Knights'* outfit, holding a huge mallet. "Hopefully, we'll have no need for my friend with the muscles to break the glass." He winked down at Roxanne. "But perhaps I'll have need for the lovely Roxanne to give me a little mouth-to-mouth."

Roxanne didn't care for the ad-lib, but the audience laughed and applauded.

"Once I'm lowered into the chamber, it will be sealed, airtight." The audience gasped as the platform turned over, pivoted. Luke was facing them again, but upside down. He began to take deep breaths, filling his lungs. Roxanne took over the patter.

"We ask for silence during the escape, and that you direct your attention to the clock." At her cue, a spotlight hit a large clock face at the rear of the stage. "It will begin ticking off the seconds the moment Callahan is immersed in the chamber. Ladies and gentlemen . . . " Luke was lowered inch by inch toward the surface of the water. Roxanne kept her eyes and her mind riveted on the audience. "Callahan will have four minutes, and four minutes only, to escape from the chamber, or we will be forced to break the glass. A doctor is standing by in case of accident."

Now she had to turn, to throw out her arm for showmanship as Luke's head broke water. She watched him lower until his body was immersed, heard the thud as the platform fit snugly into place on top of the tank. His hair swirled, floating, as his eyes, brilliantly blue, met hers.

Then the thin white curtain lowered, covering all four sides of the chamber.

The clock began to tick.

"One minute," Roxanne announced in a voice that revealed nothing of her inner turmoil. She imagined Luke out of the cuffs. Willed him out of them. He would already be unlocking the chains.

There were murmurs from the audience as the clock rounded two minutes. Roxanne felt the sweat spring cold on her palms, the back of her neck, the small of her back. He was always out in three, three-twenty tops. She could see vaguely through the white cloth a shadow of movement.

He had no way to call for help, she thought frantically as the clock neared the three-minute mark. No way to signal if his lungs hitched and ran out of air. He could die before they ripped the curtain aside, before Mouse could smash the glass. He could die alone and in silence, chained to his own ambition.

"Three minutes," she said, and now hints of her fear leaked through and caused the audience to lean forward.

"Three twenty," she said and turned panicked eyes to Mouse. "Three twenty-five. Please, ladies and gentlemen, remain calm. Remain seated." She gulped in air, imagining Luke's lungs searing. "Three minutes, forty seconds."

A woman in the back began to shout hysterically in French. It caused a chain reaction of alarm to ripple along the rows until the audience was abuzz. Many had leaped to their feet as the clock neared the four-minute mark.

"Oh, Mouse, God." With eight seconds to go, Roxanne tossed showmanship aside and ripped at the curtain. It came tumbling down just as Luke shouldered the platform aside. He surfaced, sleek as an otter, and sucked in a greedy breath. His eyes were alight with triumph as the audience erupted with shouts and applause. It had been worth the extra thirty seconds he'd waited, freed, beneath the water.

He stood, dragging air in, one hand lifted. He was already planning to add that little extra bit of drama to the next show. Hooking his arms around the platform, he rode it up away from the chamber and down again to the stage. He stood dripping, taking his bows.

On impulse he grabbed Roxanne's hand, bending gallantly over it and kissing her fingers to the delight of the romantic French.

"Your hand's shaking," he noted under the cover of applause. "Don't tell me you were worried I wouldn't make it out."

Rather than snatch her hand back as she would have preferred, she smiled at him. "I was afraid Mouse would have to break the glass. Do you know how much it would cost to replace?"

"That's my Roxanne." He kissed her hand again. "I love your avaricious mind."

This time she did pull her hand away. His lips had lingered on her skin too long for comfort. "You're dripping on me, Callahan," she said, and stepped back to let him take the spotlight alone.

IT KILLED ROXANNE to have to sit and wait. It was degrading, she thought, pacing the parlor while Lily sprawled comfortably on the couch and watched an old black-and-white on TV.

It was like sitting by the phone for hours and hoping the jerk who took you out to the movies would call and ask you out again. Making a woman wait was so typically male.

She said as much to Lily and was answered by a murmur of agreement.

"I mean, they've done it since the dawn of time." Roxanne plopped into a chair, rose restlessly again to pull open the sheer drapes to watch the City of Lights twinkle. "Cavemen went off hunting and left the women by the fire. Vikings raped and pillaged while the womenfolk stayed home. Cowboys rode off into the sunset, men went down to the sea in ships and soldiers marched off to war. And where were we?" Roxanne demanded, her vivid floral robe swirling as she spun around. "Standing on widow's walks, waiting at train stations, wearing chastity belts or sitting by the damn phone. Well, I don't want to let a man dictate my life."

"Love." Lily blew her nose heartily as the credits rolled. "It's love that dictates, honeybunch, not a man."

"Well, the hell with that."

"Oh, no. It's the best there is." Lily sighed, satisfied with the romance, the tragedy and the good cry. "Max is only doing what he thinks is right for you."

"What about what I think is right?" Roxanne demanded.

"You'll have all the time in the world for that." Lily shifted, tucking her favorite robe—a peacock silk trimmed in pink ostrich feathers—under her. "The years go so fast, Roxy. You can't imagine it now, but before you know it they start whizzing by. If you don't have love in them, you end up empty. Whatever you choose as right, if love's sprinkled through it, it will be right."

There was no use arguing with Lily, Roxanne thought. She was a bred-in-the-bone romantic. Roxanne prided herself on being a more practical woman. "Didn't you ever want to go with them? Didn't you ever want to be a part of it?"

"I am a part of it." Lily smiled, looking young and pretty and content. "My being here's part of it. I know Max'll walk in that door, and he'll have that look in his eyes. That look that says he's done just what he wanted to do. And he'll need to tell me, to share it with me. He'll need me to tell him how smart and clever he is."

"And that's enough?" Despite her love for both of them, Roxanne found it amazing, appalling. "Being a sounding board for Max's ego?"

Lily's smile faded. The flash in her eyes turned the soft blue to marble. "I'm exactly where I want to be, Roxanne. In all the years I've been with Max he's never once used me, or deliberately hurt my feelings. That may not count for much with you, but for me, it's more than enough. He's gentle and kind and gives me everything I could want."

"I'm sorry." And she was as she reached out to take Lily's hand.

Sorry that *she* had hurt Lily's feelings. Sorry, too, that her independent soul couldn't understand. "I'm feeling nasty that they left me behind, and I'm taking it out on you."

"Sweetie, we can't all think alike, or feel alike, or be alike. You . . . " Lily leaned forward to take Roxanne's face in her hands. "You're your father's daughter."

"Maybe he'd rather have had a son."

Lily's fingers tightened. "Don't even think it."

"Luke's out with him." Bitterness leaked through the crack in her ego. "I'm sitting here twiddling my thumbs."

"Roxy, you're only seventeen."

"Then I hate being seventeen." She sprang up again, silk swirling around her as she marched to the window and threw it open. She drank in air like water. "I hate having to wait for everything, having everyone say there's plenty of time."

"Of course you do." There was a smile on Lily's lips and fresh tears in her eyes as she studied Roxanne. She's so beautiful, Lily thought. So full of needs. How desperate it was to be seventeen. How wonderful and horrible to be caught on that razor's edge of womanhood. "I can give you some advice, but it might not be what you want to hear."

Roxanne lifted her face to the soft spring night and shut her eyes. How could she explain to Lily these burning, pumping needs inside her when she couldn't explain them to herself? "Advice never hurts, taking it often does."

Lily laughed because it was one of Max's sayings. "Compromise." Roxanne groaned at the word, but Lily plowed on. "Compromise isn't so painful if you're the one setting the terms." She rose, pleased when Roxanne turned toward her, a thoughtful gleam in her eyes. "You're a female, do you want to change that?"

Roxanne's lips curved as she remembered her own relief and pride when her breasts had finally begun to bud. "No. No, I don't."

"Then use it, honey." Lily laid a hand on Roxanne's shoulder. "Using it doesn't have to be the same as . . . "

"Exploiting it?" Roxanne suggested, and Lily beamed.

"That's it. You take advantage of what you've got. Make it work for you. Your brains, your looks, your womanhood. Baby, the women who've done that have been liberated for centuries. Men didn't always know it, that's all."

"I'll think about it." One decisive nod, then she kissed Lily's cheek. "Thanks." She stiffened when she heard the key in the lock, and forced herself to relax. Beside her Lily was already vibrating with excitement. It baffled Roxanne, and delighted her. After all the years they'd been together, she mused as Max swung through the door, he can still make her feel that way.

She wondered, fleetingly, if there would ever be someone who could give her that kind of gift.

Luke strolled in behind Max, grinned and tossed Roxanne a pouch.

"Still awake?" Filled to the brim with his victory, Max was already kissing Lily. "What more can a man want, Luke, than to come home after a successful venture and find two lovely ladies awaiting him?"

"A cold beer," Luke answered as he headed toward the mini-bar. "It must have been a hundred-twenty in that vault once we killed the power." Luke popped open a beer and gulped half of it down his dry throat.

He looked like a barbarian, Roxanne thought, jiggling the pouch in her hand. Dark, sweaty, overtly male. Because watching him made her own throat go dry, she turned back to her father. Now this was a man, she thought, pleased, who understood class. An aristocratic pirate, his moustache gleaming, his black trousers meticulously pressed, the dark cashmere sweater smelling lightly of his cologne.

There were thieves, she decided as she sat on the arm of the couch, and thieves.

"Mouse and LeClerc?" Lily asked.

"Both gone off to bed. I invited Luke in for a nightcap. My dear boy, perhaps you could open a bottle of that chardonnay we have chilled."

"Sure." While he uncorked the bottle, he glanced at Roxanne. "Don't you want to see what's in the pouch, Rox?"

"I suppose." She hadn't wanted to seem anxious. Certainly didn't want to give either of them too much of a reaction. But when she poured the contents of the pouch in her hand no amount of willpower could still her gasp. "Oh," she said as diamonds sizzled against her skin. And again, "Oh."

"Spectacular, aren't they?" Max took the pouch and poured the remaining stones into Lily's cupped hands. "Russian whites, round cut, perfect quality. What do you say, Luke, a million-five?"

"Closer to two." He offered Roxanne a glass of wine, set Lily's on the table.

"Perhaps you're right." Max murmured a thanks when Luke brought him a glass. "It was tempting to be greedy, I admit. Standing there in that vault." With his eyes closed, he could see it. "All that utilitarian steel gleaming, and inside a treasure trove of emeralds, sapphires, rubies. Ah, Lily, the artistry. Necklaces dripping with color. Squarecut, pear-shaped, baguettes, tiffanies." He sighed. "But these handsome fellows will be much simpler to transport and invest."

Luke remembered one piece in particular, a dramatic symphony of emeralds, diamonds, topaz and amethyst worked into a hammered gold collar in Byzantine style. He'd imagined slipping it around Roxanne's neck, lifting all that heavy hair, fixing the clasp. She'd have looked like a queen wearing it.

He would have tried to tell her that he'd needed to see her wear it, needed to give her something no one else could.

And she would have laughed.

Luke shook his head as Max's voice penetrated his fantasy. "What? Sorry?"

"Something on your mind?"

"No." With an effort of will he banished the image and his

180

scowl. "I'm tired, that's all. It's been a long day, I'm going to turn in."

Maternal instincts were stronger than the flash of gems. Lily forgot about the diamonds sparkling in her hands. "Honey, don't you want a sandwich or something? You hardly touched your dinner."

"I'm fine." He kissed her, the left cheek, then the right, in a habit he'd developed over the years. "Good night, Lily. Max."

"An excellent job, Luke," Max put in. "Sleep well."

He opened the door and tossed a look over his shoulder. They were gathered close. Max in the center with Lily nestled under his arm, Roxanne on the arm of the couch, her head resting against her father's side, her hand full of icy white stones.

Family portrait, he thought. His family. His eyes shifted to Roxanne's, held. He'd do best to remember she was family. "See you, Rox."

He shut the door and walked across the hall to his own room, where he knew he would spend what was left of the night dreaming about a prize much more unattainable than diamonds.

SHE RUBBED HIS NOSE in it that very next day. The minute rehearsal was over, Roxanne hopped on the back of a motor scooter behind a blond Adonis. She sent a cheery wave, linked her arms around the French bastard's waist and blasted off into the reckless Parisian traffic.

"Who the hell was that?" Luke demanded.

Max stopped by a flower vendor and purchased a carnation for his lapel. "Who was who?"

"That jerk Roxanne just raced off with?"

"Oh, the boy." Max sniffed the red blossom before slipping the stem through his buttonhole. "Antoine, Alastair, something of the kind. A student at the Sorbonne. An artist, I believe."

"You let her ride off with some guy you don't know?" It was

outrageous. It was inconceivable. It was unbelievably painful. "Some *French* guy?"

"Roxanne knows him," Max pointed out. Delighted with life in general, he took a deep breath of air. "When Lily finishes changing, I believe we'll all have lunch in some quaint outdoor café."

"How can you think about eating?" Luke spun on his heel and fought the urge to put his hands around Max's throat. "Your daughter's just driven off with a perfect stranger. He could be a maniac for all you know."

Max chuckled and decided to choose a dozen roses from the vendor's cart for Lily. "Roxanne can handle him perfectly well."

"He was staring at her legs," Luke said savagely.

"Yes, well. It's difficult to blame him. Ah, here's Lily." He presented her with the roses and a sweeping bow that made her giggle.

ROXANNE HAD A PERFECTLY wonderful time. A picnic in the countryside, the scent of wildflowers, a French artist who read her poetry under the shade of a chestnut tree.

She'd enjoyed the interlude, the soft, stirring kisses, the whispered endearments in the world's most romantic language. She slipped back into her room half dreaming, with a secret smile on her lips and stars in her eyes.

"What the hell have you been doing?"

She muffled a shriek, stumbled back and stared at Luke. He was sitting in the chair by the window, a bottle of beer in his hand, the stub of a cigar in the ashtray beside him and murder in his eyes.

"Damn it, Callahan, you scared me to death. What are you doing in my room?"

"Waiting for you to decide to come back."

Once her heart started beating again, she pushed her hair from her shoulders. It was windblown from the drive, and made him think of a woman just rising out of bed after an interlude of hot, reckless sex. It was one more reason for murder.

"I don't know what you're talking about. I've got a good hour before we have to leave for the theater."

She'd let the son of a bitch kiss her. Oh, he knew it. She had that look about her, those soft, swollen lips, the heavy eyes. Her shirt was wrinkled. She'd let him lay her back on the grass and . . .

He couldn't bear to think of it.

It was bad enough when they were home and she took off with American guys. But French.

Every man had his limit.

"I'd like to know what happened to your brain. What did you think you were doing, going off with some smarmy French creep named Alastair?"

"I went on a picnic," she tossed back. "And he isn't smarmy or a creep. He's a sweet, sensitive man. An artist." She threw that out like a gauntlet. "And for your information, his name is Alain."

"I don't give a flying shit what his name is." Luke rose slowly. He was still under the delusion that he had control. "You're not going out with him again."

For an instant she was too stunned to speak. But only for an instant. "Who the hell do you think you are?" She advanced on him to shove the heel of her hand in his chest. "I can go out with whomever I want."

He snagged her wrist and brought her up hard against him. "Like hell."

Her chin snapped up, her eyes sizzled. "Who do you think's going to stop me? You? You've got no say in what I do, Callahan. Not now, not ever."

"You're wrong." He said it between his teeth. His hand had dived into her hair, fisted there. He couldn't seem to stop it. He could smell her, and the lingering tang of grass, of sunlight. Wildflowers. It plunged him into a murderous rage to think some-one else had been this close. Close enough to touch. To taste. "You let him put his hands on you. If you do that again, I'll kill him."

She would have laughed the threat off, or shouted it off. But she saw the naked truth in his eyes. The only way to combat the fear that sprang into her throat was with fury. "You're out of your mind. If he put his hands on me it was because I wanted him to. Because I like it." She knew it was the wrong thing to say, but was as helpless to stop fanning the flames as Luke had been to stop them from igniting. "And I want yours off. Now."

"Do you?" His voice was soft, smooth as silk. That frightened her more, much more, than his sneering threats. "Why don't we just call this a free lesson?" He damned himself even as he brought his mouth down to cover hers.

She didn't struggle, didn't protest. She wasn't sure she continued to breathe. How could she when the heat flashed so fast and hot it incinerated everything? Even thought. This was nothing, nothing like the soft, gentle kisses of the artist. Nothing like the awkward or arrogant embraces of the boys she'd dated. This was raw, it was primitive, it was terrifying. She wondered if there was a woman alive who would want to be kissed any other way.

His mouth fit over hers perfectly. The scrape of the skin he'd neglected to shave only added to the dizzying knowledge that at last, at long last, she was being held by a man. Naked aggression, frustrated passion, pure rage, erupted from him, into her, creating a kiss beyond anything she'd experienced. That single, wild moment was everything she'd dreamed of.

With his hand still fisted in her hair he dragged her head back. If he was going to hell, he would at least have the satisfaction of knowing it had been worth it. He didn't think, didn't dare to think, but plunged his tongue between her parted lips and filled himself on her.

She was everything he'd imagined and more. Soft, strong, sexy. The moan came from her instant and torrid response. The way her body strained and trembled against his, the way her mouth met demand for hot, violent demand. Her lips clung to his, forming his name. He swallowed her moans like a starving man swallows a crust of bread.

He wanted, desperately wanted, to tumble her onto the bed. To tear her clothes aside and drive himself into her. To feel her arch as she closed around him. He couldn't breathe for wanting it.

It was like being closed in a box. Trapped. Running out of air. His heart and lungs were straining. He had no control over them. No control over anything.

He jerked back, fighting for air, and some rag of sanity. She was still wrapped around him, her eyes dark and heavy, her lips soft, parted and eager for more. Waves of shame and need washed over him, warring tidal waves that had him shoving her roughly aside.

"Luke—"

"Don't." He was hard as iron and twitchy as a stallion. If she touched him now, only touched him, he would take her like an animal. To protect her from that, he cloaked himself with all the fury he felt for what he'd nearly done, and aimed it straight at her. "Free lesson," he repeated and pretended he didn't see her lips part in shock, or her eyes glitter with hurt. "That's the kind of treatment you're asking for if you go out with men you don't know."

She had pride, and was enough of an actress to use it to mask devastation. "Odd, isn't it? You're the only one who's ever treated me that way. And I know you. Or thought I did." She turned her back on him and stared out the window. She wouldn't cry, she promised herself. And if she did, he wouldn't see it. "Get out of my room, Callahan. If you touch me that way again, you'll pay for it."

He was already paying for it, Luke thought. He curled his hand into a fist before he could give in to the urge to stroke her hair. To beg. Instead he walked to the door. "I meant what I said, Roxanne."

She aimed a glittering look over her shoulder. "So did I."

Chapter Thirteen

Roxanne took Lily's advice and compromised with Max— though Roxanne preferred to think of it as a deal. She would register at Tulane University and give her college education serious attention. If after one year she was still determined to join her father's less public show, she would be taken on as an apprentice.

It suited Roxanne perfectly. First, because she enjoyed the process of learning. Second, because she had no intention of changing her mind.

The demands of her stage career and her education had the added benefit of leaving her limited free time. She spent as little as possible in Luke's company.

She would have forgiven him for the shouting, even for the orders. Certainly she would have forgiven him for the kiss. But she would never forgive him for turning one of the most glorious moments of her life into nothing more than a lesson offered from master to student.

She was too professional to allow it to interfere with her work or his. When rehearsal was called, she rehearsed with him. They performed together night after night with none of their inner feelings bubbling up from beneath the slick surface of the act.

If the troupe went on the road, they traveled together without incident—polite strangers who shared a plane or train or car from place to place.

Only once, when Lily expressed concern that Luke's escapes were becoming more complex and more dangerous, did any of the trapped turmoil escape.

"Let him be," Roxanne had shot back. "Men like him always have something to prove."

Her small and sweet revenge was in dating a succession of attractive men. She brought them home often, for dinner, parties, study groups. It gave her a great deal of pleasure to know her current beau—as Lily was wont to call them—was in the audience during the performance. It gave her a great deal more pleasure to know that Luke was aware of it.

She leaned toward the scholarly type, because she was attracted to a keen mind. And, deviously, because she knew that none of Max's prodding had pushed Luke beyond his single year of college. It was so satisfying to mention, casually, that Matthew was a law student, or that Philip was working on his master's in economics.

For herself, Roxanne had chosen to study both art history and gemology. Her purpose, much to Max's delight, was to enhance her knowledge of what she now termed her hobby. If one was going to steal great works of art and fine gems, she'd informed her father, one should have a solid understanding of the background and value of the take.

Max was proud to have a daughter with vision.

He was pleased, too, that his reputation as a performer and respect for his troupe had grown. He treasured his magician-of-the-year award from the Academy of Magical Arts. He no longer found it necessary to avoid national exposure. The Nouvelles had two successful television specials under their belts, and Max had recently signed a contract to write a definitive book on magic.

A month before, he'd relieved a Baltimore matron of an opal

and diamond brooch, with matching earrings. He'd used his share of the profits—after tithing—to pay for his research into what had become his biggest interest: the philosophers' stone.

To some it was a legend. To Max it was a goal, one he needed badly now that his dual careers had reached their zenith. He wanted to hold it, that rock that was a magician's dream. Not simply to turn iron into gold, but as a testament to all he had learned, accomplished, taken and given back over his lifetime. Already he had gathered books, maps, scores of letters and diaries.

Tracking down the philosophers' stone would be Maximillian Nouvelle's greatest feat. Once he had it, he thought—hoped—that he could ease into retirement. He and Lily would travel the world like vagabonds while their children carried on the Nouvelle tradition.

As New Orleans settled down into a chill, rainy winter, Max was at peace with the world. The occasional twinge the damp weather brought to his hands was overcome with a couple of aspirin, and easily ignored.

ROXANNE LIKED THE RAIN. It gave her a cozy, dreamy feeling to watch it patter on the sidewalk, run down the glass of the window. She stood on the covered balcony outside of Gerald's apartment and watched the thin, chilly curtain chase away the pedestrians. If she took a deep breath she could smell the café au lait Gerald was brewing in his tiny kitchen.

It was nice to be here, she thought, taking this rainy night off. She enjoyed Gerald's company, and found him smart and sweet. A man who liked to listen to Gershwin and view foreign films. His little apartment over a souvenir shop was crammed with books and records and VCR tapes. Gerald was a student of the cinema, and had already collected more movies than Roxanne imagined she would see in her lifetime.

Tonight they were going to watch Ingmar Bergman's *Wild Strawberries*, and Hitchcock's *Vertigo*.

"Aren't you cold?" Gerald stood inside the narrow doorway, holding out a sweater. He was perhaps a half inch shorter than Roxanne with broad shoulders that gave the illusion of more height. He had lank, sandy hair that fell—endearingly, she thought—onto his forehead. He had chiseled, leading-man looks that reminded her faintly of Harrison Ford. His mild brown eyes were given distinction by the dignified tortoiseshell glasses he wore.

"Not really." But she came back inside. "It doesn't look like there's a soul in the city tonight. Everyone's snuggled in."

He set the sweater aside. "I'm glad you're snuggled in here."

"Me too." She gave him her lips in a light kiss. "I like it here." They'd been seeing each other on and off for nearly a month, but this was the first time Roxanne had been to his apartment.

It was pure struggling student. Movie posters adorned the walls, the sagging couch was covered with a faded bedspread, the scarred wooden desk shoved into the corner was laden with books. His electronic equipment, however, was state-of-the-art.

"I guess these home-movie things are the wave of the future."

"By the end of the decade, VCRs will be as common as television sets in the American home. Everyone will own video cameras." He grinned and patted his own. "Amateur directors will spring up everywhere." He touched her hair, a wild tangle of curls she'd recently cut to chin length. "Maybe you'll let me make a movie of you sometime."

"Of me?" The idea made her laugh. "I can't imagine."

He could. Taking her hand, he led her to the couch. "Bergman first, okay?"

"Fine." She picked up her coffee and settled back into the crook of his arm. Gerald pushed some buttons on his remote. One to engage the VCR, the other to start the camera he had strategically placed between stacks of books.

Roxanne supposed she was plebeian, but Bergman didn't grab her. Give me a car chase any day, she thought as she struggled to keep her mind on the slow-moving black-and-white art flickering on the screen.

She didn't mind having Gerald's arm around her. He smelled of peppermint mouthwash and mild, inexpensive cologne. She didn't object to the light trail his fingers made up and down her arm. When he shifted to kiss her, she had no trouble tilting her head back and accepting the offer.

But when she tried to ease away, he tightened his hold.

"Gerald." She gave a light laugh as she turned her head away. "You're going to miss the movie."

"I've seen it before." His voice was thick and breathless as he ran kisses down the side of her throat.

"I haven't." She wasn't worried, not really. A little annoyed perhaps that he was making such an obvious and fevered move, but not worried.

"Don't you find it erotic? The imagery, the subtleties."

"Not really." Tedious was what she found it, just as tedious as she found the fact that he was pressing her back against the cushions of the couch. "But then I'm probably too literal-minded." She blocked his mouth, but wasn't quick enough to stop his fingers from fumbling with the buttons of her blouse. "Stop it, Gerald." She didn't want to hurt him, his feelings or otherwise. "This isn't why I came here, and it isn't what I want."

"I've wanted you since the first time I saw you." He managed to pry her legs apart and began to grind his erection against her. Roxanne felt the first licks of panic sneak through the annoyance. "I'm going to get you naked, baby, and make you a star."

"No, you're not." She struggled in earnest when his hand closed over her breast and squeezed. Growing fear had her voice shaking. A mistake, she realized instantly as his breathing quickened with excitement. "Damn it, get off me." She bucked like a bronco, heard her blouse rip.

"You like it rough, baby? That's okay." He grabbed at the zipper of her jeans with sweaty, impatient hands. "That's good. Better visual. We'll watch it after."

"You son of a bitch." She never knew whether it was timing or

190

terror that had her elbow swinging over, knocking hard enough against his temple to make him rear back. She didn't hesitate, but balled her hand into a fist and slammed it against his nose.

Blood fountained out, splattering her blouse, making him yelp like a kicked puppy. His hands flew up to his face, knocking his glasses askew. Roxanne scrambled up, grabbed her canvas bag and brought it against the side of his face in a vicious, two-handed swipe.

His glasses soared across the room. "Hey, hey." Blood dripped through his fingers as he goggled up at her. "You broke my fucking nose."

"You try that again with me, or anyone else I hear about, I'll break your fucking dick."

He started to rise, then sank back down again when she lifted both fists in a boxer's stance.

"Come on," she taunted. There were tears in her eyes now, but they weren't from fear. It was pure rage. "You want to take me on, you bastard?"

He shook his head, grabbing a corner of the bedspread to stanch the flow of blood from his nose. "Just get out. Jesus, you're crazy."

"Yeah." She felt the hysteria bubbling up. She wanted to hit him again, she realized. She wanted to beat and punch and pummel until he was as frightened and helpless as she had been moments before. "You remember that, creep, and stay away from me." She slammed out, leaving him babbling about hospitals and lawsuits.

Roxanne was a block away and searching for a cab when it hit her. Make you a star? Watch it after? A scream of rage burst out as it sank in.

The son of a bitch must have been filming the whole thing.

IT WAS LIKE FALLING into a nightmare. Though the rain had slowed to a drizzle, it was a cold, miserable night. Nothing could have suited Luke's mood more perfectly.

In his hand was a letter, a letter that had dragged him back over the jagged distance to the past. Cobb. The bastard had found him. Standing in the Nouvelle courtyard with the thin rain sneaking under the collar of his jacket, Luke wondered why he had ever allowed himself to believe in escapes.

No matter how clever he'd been, how successful, how strong, he could be jerked back into that small, frightened boy. It had only taken a few words on paper.

Callahan—long time no see. I'm looking forward to talking about old times. If you don't want to lose your classy situation meet me tonight at ten at Bodine's on Bourbon. Don't try no disappearing act, or I'll have to have a nice, long talk with your pals the Nouvelles. Al Cobb

He'd wanted to ignore it. He'd wanted to laugh and tear the paper into tiny, insignificant pieces to show just how little it had meant to the man he'd become. But his hands had shaken. His stomach had twisted into slick, tiny knots. And he'd known, as he'd always known, that he couldn't escape from where he'd come from. Or what he'd lived through.

Still, he wasn't a child afraid to face the monster in the closet. He balled the paper into his pocket and stepped toward the street. He'd face Cobb tonight, and somehow find a way to vanish him and everything he stood for.

The rain dampened his jacket, his shoes and his mood. He hunched his shoulders, swore at nothing in particular and started toward the corner. When a cab veered toward the curb, he hesitated, debating about whether it would improve his frame of mind to take a dry ride rather than a wet walk.

He forgot both possibilities as he watched Roxanne alight. She was a handy target for his frustration.

"Back so soon?" he called out. "Didn't your four-eyed friend keep you entertained?"

"Kiss ass, Callahan." She kept her head down as she hurried by him, hoping to slip into the house unseen. But Luke was feeling just ugly enough to taunt her.

"Hey." He snagged her arm and spun her again. "You got some—" He stopped dead when he saw the state of her clothes. Beneath her bright jacket, the boxy cotton blouse was torn and splattered with blood. Panic hammered through him as he grabbed both of her shoulders, fingers digging in. "What happened to you?"

"Nothing. Leave me alone."

He gave her one hard shake. "What happened?" His voice seemed to be caught in his throat, squeezing out over razor blades. "Baby, what happened?"

"Nothing," she said again. Why was she starting to shake now? she wondered. It was all over. Over and done. "Gerald had a different idea on what I was doing in his apartment than I had." She tossed her chin up, ready for a lecture. "I had to disabuse him of the notion."

She heard Luke suck in his breath—not in shock. It was more like an animal snarling. When she glanced up at his face, her unsteady pulse went haywire. His eyes were like glass, the kind that leaves deep jagged gashes on flesh.

"I'll kill him." His fingers dug into her shoulders hard enough to make her yelp. He released her so quickly, Roxanne stumbled back. By the time she'd regained her balance, she had to run to catch him.

"Luke. Stop this." She snatched at his sleeve. Though her heart dropped to her knees when he rounded on her, eyes glowing, teeth bare, she hung on. "Nothing happened. Nothing. I'm all right."

"You've got blood all over you."

"None of it's mine." She tried a smile, scraping her wet hair out of her face. "Come on, I appreciate the white knight routine, but I took care of it. You don't even know where the jerk lives."

He'd find him. Somehow Luke knew that he could track the

193

bastard down like a wolf tracking a rabbit. But Roxanne's hand was trembling on his arm.

"Did he hurt you?" It was an effort to keep his voice steady and calm, but he thought she needed it. "Tell me the truth, Rox. Did he rape you?"

"No." She didn't resist when Luke's arms came around her. It wasn't fear that was making her shake, she realized. It was a haunting sense of betrayal. She had known Gerald, she'd liked him, and he'd been prepared to force sex on her. "No, he didn't rape me. I swear."

"He ripped your shirt."

This time her smile was a little steadier. "He said I broke his nose, but I think I just bloodied it." She laughed and settled her head on Luke's shoulder. It felt so good to be there, standing in the rain with him, feeling that hard, steady beat of his heart. Whenever things got really bad, she mused, Luke was there. There was a comfort in that. "You should have heard him squeal. Luke, I don't want Max or Lily to know. Please."

"Max has a right—"

"I know." She lifted her head again. Rain trickled down her face like tears. "It's nothing to do with rights. It would hurt him, and frighten him. And it's over now, so what could he do?"

"I won't say anything. If—"

"I knew there'd be an if."

"If," Luke repeated, tucking a finger under her chin, "you agree to let me talk to this creep. Satisfy myself that he's going to stay away from you."

"Believe me, I don't have anything to worry about. He might even take out a warrant so I won't be able to go within five hundred feet of him."

"I talk to him, or I talk to Max."

"Damn it." She sighed, considered her options, then shrugged. "Okay, I'll tell you where to find him, if—"

"Yeah, right. If?"

"You swear it's just talk. I don't want or need you to go beat someone's face in for me anymore." She smiled again and knew they both thought of Sam Wyatt. "I did that all by myself this time."

"Just talk," Luke said. Unless he decided more was necessary.

"Actually, you could do me a favor." She eased away because this was a tough one. "I'm not positive, but I think . . . from something he said when he was, well . . . "

"What?"

"I think he had a camera on somewhere. Filming the event, you know?"

Luke opened his mouth, shut it again. Perhaps it was for the best that he was stunned speechless. "Excuse me?"

"He's a film major," she hurried on. "Really hung up on movies, and this video craze. That's why I went to his apartment. To watch a couple of classic films. And he . . . " She blew out a breath that fogged in the air then washed away in the rain. "I'm pretty sure he had a camera on, so we could enjoy watching ourselves after."

"That fucking perverted asshole."

"Well, yeah, but I was wondering, if you insist on talking to him, if you could make him give you the film or the tape or whatever the hell it is."

"I'll get it. If you ever pull something like this again—"

"I pull?" She slapped her hands on her hips. "Look, pea brain, I was nearly raped. That makes me a victim, get it? I didn't do anything to deserve that kind of treatment."

"I didn't mean—"

"Hell with that. It's just like a man." She whirled away, paced two steps then spun back. "I must have been asking for it, right? I lured that poor, helpless man into my web then cried foul when things got heavy."

"Shut up." He pulled her against him and held tight. "I'm sorry. I didn't mean anything like that. Christ, Roxanne, can't you understand you scared me? I don't know what I'd have done if he'd . . . "

He pressed his mouth to her hair. "I don't know what I'd have done."

"All right." Another tremor hit her, rippling down her spine. "It's all right."

"Okay." He was murmuring, stroking, trying to comfort, even as his mouth sought hers. "No one's going to hurt you again." There was rain on her lips. He kissed it away, gently, sweetly, then went back for more. Her arms came up to wind strong and sure around his neck even as her body melted like wax against him. He gave himself a moment, one glorious moment to hold her, and pretend it could be real.

"Feeling better?" His smile was strained as he drew her away.

"I'm feeling something." Her voice was like the fog that snaked along the ground at their feet. When she lifted a hand to his cheek, he grabbed it, pressed his lips to the center of her palm. She wondered the rain didn't sizzle off as it struck her.

"Rox . . . we'd better—" He broke off as a man walked through the curtain of rain. Luke started to simply shift Roxanne aside, then he looked at Cobb's face, at Cobb's eyes, and felt his life turn upside down.

How foolish he'd been to forget even for a moment that he had his own demons to face that night.

But if he could do nothing else, he could prevent that ugliness from touching Roxanne.

"Go inside," he ordered.

"But, Luke—"

"Go in. Now." He pulled her toward the gate and the courtyard. "There's something I have to do."

"I'll wait."

"No, don't." When he turned, she had one glimpse of his eyes, and the torment in them.

Luke walked through the rain to confront an old nightmare.

*

"Been awhile, kid." Al Cobb sat in the dingy Bourbon Street strip joint smoking a Camel. It was his kind of setting, the women with tired eyes bumping hips and twirling pasties, the smell of stale drunks and impersonal sex. He'd known Luke would follow him in.

Luke had draped one arm over the back of his chair. He was forcing himself to relax, using every ounce of will to prevent those nasty flashbacks from sneaking into his mind. "What do you want?"

"A drink, a little conversation." Cobb let his eyes crawl over the cocktail waitress's breasts and roam down to her crotch. "Bourbon, a double."

"Black Jack," Luke told her, knowing his usual beer wouldn't have the fire to purge.

"A man's drink." Cobb grinned, showing tobacco-stained teeth. Years of hefting the bottle hadn't been kind to him. Even in the dim light Luke could see the maze of broken capillaries in his face, those twisted red banners of the dedicated drunk. He'd put on too much weight around the middle so that his knit shirt stretched and strained over the girth.

"I asked you what you wanted."

Cobb said nothing as their drinks were set down. He lifted his, took a deep swallow and watched the stage. An improbably built redhead was peeling away a French maid's uniform. She was down to her G-string and a pair of feather dusters.

"Je-sus, look at the tits on that bitch." Cobb downed his drink and signaled for another. He grinned over at Luke. "What's the matter, boy, don't you like looking at boobs?"

"What are you doing in New Orleans?"

"Having me a little holiday." Cobb licked his lips while the dancer bounced her abundant breasts and squeezed them together. "Figured since I was in the neighborhood, I'd look you up. Ain't you going to ask about your mother?"

Luke sipped carefully at the whiskey, letting the heat slide down into his gut and thaw frozen muscles. "No."

"That's unnatural." Cobb clucked his tongue. "She's living in Portland now. We still get together from time to time. She started to charge for it, you know?" He gave Luke a lascivious wink, pleased when he saw the muscles in his jaw clench. "But old Maggie, she's sentimental enough to give me a free pop when I come knocking. Want I should give her your best?"

"I don't want you to give her anything from me."

"You got a shitty attitude." Cobb tossed back more bourbon while the music grew louder, more raucous. One of the men tried to climb onstage and was tossed out. "Always did. You'd stayed around a little longer, I'd have beaten some respect into you."

Luke leaned forward, eyes glittering. "Or you'd have turned me into a whore."

"You had a roof over your head, food in your belly." Cobb shrugged and continued to drink. "I just expected you to pay for it." It didn't occur to him to be afraid of Luke. His memory was keen enough to recall how easily he'd cowed the boy with a few solid whacks of the belt. "But that's behind us now, ain't it? You're a big fucking deal these days. Coulda knocked me over with a whiff of gin when I saw you on the TV." He snorted into his bourbon. "Doing magic tricks for chrissake. Learned how to wave your magic wand, did you, Luke?" He roared with laughter at his own joke until tears sparkled in his eyes. "You and that old man got yourself a couple of prime pieces of ass out of it."

The laughter died into choking when Luke grabbed him by the collar. Their faces were close now, close enough for Luke to smell the whiskey on Cobb's breath over the barroom stink of liquor and smoke. "What do you want?" he repeated, spacing each word.

"You want to take me on, boy?" Always ready to brawl, he wrapped his meaty fingers around Luke's wrists. He was surprised by the strength he found there, but never doubted his own superiority. "Want to go head-to-head with me?"

He did, so badly his body shook with a need as basic as sex. But there was a part of him, buried deep, that was still a terrified little boy who remembered the snap of a leather belt, and the sear of it against tender flesh. "I don't want to be in the same state with you."

"It's a free country." Because he was smart enough to know that a fight wouldn't get him what he'd come for, Cobb jerked away and ordered another drink. "Problem with that is you got to pay for every damn thing. You're making good money with your magic tricks."

"Is that what you want?" Luke would have laughed if disgust hadn't blocked his throat. "You want me to give you money?"

"Helped raise you, didn't I? I'm the closest thing to a father you had."

Now he did laugh. There was enough fury in the sound to have the people nearby glance over warily. "Fuck off." Before he could rise, Cobb took hold of his sleeve.

"I can make trouble for you, and for that old man you're tangled up with. All I got to do is make a couple of calls to some of them reporters. What do you think the TV producers would think once they read about you? Callahan—that's what you call yourself now, ain't it? Just plain Callahan. Escape artist and male prostitute."

"That's a lie." But he'd paled, and Cobb saw it. All those memories flooded back, the fat hands pawing, groping, the sweat and heavy breathing. "I didn't let him touch me."

"You don't know what happened after I kicked you senseless." Cobb was pleased to see the bluff take root. He fed on the horror, the doubt, the revulsion in Luke's eyes. "One way or the other, people'd wonder, wouldn't they? People like that hot little number you were making time with a little while ago. You think she'd let you dip your wick once she found out you were blowing freaking fags when you were twelve?" He grinned, with hate in his eyes. "Don't matter if it's a lie or the God's truth, boy, not once it's in print."

"I'll kill you." Nausea weakened Luke's voice and had sweat pearling on his forehead.

"Be easier to pay me." Confident he could run the show, Cobb took out another cigarette. "I don't need much. Couple thousand to start." He blew smoke in Luke's direction. "Starting tomorrow. Then I'll drop you a line now and then, telling you how much I want and where to send it. Otherwise ... I go to the press. I'd have to tell them how you sold yourself to perverts, how you took off from your poor, grieving mother, how you got tangled up with that Nouvelle. Seems to me he broke a law or two taking in a runaway. Then again, it might sound like he had other uses for you. You know." He smiled again, satisfied with the revulsion on Luke's face. "I could make people wonder if he didn't get for free what you sold to others."

"Keep Max out of it."

"Be glad to." Cobb spread his hands in cooperation. "You bring me two thousand tomorrow night, right here. That's a show of good faith. Then I'll be on my way. You don't show, I'll just have to make me a call to the *National Enquirer*. I don't guess all the little boys and girls, and their mommies and daddies, would have much use for a magician who had a taste for young meat? Nope." He took another drag. "Can't see you doing another performance for the Queen of England when you're accused of buggery. That's what those limeys call it. Buggery." Cobb laughed again as he rose. "Tomorrow night. I'll be waiting."

Luke sat where he was, fighting just to breathe. Lies, fucking lies. He could prove it, couldn't he? His hand shook as he reached for his glass. No one would believe, could possibly believe that Max had ...

Sickened, he pressed the heels of his hands against his eyes.

Cobb was right; once it was in print, once people started to question and whisper, it wouldn't matter. The stain would be there, the shame and the horror.

If he could stand it for himself, he couldn't bear the thought of any of it touching Max or Lily. Or Roxanne. Sweet God, Roxanne. He squeezed his eyes shut as he downed the rest of his whiskey. He ordered another and settled down to get miserably drunk.

*

She was waiting for him. Roxanne had gone inside and slipped into her room unnoticed. A long, hot bath had soothed most of the aches, and some of the frustrations. Then she'd settled herself on the balcony to wait.

She saw him stumble through the drizzle and fog. Watched him weave and stop, and start again with the exaggerated care of a drunk. Her worry and confusion vanished in a white-hot rage.

He had left her and her humming nerve ends standing in the rain, and had gone off to find a bottle. Or several bottles by the look of him. Roxanne stood, jerked the belt of her robe tight—like a soldier gearing for battle—then rushed down to intercept Luke in the courtyard.

"You imbecile."

He teetered back, tried to maintain balance on the suddenly slanting bricks and grinned stupidly. "Babe, whatcha doing out in the rain? Catch cold." He took a staggering step forward. "Christ you look pretty, Roxy. Drives me nuts."

"Obviously." It didn't seem like much of a compliment when the words were slurred almost beyond recognition. She reached out to grab his arm in reflex when he swayed. "I hope you pay for this in the morning."

"T'morrow night," he muttered while his head went round and round on his shoulders. "Gotta pay tomorrow night."

"You should live so long." She sighed, but took his weight, draping one of his arms over her shoulders. "Come on, Callahan, let's see if we can get a drunk Irishman to bed without waking up the house."

"My great-grandfather came from county Sligo. The old lady told me that once. Did I mention it?"

"No." She grunted a bit with the effort of dragging him toward the side door.

"Supposed to have a voice like an angel. Sang in the pubs, you know." Rain washed over his face, cool and sweet, when his head fell back. "Sumbitch was never my father. Nothing of him inside me."

"No, there's just a gallon of whiskey inside you from the way you stink."

He grinned and bumped heavily against the door before she could open it. "Sorry. You smell good, Rox. Like rain on wild-flowers."

"Ah, the Irish poet." And her face flushed as she braced Luke upright with one hand and pushed the door open with the other.

"I'm just as glad you don't have tits like that broad tonight. I don't think I'd like it."

"What broad?" Roxanne demanded in a stage whisper before she hissed out a breath. "Never mind."

"I don't get much of a thrill watching some babe strip when there's a couple dozen guys in the room. One-on-one's more my style, you know?"

"Fascinating." She didn't feel the least remorse when she turned and rammed him into the kitchen counter. "Leaves me in the rain and runs off to a strip joint. You're a prince, Callahan."

"I'm a bastard," he said with drunken cheer. "Born that way, die that way." He reeled around as she tried to steer him toward the back stairs. "Maybe I should just kill him. Cleaner that way."

"No, you promised me you'd just talk to him."

Luke ran a hand over his face to make sure it was still there. "Talk to who?"

"Gerald."

"Yeah, yeah." He tripped on the first step, and though he went down hard, he didn't seem to notice. To Roxanne's dismay he simply stretched out on the staircase and prepared to go to sleep. "It's scary, so fucking scary when he comes at you that way. And you know you might not be able to stop it. Grabbing you, slob-bering on you. Oh, Christ . . . " His voice died to a bleary whisper. "Don't want to think about it."

"Then don't. Think about getting upstairs."

"Gotta lie down," he muttered, all irritation when she pulled and tugged at him. "Let me alone."

"You're not going to pass out here, like the drunken jerk you are. Lily'll worry sick over you if she finds you here."

"Lily." He sighed, crawling up the steps at Roxanne's prodding. "First woman I ever loved. She's the best. Nobody's ever going to hurt Lily."

"Of course not. Come on, just a little farther." Her struggles had her robe spreading open. From his vantage point, Luke had an excellent and disturbing view of smooth, white thigh. Even the whiskey couldn't stop his blood from heating. "Going to hell," he said on a groaning laugh as Roxanne shushed him. "Straight to hell. Christ, I wish you'd wear something under your robe once in a while. Let me just—" But as he reached out to touch, just to touch that smooth white skin, he landed in a heap on the top landing.

"On your feet, Callahan," Roxanne hissed in his ear. "You're not going to wake up Max and Lily."

"Okay, okay." He tried to swallow, but his spit tasted like poison. He made it to his knees on his own, then did his best to stand upright when Roxanne dragged him to his feet. "Am I going to be sick?" he asked as nausea curled in his belly.

"I hope so," she said between her teeth as she half carried, half dragged him to his bedroom. "I sincerely hope so."

"Hate that. Makes me feel like that time Mouse gave me my first cigarette. Not getting drunk anymore, Rox."

"Right. Here we—Shit."

He pitched toward the bed. Though she was quick, she wasn't quite quick enough to avoid going down with him. He landed on her with enough force to steal her breath.

"Get off me, Callahan."

His answer was an unintelligible mutter. Because his breath reeked of Jack Daniel's, she turned her head away. His lips nuzzled sleepily at her throat.

"Cut it out. Oh ... damn." The curse ended on a muffled groan. Pleasure, heavy and dark, crept into her when he cupped a hand over her breast. He didn't grope, didn't squeeze, he simply possessed.

"Soft," he murmured. "Soft Roxanne." His fingers caressed over the thin silk, lazily, absently while his lips rubbed flesh.

"Luke. Kiss me." Her body was already floating as she tried to turn her mouth to his. "Kiss me like you did before."

"Mmm-hmm." He gave a long, windy sigh, and passed out.

"Luke." She shook his shoulders. It couldn't be, she told herself, not twice in one night. But when she took a handful of his hair to pull his head back, she saw that he was out cold. Grinding her teeth and swearing under her breath, she shoved his inert body aside.

She left him sprawled crossways on the bed, fully dressed, and went off to try the time-honored remedy of a cold shower.

Chapter Fourteen

He nearly killed himself. Between a vicious hangover and a precarious emotional state, Luke found his timing and his equilibrium were off. He knew better. There were rules, hard and fast rules governing the art of escapology. They quite simply fashioned the border between life and death.

But the choice of playing by the rules and ignoring pride left little room for maneuvering. Luke went forward with the escape segment of the first show, allowing himself to be straitjacketed, shackled and leg-ironed before folding himself into an iron chest center stage.

It was hot, black and all but airless inside. Like a tomb, like a vault. Like a closet. As always, he felt that initial bolt of panic. Being trapped.

No way out, boy, Cobb's voice chortled inside Luke's head. *No way out until I let you out. And don't you forget it.*

That old, helpless fear swept into him, grinning masked bandits hunched in the shadows ready to ambush control. He took slow, shallow breaths to beat the nerves back as he worked on freeing his hands.

He could get out. He'd proven time and time again that no one would keep him locked up ever again. Focusing, focusing, he turned the next corner.

Cobb was waiting for him.

I got the key, you little bastard, and you'll stay right where I put you. It's time you remember who's boss around here.

The image of the closet came back, the small boy sobbing, beating his bound hands raw against the door. Luke's breath hitched as his heart knocked fitfully against his ribs, echoing in his spinning head. The lingering nausea churned in his stomach like a sea of acid. Fear came back, skittering like tiny insects along his sweaty skin.

He hissed with pain as the irons bit into his wrists. For one blind moment, he fought them like a desperate man fighting his shackles on his way to the gallows. And he smelled the coppery scent of his own blood.

Breathing too fast, he told himself, unnerved by the helpless, whooshing sound of his own lungs struggling for oxygen. Calm down, damn it, calm down.

He twisted his body; the familiar and expected twinge as he manipulated his joints helped. His shoulder shifted into an impossible position, allowing him to slither and slide in the straitjacket.

The pounding at his temples had him cursing Jack Daniel's. He was forced to stop again, to gather enough composure to float by the pain.

He was light-headed, a sensation that reminded him too vividly of his condition the night before—and Roxanne. The flashes came, even when he fought to hold them back and concentrate on freeing his arms. Her skin, that soft white skin and his hands moving over it. Her body, curved and yielding under his.

Oh God, Jesus God, had he seduced her, had he used his own turmoil and drink as an excuse to act on the fantasy that had been plaguing him for years?

The sweat was running off Luke in thin hot rivers. He'd lost track of the time, a huge mistake. If he'd had the breath left he would have cursed himself. By the time he was free of the strait-jacket, his tortured muscles and joints were screaming. He had only to beat on the box—beat on it as he had once beat on a closet door.

They'd open it, let him out, let him gulp in fresh air. His head lolled back, rapping sharply against the side of the trunk. White-hot pain seared into his head, and images danced behind his closed eyes.

Cobb leering, spouting gut-clenching lies.

He could take care of Cobb, Luke promised himself as he grayed out. It only took money.

Roxanne. Those pictures of Roxanne on the tape he'd terrified out of Gerald. He could hear the sound of her blouse ripping, the muffled demands to be released. He could see the spray of blood, almost smell it as she'd fought herself free.

And how she'd looked, bloody Christ, how she'd looked standing there, fist clenched and ready, body poised like an Amazon, valor shimmering around her and fear and rage shining in her eyes.

He'd wanted to hold her then, to stroke the tremors away. Just as he'd wanted to beat the already bruised and battered Gerald to a slimy pulp.

But as furious as he'd been, he'd been equally ashamed. Had he, blind with drink and lust, done to Roxanne what Gerald had only attempted?

No. He was being a fool. Hadn't he awakened, sick, aching *and* fully dressed? Right down to his shoes. The taste in his mouth hadn't been Roxanne, but the dead skunk flavor of stale whiskey.

Desire and blackmail. Well, neither was worth dying for. He lifted an unsteady hand and slapped himself hard, once, twice so that the shock of pain cleared most of the mists in his brain.

He went to work on the leg irons, sipping cautiously at the thinning air.

*

"IT'S TOO LONG." Roxanne heard the skitter of panic in her own voice as she grabbed at her father's sleeve. "Daddy, he's two full minutes over."

"I know." Max closed a hand that had gone ice cold over his daughter's. "He has time yet." There was no use telling her that he'd taken one look at Luke's pale, hollow-eyed face in the dressing room and had demanded he cancel his part of tonight's performance.

Just as there was no use telling her that Luke had overruled him. The boy was a man now, and the lines of power were shifting.

"Something's wrong." She could imagine him unconscious, smothering helplessly. "Damn it." She whirled around, intending to streak to the wings to snatch the keys from Mouse. Before she'd taken a step, the lid to the box crashed open.

Suitably impressed, the audience applauded. Drenched with sweat, Luke took his bows and filled his starving lungs. When Max saw him sway, brace himself, he signaled to Roxanne and immediately stepped forward to distract the crowd with sleight of hand.

"Idiot. Jerk. Flea brain." She hurled insults between the clenched teeth of a bright smile as she took his arm and led him offstage. "What the hell were you trying to do?"

Lily was right there with a tall glass of water and a towel. Luke gulped down every drop. The fact that he still felt faint mortified him.

"Get out, mostly," he said as he rubbed sweat from his face. When he staggered, Roxanne wrapped her arms around him. Her heart beat like thunder in her ears as she continued to berate him.

"You had no business going in there tonight after spending last night in a bottle."

"My business *is* going in there," he reminded her. It felt good, too good, to have her holding him steady. He pulled away and headed for his dressing room. Like an angry terrier, Roxanne stayed on his heels.

"Show business does not mean you have to kill yourself. And if you—" She stopped at the door to his dressing room. "Oh, Luke, you're bleeding."

He glanced down where the blood seeped from his wrists and ankles. "Had a little trouble with the leg irons." He shot a hand up to stop her before she could rush in. "I want to change."

"You need to have those cleaned up. Let me—"

"I said I want to change." Now it was the cool look in his eyes that stopped her. "I can take care of it myself."

She pressed her lips together to keep them from trembling. Didn't he know that a cold dismissal hurt her a hundred times more than an angry word? Her chin came up. Of course he did. Who knew better?

"Why are you treating me like this, Luke? After last night—"

"I was drunk," he said sharply, but she shook her head.

"Before, you weren't drunk before. When you kissed me."

Little licks of fire curled in his gut. A man would have to be blind not to see what she was offering with her eyes. He felt sick, needy and tired to the bone. "You were upset," he managed with remarkable calm. "So was I. I was trying to make you feel better, that's all."

Pride flared. "You're a liar. You wanted me."

He gave her a smile calculated to insult. He had that much self-control left. "Babe, if I've learned anything in the past ten years, it's to take what I want." His hands curled into fists at his sides, but his eyes stayed lightly amused. "Weave your little fantasy around your pin-striped college boys. Now I've got things to do before the next show."

He closed the door smartly in her face, then leaned heavily against it.

Close call, Callahan, he thought, closing his eyes. In more ways than one. Because his aches were demanding attention, he pushed away to search out some aspirin. He had to go see Cobb, and he would be armed with two thousand dollars and a clear head.

*

209

No one knew the value of timing better than Maximilian Nouvelle. He waited patiently through the second show, making no comment, voicing no criticism. He firmly overrode both Lily's and Roxanne's objections when Luke lowered himself into the iron box for the late audience. Max was in a position to know that if a man didn't face his personal demons, he would be swallowed whole by them.

At home, he politely invited Luke into the parlor for a nightcap and moved inside to pour two snifters of brandy before the invitation could be accepted or declined.

"I'm not much in the mood for a drink." Luke's stomach swayed sickly at the thought of alcohol.

Max merely settled into his favorite wing chair, warming the bowl of the snifter in his hands. "No? Well, then you can keep me company while I have mine."

"It's been a long night," Luke began, hanging back.

"It certainly has." Max lifted one long-fingered hand, gesturing to a chair. "Sit."

The power was still there, the same force that had once compelled a twelve-year-old boy to wait by a darkened stage. Luke sat, took out a cigar. He only ran it between his fingers as he waited for Max to speak.

"There are all manner of methods of suicide." Max's voice was mild, like a man settling back to tell a story. "But I have to admit that I consider any and all of them a form of cowardice. However." Gesturing with one hand, he smiled benignly. "A choice of that nature is highly personal. Would you agree?"

Luke was lost. Since he'd learned long ago to be cautious with words when Max was laying a trap, he merely shrugged.

"Eloquently put," Max said with a bite of sarcasm that had Luke's eyes narrowing.

"If you contemplate the choice again," Max continued after a sip of brandy and an "ah" of appreciation for its flavor, "I would suggest a quicker, cleaner method, such as the use of the handgun on the top shelf of my bedroom closet." Before Luke could do more than blink in surprise, Max had lunged forward, one hand still delicately cupped around the glass bowl, the other dragging hard on the collar of Luke's shirt. When their faces were close, Max spoke with a quietly intense fury that mirrored the look in his eyes. "Don't ever use my stage again, or the illusion of magic, for something as cowardly as ending your life."

"Max, for God's sake." Luke felt the strong, wiry fingers close around his throat, squeeze off his words, then release.

"I've never lifted a hand to you." Now the control that had cloaked Max through the second show and beyond began to crack so that he had to rise and turn away as he spoke. "A decade now, and I've kept that promise I made to you. I'm warning you now, I will break it. If you ever do such a thing again, I will beat you sensible." He turned back, measuring Luke with dark, gleaming eyes. "Naturally, I'd be forced to have Mouse hold you down while I did so, but I promise you I know where to strike to hurt a man most."

The outrage came first. Luke sprang to his feet with it, furious dares and denials hot on his tongue. It was then he saw in the flash of the lamp-light that Max's eyes weren't gleaming with temper, but with tears. It humbled him more than a thousand beatings would have done.

"I shouldn't have done the bit tonight," he said quietly. "My timing was off. I had problems I wasn't able to push out of my mind. I knew it, but I couldn't . . . I wasn't trying to hurt myself, Max, I swear it. It was stupidity, and pride."

"Amounts to the same, doesn't it?" Max drank again to clear the thickness from his voice. "You drove Lily to tears. That's difficult for me to forgive."

For the first time in years, Luke felt that clammy fear—that he would be turned away. That he would lose what had become so precious to him. "I didn't think." He knew it was a weak excuse. Part of him wanted to pour out his reasons. But if he could do nothing else, he could spare them that. "I'll talk to her. Try to make it right."

"I expect you will." Calmer now, Max reached out to lay a hand on Luke's shoulder. There was comfort in that, and a wealth of understanding that needed no words. "Is it a woman?"

Luke thought of Roxanne, and how his hands burned to touch her. That had been part of what had clogged his brain, topped off by Cobb and too much drink. He could only shrug.

"I could tell you that no woman is worth your life, or your peace of mind. But of course, that would be a lie." His lips curved now, and his fingers squeezed lightly. "There are some, and a man is both blessed and cursed to find them. Would you like to talk about it?"

"No," Luke managed in a strangled voice. The idea of discussing his dark and driving desire for Roxanne with her father had him hovering between a laugh and a scream. "I've got it under control."

"Very well. Perhaps you'd like to hear about the next job."

"Yes. Fine."

Satisfied the air was clear once more, Max sat again, settled back. "LeClerc has come across some interesting information. A certain high-ranking politician keeps a mistress in the rich suburbs of Maryland near our nation's capital." Max paused to drink. Interest caught, Luke reached for his own snifter. His stomach no longer felt like a minefield. "Our public servant is not above accepting bribes—a particularly foul way of making a living in my estimation, but there you have it. In any case, he's wise enough not to use his bonuses to inflate his own lifestyle and cause speculation. Instead, he quietly invests in jewelry and art, and keeps his investments with his mistress."

"She must be a hell of a lay."

"Precisely." Max inclined his head, brushed a finger over his luxuriant moustache. "It's difficult to imagine why a man who would cheat on his wife and his constituents would then trust the woman who helps him cheat with nearly two million in trinkets." Max sighed a bit, as always baffled and delighted with the capriciousness of human nature. "I would hardly admit this in front of the delightful ladies of our house, but a man is not led by the nose, but by the dick."

Luke grinned. "I thought the way to a man's heart was through his stomach."

"Oh, it is, dear boy, it is. As long as it's by way of the crotch. We are, after all, an animal with intellect, but an animal nonetheless. We bury ourselves in a woman, don't we? Quite literally. How many among us can resist that illusion of returning to the womb?"

Luke lifted a brow. "I wouldn't say that was what was on my mind when I'm bouncing on a woman."

Max swirled his brandy. It had been a roundabout way to get the boy to talk, but Max often preferred a circular route. "My point, Luke, is that at a certain stage—thank God—the intellect clicks off and the animal takes over. If you're doing everything right, you're not thinking at all. Thought comes before—in the attraction, the pursuit, the seduction, the romance. Once a man's inside a woman, once she surrounds him, the mind turns off and control is forfeited. I suppose that's why sex is more dangerous than war, and much more desirable."

Luke could only shake his head. "It's not that difficult to enjoy the experience, and keep your mind focused."

"Obviously you haven't found the right woman. But you're young yet," Max said gently. "Now." He leaned forward. "About our trip to Washington."

IT TOOK SIX MONTHS in the planning. Details needed to be refined and polished as carefully as the stage show the Nouvelles would perform at the Kennedy Center.

In April, when the cherry blossoms were in rich and fragrant bloom, Luke traveled to wealthy Potomac, Maryland. Disguised with a pin-striped suit, a blond wig and a trimmed beard, he made the rounds with an eager real estate agent. With a clipped Boston accent, he assumed the identity of Charles B. Holderman, the representative of a wealthy New England industrialist who was interested in a home in D.C.'s elegant suburbs.

He appreciated the trip for what it was, and for the added benefit of distance from Roxanne. She'd taken her revenge in the sneakiest and most effective of ways. By acting as though nothing had ever happened.

Luke hadn't fully relaxed in months, and looked on the trip as a kind of working vacation. There was the added benefit of having a suite of rooms in the quietly dignified Madison, indulging in tourism—he particularly enjoyed the Smithsonian's array of gems—and simply being alone.

He toured the listed houses with the real estate agent, hemmed and hawed over building lots and locations. The questions he asked as the representative of a prospective buyer paralleled what he needed to know as a potential thief.

Who lived in the neighborhood and what did they do? Were there any loud dogs? Police patrols? What company would be recommended for installing a security system? And so on.

Later that day Luke approached Miranda Leesburg straight on. He strolled up her flower-lined flagstone walk and knocked on her oak and stained-glass front door.

He already knew what to expect. He'd studied the pictures of the sharp and sleek thirty-something blonde with a killer body and blue ice eyes. With resignation, he heard the high-pitched barking of a pair of dogs. He'd known she had two Pomeranians, it was just too bad they were yappers.

When she opened the door he was surprised to see the sleek blond hair pulled ruthlessly back in a ponytail and the sharp-featured, canny face damp with sweat. There was a towel around Miranda's neck. The rest of that lush, boldly curved body was snugged into a scant, two-piece exercise suit in vivid purple.

214

She scooped up both dogs, soothing them against breasts that rose like snowy white moons above the thin swatch of spandex.

Luke didn't lick his lips—but he thought about it. He began to understand why the good senator kept this little prize tucked away.

In photographs she was lovely in a cool, detached and obvious way. In person she shot out enough sex appeal to strike a man blind at sixty paces. Luke was much closer than that.

"I beg your pardon." He smiled and spoke with Charles's Yankee accent. "I'm sorry to disturb you." The dogs were still yapping and he had to pitch his voice over the din. "I'm Holderman, Charles Holderman."

"Yes?" She looked him up and down, much as she might if he were a sculpture she was contemplating in a gallery. "I've seen you around the neighborhood."

"My employer is interested in some property in the area." Luke smiled again. Holderman's proper maroon tie was beginning to strangle him.

"Sorry, my house isn't on the market."

"No, I realize that. I wonder if I might have a moment of your time? We could speak out here if you'd be more comfortable."

"Why would I be more comfortable outside?" She arched one delicately sculpted brow as she sized him up. Young, well built, repressed. She bent down to set the dogs on the polished hard-wood—the movement put a marvelous strain on the spandex—and gave them both a little pat on the rump to send them skittering off. With her lover out of town for nearly two weeks on a fund-raising tour, she was bored. Charles B. Holderman looked like an interesting diversion. "What did you want to speak to me about?"

"Ah, landscaping." He managed to keep his eyes from skimming down to the slopes of her breasts. "My employer has very specific requirements for grounds and gardens. Yours comes quite close to meeting them. I wonder, did you construct the rock garden in your side yard yourself?"

She laughed, patting the towel to her breasts, her gleaming midriff. "Darling, I don't know a pansy from a petunia. I use a service."

"Ah. Then perhaps you could give me a name, a number." The ever efficient Holderman took a slim, leatherbound book from his breast pocket. "I'd appreciate it very much."

"I suppose I could help you out." She tapped a finger to her lips. "Come on in. I'll dig up the card."

"That's very kind of you." Luke put the book away and filled his mind instead with the details of the foyer, the front stairs, the size and number of rooms off the hallway. "Your home is lovely."

"Yeah, I had it redecorated a few months ago."

It was all pastels and floral prints. Restful, feminine. The lush body in the vivid slashes of purple added a shock of sex. Like passion in a meadow.

Luke paused to distract himself and admired a Corot painting. "Exquisite," he said when Miranda looked questioningly over her shoulder.

"You into paintings?" She pouted a little as she turned back to his side to study it with him.

"Yes, I'm quite an admirer of art. Corot, with his dreamy style, is a favorite of mine."

"Corot, right." She didn't give a damn about the style, but she knew the value of the painting to the last cent. "I can never figure out why people want to paint trees and bushes."

Luke smiled again. "Perhaps to make people wonder who or what is behind them."

She laughed at that. "That's good, Charles, very good. I keep a card file in the kitchen. Why don't you join me for something cold while I find you your landscaper?"

"It would be a pleasure."

The kitchen carried through the soft, female charm of the rest of the house he'd seen. Potted African violets sat in sunbeams on mauve and ivory tiled counters. The appliances were streamlined and unobtrusive. A round glass table with a quartet of padded ice-cream-parlor chairs stood in the center of the room on a pale rose rug. Incongruously, the hard-edged pulse of Eddie Van Halen's screaming guitar spouted through the kitchen speakers.

"I was working out when you knocked." Miranda moved to the refrigerator for a pitcher of lemonade. "I like to keep in shape, you know?" She set the pitcher down and skimmed her hands over her hips. "That kind of music makes me sweat."

Luke rolled his tongue inside his mouth to keep it from hanging out and answered as Holderman would. "I'm sure it's stimulating."

"You bet." She chuckled to herself as she took out two glasses and poured. "Sit down, Charles. I'll find that card for you."

She set the glasses on the table with a quick chink of glass to glass, then brushed lightly against him as she walked over to a drawer. Her musky scent went straight to his grateful loins. Loins, he thought now, he hadn't been able to put to good use since he'd passed out courtesy of Jack Daniel's on top of Roxanne.

Down boy, he thought and straightened the knot of his tie before reaching for his drink.

"Beautiful day," he said conversationally as she rummaged through the drawer. "How fortunate that you can be home to enjoy it."

"Oh, my time's pretty much my own. I own a little boutique in Georgetown. Keeps the wolf from the door, you might say, but I have a manager that handles the day-to-day nuisances." She took a business card from the drawer and stood flipping the end against her palm. "Are you married, Charles?"

"No. Divorced."

"Me too." She smiled, pleased. "I discovered I like having the house, and my life, to myself. Just how long will you be in the area?"

"Oh, only a day or two longer, I'm afraid. Whether or not my employer purchases property here, my business will be completed."

"Then it's back to . . ."

"Boston."

"Hmm." That was good. In fact, it was perfect. If he'd been staying longer, she would have dismissed him with the drink and the landscaper's card. As it was, he was the answer to a long and frustrating two weeks. Every so often—every so discreetly often—Miranda liked to change partners and dance.

She didn't know him, and neither did the senator. A quick, anonymous fuck would do a lot more for her state of mind than an hour on the damn Nautilus.

"Well . . ." She slid her hand down to rub it lightly over her crotch. "You could say you'll be—in and out."

Luke set down his glass before it slid out of his hand. "In a manner of speaking."

"Since you're here now." Watching him, she slipped the business card down into the triangle of her spandex bikini. "Why don't you take what you need."

Luke debated for nearly a heartbeat. It wasn't going precisely the way he'd imagined. But, as Max was wont to say, an ounce of spontaneity was worth a pound of planning. "Why don't I?" He rose and, moving much faster than she'd given him credit for, hooked a finger under the slanted line of spandex. She was hot and wet as a geyser.

Even as she arched back in shock, the first lusty cry tumbling from her lips, he'd dragged the material down. In two quick moves, he'd freed himself and plunged violently into her. The first orgasm took her by surprise. Damned if he'd looked that clever.

"Oh, Christ!" Her eyes popped wide with pleasure. Then his hands had cupped her hips and had lifted her up in surprisingly strong arms so that her legs were wrapped around his waist. She managed a few gargled gasps and held on for the ride of her life.

He watched her. His blood was pumping hot and fast, his body was steeped in the velvet lightning that was sex. But his mind—that was clear enough so that he could see the faint lines around her eyes, the quick darts of her tongue. He knew the dogs had scrambled in, nervous and curious at the sounds their mistress made. They were crouched under the glass table, yapping.

Van Halen was wailing on the speakers. Luke set his rhythm to theirs, down and dirty. He could count her climaxes, and saw that the third he gave her left her dazed and limp. It was his pleasure to gift her with another before he succumbed to his own. But even as he reached flash point, he had enough control to keep her from rapping her head back against the white oak cabinet door—and enough to prevent her from snatching at his hair and dislodging the wig.

"Sweet God." Miranda would have slid bonelessly to the floor if he hadn't held her up with that easy, eerie strength. "Who'd have thought you had all that under that Brooks Brothers suit?"

"Only my tailor." A bit belatedly, he tilted her head back for a kiss.

"When did you say you had to leave?"

"Tomorrow night, actually. But I have some time today." And he might as well use it to case the house. "Do you have a bed?"

Miranda wound her arms around his neck. "I've got four of them. Where do you want to start?"

"You look pleased with yourself," LeClerc noted when Luke dropped his suitcases in the foyer of the house in New Orleans.

"Got the job done. Why shouldn't I look pleased?" Luke opened his briefcase and took out a notebook filled with notes and drawings. "The layout of her house. Two safes, one in the master bedroom, another in the living room. She's got a Corot in the downstairs hallway and a goddamn Monet over her bed."

LeClerc grunted as he scanned the notes. "And just how did you discover the painting and the safe in her bedroom, *mon ami*?"

"I let her fuck my brains out." Grinning, Luke peeled off his leather jacket. "I feel so cheap."

"*Casse pas mon cœur*," LeClerc muttered, amusement gleaming in his eye. "Next time I'll see that Max sends me."

"*Bonne chance*, old man. An hour with that lady would have put you in traction. Sweet Christ, she had moves you wouldn't—" He broke off when he heard a sound at the top of the stairs. Roxanne stood there, one hand gripping the banister. Her face was blank, coldly so, but for two flags of color that could have been embarrassment or fury and rode high on her cheeks. Without a word, she turned and disappeared. He heard the echo of her door slamming.

Now he did feel cheap, and dirty. He would have rejoiced to strangle her for it. "Why the fuck didn't you tell me she was here?"

"You didn't ask," LeClerc said simply. "*Allons*. Max is in the workroom. He'll want to hear what you found out."

Upstairs, Roxanne lay prone on her bed, fighting back a horrible urge to hurl breakables. She wouldn't give him the satisfaction. She didn't need him, didn't want him. Didn't care. If he wanted to spend his time screwing overendowed tarts, it was strictly his business.

Oh, but damn him to a fiery hell for enjoying it.

There were a dozen—well, at least a half dozen—men who would be more than happy to relieve her of the burden of her virginity. Maybe it was time to pick one out.

She could brag, too, after all. She could flaunt her sexual exploits under his nose until he choked on them.

No, she'd be damned if she'd make a decision like that out of pique.

And she'd be double damned, she decided, sitting up, if she'd wait in the wings this time while the men had all the fun. When they moved on the house in Potomac, she was going to be right there with them.

Come hell or high water.

"I'm fully prepared, Daddy." Roxanne transferred a neatly folded blouse from her suitcase to a drawer in her room at the

Washington Ritz. "And I've kept my part of the bargain." She arranged lingerie tidily in the drawer above. "I've completed my first year at Tulane, with a three point five grade average. I fully intend to do the same when classes start back in the fall."

"I appreciate that, Roxanne." Max stood at the window. Behind him, the Washington summer baked the pavements and rose again in oily waves. "But this job has been months in the planning. It's wiser for you to make your debut, as it were, with something smaller."

"I prefer starting at the top." With the careless precision of the innately tidy, she began to hang dresses and cocktail wear in the closet. "I'm not a novice, and you know it. I've been a part of this aspect of your life—behind the scenes, unfortunately—since I was a child. I can pick a lock as well, and often quicker than LeClerc." Conscientiously, she shook a fold out of a silk skirt. "I know a great deal about engines and mechanics thanks to Mouse." After closing the closet doors, she shot her father a bland look. "I know more about computers than any of you. You know yourself that kind of skill is invaluable."

"And I've appreciated your help in the early stages of this job. However—"

"There's no however, Daddy. It's time."

"There are physical aspects as well as mental," he began.

"Do you think I've been working out five hours a week for the last year for my health?" she tossed back. They'd reached a cross-roads. Roxanne chose her path and planted her fists on her hips. "Are you standing in my way because you're having fatherly qualms about leading me down a dishonest path?"

"Certainly not." He looked shocked, then affronted. "I happen to consider what I do an ancient and valuable art. Thievery is a time-honored profession, my girl. Not to be confused with these hooligans who mug people on the street, or bloodthirsty klutzes who burst into banks, guns blazing. We're discriminating. We're romantic." His voice rose in passion. "We're artists."

Chapter Fifteen

THE KENNEDY CENTER LENT ITSELF TO LARGE-SCALE ILLUSIONS, as did the network television cameras that were filming the event for a special to be aired in the fall. Max had staged the one-hundred-and-two-minute show like a three-act play, with full orchestra, complex lighting cues and elaborate costumes.

It began with Max alone on a darkened stage, caught in the moonlike beam of a single spotlight. He was draped in a velvet cloak of midnight blue that was threaded with shimmering silver. In one hand he held a wand, also silver, that glinted in the light. In the other he cupped a ball of crystal.

So Merlin might have looked as he plotted for the birth of a king.

Sorcery was his theme, and he played the mystic necromancer with dignity and drama. He lifted the ball onto the crown of his fingertips. It pulsed with lights as he spoke to the audience of spells and dragons, alchemy and witchcraft. While they watched, already snagged by the theatrics, the ball began to float—along the folds of the velvet cloak, above the tip of the magic wand, spinning high above his head at a shouted incantation. All the while it pulsed with those inner lights, flickering scarlet and sapphire, amber and emerald onto his uplifted face. The audience gasped as the ball plummeted toward the stage, then applauded when it stopped, inches before destruction, to rotate in a widening circle, rising, rising toward Max's outstretched hands. Once more he held it poised on his fingertips. He tapped it once with the shimmering wand and tossed it high. The ball became a shower of silver that rained down on the stage before it went black.

When the lights came up again, seconds later, it was Roxanne who stood center stage. She was all in glimmering silver. Stars glittered in her hair, along the arms the column of sequins left bare. She stood straight as a sword, her arms crossed over her breasts, her eyes closed. When the orchestra began to play a movement from Beethoven's Sixth Symphony, she swayed. Her eyes opened.

She spoke of spells cast and love lost, of witchery gone wrong. As she uncrossed her arms, lifted them high, sparks flew from her fingertips. Her hair, a flame of curls nearly to her shoulders, began to wave in an unseen wind. The spotlight widened to show a small table beside her, on it a bell, a book and an unlit candle. Cupping her palms, she made fire in them, flames rising and ebbing as if breathing. As she passed her hands over the candle, the flames guttered in her palms and spurted from the wick in a shimmer of gold.

A flick of her wrist, and the pages of the book began to turn, slowly, then faster, faster, until it was a whirl. The bell rose from the table between her outstretched palms. As she swayed her hands, it tolled. Suddenly, beneath the table where there had been only space three candles burned brightly. Their fire licked up and up until the table itself was aflame with Roxanne standing behind it, her face washed in its light and shadows. She threw her arms out and there was nothing left but smoke. At the same instant another spotlight shot on. Luke was there, upstage left.

He wore sleek black trimmed in glistening gold. Lily's clever makeup had accented his cheekbones, arched his brows. Nearly as long as hers, his raven hair flowed free. He looked to Roxanne like a cross between a satyr and a pirate. Her traitorous heart gave one thump before she quashed the flicker of need.

She faced him across the stage with smoke twining between them. Her stance was a challenge, head thrown back, one arm up, the other held out to the side. A streak of light shot from her fingertips toward him. He lifted a hand, seemed to catch it. The audience erupted with applause as the duel continued. The combatants moved closer together, whirling smoke, hurling fire as the stage lights came up rose and gold, simulating sunrise.

Roxanne threw her arm over her eyes, as if to shield herself. Then her arms fell limply, her head drooped. The silver gown sparkled, hissing with light while she swayed, as if her body were attached by strings to Luke's hands. He circled her, passing those hands around her, inches from touching. He passed his spread hand in front of her eyes, indicating trance, then slowly, slowly gestured her back, farther back. Her feet lifted from the stage. Her back stayed straight as a spear as he floated her up until she lay on nothing more than wisps of blue smoke.

He whirled once, and when he faced the stage again he held a slim silver ring. Graceful as a dancer, he moved from her feet to her head, sliding her body through the circle. Unrehearsed, he leaned forward, as if to kiss her. He felt her body stiffen as his lips halted a breath away.

"Don't blow it, Rox," he whispered, then whipped off his cape, tossed it over her. It held for a moment before the form beneath it seemed to melt away. When the cape fluttered to the floor, Luke held a white swan cradled in his arms.

There was a crash of thunder from backstage. Luke bent for his cape, praying the damn swan wouldn't take a nick out of him this time. He crouched, swirling the cape over his head. And vanished.

"I didn't care for the ad-lib," Roxanne told Luke the minute she caught up with him.

"No?" He handed off the swan to Mouse and smiled at her. "I thought it was a nice touch. How about you, Mouse?"

Mouse stroked the swan—he was the only one who could without endangering fingers. "Well . . . I guess. Gotta give Myrtle her snack."

"See." Luke gestured after Mouse's retreating back. "Loved it."

"Try it again and I'll do a little ad-libbing myself." She stabbed a finger into his shirt. "You'll end up with a bloody lip."

He caught her wrist before she could storm away. From the sound of the applause he knew that Max and Lily were keeping the momentum high. His own emotions were a rising riot. He wasn't sure he'd ever felt better in his life.

"Listen, Rox, what we do onstage is an act. A job. Just like what we're going to do tomorrow night in Potomac." Some inner demon had him shifting his body, effectively sandwiching her between it and the wall. "Nothing personal."

The blood was humming in her head, but she dredged up a friendly smile. "Maybe you're right."

He could smell her—perfume, greasepaint, the slight muskiness of stage sweat. "Of course I'm right. It's just a matter of—" His breath wolfed out as she rammed an elbow into his gut. She slipped easily away and smiled with a lot more sincerity.

"Nothing personal," she said sweetly. She stepped inside her dressing room, shut—and locked—the door. It was time for a costume change.

The next time she had to deal with him they were nearly nose to nose with only a thin sheet of plywood between them. They were locked in a trick box and had only seconds before transmutation.

"Pull that again, babe," Luke hissed even as they were flipping positions. "I swear I'll hit you, back."

"Oh! I'm shaking." Roxanne sprang out of the box in Luke's place to thunderous applause.

They took their bows graciously after the finale. Luke pinched her hard enough to bruise. Roxanne trod heavily on his instep.

He bowed with a flourish, pulling roses out of thin air and

offering them to her. She accepted them, but before she could dip into the curtsy, he moved. No way was he going to allow the blow to go unrewarded. He arched her back in an exaggerated dip and kissed her.

Or it appeared to be a kiss to the delighted audience. He bit her.

"You bastard." She forced her throbbing lip to spread into a smile. They stepped back as Max made his final entrance. Luke took Roxanne's hand. His eyes popped wide when she gripped his thumb and twisted.

"Jesus, Rox, not the hands. I can't work without my hands."

"Then keep them off me, pal." She released him, satisfied with the idea that his thumb would be aching every bit as much as her bottom lip. Together they joined Max and Lily center stage for a final bow.

"I love show business," Roxanne said with a breathy laugh.

The pure good humor in her voice scotched Luke's notion of booting her in the rump. He took her hand again, with more caution. "Me too."

SHE DIDN'T FIND THE BENEFITS too shabby either. The elegant White House reception put the perfect cap on the evening. Max, she knew, was staunchly apolitical. He voted, considering it his right and his duty, but more often than not pulled the lever with the same kind of careless glee with which he gambled.

Max thought nothing of drawing to an inside straight.

It wasn't the politics of Washington that appealed to Roxanne. It was the formal, often pompous ambience those politics generated. A far cry from New Orleans, she thought, admiring the richly dressed and somewhat stuffy dancers swirling around the ballroom floor.

"You seem to have made magic work for you."

Roxanne turned, her pleasant, company smile fading into simple shock. "Sam. What are you doing here?"

227

"Enjoying the festivities. Almost as much as I enjoyed your performance." He took her hand, bringing her stiff fingers to his lips.

He'd changed considerably. The thin, poorly attired teenager had groomed himself into a slim, impeccable man. His sandy hair was as conservatively cut as the tuxedo he wore. On his hand glittered one discreet diamond ring. Roxanne caught a whiff of masculine cologne as his lips brushed her skin.

He was clean-shaven, as well polished as the gleaming antiques that littered the White House. Like the air they breathed, he exuded the strong, unmistakable aura of wealth and success. And like politics, she thought, beneath that glowing aura, was the faint stink of corruption.

"You've grown up, Roxanne. And beautifully."

She slipped her hand away from his. Her flesh tingled where he'd touched, as if she'd reached too close to a current that might prove fatal. "I could say the same about you."

His teeth flashed. Those he'd lost in his fight with Luke had been nicely replaced. "Why don't you—while we dance."

She could have refused, flatly, politely, flirtatiously. She had the skill for it. But she was curious. Without a word she moved with him out on the floor and joined the flow of dancers.

"I could say," she began, more than a little surprised to find him graceful and accomplished, "that the White House is the last place I would have expected to see you again. But—" She met his eyes. "Most cats land on their feet."

"Oh, I always planned to see you—all of you—again. Odd how fate would make it here in such . . . powerful surroundings." He drew her closer, enjoying the way she held that slim, soft body rigid and still managed to follow his lead as fluidly as water. "The act tonight was quite a step up from those little bits of business at that grimy club in the Quarter. Better even than the show Max devised for the Magic Castle."

"He's the best there is."

"His talent is phenomenal," Sam agreed. He dipped his face

down to hers, watched her eyes narrow. The sexual punch was like a brick to the gut. He shifted, just enough so that she'd feel his arousal. "But I must admit it was you and Luke that held me breathless. A very sexy little number that."

"An illusion," she said coolly. "Sex had nothing to do with it."

"If there was a man unstirred when you levitated under his hands, they were dead and buried." And how interesting it would be, he thought, to have her. To feel *her* stir, willing, unwilling, under his hands. A beautiful payback it would be, with the added benefit of hot, greedy sex. "I can assure you, I'm alive."

Her stomach muscles were knotted, but she kept her gaze level. "If you think I'm flattered by the bulge in your pants, Sam, you're mistaken." She had the satisfaction of seeing his lips tighten in anger before she continued. And yes, she noted, his eyes were the same. Sly, canny and potentially mean. "Where did you go when you left New Orleans?"

Now he not only wanted to take her, but wanted to hurt her first. "Here and there."

"And here and there led you . . . " She gestured. "Here?"

"On a circular route. At the moment, I happen to be the right-hand man of the Gentleman from Tennessee."

"You're joking."

"Not at all." He spread his palm over the small of her back. "I'm the senator's top aide. And I intend to be a great deal more."

It took her only a moment to recover. "Well, I suppose it fits, since politics is the ultimate con game. Won't your past indiscretions interfere with your ambitions?"

"On the contrary. My difficult childhood gives me a fresh and sympathetic perspective on the problems of our children—our most valuable natural resource. I'm a role model—showing them what they can make of themselves."

"I don't suppose you put using an ignorant child to help you steal from her friends on your résumé."

"What a team we made." He chuckled as if his betrayal had

been nothing more than a joke. "How much better a team we might make now."

"I'm sorry to say the idea revolts me." She smiled with a flutter of lashes. When she started to step away, he gripped her hand hard enough to make her wince.

"I believe there are some things best left behind the fog of memory. Don't you, Roxanne? After all, if you suddenly felt the urge to gossip about an old acquaintance, I might have to do the same." His eyes were hard as he jerked her closer. To the casual onlooker it would appear they were contemplating a kiss. "I didn't leave New Orleans right away. I made it my business to watch, to ask questions. To learn all manner of things. Unless I'm very much mistaken, you'd prefer those things to be kept quiet."

She felt her color drain. Of all the things she could control, she had never been able to outwit the traitorously delicate skin of a redhead. "I don't know what you're talking about. You're hurting me."

"I'd prefer to avoid that." He lightened his grip. "Unless it were under more intimate circumstances. Perhaps a quiet midnight supper, where we can renew old acquaintance."

"No. I realize it might be a blow to your ego, Sam, but I really have no interest in your past, your present or your future."

"Then we won't talk business." He pressed his mouth to her ear and murmured a suggestion so blatant Roxanne wasn't certain whether to cringe or laugh aloud. She didn't have the chance to do either as a hand gripped her arm and jerked her back.

"Keep your hands off her." Luke's face was alive with fury as he stepped between Roxanne and Sam. He was sixteen again, and ready to rumble. "Don't ever touch her."

"Well, it appears I've stepped on some toes." In marked opposition to Luke's harsh whisper, Sam spoke jovially. He'd been right, after all. Not all the sparks he'd seen flying around onstage had been the result of special effects and magic.

"Luke." Well aware that heads were turning in their direction,

Roxanne slipped a hand through his arm. It gave her the opportunity to dig her nails into his flesh. "A reception at the White House isn't the place to cause a scene." She was smiling gaily as she spoke.

"Sensible and beautiful." Sam nodded toward her, but kept his eyes on Luke. It was still there, and Sam was glad of it. The greasy pool of jealousy and hate still lapped in his gut. "I'd listen to the lady, Callahan. After all, this is my turf, not yours."

"Do you know how many bones you have in your hand?" Luke spoke pleasantly while his eyes continued to promise murder. "If you touch her again, you'll find out. Because I'll break each and every one of them."

"Stop it. I'm not a bone for the two of you to snap over." With relief, she saw her father and Lily making their way through the crowd. "Let's get through it, shall we? Daddy!" Bright enthusiasm bubbled out as she turned toward Max. "You won't believe who's here. It's Sam Wyatt. After all this time."

"Max." Smooth as a snake, Sam offered a hand, then took Lily's fingers in his free one to kiss. "And Lily. More beautiful than ever."

"You'll never guess what Sam's up to these days." Roxanne continued to chatter as if they were old, dear friends reunited.

Max wasn't one to hold a grudge. Nor was he a man to let down his guard. "So, you settled on politics."

"Yes, sir. You could say I owe it to you."

"Could you?"

"You taught me showmanship." He grinned, a political poster for success and youthful energy. "Senator Bushfield, sir." Sam waylaid a trim, balding man with tired brown eyes and a lopsided smile. "I imagine you've met the Nouvelles."

"Yes, yes." The Tennessee twang was rich and hearty despite the fatigue on the senator's face. "Delightful show, as I told you, Nouvelle."

"I didn't mention you before, Senator, because I wanted to surprise my old friends." With an amused glance at Luke, Sam laid a hand on Max's shoulder. "I once spent several months as apprentice magician to the master."

"You don't say?" Bushfield's eyes lit with interest.

"But I do." Sam smiled and wove a tale of a confused, disenchanted youth taken in and given direction by the kindness of a generous man and his family. "Unfortunately," he concluded, "I was never adept at performing. But when I left the Nouvelles it was with a fresh purpose." He laughed and ran a finger surreptitiously down Roxanne's spine. "I wouldn't be where I am today without them."

"I'll tell you this." Bushfield thumped Sam paternally on the back. "This boy here's going places. Sharp as a tack and slippery as an eel." He winked at Max. "He may not've been good at hocus pocus, but he sure can charm the pants off the constituents."

"Sam was never lacking in charm," Max said. "Perhaps in focus."

"I'm focused now." He aimed a look at Luke. "I know just how to do what needs to be done."

"THE SLIMY SON OF A BITCH had his hands all over you."

Roxanne merely sighed. It was hard to believe that Luke was playing the same tune. Maybe it was because she'd managed to avoid him for the best part of twenty-four hours. "We were dancing, stupid."

"He was drooling on your neck."

"At least he didn't bite." She shot Luke a superior smile and leaned back. Mouse was driving silently through the suburbs, making slow sweeps of the area around Miranda's house. "Get your mind out of the gutter, Callahan, and back on the job."

"I'd like to know what he's got in his head," Luke muttered. "It's bad luck running into him like this."

"Luck is luck, my boy," Max commented from the front seat. "What we do with it determines whether it's good or bad." Satisfied with the atmosphere, Max stripped out of his suit jacket and the false shirt front that hid a thin black sweater.

In the rear seat, Luke and Roxanne made similar transformations. "Keep away from him."

"Kiss ass."

"Children." Max shook his head as he glanced back. "If you can't behave, Daddy won't take you to find hidden treasure. Thirty-five minutes," he said to Mouse. "No more, no less."

"'Kay, Max." He slipped the car to the curb, then swiveled around. There was a big, happy grin on his face. "Break a leg, Roxy."

"Thanks, Mouse." She leaned up to kiss him before climbing out of the car.

It was a still, humid night. The light from the thumbnail moon was almost obscured by haze, and the heat hung in the air like a cowl. She could smell roses, jasmine and grass newly mowed, and the damp woody aroma of mulch recently watered.

They moved like shadows over the lawn, slipping past azaleas no longer in bloom and summer perennials just starting to bud. Another shadow streaked past them, causing Roxanne to bump heavily against Luke. Her heart jammed hard at her ribs.

But it was only a cat, racing off to find a stray mouse or a mate. "Nervous, Rox?" Luke's teeth flashed in the dark.

"No." Annoyed, she hurried on, comforted by the solid bounce of her leather pouch against her thigh.

"They got some woods around here," he whispered close to her ear. "But I doubt there's wolves. A couple wild dogs maybe."

"Get a life." But she looked uneasily into the shadows for yellow eyes or fangs.

As planned, they separated at the east corner of the house, Luke to cut the phone wires, Max to disengage the alarm system.

"It takes a light touch," Max patiently instructed his daughter. "One must not hurry or be overconfident. Practice," he said, as he had done countless times over rehearsals. "An artist can never get enough practice. Even the greatest ballerina continues to take classes all of her professional life."

She watched him spreading and stripping wires. It was a hand-cramping, tedious job. Roxanne held the light steady and watched every move he made.

"There's a unit inside that operates on a code. It's possible, with finesse, to jam it from out here."

"How do you know when you have?"

He smiled and patted her hand, ignoring the grinding ache in his fingers. "Faith, coupled with intuition and experience. And ... that little light up there will go out. *Et voilà*," he whispered when the red dot went blank.

"Six minutes gone." Luke crouched behind them.

"We won't cut the glass." Max continued to instruct as he moved to the rear terrace door. "It's wired, you see. Even with the alarm off, it's tricky—and much more time-consuming than picking the lock."

He took out his set of picks, a gift some thirty years before from LeClerc. With some ceremony, he handed them to Roxanne. "Try your luck, my love."

"Jesus, Max, it'll take her forever."

Roxanne took a moment to scowl at Luke before bending to her task. Not even he could spoil the moment for her. She worked as her father had told her. Patiently. With hands as delicate as a surgeon's, she operated on the lock. Her ear close to the door, her eyes serenely closed.

She was imagining herself inside the lock, easing at the tumblers with gentle hands. Shifting, cajoling, maneuvering.

A smile curved softly on her lips as she heard the click. Ah, the power of it.

"It's like music," she whispered, and brought proud tears to Max's eyes.

"Two minutes, thirty-eight seconds." He glanced over at Luke as he hit the button on his watch. "As good, I believe, as you've done."

Beginner's luck, Luke thought, but was wise enough to keep the opinion to himself. They slipped through the door single file, and again separated.

Luke's layout of the house had been so complete they had needed to bribe no one for blueprints. Roxanne's assignment was the paintings. She cut them carefully from their frames and rolled Corots, Monets, a particularly fine Pissarro street scene into the knapsack on her back before joining her father in the living room.

She knew better than to disturb him at work. His fingers flicked at the safe dial. Roxanne thought he looked like Merlin, deftly brewing his spells. Her heart swelled.

They exchanged grins as the door eased open.

"Quickly now, dear." He opened velvet boxes and long flat cases, dumping the contents into her pouch. Wanting to prove she'd learned well, Roxanne removed a loupe and under the beam of her flashlight examined the stones in a sapphire brooch.

"Berlin-blue," she murmured. "With an excellent—"

It was then they heard the yip of a dog.

"Oh, shit."

"Easy." Max laid a quieting hand on her arm. "At the first sign of trouble, you're out the door and back to Mouse."

Her nerves jittered like banjo strings, but loyalty hung tough. "I won't leave you."

"You will." Moving fast, Max emptied the safe.

Upstairs, Luke scowled at the growling Pomeranians. He hadn't forgotten them. He knew, from his own afternoon there, that they made a habit of sleeping on their mistress's bed.

That was why he had two meaty bones in his pouch.

He took them out, freezing when Miranda grumbled sleepily at the dogs and rolled over. Then he crouched, a shadow in the shadows, and gestured with the bones.

He didn't speak, didn't dare take the risk even when Miranda began to snore lightly. But the dogs didn't need any verbal prompting. Scenting the snack, they scrambled off the bed and snapped their jaws.

Satisfied, Luke pulled out the false front on the section of bookshelves and went to work on the safe.

It was a bit distracting having the woman sleeping in the room. Not that he hadn't burgled a home with a woman snoring close by before. But he'd never done so with a woman he'd shared the bed with.

Added an interesting angle, he thought.

And wouldn't you know that the luscious Miranda slept buck naked?

The excitement, always vaguely sexual, that he felt on lifting a lock increased dramatically. By the time he had the safe open, he was rock hard and struggling to hold back laughter at the absurdity of the situation.

He could always climb into bed with her and seduce her while she was half asleep. After all, he had the added benefit of knowing what moves she preferred.

And she'd recognize him in the dark, he had no doubt.

It would be a thrill, undoubtedly, but time was against him.

Of course, there were proprieties and priorities. As Max would have said. Then again, he was the same one who said strike while the iron was hot.

Christ Almighty, Luke thought, his personal iron was currently hot enough to melt stone.

Too bad, baby, he thought, taking a last glance at the sprawled Miranda. He wondered if she'd have considered a quick roll payment for the loss of the jewels. Then he had to stifle another laugh as he hobbled from the room.

"You're two minutes behind." Roxanne stood at the base of the stairs, hissing at him. "I was about to come up." Her eyes narrowed against the dark. "Why are you walking like that?"

Luke only snorted with muffled laughter and kept limping down the stairs.

"Are you hurt? Are you—" She broke off when she saw just what was hampering him. "Christ, you're a pervert."

"Just a healthy all-American boy, Roxy."

"Sick," she tossed back, unreasonably jealous. "Disgusting."

"Normal. Painful, but normal."

"Ah, children." Like a patient schoolteacher, Max signaled. "Perhaps we could discuss this in the car?"

Roxanne continued to whisper insults as they hurried across the lawn. By the time they reached the car, the simple thrill of the entire evening took over. She tumbled in behind Mouse, laughing. She kissed him, even as he drove the car sedately down the street. There was another smacking kiss for Max, and because she was feeling generous—and perhaps just a little vindictive—she turned and pressed her lips firmly to Luke's.

"Oh, God."

"I hope you suffer." Leaning back, she hugged the gem-packed pouch to her breasts. "Okay, Daddy. What do we do for an encore?"

Chapter Sixteen

ROXANNE PACED RESTLESSLY FROM BEADED LAMPSHADE TO picture frame, from crystal wand to jeweled box in Madame's shop. In faded jeans and an oversized New Orleans Saints T-shirt, she looked precisely like what she was. A newly graduated college student waiting for her life to begin.

Madame carefully counted out her customer's change. After thirty years in business she continued to eschew modern distractions such as a cash register. The old, hand-painted cigar box under the counter served her well enough.

"Enjoy," she said, shaking her head as her customer left the shop with a stuffed parrot under his arm. Tourists, she thought, would buy anything. "So, *pichouette*, you come to show me your new college diploma?"

"No. I think Max is having it bronzed." She smiled a little, toying with a china cup that had a chip on its gold rim. "You'd think I'd discovered the cure for cancer instead of slogging my way through four years at Tulane."

"Graduating fifth in your class is not so small potatoes."

Roxanne jerked a shoulder in easy dismissal. She was restless, oh so restless, and couldn't quite find the root of it. "It only took application. I have a good memory for details."

"And this troubles you?"

"No." Roxanne set the cup down and took a steadying breath. "I'm worried about my father." It was a relief to say it aloud. "His hands aren't what they were."

It was something she could speak with no one about, not even Lily. They all knew that arthritis was gaining on Max, swelling his knuckles, stiffening those agile fingers. There had been doctors, medication, massage. Roxanne knew that the pain was nothing compared to the fear of losing what he held most dear. His magic.

"Even Max can't cause time to vanish, *petite*."

"I know. I understand. I just can't accept. It's affecting him emotionally, Madame. He broods, he spends too much time alone in his workroom and with his research on that bloody magic stone. It's gotten worse since Luke moved out last year."

Madame lifted a brow at the bitterness. "Roxanne, a man becomes a man and needs his own place."

"He just wanted to bring women in."

Madame's lips twitched. "This is reason enough. He's only a short distance, still in the Quarter. Does he not continue to work with Max?"

"Yes, yes." Roxanne waved a hand in dismissal. "I didn't mean to get off the subject. It's my father I'm concerned about. I can't reach him the way I used to, not since he's become obsessed with that damn stone."

"Stone? Tell me, what is this stone?"

Roxanne wandered over to the counter. She picked up the tarot deck Madame left there and began to shuffle. "The philosophers' stone. It's a myth, Madame, an illusion. Legend has it that this stone could turn anything it touched into gold. And . . . " She glanced up significantly. "Give youth back to the aged. Health to the ill."

"And you don't believe in such things? You, who have lived your lifetime in magic."

"I know what makes magic work." Roxanne cut the cards and began a Celtic cross. "Sweat and practice, timing and misdirection. Emotion and drama. I believe in the art of magic, Madame, not in magic stones. Not in the supernatural."

"I see." Madame cocked a brow at the cards on the counter. "Yet you seek your answers there?"

"Hmm?" Caught up in interpreting the spread, Roxanne frowned. Then flushed. "Just to pass the time." Before she could gather the cards up, Madame caught her hand.

"A shame to disturb a reading." She hunched over the cards herself. "The girl is ready to become a woman. There's a journey ahead, soon. Both figuratively and literally."

Roxanne smiled. She couldn't help it. "We're taking a cruise. North, up the Saint Lawrence Seaway. We'll perform, of course. Max sees it as a working vacation."

"Prepare for changes." Madame tapped the Wheel of Fortune. "The realization of a dream—if you're wise. And the loss of it. Someone from out of the past. And sorrow. Time to heal."

"And the Death card?" It surprised Roxanne that her skin prickled when she looked at the grinning skeleton.

"Death chases life from the first breath." Madame stroked the card with a gentle finger. "You are too young to feel it whispering at your ear. But this is death that is not death. Go on your journey, *pichouette*, and learn."

LUKE WAS MORE THAN READY to go. There was nothing he could think of he'd rather do than get out of town. The latest payment to Cobb sat on his coffee table, addressed and stamped.

The demand for money had been as steady as mortgage payments over the years. Two thousand here, four there, to an average of fifty thousand annually.

Luke didn't mind the money. He had plenty of that. But he'd yet to control that greasy wave of nausea each time he found a plain postcard in his mailbox.

2K, it might say. Or perhaps when Cobb's luck was running thin, 5K, and the post office box. Nothing more.

Luke had had four years to reconsider the extent of Cobb's brainpower. The man was much smarter than Luke had ever given him credit for. A fool would have pushed for the big score and quickly dried the well. But Cobb, good old belt-wielding Al, knew the value of a steady trickle.

So Luke was more than ready to get away—from the postcards, from the dissatisfied tickle at the back of his neck, from worry over Max's overpowering obsession with a nonexistent magic rock.

They'd be too busy on the ship to worry about such things with performances, ports of call and the tidy job they had planned for Manhattan.

When they did have free time, Luke planned to plop himself down by the pool, clamp headphones on his ears and bury his nose in a book while some nubile strolling cocktail waitress kept the cold beer coming.

All in all, life was good. He had a bit more than two million in his Swiss accounts, that much again floating in various stocks, bonds and money markets in the States, along with some modest real estate investments. In his closet hung suits from Savile Row and Armani, though he still preferred denim by Levi's. Perhaps he was more at home in Nikes, but there were highly polished Gucci shoes in his rack, and a selection of John Lobb boots. He drove a vintage 'Vette and piloted his own Cessna. He indulged in imported cigars and French champagne and had a weakness for Italian women.

All in all, he figured the half-starved pickpocket had turned himself into a discriminating, cosmopolitan man.

What it cost him to maintain the image was a bit of blackmail—and the repression of one small, nagging, incessant need.

Roxanne.

But then, Max had taught him never to count the cost, unless it was pride.

Luke took a mug of coffee onto his terrace to watch the action down in Jackson Square. There were girls in pretty summer dresses, babies in strollers, men with cameras slung around their necks. He spotted three black kids tap dancing. Their feet were moving like fury. Even with the distance, he could hear the cheerful click and clatter of their shoes on the concrete. They'd drawn a crowd, and that pleased him.

The woman he'd heard on that first day in New Orleans no longer sang in the Quarter. He missed the sound of her, and though he'd never quite had the same emotional tug toward anyone else, it satisfied him to see the cardboard boxes of the street performers fill with silver.

Without Max, he thought. Without Max and Lily he could have done much worse than dance for pennies.

That brought a frown to his eyes. He knew why Max was handing over more and more of the sleight of hand and close-up work to him and Roxanne. He thought he even understood why Max was devoting so much of the time he'd once earmarked for preparing the act toward the damn philosophers' stone. And understanding hurt.

Max was getting old, right in front of Luke's eyes.

A knock on the door had him turning reluctantly away from the street scene. But when he opened it, there was only pleasure.

"Lily." Luke bent to kiss her, to breathe in the wonderfully familiar Chanel before taking the various bags and boxes she carried.

"I was shopping." She giggled, patting her fluffy blond hair back into place. "I guess that's obvious. I got the urge to stop by. Hope it's okay."

"It's always okay." He dumped her purchases on an overstuffed chair beside a Belker table. "Ready to give Max his walking papers and move in with me?"

242

She laughed again, that bubbly, champagne sound that he loved. Past forty now, she remained as lush and pretty as she'd been when Luke had first seen her strut across the stage. It took a bit more woman's magic to maintain the illusion, but Lily had an endless store of it.

"If I did, it would be to give those ladies of yours the once-over as they sashay in and out."

"I'd give them all up, for the right lady."

Lily didn't laugh this time, but there was a different sort of amusement in her eyes. "Oh, I'm sure you would, honey. I'm getting old waiting for you to make the next move. But," she continued before he could speak, "I didn't come by to talk about your love life—fascinating though it may be."

He grinned. "You're going to make me blush."

"Fat chance." She was proud of him, so proud it almost burst her heart. He was tall and trim and gloriously handsome. And more, much more than that, there was a goodness inside of him that she knew she had nurtured herself. "I dropped by to see if you needed any help packing—or if you needed anything while I was shopping. Socks, underwear?"

He couldn't help it. Setting the mug down he cupped her face in his hands and kissed her again. "I love you, Lily."

Pleasure had her cheeks blooming. "I love you, too. I know how men hate to pack and shop for undies and stuff."

"I've got plenty."

"They've probably got holes in them, or the elastic's gone."

Sober-eyed, he lifted a hand in an oath. "I swear to God, I didn't pack a single pair of jocks that I'd be ashamed to wear if I were in an accident."

She sniffed, but her eyes were laughing. "You're making fun of me."

"Yeah. How about some coffee?"

"I'd rather something cold, if you have it."

"Lemonade?" He headed back toward the kitchen. "I must have

had a premonition that you'd drop by when I squeezed those damn lemons this morning."

"You made it fresh? Yourself?" She was as proud of that as she would have been if he'd won the Nobel prize.

He took out a squat pitcher of pale green glass and matching glasses. His kitchen was neat and small, with an old-fashioned two-burner gas range and a short, round-edged refrigerator. Lily thought the herbs potted on the windowsill were the sweetest things.

"I know you're competent." It hurt only a little that he could do so easily without her. "You always could do anything you set your mind on." She took the glass he offered and rattled the ice in it, wandered back into the living room. "You have such good taste."

He lifted a brow, noting the way she ran fingertips over the curve of his love seat, the surface of an antique commode. "I got it through osmosis."

"From Max, I know. Me, I have terrible taste. I just love tacky things."

"Whatever I got, I got from both of you." Taking her hand, he drew her down with him on the love seat. "What's this all about, Lily?"

"About? I told you, I just stopped by."

"You've got worry in your eyes."

"What woman doesn't?" But her eyes slid away from his.

He brushed his knuckles over her cheek. It was soft as a baby's still. "Let me help."

That was all it took to crumble the fragile wall she'd managed to build before knocking on his door. Tears blurred her vision as he took her glass, set it aside, then drew her into his arms.

"I'm being silly. I know I am, but I can't help it."

"It's all right." He kissed her hair, her temple, and waited.

"I don't think Max loves me anymore."

"What?" He'd meant to be sympathetic, comforting, support-ive. Instead he jerked back, laughing. "What a crock. Oh, shit," he muttered as she dissolved into helpless sobs. "Don't. Come on, Lily, don't cry." Women's tears remained the one thing he had no defense against. "I'm sorry I laughed. What makes you say such a crazy thing?"

"He—he—" It was the best she could do as she wailed against his shoulder.

Change tactics, Luke thought, and stroked her back. "Okay, okay, baby, don't you worry. I'm going to go right over and beat him up for you."

That brought a gurgle of laughter to mix with tears. She wasn't ashamed of the laughter, or the tears. She'd learned never to be ashamed of what felt good. "I just love him so much, you know? He's the best thing that ever happened to me. You don't even know what it was like before."

"No." He sobered, resting his cheek on her hair. "I don't."

"We were so poor. But that was okay, because my mama was wonderful. Even after Daddy died, she held everything together. She'd always see to it there was a little extra, for a movie, or an ice cream. I didn't know, not till later, that she took money from time to time from men. But she wasn't a whore." Lily lifted her tear-streaked face. "It was just a way to take care of her kids."

"Then you can be proud of her."

No mother, she mused, had ever had a wiser son. "I got married before. Max knows about it, but nobody else."

"Then nobody else'll know now, if that's what you want."

"It was a mistake, such an awful mistake. I was just seventeen, and he was so good-looking." She smiled a little again, knowing how silly it sounded. "I got pregnant, so we got married. He didn't like being poor, or having a wife who got sick in the mornings. He knocked me around some."

She felt Luke tense, felt a little curl of shame, and hurried on. "When he kept it up, I told him I was leaving. My mama'd raised me better than to be a punching bag. He told me my mama was a whore and so was I. He beat me good that time, and I lost the baby." She shuddered once, from old memory. "It messed me up inside so they said I wouldn't be able to have another."

"I'm sorry." And helpless, he thought. Completely helpless.

"I'm telling you so that you can understand where I came from. About that time my mother died. I think knowing how hard she'd worked so that I could have good things helped me get strong. So even when he came by and said how he was sorry and he'd never hit me again, I did leave him, and I got work at a carnival. Told fortunes, worked some of the booths. Small cons. That's how I met Max.

"He was magic even back then. Him and little Roxanne. I guess I loved them both so much right off I nearly burst with it. He'd lost his wife, and maybe a little bit of himself, too. And I wanted him, so I did what any smart woman would do and seduced him."

Luke held her closer. "I bet he put up a hell of a fight, didn't he?"

That made her laugh, and sigh. "He could have taken what I gave him and left it at that. But he didn't. He took me in. Treated me like a lady. He showed me the way it's supposed to be between a man and a woman. He made me family. Most of all he loved me—just for me, you know what I mean."

"Yeah, I do. But I don't think it was all one-sided, Lily. I figure you gave as good as you got."

"I always tried. Luke, I've loved him for almost twenty years now. I just don't think I could stand to lose him."

"What makes you think you could? He's nuts about you. That's one of the things that always made me feel the best, the way the two of you are with each other."

"He's pulling away." She took a couple of steadying breaths to strengthen her voice. "Oh, he's still sweet to me, when he remembers I'm around. Max would never hurt me, or anybody on purpose. But he spends hours and hours alone, going through books and notes and journals. That damn stone." She sniffled, digging into her pocket for a lace hankie. "At first I thought it was kind of interesting." She blew her nose. "I mean, suppose there really was such a thing? But he's gotten so caught up in it there's hardly room for anything else. And he's forgetting things." She worried her bottom lip and wrung her hands. "Just little things. Like appointments and meals. We were nearly late for a perform- ance last week because he forgot all about it. I know he's worried because he can't do some of the sleight of hand anymore, and it's affecting his . . . " She trailed off, wondering how it could be put delicately. "What I mean to say is that Max has always been, well, robust, sexually. But lately we hardly ever . . . you know."

He did, but devoutly wished he didn't. "Well, I, ah."

"But I don't just mean the performance, so to speak. The romance of it. He doesn't turn to me in the night anymore, or take my hand, or look at me that way." Another tear bloomed over and slid down her cheek.

"He's distracted, Lily. That's all. All that pressure to do another special, to write another book, to go back and tour Europe. Then the jobs. Max has always taken too much on himself in the plan- ning and execution." He wasn't going to mention that on their last job, he found Max standing in front of an open safe as if in a trance. Or that it had taken Max nearly five minutes to come back to himself and remember where he was and what he was doing.

"You know what I think," he said, taking the useless swatch of lace and drying Lily's eyes himself. "I think you're as stressed out as Max is—what with Rox's graduation, getting ready for this summer gig. And I—wait!" He grabbed her hand, turning it palm up. "I see a long sea voyage," he continued as Lily gave a watery chuckle. "Moonlit nights, salty breezes. Romance." He winked at her. "And great sex."

"You don't read palms."

"You taught me, didn't you?" He pressed his lips to her palm, then curled her fingers in his. "You're the most beautiful woman I've ever known, and Max loves you—nearly as much as I do. Hey, don't start dripping again, please."

"Okay." She blinked furiously at tears. "Okay."

"I want you to trust me when I say it's all going to be fine. We're going to get away for a little while, relax and drink champagne cocktails on the poop deck."

"Maybe he does just need to rest." Her shoulders shifted in one last sigh. "I wasn't going to dump on you, Luke, really I wasn't. But I'm awful glad you were here."

"Me too. You dump anytime you like."

"I'm done." Brushing tears from her lashes, she sat up. "Sure you don't want me to pack for you?"

"Already done. I'm as anxious to leave in the morning as you."

"I'm anxious all right." Recovered, she reached for her lemonade and sipped to ease her raw throat. "But I haven't packed a thing. Roxanne's got everything all neat and tidy, and in only two cases. I don't know how she does it."

"The brat's been an organization maniac since she was eight."

"Hmm." She sipped again, watching Luke. "She's not eight anymore. Wait till you see the cocktail dress she bought for the captain's party."

Luke merely shrugged and sat back. "How about you? Any sexy numbers in those bags?"

"A few."

Knowing just how much Lily enjoyed displaying her purchases, Luke played along. "Going to show me?"

"Maybe." She fluttered still damp lashes and turned to set her glass down again. Her glance passed over the letter he'd left on the table, then cut back to it and froze. "Cobb." Nerves fluttered in her throat. "Why are you writing to him?"

"I'm not." With a vicious inner curse, Luke scooped up the letter and jammed it in his pocket. "It's nothing."

"Don't lie to me." Her voice was suddenly brittle as glass. "Don't ever lie to me."

"I'm not. I said I wasn't writing to him."

"Then what's in the envelope?"

248

His face went blank and still. "It's nothing to do with you."

She said nothing for a moment, but a dozen varied emotions played across her tear-streaked face. "You're everything to do with me," she said quietly as she rose. "Or so I thought. I'd better go."

"Don't." He swore again, violently, and put a hand on her arm. "Damn it, Lily, don't look at me like that. I'm handling this the only way I know how. Leave it to me."

"Of course." She had a way, as certain women did, of being perfectly agreeable, and cutting a man off at the knees. "You'll be at the house by eight, won't you? We don't want to miss the flight."

"Damn it all to hell. I'm paying him, all right? I send him some money now and again and he leaves me alone." His eyes were fierce and deadly. "He leaves all of us alone."

With a nod, Lily sat again. "He's blackmailing you?"

"That's a polite term. A bloodless term." Furious with himself, Luke stalked to the window. "I can afford to be polite."

"Why?"

He only shook his head. Not to her, not to anyone would he speak of it. Not of what had been, nor the nightmares that plagued him a day or two after he found that plain white postcard in his mailbox.

"As long as you pay him, he'll never go away." Lily spoke quietly from just behind him. Gently, she laid a hand on his back. "He'll never leave you in peace."

"Maybe not. But he knows something I'm ashamed enough of that I'm willing to pay him to keep to himself." The tap dancers had gone off to other pastures, Luke thought. Pigeons fluttered in the park. "And he can insinuate a great deal more, twist lies with truth in such a way that I couldn't live with it. So it costs me a few thousand a pop for this kind of illusionary peace. It's worth it to me."

"Don't you know he can't hurt you anymore?"

"No." He turned back then, torment in every muscle. "I don't. Worse, I don't know who else he could hurt. I won't chance it, Lily. Not even for you."

"I won't ask you to. I will ask that you trust me enough to come to me. Always." She stood on tiptoe to kiss his cheek. "I know I'm silly, flighty—"

"Stop."

She only laughed. "Honey, I know just what I am. And I'm not sorry about it. I'm a middle-aged woman who wears too much makeup and who'll die without letting the first gray hair show. But I stand behind those I love. I've loved you for a long time. You send that check if you feel a need to. And if he asks for more than you can spare, you come to me. I've got my own put aside."

"Thanks." He cleared his throat. "But he doesn't squeeze too hard."

"There's one more thing I want you to remember. There's nothing you've done or could do I'd be ashamed of." She turned and began to gather her bags. "I'd better get on home. It's going to take me half the night to figure out what to pack. Oh, goodness." She pressed her hands to her cheeks. "I have to fix my face first. I can't go out in public with mascara all over." She dashed toward the bathroom, purse in tow. "Oh, Luke, you know you could come on home with me, spend the night in your old room. Might be easier getting things together in the morning."

It might at that, he mused, and dipped his hands into his pockets. It would be even better to go home, even if just for one night.

"Let me get my bags," he called out to her. "I'll drive you home in style."

Chapter Seventeen

THE ACCOMMODATIONS FOR THE ENTERTAINERS ABOARD THE *Yankee Princess* weren't quite as luxurious as Roxanne might have hoped. Because of their special guest-star status, they had been given outside cabins—slightly above water level.

The two-berth cabin was tiny enough that she was grateful she wouldn't be required to share its space over the next six weeks. Her practical nature tugged her away from the porthole to unpack the contents of her two suitcases. As a matter of habit, everything was neatly folded or hung in the stationary bureau and gnome-sized closet. She was romantic enough to want to hurry and be on deck when the whistle blew to signal castoff.

She took time to set out the antique bottles and jars she'd collected over the years, all carefully filled with perfumes and lotions. They'd been a bitch to pack against breakage, and she knew plastic would have been wiser. But seeing them there, all those pretty shapes and colors, made her smile. The extra weight and trouble had been worth it.

She checked herself in the mirror first, glad that her hair had grown back to past her shoulders after her rash decision two years before to crop it chin length. It, too, was a great deal of trouble, taking enormous amounts of time to dry and groom. But she was vain enough to consider the time and effort well spent.

Pleased that the piped-in music included a classical station, she touched up her makeup—a bit more bronze shadow on the lids, a whisper of extra blusher along the cheekbones. That wasn't vanity—precisely—she assured herself. Part of the job the Nouvelle troupe had taken on was to mix and mingle with the passengers, to make themselves companionable, presentable and pleasant.

It was little enough to pay for a six-week run on an elegant floating hotel.

Grabbing her roomy canvas bag, she headed out, and up. Boarding passengers were already roaming the narrow passageways, seeking their rooms or exploring. Piles of luggage were stacked in front of cabin doors. Larceny tugged gleefully at Roxanne's heart. It would be so pitifully simple to pluck a bit here, snatch a bit there. Like picking daisies, she mused, smiling at a round-bellied man in a baseball cap who inched by her.

There'd be time for fun and games, she reminded herself. Six long weeks' worth of time. But this afternoon she was on vacation. She turned at the top of the stairs and wound her way through the Lido Lounge, out to the deck at the stern, where eager passengers were sipping their complimentary cocktails, taking videos or simply leaning at the rail waiting to wave good-bye to the Manhattan skyline.

She took a hurricane glass filled with blush pink liquid from the tray of a waiter and, sipping the oversweet rum drink, sized up her fellow sailors.

At a guess, Roxanne gauged the mean age to be sixty-five. There were a few families with children, a sprinkling of honeymooners, but for the most part there were older couples, elderly singles and a scattering of aging gigolos on the prowl.

"Maybe we should call it the Geriatric Boat," Luke said close to her ear and nearly had her spilling the rum concoction.

"I think it's sweet."

"I didn't say it wasn't." Despite her barbed tone, he slipped a friendly arm around her shoulders. He'd decided if they were going to be in such relatively close quarters for the next few weeks, they should try to be civil. "Check this dude."

He'd bypassed the rum for a bottle of Beck's and gestured with it toward a dapper, silver-haired gentleman wearing a double-breasted navy blazer and natty white trousers. He already had a cluster of admiring female senior citizens around him. "Joe Smooth."

"Of the Palm Beach Smooths," she said, amused. "What do you want to bet he does a mean cha-cha?"

"Probably got a rumba or two in him. And there." He gestured again, using only an arched eyebrow to have Roxanne's gaze shifting. Near the portside rail was a big, frowsy blonde in a shocking-pink jogging suit. She had a camera and a pair of binoculars slung around her neck, and was busily lifting one then the other in between sips of her rum surprise. "Sally Tourist."

"Snob."

He only grinned. "Come on, you pick one."

She scanned the deck, then touched her tongue to her top lip. "Mmm. I'll take him. Tom Terrific."

Luke studied the ship's officer, bronzed and blond and gorgeous in his dress whites. His mood immediately soured. "If you go for that type."

"I do." Unable to resist, she heaved an exaggerated sigh. "Oh, I do. Look, there's Mouse." Roxanne gave a wide wave to bring him over. "What do you think?"

"It's great." His big, pale face was flushed with pleasure. Muscles bulged beneath the cropped sleeves of the flowered shirt Lily had picked for him. "They let me go down in the engine room. I gotta check the equipment for the show and all, but later, they said, I could go up on the bridge and everything."

"They got any women down there?" Luke asked.

"In the engine room?" Mouse grinned and shuffled. "Nah. 'Cept in pictures on the walls."

"Stick with me, pal. I'll find you some real ones."

"Leave him alone, you walking hormone." In defense of Mouse, Roxanne slipped a hand through his arm. "Listen." She squeezed as the ship blew two long blasts. "We're casting off."

"One deck up," Luke murmured when she began to crane her neck.

She looked up and saw them. Lily, looking festive in a flowing blue sundress, Max dashing in an off-white jacket and navy pants, and LeClerc, hovering like a shadow behind them.

"He's going to be fine." Luke took her hand, linking fingers.

"Of course he is." She shook away the seeds of doubt. "Let's go up. I want to get some pictures."

IT WASN'T GOING TO BE a walk on the beach. The first onboard staff meeting dispensed with any notion that the next six weeks would be a free ride. The Nouvelles would give a mini-performance that night to welcome the passengers on board, along with shortened acts from the other entertainers. A French chanteuse, a comedian who spiced up his monologues with juggling and the six-member song-and-dance group who made up the Moon-glades.

In addition to their act, they were asked to assist in daily activities from bingo to shore excursions. When it was discovered that Roxanne spoke fluent French, she was immediately dragooned to help the ship's two interpreters.

Rules were also dispensed. Being friendly and personable with the passengers was mandatory. Being intimate was not. Accepting tips was not permitted, drunkenness was frowned on. Meals were to be taken only after the passengers had dined. And, in the event of trouble at sea, all members of the crew and staff would man the lifeboats only after all passengers were safe.

There was some groaning from the more seasoned members of

the staff when weekly assignments were handed out. The cruise director, Jack, a youthful vet with ten years' experience on cruise ships, took it in stride. "If there's anything you need, just ask. And don't pay any attention to these gripers. Most of the extra work with the passengers is pure fun."

"So he says." A tall, slender blonde called Dori aimed a considering smile at Luke. "Let me know if you need any help getting adjusted." She smiled at Roxanne to include her in the invitation. "We've got a very shaky run-through rehearsal scheduled at three-thirty in the movie theater. That's on the Promenade Deck, aft."

"And first show's at eight," Jack finished. "Take some time to get familiar with the ship's layout."

ROXANNE WAS GIVEN A *Yankee Princess* T-shirt in fuchsia, a name tag to pin on and a pat on the back for luck. She toured the ship, rehearsed, then toured the ship some more, answering questions, smiling, wishing passengers a good voyage.

As afternoon slid toward evening, she managed to snag an apple and a few hunks of cheese from the buffet the passengers had decimated and smuggled them into the dressing cum storage room where she and Lily were to change for the first show.

"There's so many of them," Roxanne said over a bite of McIntosh. "And they want to know everything."

"Everyone's so nice and friendly." Lily avoided crashing into a cardboard jail cell and wriggled into costume. "Why, I met people from all over the country. It's really like being on the road again."

"Max likes it, doesn't he?"

"He loves it. He already loves it."

That was enough for Roxanne, even though she had to press a hand to her stomach as the ship rolled. "Do you think this is going to keep up?"

"What, honey?"

"The movement." She blew out a breath, setting the apple aside to reach for her costume.

"Oh, the ship? It kind of feels like being in a cradle, doesn't it? Nice and soothing."

"Yeah. Right." Roxanne swallowed hard.

She managed to get through the first show before the soothing cradle she was in had her dashing down to her cabin. She was just finished being sick when Luke walked in the tiny head.

"I locked the door," she said with all the dignity she could muster while sitting on the floor.

"I know. It took me nearly thirty seconds to open it."

"What I meant was, since I locked it, that probably meant I wanted to be alone."

"Mmm-hmm." He was busy running cool water on a washcloth. He helped her up and led her out to the bed. "Sit. Put this on the back of your neck."

He did it himself and drew a long, grateful sigh from her. "How'd you know I was sick?"

He flicked a hand over the emerald spangles of her dress. "Your face was the same color as your costume. Dead giveaway."

"I'm okay now." Or she hoped she was. "I'll get used to it." Her eyes were a little more than desperate when she lifted them to his. "Don't you think?"

"Sure you will." It was a rare thing to see Roxanne Nouvelle vulnerable—so rare he had to resist an urge to gather her close and make it all go away. "Take a couple of these." He held out two white pills.

"I don't suppose they're morphine."

"Sorry. Just Dramamine. Down them with a couple of sips of this ginger ale. There you go." As competent as a nurse, he turned the cloth over and pressed the cooler side to her neck again. "If it doesn't let up, the ship's doctor'll take care of it."

"Stupid." More annoyed than embarrassed, she sipped more ginger ale and prayed for it to settle. "I could ride everything in the carnival and never feel a thing. One night on a boat and I'm whipped."

"It'll pass." Since her color was nearly normal again, he judged it already was passing. "If you're feeling shaky, we can cover for you in the second show."

"No way." She rose, willing her legs and her system to steady. "A Nouvelle never misses a cue. Give me a minute." She retreated to the bathroom to rinse out her mouth and check her makeup. "I guess I owe you one," she said when she came out again.

"Babe, you owe me a lot more than one. Ready?"

"Sure, I'm ready." She opened the door, stepped out. "Luke, we don't have to mention this, do we?"

He lifted his brows. "Mention what?"

"Okay." She smiled at him. "I owe you two."

SINCE THERE WAS NO RECURRENCE of seasickness over the next day or two, Roxanne was forced to consider that the motion of the boat had only been a contributing factor to the whole that had been made up of stress, rum on a nearly empty stomach and nerves. It wasn't a particularly pleasant admission for a woman who had always prided herself on being able to handle anything that came her way. Her days were too full, however, to allow her to dwell on it.

Jack had been right, she decided. The majority of the work required was pure fun. She enjoyed the passengers, and the games and events scattered through the daily schedule designed to keep them entertained. The rest of her family seemed to be getting into the spirit of things as well. Max and Lily judged a dance contest, Mouse spent most of his spare time haunting the engine room and crew quarters and LeClerc found a trio of poker buddies.

The stress she hadn't been aware of carrying on board with her began to dissipate with each passing hour. It might have faded completely if Roxanne hadn't turned toward the stairway on the Laguna Deck and seen Max standing there, looking lost.

"Daddy?" He didn't respond, so she stepped closer and touched his arm. "Daddy?"

He jolted, and she saw the panic streak into his eyes. In that instant, her blood froze. She saw more in his eyes than panic; she saw total confusion. He didn't know her. He was staring into her face and he didn't know her.

"Daddy," she said again, unable to keep a tremor from her voice. "Are you all right?"

He blinked, a muscle working furiously in his jaw. Like a cloud slowly lifting, the confusion faded from his eyes to reveal annoyance. "Of course I'm all right. Why wouldn't I be?"

"Well, I thought you—" She fought a smile onto her face. "I guess you're turned around. I keep doing that."

"I know exactly where I'm going." Max felt the pulse throbbing at the base of his neck. He could almost hear it. He hadn't known. For a moment, he hadn't been able to remember where he was or what he'd been doing. Stark fear had him snapping at his daughter. "I don't need anyone snooping around after me. And I don't appreciate being nagged about my every move."

"I'm sorry." The color ebbed from her cheeks. "I was just going up to your cabin." There was a book tucked under his arm, she noted. A tattered, antique book on alchemy. "I certainly didn't mean to nag." Cloaked in injured pride, she moved stiffly around him.

A wave of shame had him reaching out. "I apologize. My mind was elsewhere."

She merely shrugged, a distinctly female gesture that could make any man grovel.

He took out his key to open his stateroom door. Mouse, LeClerc and Luke were already waiting.

"All right, my pets." Max pulled out the single chair that stood by the bureau, and sat. "Time to get down to business."

"Lily isn't here yet," Luke pointed out, concerned when Max looked blankly around the room.

"Ah, well."

Roxanne plunged into the uncomfortable silence. "They've already got at least a dozen passengers signed up for the talent show at the end of the week. It should be a kick."

"How much do you want to bet someone does 'Moon River'?" Luke asked.

Roxanne was nervously rubbing her hands together, but she smiled. "No bet. I heard Mrs. Steiner tap dances. Maybe—" She paused, relieved when Lily hurried in.

"Sorry I'm late." She was prettily flushed and weighed down with purse and camera. "They were having an ice-carving demonstration out by the pool, and I got caught up. He made the most incredible peacock." She smiled at Max, who only gestured absently.

"All right then, what have we got?"

LeClerc linked his hands behind his back. "DiMato in cabin seven sixty-seven. Diamond earrings—probably two-carat, Rolex watch and a five- to six-carat sapphire pendant."

"The DiMatos are the ones celebrating their fiftieth wedding anniversary," Roxanne put in, plucking one of the grapes from the fruit basket on the bureau. "The pendant was her anniversary present. They're awfully sweet together."

Max smiled, understanding. "Something else then?"

"Well, Mrs. Gullager in six twenty," Roxanne offered. "A ruby set, cuff bracelet, necklace, earrings. Looks heirloom."

"Oh, she's the dearest thing." Lily sent Roxanne a pleading look. "I had tea with her the other day. She lives in Roanoke, Virginia, with her two cats."

"Another contender?" Max gestured to the room at large.

"There's Harvey Wallace in four thirty-six." Luke shrugged. "Diamond cuff links, stick pin, another Rolex. But ... Shit, he's such a funny old guy."

"He's nice," Mouse put in. "He told me all about this De Soto he rebuilt in 1962."

"Jamisons," LeClerc said between his teeth. "Cabin seven ten. Diamond ring, square cut, approximately five carats. Ruby ring, possibly Burmese, same carat weight. Antique emerald brooch—"

"Nancy and John Jamison?" Max interrupted. "I had a delightful time playing bridge with them on the Promenade Deck just yesterday. He's in food processing and she owns a bookstore in Corpus Christi."

"*Bon Dieu*," LeClerc muttered.

"We're a sentimental lot, aren't we?" Roxanne patted LeClerc's hand. "And an embarrassment to you, I'm sure." After choosing another grape, she folded her legs under her. "I don't see how we can steal from people we're all but living with day in and day out. Especially when we like them so much."

Max steepled his hands, tapped his fingers against his chin. "You're quite right, Roxanne. Once an emotional attachment's made, the fun goes out of it." He scanned the room, gauging faces. "Are we agreed then? No marks this week?"

He got a nod from everyone but LeClerc, who only ground his teeth.

"Cheer up." Luke picked up Max's remaining mineral water and toasted. "We've got the best part of six weeks. Someone's bound to come on board we don't like."

"Then we're adjourned."

"Have you got a minute?" Luke asked Max as everyone made to leave.

"Of course."

Luke waited until they were alone, but still took the precaution of keeping his voice low. "Why the hell are you doing this to Lily?"

Max's mouth fell open. "I beg your pardon?"

"Damn it, Max, you're breaking her heart."

"That's absurd." Highly insulted, Max rose from the chair to pick up his book. "Where did you get such a ridiculous notion?"

"From Lily." Too angry for respect, Luke snatched the book away and tossed it onto the bed. "She came to see me the day before we left for New York. Damn you, you made her cry."

"I? I?" Shaken by the thought, Max sat again. "How?"

"Neglect," Luke tossed out. "Disinterest. You're so fucking obsessed with some magical stone, you can't see what's happening in front of your face. She doesn't think you love her anymore. And after seeing the way you behaved toward her over these last couple of days, I understand just how she got the idea in her head."

Very pale, very still, Max stared at Luke. "That is a completely asinine notion. She has no reason to doubt my feelings."

"Really?" Luke sat on the edge of the bed, leaned forward. "When's the last time you bothered to tell her what they are? Have you sat in the moonlight with her and listened to the sea? You know how much she counts on the little things, but have you stirred yourself to give any of them to her? Have you used this bed for anything but sleeping?"

"You go too far." Max stiffened like a poker. "Much too far."

"The hell I do. I'm not going to stand by and see that hurt look in her eyes. She'd crawl over glass for you, and you can't even bother to give her ten minutes of your valuable time."

"You're wrong." Max stared down at his clenched fist. "And if Lily feels as you say, she's quite mistaken. I love her. I've always loved her."

"Could have fooled me. You didn't even look at her when she walked in here."

"That was business," he began, then cut himself off. He'd always prided himself on honesty, in his own way. "Perhaps I've been a bit distracted lately, and more than a little self-involved." He lifted his gaze from his aching hands. "I would never hurt her. I'd cut out my own heart before I'd hurt her."

"Tell her." Luke turned for the door. "Not me."

"Wait." Max pressed his fingers to his eyes. If he'd made a mistake, he'd do whatever was necessary to correct it. The faintest smile touched his lips. And he'd correct it in style. "I need a favor."

The fact that Luke hesitated showed Max just how deep the temper went. And how deep his own sins. "What?"

"First, I'd like to keep this conversation between us. Second, after the last performance tonight, I'd appreciate it if you'd detain Lily, keep her away from the cabin for about thirty minutes. Then I'll need you to be certain she comes directly here."

"All right."

"Luke?"

He had his hand on the door, but paused and glanced back. "Yeah?"

"Thank you. Now and again a man needs someone to make him face his shortcomings, and his blessings. You've done both."

"Just make it up to her."

"Oh, I will." Max smiled then, fully. "That, at the very least, I can promise."

"WE DONE GOOD." Roxanne dropped heavily into a chair in the corner of the disco. The second performance of the evening had gone as successfully as the first.

"We knocked them dead." Luke sat down, stretched out his legs. "Of course, with a crowd this age, that's not too hard."

Roxanne snickered. "Don't be gruesome. Be useful and go get me and Lily drinks."

"Oh, I think I should skip it." Lily looked around the hotly lit room for a glimpse of Max. "You young people should enjoy yourselves."

"No way." Luke grabbed her hand. "You're not ducking out on me without a dance." He pulled her laughing out on the floor where Michael Jackson was telling everyone to beat it.

"That your competition?" Dori plopped down on Luke's vacated chair.

"She's a tough act to follow."

"She's pretty great," Dori agreed and snagged a waitress's attention. "I mean besides being a real sweetheart, just look at that body. Want a drink?"

"Glass of white wine," Roxanne decided. "A pink lady for Lily and a Beck's for Luke."

"Make it two Beck's," Dori said, then leaned over the table again. The music was loud, but not oppressive. There were a smattering of passengers on the dance floor gyrating to Jackson's driving rhythm.

When their drinks were served, she said, "First round's on me. I really like working cruise ships. Most people come on with a mind-set to have fun. Makes it easier. And you get to meet so many different types. Speaking of which." She took a deep sip of beer. "What's the story on him?"

Roxanne glanced over to where Luke was twirling Lily under his arm. "Story?"

"I mean, he's gorgeous, dynamic, single. Straight, right?"

Roxanne chuckled. "Definitely heterosexual."

"So how come you haven't jumped on it?"

Roxanne choked on her wine. "Jumped? Jumped on it?"

"Roxanne, he's a mouth waterer." To prove her point, Dori traced her tongue around her lips. "I'd take the leap myself except I don't like to swim in someone else's pool."

After a deep breath, Roxanne shook her head. "You lost me, Dori."

"The two of you. It's so obvious."

"Oh? What's obvious?"

"There's enough sexual friction between you to set the ship on fire."

Since the color was fluctuating in her cheeks, Roxanne hoped it could be blamed on the flashing lights of the disco. "You're reading it wrong."

"Oh yeah?" Dori looked back at Luke, drank, then swiveled back to Roxanne. "Are you saying you don't want him?"

"No. I mean, yes. I mean ..." She wasn't used to being flustered. "What I mean is things aren't that way with us."

"Because you don't want them to be?"

"Because . . . because they aren't."

"Uh-huh. Well, I don't like to poke my nose in."

Roxanne had to laugh. "Oh, I could see that right off."

"Anyway." Dori grinned engagingly. "If I were to poke it in, I'd offer this simple, time-honored advice. Intrigue, confuse, seduce. And if that doesn't work, jump his bones. Got to go."

"Yeah. See you." Roxanne stared into her wine, drawing lines down the outside of the glass with her fingers. Her thoughts were such that she jolted when Luke and Lily sat down again.

"Oh, that was fun." Nearly out of breath, Lily reached for her drink.

"Finish that off, and we'll do it again."

"Not on your life." She waved a hand. "Go do it with Roxy."

Roxanne choked again and blushed scarlet.

"Take it easy." Luke thumped her on the back. "Want to dance, Rox?"

"No. Ah, maybe later." Her whole body was tingling. Her heart picked up the rhythm of the bass and thudded against her ribs. Sexual friction? Was that what this was? If so, it was deadly. She sipped again, more cautiously. Intrigue. All right, she'd give it a shot. "I liked watching the two of you out there." She touched a hand lightly to the back of Luke's. "You've got some good moves, Callahan."

He stared at her. What was that gleam in her eye? In another woman, he would have taken it as an invitation. In Roxanne, he wondered where she'd bite or scratch first. "Thanks." He picked up his beer and casually checked his watch.

"Got a late date?" Roxanne purred.

"What? No."

Now, wasn't this interesting? Lily mused. A little cat and mouse, with Roxanne in the role of cat. "You two should take a nice stroll out on deck. It's gorgeous tonight."

"Good idea. Why don't we all do that?" Luke grabbed Lily's

hand and watched Roxanne warily. He had ten more minutes to detain Lily, then he thought it might be wise to run for his life.

"No, no, I'm a little tired." Lily feigned a huge yawn. "I'll just go down and turn in."

"You haven't finished your drink." Luke sat again, kept his hand firmly on Lily's. "And I've been meaning to ask you . . . " What? What? "Ah, if you think it's going to rain tomorrow in Sydney?"

"Australia?" Lily said, big-eyed.

"No, Nova Scotia. We're docking there in the morning. I've, ah, got a couple hours off, and thought I'd go into town and look around."

Why, he's nervous, Roxanne realized, and found it oddly endearing. And exciting. "So do I," she murmured. "Want company?"

"Well . . . "

"I really am tired." Lily yawned again and shook her hand free of Luke's. "Enjoy yourselves."

Shit, Luke thought. He had to hope it was close enough. "I'm a little tired myself." Luke stood as Lily walked off. And made a small, gagging sound when Roxanne rose as well, her body bumping against his.

"A walk on deck would help you sleep better." She tilted her head back so that they were eye to eye and nearly mouth to mouth. He could feel his lips tingle.

"Nope." He thought of all the things he'd like to do with her, to her, in the salt-sprayed moonlight. "I can guarantee it wouldn't. You should turn in, too."

"I don't think so." She trailed a finger down his arm. "I imagine there's someone around who'd like to dance, or walk." She brushed her lips lightly over his. "Good night, Callahan."

"Yeah." He watched her stroll away, then lean over a table where a few of the entertainers were having drinks. He doubted he'd sleep a wink.

*

LILY UNLOCKED THE DOOR of her cabin, smiling at the image of Roxanne and Luke walking hand in hand in the moonlight. She'd waited a long time to see her two children find each other. Maybe tonight, she thought, and opened the door to music, candlelight and roses.

"Oh." She stood there, silhouetted by the backlight from the passageway. Max stepped away from the table where a bottle of champagne was open and waiting. He crossed to her, offering a single pink rose.

He said nothing, only took her hand and brought it to his lips as he eased the door shut behind her. Locked it.

"Oh, Max."

"I hope it's not too late for a small bon voyage celebration."

"No." She pressed her lips together to hold back tears. "It's not too late. It's never too late."

Cupping her face in his hand, he tilted her head back. "My heart," he murmured. His lips were soft and strong against hers. Then the kiss deepened, lengthened as their tongues met in a slow, familiar dance.

When he drew her back, the old twinkle she adored was in his eyes. "Perhaps I could ask one small favor."

"You know you can."

"That crimson negligee you packed? Would you put it on while I pour the wine?"

Chapter Eighteen

HE'D FINALLY FIGURED IT OUT. IT TOOK LUKE A COUPLE OF days, and an equal amount of uncomfortably restless nights, but he finally got a handle on it.

She was trying to drive him crazy.

It was the only reasonable explanation for Roxanne's behavior. It wasn't that she smiled at him so often. It was the *way* she smiled. With that oddly female light in her eyes that was invitation, challenge and amusement melded together. He couldn't even blame the fact that she'd cornered him into one of the ballroom dancing demonstrations—under the guise of staff participation—so that he'd had to hold her in his arms, breathing in the scent of her hair while her hips twitched in a rumba under his hand.

It wasn't possible to point to the fact that she'd run into him that afternoon in Quebec City after completing her role as interpreter on one of the shore excursions—or that she'd made him enjoy being hauled from shop to shop buying gifts and souvenirs, eating ice cream and weaving through crowds of tourists on the long narrow streets to listen to a musician play the concertina.

To be fair, he couldn't blame the fact that she made certain a day didn't pass without giving him one of those light, butterfly kisses that stirred the juices the way a crust of bread would heighten the hunger of a starving man.

No, he couldn't blame any one of those things—until he put them all together with the less tangible but equally effective vibrations she seemed to emit whenever he was within five feet of her.

He grumbled to himself all the way up the outside stairway from the Lido Deck to Promenade, from Promenade to Royal. He wasn't some freaking messenger boy, and he'd nearly told Jack as much. But it would have been hard to explain why he objected so strenuously to asking Roxanne if she'd help greet passengers in the reception line for the captain's farewell party.

They were still docked in Quebec City. From the high rail he could see the pretty hills, the steep streets, the elegance of the towering Chateau Frontenac. It had been fun to wander through the old town with her, hearing her laugh, watching her eyes light up.

He didn't know how he was going to get through the next five weeks being so goddamn brotherly.

He turned. Most of the deck chairs were empty. Because they wouldn't sail until seven that evening, many of the passengers would stay ashore until deadline. Those who preferred relaxing on board were two decks below, indulging in the delicate pastries being served at tea.

But Roxanne was here, stretched out on a deck chair, mirrored sunglasses shading her eyes, a book in her hands, and an unbearably tiny bikini covering no more than was required by law.

Luke swore viciously under his breath before crossing to her.

She knew he was there, had known from the moment he reached the top of the stairs and turned toward the rail. She'd been staring at the same page in her novel for five full minutes, and was grateful for the time to whip her heart rate under control.

Leisurely she turned the page then reached out for the luke-warm soft drink on the table beside her.

"You like to live dangerously."

She glanced up, arched a brow, then tipped her glasses down just far enough to look over the tops. "Do I?"

"A redhead sitting in the sun's just asking to burn." In truth her skin had neither burned nor tanned. It had simply bloomed, gorgeously, like a ripening peach.

"I don't stay out long." She smiled and pushed her glasses back into place. A healthy ripple of lust swam through her. "And I'm just slathered all over with lotion." Very slowly, she skimmed a fingertip up a glistening thigh. "Did you give Lily the lace fan you bought her?"

"Yeah." To make certain they behaved, Luke tucked his itchy hands in his pockets. "You were right. She was crazy about it."

"See? You only have to trust me."

She shifted, only a little, but he was aware of every muscle, every detail. The tiny hoops in her ears, the glint of the delicate gold chain with its slim amethyst crystal around her neck, the way her hair curled riotously where she tied it on top of her head, the erotic scent of the lotion she'd slicked over her skin.

Murder was too good for her.

"Jack wanted to know if you could do the reception line tonight. One of the girls is fighting off a virus."

"Oh, I think I could manage that." She slid her foot up the chair and lazily scratched her knee. "Want a sip?" She offered the watered-down Coke. "You look hot."

"I'm fine." Or he would be once he managed to move the feet that seemed nailed to the deck by her chair. "Shouldn't you go in and get ready?"

"I've got plenty of time. Do me a favor?" She stretched once, catlike, before she picked up the bottle of lotion and tossed it to him. "Do my back, okay?"

"Your back?"

"Um-hmm." Shifting again, she lowered the back of the chair, rolled over and snuggled down. "I can't reach it."

He was surprised the lotion didn't geyser out the top as he squeezed the bottle so tightly. "Your back looks fine."

"Be a pal." After pillowing her head on her hands, she sighed like a woman relaxed. But behind the mirrored lenses her eyes were open and watchful. "It wouldn't do for me to ask one of the deckhands."

That did it. Setting his teeth, he crouched down and squeezed lotion on her shoulder blades. She sighed again, her lips curving.

"Feels good," she murmured. "Warm."

"Having the bottle in the sun could account for it." He began to spread the lotion with his fingertips, objectively, he thought. After all, it was only a back. Skin and bone. Soft, satiny skin. Long, delicate bones. She moved sinuously under his hands, and he bit back a moan.

Her toes were curling. His hands were magic on her slippery skin, conjuring up images, lighting fires, fogging the brain. Still, Luke wasn't the only one who knew about image and control. Her voice might have been husky when she spoke, but Roxanne thought that could be attributed to a state of relaxation as easily as arousal.

"You have to unhook the top."

The hands circling her back paused. Her glasses tossed back the reflection of his stunned face. "Excuse me?"

"The top," she repeated. "Unhook it or I'll get a line."

"Right." No big deal, he told himself, but his fingers reached and pulled back from the simple hook twice before he was satisfied with his willpower.

Now Roxanne did close her eyes, the better to absorb each rippling sensation. "Mmmm. You could get a job belowdecks with Inga."

"Inga?" Odd, he didn't think he'd ever noticed how subtly her back tapered down to her waist.

"The masseuse. I had a thirty-minute session last night, but she's got nothing on you, Callahan. Daddy's always admired your hands, you know?" Her chuckle was shaky as he trailed his fingers down to the small of her back. If she didn't laugh, she'd groan. "For entirely different reasons, of course. As for me, I . . ." She trailed off on a throaty sigh when he smoothed his palms down her rib cage.

Good God, her bones were melting under his hands. It was an impossibly erotic sensation to have her grow warmer, more fluid with each stroke. The nape of her neck tempted him desperately. His mouth watered at the thought of pressing his lips just there, tasting that lotion-slicked skin and feeling her tremble. It took little imagination to conjure a fantasy of her rolling over, that ridiculous band of emerald falling away as she let him explore those sleek curves. She'd groan for him, reach for him, open for him.

And then, at last then . . .

It was the sound of his own unsteady breathing that pulled him back. His hands were poised on the sides of her breasts, his fingers on the point of sliding beneath to claim that silky fullness.

She was trembling, as obviously and completely aroused as he.

They were on an open deck, he thought in disgust. In full sunlight. Worse, much worse, they were as closely related as two people could be without sharing blood.

He snatched his hands back, capped the bottle after two fumbling attempts. "That'll do it."

Her system shuddered with the broken promise of fulfillment. Roxanne lifted her head, bringing one hand up automatically to hold the loosened top in place, using the other to lower her glasses again. This time the eyes behind them were dark and heavy. "Will it?"

Furious with the ease with which she could undermine his willpower, he clamped tense fingers on her jaw. "I've just seen to it you won't get burned, Rox. Do us both a favor, and keep your distance from the heat."

She forced her lips into a smile. "Which one of us are you afraid for, Callahan?"

271

Because he didn't know the answer, he pulled back and stood. "Don't push your luck, Roxy."

But she intended to push it, she thought when he strode across the deck and down the iron stairs. She intended to push until it broke, one way or the other.

"Who you mad at, *loup*?"

"No one." Luke stood with LeClerc outside the casino, watching the dancers sway on the postage-stamp dance floor in the Monte Carlo Lounge. The quartet of Polish musicians was playing "Night and Day" with a touch of bebop.

"So why you scowl?" LeClerc yanked at the detested tie he was obliged to wear on this last formal night of the first cruise. "That look in your eye makes the menfolk back away, and the women sigh and shiver."

Despite his mood, Luke's lips twitched. "Maybe that's how I like it. Where's that silver-haired French fox you've been sniffing around?"

"Marie-Clair. She'll be along." LeClerc chewed on his pipe while Luke lit a cigar. "A handsome woman, that. Meat on the bone and fire in the belly." He grinned, making the pipe stem rattle against his teeth. "A rich widow is a gift from God to a man. She has jewelry. Ah." He kissed his fingers and sighed. "Last night, I held her opal pendant in my hand. Ten carats, *mon ami*, perhaps twelve, circled by a dozen ten-point diamonds. But you and the rest, you make me feel guilty for even thinking about taking it from her. So tomorrow, I will bid her *adieu*, and she will go home to Montreal with her opal and her diamonds, with a ruby ring of exquisite proportion, and numerous other treasures that break the heart. Only her virtue will I have stolen."

Amused, Luke laid a hand on LeClerc's shoulder. "Sometimes, *mon ami*, that is enough." He glanced toward the forward entrance of the lounge.

Roxanne stood with her hand being kissed by the ship's first officer. The fact that the man was tall and bronzed and Greek was bad enough. Insult was added to injury by the sound of Roxanne's low laughter.

Her dress was a short, shimmery swath of aquamarine. Without benefit of straps, it left Roxanne's arms and shoulders bare. It dispensed with a back altogether. What little material there was draped low at the hips and stopped teasingly at mid-thigh.

The skin she'd warmed in the sun that afternoon glowed pale gold against the dreamy blue. She caught up her hair in a jeweled pin so that its mass tempted a man to free it and watch it spill fire.

"She's not going to get away with it."

"Eh?"

"I know what she's up to," Luke said under his breath. "And it's not going to work." He stalked off to the bar to indulge in a single whiskey. LeClerc stayed where he was and chuckled.

"It's already worked, *mon cher loup*. The wolf is trapped by the vixen."

Two hours later, Roxanne stood in the shadows behind the stage awaiting her first cue. The show on the last night of the cruise involved all the entertainers. For their part, the Nouvelles intended to leave them gasping.

Max and Lily were cashing in by leading off with one of their variations on the Divided Woman. The moment Lily was put back together for bows, Luke dashed out to keep the crowd warm with patter and pickpocket routines.

While explaining the escape he planned with handcuffs and a locked trunk, he called for two volunteers from the audience, then proceeded to steal them blind, to the delight of the onlookers.

A shake of hands, and he dangled the first man's watch behind his head, while continuing to distract his two baffled volunteers with the handcuffs he offered for examination. He lifted wallets, penknives and pocket change from under their noses.

"Now, once they're locked on, I'll have thirty seconds. Harry?" He smiled at the short, bespectacled man beside him. "I can call you Harry?"

"Sure."

"Well, Harry, I'm going to want you to time me. Got a second hand on your watch?"

"Oh, yeah." All cooperation, Harry turned his wrist and frowned at his bare wrist.

"He's really good, isn't he?" Dori peeked over Roxanne's shoulder.

Luke finished up the routine, making both men grin sheepishly as he passed back their belongings. The orchestra struck up a lively tune, indicating the finish. "You were great. You can relax now. Take it easy." He winked, handing Harry the tie he'd removed from the man's neck. Then he made a business out of brushing down Harry's shirt, fussing with his jacket, tugging the sleeves.

"What's he doing? Playing valet?" Dori demanded.

"Just watch."

Luke tugged and smoothed and plucked, then stuck out his hand again for a last hearty shake. As Harry turned to walk off-stage, Luke grasped the back of his shirt collar. A flick of the wrist and he held Harry's baby-blue Arrow while the man goggled down at his bare chest showing beneath his suit jacket.

"Holy cow! How'd he do that? How'd he get the arms out of the jacket?"

Roxanne laughed, as she did every time she watched Luke pull off that particular trick. "Sorry, trade secret." Roxanne grinned as she left to make her entrance.

She was working with Luke at this point, flying through a fast-moving sleight-of-hand duel from either side of the stage. Her costume mirrored his as well, a tailored tux with spangled lapels. Precision timing was as essential as dexterity. Objects appeared and disappeared out of their hands, multiplied and changed color and size.

To cap off the act, Luke made good on his promise of the trunk escape, cajoling what appeared to be reluctant assistance from Roxanne.

"Come on, Roxy, don't embarrass me in front of all these nice people."

"Do it yourself, Callahan. I know what happened last time."

Luke turned toward the audience and spread his hands. "So she vanished for a couple of hours. I got her back eventually."

"No."

"Give me a break." She shook her head again, and he sighed theatrically. "Okay, just hold up the curtain for me then."

She studied him through narrowed, suspicious eyes. "You just want me to hold up the curtain."

"Yeah."

"No funny business?"

"Absolutely not." He turned to the side with an exaggerated wink.

"Okay. I'll do it, but only because the audience is so great. Tell you what, I'll even do the cuffs for you."

She dangled them, making the audience howl with laughter as Luke opened his eyes wide and patted his pockets.

"Pretty slick, Roxanne."

"I've got plenty of tricks up my sleeves. Assume the position, Callahan."

The music bounced out again as he offered his wrists. With big, exaggerated moves, Roxanne clamped the cuffs, locked them and pulled out a chain to wrap around his hands for good measure. She then turned the trunk in a circle, opening the lid so everyone could see it had four sides and a bottom. Luke climbed in and, taking advantage of his imprisoned hands, she bent to give him a hard kiss.

"For luck." Then she shoved his head down and lowered the top. She fastened the bolts, taking a key from her pocket to lock

275

each one. Using a four-sided white curtain, she stood on the lid, letting the material drop until it had covered everything from her chin down.

"On the count of three," she called out. "One. Two."

Her head disappeared and Luke's popped up. "Three."

The audience erupted with applause, continuing to thunder it out after Luke dropped the curtain. He wore a white tux now, spangled with silver. He took his bow with a flourish before glancing absently over his shoulder. Banging sounded from inside the box.

"Whoops. Forgot something." He snapped his fingers and revealed a key. After using it to unlock the trunk, he pushed the bolts back and threw up the lid.

"Cute, Callahan. Real cute."

He only grinned, reaching down and lifting Roxanne out of the trunk into his arms. She, too, wore a white tuxedo, and now her hands were cuffed and chained. He took a final bow with her in his arms, then carried her offstage.

"Got it?" he murmured.

"Almost. Now."

He turned back toward the applause. He still carried her, only now her hands were free and his were cuffed.

"You could have been a couple seconds faster," he complained when he set her down in front of her dressing room. "You were a beat behind all during the sleight of hand."

"No, you were a beat ahead." She smiled because she'd felt how hard his heart had been thumping when he'd carried her offstage. "Want to fight, Callahan?"

"No. Just work on your damn timing."

"I've got it down," she murmured when he turned away.

SHE CERTAINLY HOPED she did. God knew she was nervous as a cat, but it was now or never. For the fifth time, she checked out her appearance in the mirror. Her hair was artfully tousled, her face just touched with the most subtle of cosmetics. The long robe of ivory silk clung lovingly to each curve. She spritzed some scent into the air, then walked through the cloud of fragrance. With her mind made up, she kept walking out her cabin door, down the passageway and across the hall to Luke's.

He'd stripped down to gray sweatpants and was trying to ease his mind toward sleep by working out the bugs in a new escape.

He only grunted when he heard the knock on the door. His absent glance up as the door opened turned into a gape when he saw Roxanne.

"What? What? Is something wrong?"

"I don't think so." She leaned back against the door. It wasn't a provocative move as much as one designed to give her legs a chance to stop shaking. She turned the lock. "I'm working on my timing," she said as she crossed the room. He rose, braced to ward her off. She had only to lay her palm against the bare skin of his chest to break through the guard and make him quiver.

"You were right." She spread her fingers wide over the thud of his heart. The sensation made her bold, reckless, needy. "About my timing? This is something I should have moved on a long time ago."

He could feel his nerves grind and scream like crashing gears. She smelled like sin. "I'm busy, Roxanne, and it's too late for riddles."

"You already have the answer to this one." With a low, careless laugh, she skimmed her hands up his chest to his shoulders. The muscles there were bunched tight. "What do you get when you put a man and a woman together alone, at night, in a small room?"

"I said—" But she moved quickly, and covered his mouth with hers. There was little he could do about the response that leaped into his system, the way a tiger leaps through the open doors of a cage. But he could keep it from going any further. He prayed to God he could.

"There." She brushed her lips over his once, twice, before drawing back just enough to smile into his eyes. "I knew you had the answer."

It cost him dearly, but he let his hands fall away and side-stepped. "Game's over. Now get lost. I've got work to do."

The hurt snuck through, fast as a stiletto, and pierced. Okay, she thought, she might bleed, but she wasn't backing down without a fight. She was at the seduction stage of Dori's advice. Damned if she'd let him see how terrified she was.

"That didn't work very well when I was twelve." She stepped closer, out of the light, into the shadows, effectively maneuvering him into the corner. "It doesn't work at all now. You watch me." The curve of her lips was witchlike, powerful in its confidence. She stepped closer yet so that his hands shot out to take her arms and prevent her body from brushing dangerously against his. "I can feel you watch me when I'm across a room. I can almost hear what you're thinking when you do." Her eyes were like dark, deep seas, and he was already drowning. When she spoke, her voice misted over him like fog. "You wonder what it would be like between us." She cupped a hand on his chin, trailing those long fingers down his jaw. Everything he felt, everything he wanted, careened from his brain to thunder in the blood. "So do I. You wonder what it would feel like to have me, to do all those secret things you've wanted to do. And so do I."

He had to fight every breath into his lungs. Each gulp he took carried the scent of her into his system until he thought he'd explode. If this was seduction, he'd never experienced it before, never imagined she could wrap the hot chains of it so expertly around him. Trapped, was all he could think. He was trapped in a cage of unspeakable needs and the only door out was his own draining will.

The lamplight shimmered in her hair. Before he could think, he'd lifted a hand and had taken a fistful of flame.

"You don't know what I want to do. If you did, you'd run screaming."

Her body leaned forward with a longing much stronger than fear. "I'm not running. I'm not afraid."

"You haven't the sense to be." But he did. He released her hair and shoved her away in one jerky movement. "I'm not one of your trusty college boys, Rox. I wouldn't be polite and make promises and tell you what you think you want to hear. I've got where I came from inside me, and it's staying there, whatever shows on the outside." She saw a flare in his eyes—self-disgust, regret, anger—she couldn't be sure. Then it was gone. "So be a good girl and run along."

She felt the prickle of tears at the back of her throat, but her head remained high, her eyes dry. "I've never been a good girl. And I'm not going anywhere."

He sighed. There was such amused exasperation in it, she winced. "Roxy, you're putting me in the position where I have to hurt your feelings." With legs that felt like brittle glass, he walked over and patted her head. A slap, he knew, would have been less insulting. "I know you worked yourself up to try out this big seduction scene. And I'm flattered, really, that you've got this crush on me."

"Crush?" she managed when she found her voice. He could see by the daggers in her eyes he'd pressed the right button.

"It's sweet, and I appreciate it, but I'm just not interested. You're not my type, babe." He leaned casually against the dresser. "You're pretty, and I'm not going to pretend that I haven't had a couple of interesting fantasies over the years where you've been costar, but let's get real."

"You . . . " The stab of rejection nearly brought her to her knees. "You're saying you don't want me."

"That's as clear as it gets." He plucked a cigar off the dresser. "I don't want you, Roxanne."

She would have believed him. His voice was so mild, so insultingly apologetic and understanding. There was a light of amusement in his eyes that sliced like a blade and the faintest of smiles on his lips. She would have believed him. But she saw that his hands were clenched into fists so tight the knuckles were white. He'd already mangled the cigar.

She kept her eyes cast down a moment, knowing she needed that long to put out the gleam of triumph in them. "Well, all right, Luke. I'll only ask one thing."

He took one measured breath, tasted relief. "Don't worry, Rox, I won't mention this to anyone."

"That's not it." She brought her head up and the staggering power of her beauty wiped the easy smile off his face. "The one thing I have to ask you is—prove it."

She reached up and untied the belt at her waist.

"Stop it." He dropped the crushed cigar and backed up. "Christ, Roxanne, what do you think you're doing?"

"Just showing you what you claim not to want." Watching him, she rolled her shoulders and sent the ivory silk slithering to the floor. There was more silk beneath it, a thin chemise of that same soft ivory trimmed in lace. While he tried to catch his breath, one slender strap slipped seductively from her shoulder. "If you're telling the truth, it shouldn't be any problem. Should it?"

"Get dressed." His voice had thickened like a drunk's. "Get out. Don't you have any pride?"

"Oh, I've got plenty of that." And it swelled as she saw the help-less desire in his eyes. "What I seem to be lacking at the moment is shame." The silk whispered against her flesh as she walked to him. "At the moment," she murmured, winding her arms around his neck, "I don't seem to have an ounce of shame." Tilting her head she nipped at his bottom lip. His groan had her letting loose one low laugh. "Tell me again you're not interested." Her lips parted, full of demands against his. "Tell me again."

"Damn you, Rox." His hands were in her hair again, fisted. "Is that what you want?" He swung her around so that she rammed into the dresser as his mouth plundered hers. "You want to see what I can do to you, what I can make you do?" The part of him that still hoped to survive grasped on to heartlessness to push her away. "You want to be used up and tossed aside?"

She threw her head back. "Try it."

He cursed her, he berated them both, every time he dragged his mouth from hers. The war raged in him even as he pulled her to the bed and tumbled onto the mattress with her. Without care, without compassion, he took his hands over her, ripping the silk, bruising flesh, hating himself for the thrill of excitement that wracked him each time she whimpered or moaned.

He'd send them both to hell, he thought. But, by God, they'd take a fast, hot ride through heaven first.

Through a maze of needs and fears she recognized his anger. And his greed. He'd lied, she thought, crying out when his mouth closed hungrily over her breast.

Oh, how he'd lied.

She twined her fingers through his hair and shuddered. This was truth, this desperate, clawing chaos of sensation was truth. All the rest was illusion, pretense, deception.

He was breathless when he lifted his head to stare at her. Breathless and beaten. But somehow the anger had vanished, like a conjurer in a puff of smoke.

Beneath him her body was vibrating, like a finely tuned engine revving to race. He could drive her, that he understood, but he was afraid, horribly afraid that he would lose control until they crashed and burned.

Knowing he was lost, he lowered his forehead to hers. "Oh, Rox," he murmured and stroked his fingers gently over her shoulders.

With no hesitation she wrapped her arms around him. "Listen to me, Callahan, if you stop now, I'll have to kill you."

The laugh was a relief, though it didn't begin to ease the tension balled in his gut. "Roxy, the only way I could stop now is if I were already dead." He lifted his head. She recognized the concentration on his face, the same as she'd seen dozens of times as he prepared for a complicated illusion or a dangerous escape. "We crossed the line, Roxanne. I can't let you go tonight."

Her smile bloomed slowly. "Thank God."

He shook his head. "You'd do better to pray," he warned her, and lowered his mouth to hers.

Chapter Nineteen

AT LAST. IT WAS THE FINAL COHERENT THOUGHT THAT passed through Roxanne's mind as Luke's mouth fixed hot and open on hers. At long last.

Another woman might have wanted soft words, slow hands, gentle persuasion. She had no need for that now. Every wish she'd ever held close, every fantasy she'd ever woven in secret was granted by the wild, willful demands of his hands and lips.

She gave him the most coveted and elusive gift a woman can grant a man. Complete surrender.

That was her power, and her triumph.

Needs that had budded slyly inside her flashed into full bloom. Fears tangled with them, creating an ache so fierce she shook from it. She hadn't known, not even in her most secret imaginings had she known it was possible to feel like this.

Helpless and strong. Dizzy and sane.

She laughed again, from the sheer glory of it, that reckless, rushing roller coaster ride, speeding uphill, plunging down whippy turns, flashing through dark, dark tunnels of secret desires. She clung, not for support, but to be sure, very sure, he joined her in that same thrilling race.

Every sigh, every gasp intensified his greed. It was Roxanne beneath him, her slim, agile body trembling at his touch, her eager mouth meeting his, her scent crowding reason from his brain.

He didn't need to think—no longer had the faculties to think. Later he would remember Max talking of the animal taking over. But for now, Luke was no more than that, taking what his body so violently craved.

The light still burned brightly, far from loverlike. The spread they'd neglected to turn down was stiff and nubby against flesh. The narrow bed swayed with the roll of the ship. But she arched against him and there was nothing but her, and what she so recklessly offered.

He wanted more, needed more, and tore the tattered remains of her chemise aside to find all of her.

Impatient, urgent, his hand streaked down and found her already hot and wet and waiting. With one rough stroke he drove her hard to a first towering climax.

She felt as though she'd been ripped in two as easily as the ivory silk. Her body jerked, convulsed, exploded before her mind had a chance to catch up. Even as she reared forward, shocked and dazzled, he was shoving her back roughly again, devouring damp, trembling flesh.

She wanted to tell him to wait, to give her a moment to catch her breath and her reason. But he dragged her ruthlessly up again until the breath was sobbing in her lungs and reason was impossible.

Ravenous, he feasted on her breasts, one, then the other, using teeth and tongue and lips so that the answering ache deep in her center spread until even her bones throbbed with it.

"Please." Her hands searched for purchase, fingers gripping urgently in the tousled spread. "Please," she moaned again without shame.

Breath heaving, he dragged the loose sweats over his hips. The blood was pounding in his head, beating mercilessly in his loins. He was quivering like a stallion when he mounted her, then cupped her hips to lift them and plunged deep.

She cried out, arching like a bow when the pain tore through her, a white flash, icy against the heat. Her hips jerked as she sought escape and ripped a moan from him.

"Oh, Jesus, Roxanne." Sweat pearled on his brow as he fought every instinct to remain still, not to hurt her again. "Sweet God."

A virgin. He shook his head in a desperate attempt to clear it even as his body vibrated on the razor's edge between frustration and completion. She'd been a virgin, and he'd slammed into her like a fucking Mack truck.

"I'm sorry. Baby, I'm sorry." Useless words, he thought as he watched the first tears spill over onto her cheeks. He levered his arms, the muscles trembling, and braced himself to slip out of her as gently as possible. "I'm not going to hurt you."

Her breath shuddered through her lips. There was pain yet, radiating pain, and a softer, deeper ache. Mixing through both was a sense of glory not yet reached. She arched her hips instinctively when she felt him retreat from her.

"Don't move." His stomach twisted into slippery knots as she drew him back in. "For God's sake don't ... " The rippling pleasure almost drove him mad. "I'm going to stop."

She opened her eyes and locked them on his. "The hell you are." Braced for the next slash of pain, she gripped his hips. She thought she heard him swear. But she couldn't be sure. For there was no pain at all, just a deep, grinding, glorious pleasure. She hurled herself into it, felt it spin and shudder through her system so that there was nothing else, nothing but the wild delight of finding a mate.

He couldn't resist. His body betrayed him, and he thanked God for it. He buried his face in her hair and let her take him.

*

285

HER BODY FELT AS DELICATE as glass. She was afraid to move for fear that she would break apart into thousands of glittery pieces. So this was what the poets wept for, she thought. Her lips curved, smugly. It had certainly been nice, though she doubted she'd compose sonnets about the event.

But this part. She sighed and risked moving her hand to stroke Luke's back. This part was lovely, lying here feeling her lover's heart thud fast and hard against hers. She could happily stay just so for days.

But he moved. Roxanne winced as the bed shifted. She was more than a little sore where Luke had invaded her. Not wanting to lose the close, warm feelings, she curled against him as he rolled onto his back.

There weren't names foul enough to call himself, he thought as he stared up at the ceiling. He'd taken her like an animal, without care, without finesse. He shut his eyes. If the guilt didn't kill him, Max would.

Until then, he had to do something to fix what he'd so heedlessly destroyed.

"Rox."

"Hmmm."

"I'm responsible."

Dreaming, she nestled her head more comfortably on his shoulder. " 'Kay."

"I don't want you to worry about it, or feel guilty."

"About what?"

"This." Impatience shimmered in his voice. Did she have to sound so sleepy, so sexy, so damned satisfied? "It was a mistake, but it doesn't have to ruin anything."

Roxanne opened one eye, then the other. The smile that had curved her lips turned into a frown. "A mistake? You're telling me what just happened here was a mistake?"

"Of course it was." He rolled off the bed, searching for his sweats before his body lured him into repeating it. "In dozens of ways." He looked back at her, setting his teeth. She was sitting up now, her tousled hair falling over her shoulders, curling seductively over her breasts. The stain of blood on the rumpled spread knocked the worst of his mounting desire out of him.

"Really?" The lovely, dreamy feeling had vanished. If Luke hadn't been so involved with cursing himself, he would have recognized the light of battle in her eyes. "Why don't you tell me some of those ways?"

"For Christ's sake, you're practically my sister."

"Ah." She folded her arms, stiffened her shoulders. It would have been a tough stance if she hadn't been buck naked. "I think the operative word there is practically. There's no blood between us, Callahan."

"Max took me in." To help him keep his sanity, Luke yanked open a drawer and found a shirt. He tossed it to Roxanne. "He gave me a home, a life. I've betrayed that."

"Bullshit." She heaved the shirt back at him. "Yes, he took you in and gave you a home. But what happened here was between us, just us. It has nothing to do with Max or betrayal."

"He trusted me." Grimly, Luke stepped over and shoved the shirt over Roxanne's head. She slapped his hands away and sprang to her feet.

"Do you think Max would be shocked and angry because we want each other?" Furious, she yanked the shirt off her shoulders and sent it sailing. "You're not my brother, damn it, and if you're going to stand there and tell me you thought of me as your sister a few minutes ago, you're a goddamn liar."

"No, I didn't think of you as my sister." He gripped her shoulders and shook. "I didn't think at all, that's the problem. I wanted you. I've wanted you for years. It's eaten me from the inside out."

She tossed her head back. The gesture was a challenge, but a soft warmth was kindling inside her. For years. He'd wanted her for years. "So you've been playing games with me, running hot then cold since I was sixteen. All because you wanted me and had it twisted around in your tiny brain that acting on it would be some sort of what—emotional incest?"

He opened his mouth, shut it again. Why did it suddenly sound so ridiculous? "Close enough."

He didn't know what response he expected from her, but it certainly wasn't laughter. She shouted with it until tears sprang to her eyes. Holding her sides, she sat on the side of the bed. "Oh, you jerk."

His pride was at stake. Damned if he'd admit that a naked woman, bowled over with laughter at his expense, could arouse him until he was ready to whimper and beg.

"I don't see that this is a laughing matter."

"Are you kidding? It's a riot." She pushed her hair out of her face and beamed at him. "And terribly sweet, too. Were you protecting my honor, Luke?"

"Shut up."

She only chuckled and scrubbed amused tears from her cheeks. "Think about it, Callahan. Really think for a minute. You're standing there, riddled with guilt over the idea of making love to a woman who used every means available to seduce you, a woman you've known most of your life—one who is not, I repeat, is not in any way, shape or form related to you. A single woman, over the age of consent. You don't think that's funny?"

He shoved his hands in his pockets and scowled. "Not particularly."

"You're losing your sense of humor." She rose then and wound her arms around him. Her naked breasts brushed his chest and she had the satisfaction of feeling his muscles quiver. But he didn't return the embrace. "I guess if you feel this way, I'll have to seduce you every time. I suppose I'm up to it." She nibbled lightly at his lips, smiling when she glanced down between them. "And it appears you are, as well."

"Cut it out." But the order lacked conviction. "Even if I've been off base about that, there are other things."

"Okay." She trailed her fingers down his back, played light kisses over his throat. "Let's hear them."

"Damn it, you were a virgin." He took her arms, pulled her back so he could escape.

"That bothers you?" She pouted a moment, thinking it through. "I always thought men got a charge out of that. You know, the *Star Trek* syndrome."

"What?"

"To boldly go where no man has gone before."

He strangled back a laugh. "Christ." He wished he had a beer—hell, he wished he had a frigging six-pack, but settled on a warm bottle of mineral water. "Look, Roxanne, the point is I didn't do it right."

"You didn't?" She tilted her head, curious. "I can't imagine there are that many ways to do it."

He choked, cautiously set the bottle down again. Not only a virgin, God help him, but impossibly, and yes, damn it, erotically innocent. "What the hell was wrong with all those college boys? Didn't they know what to do with you?"

"I imagine they did—if I'd wanted them to do anything." She smiled again, secure in her power. When she spoke again, her voice was soft. "I wanted you to be the first." She saw the raw emotion in his eyes as she stepped to him again. "I only wanted you."

No one and nothing had ever moved him more. Gently, he touched a hand to her hair. "I hurt you. If you stay with me I'll probably hurt you again. What I said before about what's inside me, it's the truth. There are things you don't know. If you did—"

"I do know." She slid a hand to his back, running fingers over scars. "I've known for years, since the day you told Max. I listened to you. I cried for you. Don't." She wrapped her arms tight around him before he could turn away. "Do you really believe that I'd think less of you because of what was done to you as a child?"

"I'm not good with pity," he said tightly.

"I'm not giving you any." Her eyes were dark and fierce when she tilted back her head. "But understanding, the kind you'll have to take, the kind you can only get from someone who's known you, and loved you all of her life."

Drained, he rested his brow on hers. "I don't know what to say to you."

"Don't say anything. Just be with me."

THERE WAS LITTLE TIME to enjoy the sensation of awakening in Luke's arms, and none at all for lazing through the morning. Roxanne took only a moment to cuddle closer as she listened to the announcements from the passageway intercom listing disembarkation structures. One long, sleepy kiss, a few groans of frustration and she was up, tugging on Luke's sweats and the T-shirt she'd rejected the night before. Holding the sweats up to her slim waist with one hand, she cracked open the cabin door and scanned the passageway. Because Luke was laughing behind her, she shot a look over her shoulder.

Her hair was tousled, her face flushed, her eyes heavy and dreamy. She looked, he thought as his breath caught, exactly like what she was. A woman who'd spent the night with her lover.

And he was her lover. Her first. Her only.

"All hands on deck, Callahan." Her voice was morning husky. "See you in fifteen minutes."

"Aye, aye."

Gripping the sweats securely, Roxanne dashed to her own cabin. A stickler for promptness, she reported to the Lido Deck within a quarter hour. Passengers were gathered in the lounges, carry-on and shopping bags pooled around them while they yawned, chatted and waited for their turn to leave the ship. Every few moments the announcement would be made in English, then in French, inviting passengers holding certain colored baggage tags to disembark. They went through red, blue, white, yellow, red with white stripes, white with green stripes. Roxanne shook hands, had her cheek kissed and exchanged hugs while the noise level gradually decreased.

By ten only crew and the small percentage of passengers cruising back to New York were on board. New passengers wouldn't trickle on board until one o'clock. Max took advantage of the lull to call a rehearsal.

It was good to see Max back in stride, she thought. A slower stride than she was used to, but without the hesitation and hitches that had worried her.

She thought she did very well, moving through card tricks, rope tricks and bigger illusions without giving away what was in her mind and heart. Images of Luke tumbling her onto the bed, flashes of memory that brought heat and pleasure were held very strictly under control. She was satisfied that no one knew the dramatic turn her life had taken but herself, and the man who had taken it with her.

But of course love is blind.

Lily sighed every time she glanced in their direction. Her romantic heart wept happy tears. LeClerc's lips twitched. Even Mouse, who'd spent most of his life oblivious to the subtle exchanges between men and women, flushed and grinned.

Only Max seemed oblivious.

"Isn't it wonderful?" Lily sighed again when she and Max took the hour of free time left to them on the nearly deserted Lido Deck with cups of bouillon and herbal tea.

"It certainly is." He patted her hand, thinking she was speaking of the quiet moment, the cooling breeze and the view of Montreal from the port side.

"It's like having your fondest dream come true." She lifted her teacup, her trio of rings sparkling. "I was beginning to think it would never happen."

"It's been a busy week," he agreed. And he hadn't had nearly enough time to continue his research on the philosophers' stone.

291

Perhaps when they docked in Sydney, he could make an excuse not to play tourist and spend a few hours with his books and notes. He was getting closer. He could feel it.

"I wonder if being on a ship like this helped. I mean, in close quarters—sort of in each other's pockets. They couldn't keep avoiding each other."

"Certainly not." Max blinked and frowned. "Who?"

"Roxy and Luke, silly." Bracing her elbows on the table, she sighed dreamily. "I bet they're strolling hand in hand through Montreal right now."

"Roxanne and Luke?" was all Max could think of to say. "Roxanne and Luke?"

"Well, sure, honey. What'd you think I was talking about?" She laughed, enjoying, as women do, that superiority over most males of the species on romance. "Didn't you see the way they were looking at each other this morning? It's a wonder the lounge didn't catch fire with all the sparks flying around."

"They always shot sparks off each other. They do nothing but argue."

"Honey, that was just a kind of mating ritual."

He choked on his tea. "Mating?" he said weakly. "My Jesus."

"Max, baby." Baffled and concerned, Lily took both of his hands. They trembled under hers. "You're not upset, not really, are you? They're so perfect for each other, and so much in love."

"You're saying that he's—that they've—" He couldn't get the words out.

"I wasn't a fly on the wall, but if this morning was any indication, I'd say they've done the deed." She'd kept her voice light, but when Max continued to stare, shell-shocked, her tone changed. "Max, you're not angry?"

"No. No." He shook his head, but had to stand. He walked to the rail like a man in a trance. His baby, he thought as a small piece of his heart ripped away. His little girl. And the boy he'd thought of as his own for so long. They'd grown up on him. Tears started in his eyes. "I should have seen it, I suppose," he murmured when Lily slipped an arm around him.

He shook his head again. The weakhearted tears were gone as he drew her closer. "Will they have what we have, do you suppose?"

She leaned her head against his shoulder and smiled. "No one could, Max."

THAT NIGHT HE CAME TO HER. She was waiting for him. No matter how sternly Roxanne told herself it was foolish, she was more nervous now than she had been before. It was a matter of control, she supposed. The night before, that first night, she had mapped the route, and had been so sure of the course.

Tonight, he would be taking her beyond.

She was grateful he hadn't come directly to her cabin after the last show, but had given her time to remove the stage makeup and change from the spangled costume into a simple blue robe. But that time alone had also worked against her, giving her heart the opportunity to beat too fast and hard.

It had been lovely that afternoon. They had done precisely what Lily had imagined for them. Strolling down Montreal's sloping sidewalks, listening to American music pouring through shop doorways, huddling together at a small table of an outdoor café.

Now they were alone again. The bouquet of flowers he'd brought her from a sidewalk vendor stood fragrantly on her dresser. The bed was neatly turned down. The deck swayed under her feet as the ship steamed south.

"It was a good crowd tonight." An idiotic thing to say, Roxanne berated herself.

"Enthusiastic." He flicked his wrist. A single white rosebud appeared in his hand. Roxanne felt her heart melt.

"Thanks." It would be fine, she told herself as she drew in the bud's bouquet. She knew what to expect now, and could look forward to the feel of his hands on her skin, the rough tumble into oblivion. The pain was fleeting after all. Surely a few moments' discomfort was a small price to pay for the lovely aftermath of lying curled in his arms.

He could read the nerves in her eyes as clearly as he could see their color. There was no use cursing himself again for his mindless initiation of the night before. At least he'd had the good sense to do nothing more than hold her throughout the rest of the night.

He touched a hand to her cheek and watched her eyes lift slowly from the rose to his face. He thanked God there was more than fear in them. He could make the fear vanish. He passed a hand in front of her face and made her laugh when she saw the candle between his fingers.

"Clever."

"You ain't seen nothing yet." He crossed to the dresser, slipping a crystal holder he'd palmed from the dining room from his pocket. He set the candle carefully in place, then snapped his fingers. The wick sputtered, caught and glowed.

A bit more relaxed, Roxanne smiled. "Shall I applaud?"

"Not yet." Watching her, he flicked off the lights, removed his jacket. "You can wait till the show's over."

Unconsciously, she brought a hand to her throat. "There's more?"

"Much more." He crossed to her. Perhaps it wasn't quite fair that he should be rewarded rather than whipped for his carelessness last night. But he was going to make it up to her. To both of them. He took the hand that was still splayed against her throat, turned it, pressed his fingers to the cup of her palm, to the fragile wrist where her pulse beat like thunder. "I told you there was more than one way, Roxanne." With her hand still tucked in his, he traced light kisses over her jawline. "But just like magic, showing's better than telling." He saw her lashes flutter down and slipped the rose from her limp fingers. "I won't hurt you again."

Her eyes opened at that. Doubts and needs warred within them.

"It's all right," she murmured, and lifted her mouth toward his in invitation.

"Trust me."

"I do."

"No, you don't." He covered her waiting mouth, drawing the kiss out and out until she swayed. "But you will," he said and swept her into his arms.

She braced herself for the onslaught. A part of her burned for the feel of those hard strong hands, that urgent, demanding mouth. But his lips were soft tonight, soft, seductive, even soothing as they whispered over hers. The breathless, confused sound she made in the back of her throat made him smile.

"I have places to take you." His tongue dipped in, toyed with hers. "Magic places."

She had no choice but to follow where he led. Her body was floating before he ended that first, sumptuous kiss. Leaving her lips trembling for more, he took his own on a languorous journey, tasting her skin, lingering at the base of her throat while her pulse fluttered under his mouth like the heart of a caged bird.

The arms that had risen to enfold him went lax. And he knew she was his.

"I want to look at you," he whispered, gently sliding her robe aside. "Let me look at you."

Her beauty scorched his heart, made his blood churn like white water. But in the flickering light he touched her with fingertips only, skimming them over curves and dips, enchanted by the contrast of his flesh against hers, bewitched by the quick tremors each gentle caress tore from her.

"We were in a hurry before." Lowering his head, he gently, very gently laved her aching nipples with his tongue. "Maybe we'll be in a hurry later." When he straightened to look at her, he rolled the damp nipple between his thumb and forefinger, pinching, tugging lightly to bring her helplessly to that staggering point between pleasure and pain. "But we'll take our time now, Roxanne." He trailed a finger down the center of her body, enjoying every quiver as he tangled through the soft triangle of hair to stroke the secret sensitive nub.

When her eyes glazed, when her breath caught and he felt the warm flow of her response, his head swam. But he only smiled.

"I want to do things to you. I want you to let me."

When he joined his mouth to hers again, he replaced his fingertips with the rose, sliding the silky petals over her breasts, teasing the nipples with its fragrant smoothness, following those subtle curves over waist and hips.

"Tell me what you like."

The breath shuddered from between her lips. She could see him in the candlelight. His chest was bare now, though she had no memory of him taking the time to shrug out of his shirt. She felt the heaviness of his arousal against her leg, and realized he was as naked as she.

"I can't." She lifted her hand to touch him through air that felt as sweet and thick as syrup. "Just don't stop."

"This?" He slid slowly down, teasing the nub of her breast with his tongue, catching it between his teeth before suckling as if he'd swallow her whole. She moaned, long and deep, thrilling him.

It was torture of the most exquisite. Drugging, aching pleasure glided through her until she thought she would die from it. The bed moaned, gave as he shifted. Her skin hummed under his hands, sang beneath the patient, questing mouth. When his tongue skimmed up her thigh, she understood there was no part of her he wouldn't claim, and nothing she would deny him.

She opened for him on a sigh of acceptance. All at once the soothing warmth exploded into heat, as if a comet had erupted in her and trailed its fire to every cell. Her cry of release trailed into a deep, throaty moan.

Still he was patient, relentlessly patient, stroking her up again, higher, waiting as she drifted down again.

Sighs and moans and whispered promises. The flicker of

candlelight and the faintest hint of a moon, the scent of flowers and passion heady on the air. These she would remember, even as her body shuddered from the patient onslaught.

Oh, he did things to her, just as he'd promised. Exquisite, impossible, delicious things.

He showed her what it was to be desired, to be cherished, and at last, at last, what it was to be taken slowly, like sailing down a quiet river into a mist.

He slipped inside her painlessly, perfectly, and she was slick and hot and more than ready. Her body rose fluidly to welcome him. He hadn't known it could be so easy, that he could feel such sweet, sweet pain as she closed around him. The rhythm built, needs swelling like music in his head.

"Roxanne." Her name came hoarsely from his throat. He clung to the reins of his control like a man fighting a wild beast. "Look at me. I need you to look at me."

His voice seemed to come from the end of the long, dark tunnel in which her body was flying. She lifted heavy lids and saw only him. His eyes were a violent blue, like the heat at the center of flame.

"You belong to me now." He crushed his mouth to hers as the climax exploded inside her. Only me, he thought and let himself follow her.

SHE WASN'T SURE she could ever move again, but when she did it was to turn her head and seek his mouth. He responded with an unintelligible murmur and rolled to shift their positions.

"Better," she sighed, now that she could breathe again. She rubbed her cheek against his chest, and settled. "I didn't know it could be like that."

Neither had he. But Luke felt it would sound foolish to say it and stroked her hair instead. "I didn't hurt you?"

"No. I feel like . . ." She made a cat-in-cream sound. "Like I've been levitated up to the moon." She stroked a hand down his chest. When she cruised her fingers over his belly, she felt the muscles quiver. Well, well, she thought, smiling to herself. The power wasn't all one-sided. That would have to be put to good use very soon.

"So . . . " She lifted her head and grinned down at him. "Just how many ways are there, anyhow?"

He lifted a brow. "Why don't you give me a couple of minutes, and I'll show you."

Drunk on her own pleasures, Roxanne shifted to straddle him. "Why don't you show me now?" she suggested and closed her mouth over his.

Chapter Twenty

BOTH LUKE AND ROXANNE WOULD HAVE HOTLY DENIED ANY suggestion that they had fallen into a cliché such as a shipboard romance. Sea breezes, brilliant sunsets and moonlit decks might influence others, but never them. They both would have shrugged off the idea of a honeymoon, yet if the honest definition for that time-honored period was an opportunity to discover, to focus on a mate and to enjoy great sex, their honeymoon had cruised into its third week.

Discoveries were made. Much to Luke's relief, he learned that he wasn't a jealous fool. He actually enjoyed the way men's heads turned when Roxanne walked into a room. He could smile when he watched her flirt or be flirted with. Both were a matter of pride and confidence, laced with a touch of arrogance. She was beautiful, and she was his.

Roxanne discovered that beyond the tough, troubled boy she'd known most of her life, the man she'd fallen in love with could be gentle and kind. The veneer of sophistication and charm was a thin coat over a smoldering bed of passions. Yet mixed with those was a keen sense of loyalty and a yearning to love no less than her own.

Both were able to focus on each other, even in a room crowded with people. They didn't need to touch or speak; a look was enough to communicate.

Perhaps that was why the last requirement for a honeymoon fell so naturally into place.

Through this fantasy of days and nights, both agreed there was only one thing missing. They had yet to choose a genuine mark. Their thief's blood grew restless. True, they had stemmed the impatience temporarily by relieving a certain Mrs. Cassell of some antique marcasite and ruby jewelry. Since the old crab had spent her seven days on board the *Yankee Princess* complaining and demanding and making Jack's life as cruise director a living hell, the Nouvelles had considered it a matter of honor to give her something genuine to complain about.

But the job had been so pitifully simple. Roxanne had only to slip into Mrs. Cassell's cabin between cues and snatch the locked jewelry case from among the pile of half-packed luggage. One glance at the mechanism had her altering the plan. Rather than strolling out again and passing the case to Luke, she used one of Cassell's own hairpins to pick the lock. Once the marcasite was snugly in the pockets of her stage tux, she relocked the case, replaced it and slipped outside again.

As planned Luke was just coming through heading aft.

"Problem?"

She smiled. "Not at all." With one brow lifted, she patted her pockets. "I just need to get something from the cabin," she said as he grinned. "I won't miss my cue."

Luke snatched her into his arms for a kiss. His clever fingers dipped into her pockets to take inventory. "You got three minutes, Rox."

It took her less than half that to secure the cache in the false bottom of her makeup case. She had time to freshen the lipstick Luke had smudged and still hit her cue dead on.

They all agreed it was an elegant set, the craftsmanship exquisite, the stones quite good. But the lack of challenge took the sweetness out of it.

The Nouvelles, one and all, yearned for work.

"Maybe we should try something in one of the ports," Roxanne said absently. She and Lily stood on deck. New passengers boarding in Montreal were dribbling out, complimentary cocktails in hand, cameras at the ready. Luke and Mouse had trekked to Olympic Stadium to watch the Expos take on the Dodgers.

"I suppose we could." Lily's mind kept drifting back to Max. She'd stirred awake before dawn and had seen him on the narrow sofa beneath the porthole, his research books spread out around him. He'd been manipulating a coin between his fingers. The second time he'd fumbled and dropped it, she'd seen the pain in his face. A pain she knew she could never ease.

"I was thinking Newport," Roxanne went on. "The place is lousy with mansions. We could at least do some legwork the next time through."

"You're so like him." Lily sighed and turned from the rail. "If you're not in the middle of a project, you're planning one. It's the only way you're happy."

"Life's too short not to enjoy one's work." Her smile was quick and wicked. "God knows I love mine."

"What would you do if it all went away?" Lily's suddenly nervous fingers began to toy with the jade pendant Max had bought her in Halifax. "If you couldn't do it anymore. The magic or the other?"

"If I woke up one morning and it was all gone? If all that was left was the ordinary?" Roxanne pursed her lips in thought, then laughed. At twenty-one, it was impossible to believe that old age would ever apply to you. "Stick my head in the first convenient oven."

"Don't say that." Lily grabbed her hand, squeezing until the bones rubbed. "Don't ever say that."

"Darling, I'm only joking." Surprise widened her eyes. "You

301

know me better. People who do something permanent like that have forgotten that nothing lasts forever. No matter how wonderful, or how awful, if you wait awhile, it changes."

"Of course it does." Feeling foolish, Lily loosened her grip, but her throat remained tight and dry. "Don't pay any attention to me, honey. I think I must be overtired."

Now that Roxanne looked, really looked, she could see the faint shadows beneath Lily's careful makeup. Surprise became concern. "Are you all right? Aren't you feeling well?"

"I'm fine." She'd lived on the stage long enough to show only what she wanted to show. "Just tired—and it's silly—but I think I'm a little homesick. I've had a yen for LeClerc's gumbo for days."

"I know what you mean." Because this so clearly mirrored her own feelings, Roxanne relaxed with a smile. "All this great food, and after a few weeks, you'd offer a hundred dollars for a cheeseburger and fries—and ten times that for an entire day where you didn't have to talk to anyone."

She needed time alone, Lily realized, before she blurted out her fears and miseries. "Well, I'm going to cheat." With a wink, she kissed Roxanne's cheek. "I'm ducking down to the cabin for an hour, giving myself a facial and a foot soak and a chapter of my romance novel."

"You're just saying that to make me jealous."

"Tell you what. Cover for me, and in an hour, I'll do the same for you."

"Deal. Anybody asks, I'll tell them you're tacking loose sequins back on your costume."

"That's a good one." She hurried off, wanting to be behind locked doors before she indulged in a good crying jag.

Alone, Roxanne glanced around the deck. New faces, she thought, new stories. She enjoyed variety, always had. But she couldn't help wishing that Luke was with her rather than chugging beer and damning umpires in two languages. It was more fun with him, studying faces, making up names and backgrounds.

By the time she'd answered the question of what it was like to work on a cruise ship for the tenth or twelfth time, she began to think an hour alone with a mud pack and a romance novel was a pretty good deal.

But she turned, her *Yankee Princess* smile in place, when her name was called yet again. The smile wavered for an instant, then held solidly. She was, after all, a pro.

"Sam. What a small, small world."

"Isn't it?" He might have stepped out of an article on cruisewear in *Gentleman's Quarterly*. His buff-colored trousers had knife-edged pleats that looked sharp enough to draw blood. His shirt was unpressed cotton—the type that cost the earth to look casual. His sockless feet were encased in Docksiders, and his arm was draped around a sleek and polished blonde. She wore billowy silk slacks in an aching blue to match her eyes, with a softly draped blouse in the same shade. Roxanne was more impressed with the simple strand of creamy pearls and their sapphire enhancer that was as big around as Mouse's thumb.

"Justine, darling, I'd like you to meet a very old friend. Roxanne Nouvelle. Roxanne, my wife, Justine Spring Wyatt."

"How nice." Justine offered a pleasant smile that didn't reach her eyes, and a quick firm handshake that pretended to be personable.

The perfect politician's wife, Roxanne decided. "My pleasure."

There were earrings as well, Roxanne noted. Two teardrop-shaped indigo stones dripping from lustrous pearls.

"I was amazed to see you on deck," Sam began. "Doubly amazed to see you're staff." His gaze skimmed down to the name tag over her breast, lingered, then rose again. "Have you given up the magic business?"

"Not at all. We'll be performing on board for the next few weeks."

"Fabulous." He'd known, of course, had made it his business to know. He hadn't been able to resist the idea of spending a week with the Nouvelles. "Justine, Roxanne is quite an accomplished magician."

"How unusual." Her lips parted in a smile that revealed perfectly aligned teeth. "Do you perform for children's parties?"

"Not yet." Roxanne took a cocktail from a passing waiter's tray. "Is this your first trip on the *Yankee Princess*?"

"On this particular ship, yes. I've done quite a bit of cruising—the Caribbean, the Mediterranean, that sort of thing." She lifted a narrow white hand to toy absently with the enhancer. The diamonds circling the sapphire burst into tiny flames of light that stirred Roxanne's blood. The arousal was as thoroughly sexual as a long, slow, wet kiss.

"How nice." It took most of her control to resist licking her lips. "I hope you'll enjoy this cruise as much."

"I'm sure I will." The sapphire winked like a seductive eye. "I was delighted when Sam suggested this cruise as part of our honeymoon."

"Oh, you're newlyweds." Knowing it was a womanly gesture, considered harmless, Roxanne studied Justine's wedding ring set. Oh yes, she thought, ten carats, emerald cut for the engagement rock, and a nice platinum band studded with channel-set diamonds for the wedding ring. She yearned for her loupe. "How perfectly lovely. Congratulations, Sam."

"Thank you. I'd love to see your family again—and Luke, of course."

"I'm sure you will. Wonderful meeting you, Justine. Enjoy your cruise."

She was smiling when she walked away. At last, they'd found a worthy mark.

LUKE TOOK ADVANTAGE of a lull to bake away fatigue in the sauna belowdecks. He doubted he'd had more than five hours' sleep a night since Roxanne had walked into his room armed with ivory silk and hot-blooded determination.

Not that he was complaining, but the sauna couldn't hurt. If nothing else it would give him a few minutes to clear his head and think through what Roxanne had told him when she'd tracked him down that afternoon.

Mr. and Mrs. Samuel Wyatt.

Of all the cruise ships in all the ports in all the world, he thought with a grimace. Well, hell, they were stuck for the next week. But he wasn't sure he shared Roxanne's enthusiasm for relieving the bride and groom of the lady's glitters.

No, he wanted to take that one slow, and careful, and calculate all the odds.

When the wooden door of the sauna room creaked open, Luke opened one eye. He shut it again and remained leaning against the back wall, the white towel carelessly hooked at his waist.

"Heard you slithered on board, Wyatt."

"And you're still pulling rabbits out of your ass for a living." Sam settled on the bench below Luke. It had taken only a few discreet inquiries to discover where Luke was spending his hour off. "And dancing to the old man's tune."

"Ever learn how to do a one-handed cut?"

"I gave up games quite some time ago."

Luke only smiled. "I didn't think so. You always had lousy hands—not good for much except pushing little girls around."

"You hold a grudge." Sam spread his arms comfortably on the bench. The years had been good to him. He'd jumped on the trend for physical fitness, and his body reflected his daily workouts with his personal trainer. He used his position, and now his wife's money, to indulge in hair-stylists, manicurists, spas where they pampered the skin. He'd slipped seamlessly into his image of a young, attractive up-and-comer. Now he had wealth to ice the cake.

"Odd," he continued, "Roxanne doesn't appear to. She was quite—friendly earlier."

It wasn't rage, as it once might have been, that Luke experienced. It was pure amusement. "Pal, she'd chew you up and spit you out."

"Really?" Sam's arms tensed against the baking wood. There was one thing his position and his money hadn't been able to give him. A sense of humor about himself. "I think she might find me more her style than you realize. A woman like Roxanne would appreciate a man of position rather than one who has never been quite able to smooth off those rough edges. You're still a loser, Callahan."

"I'm still a lot of things." Luke opened his eyes and, tilting his head, studied Sam's face. "They did a good job on your nose. Nobody'd know it had been broken." He stretched lazily then climbed down. "Except me, of course. See you around."

Sam clenched and unclenched his fists as the door swung shut behind Luke. It appeared his old friend needed a harder lesson. A telegram to Cobb, perhaps, Sam thought, forcing his angry muscles to relax. It was time to squeeze harder.

He opened his fist and studied the smooth palm where the manicured nails had bitten deep.

Much harder, he decided.

"I TELL YOU IT'S PERFECT." Roxanne scowled from face to face. The meeting between shows in her father's cabin was not going according to her plans. "Any woman who wears rocks like that in the afternoon has to be loaded with them. And any woman who'd marry a scum like Sam deserves to lose them."

"Be that as it may." Max steepled his fingers and struggled to focus his concentration. "It's risky to steal from someone you know, and who knows you, particularly in a situation as narrow as this."

"We could do it," she insisted. "LeClerc, if I got you photos and detailed descriptions of some of the better pieces, how long would it take for your contact to make up paste replicas?"

"A week, perhaps two."

She nearly snarled. "If you put a rush on it."

He began to consider. "If we sweetened the pot, four or five days. But, of course, this doesn't include delivery time."

"That's what Federal Express is for. We switch them." She swung back to her father. "The last night of the cruise. By the time Justine gets home and notices any difference, we're clear." She waited impatiently for a response. "Daddy?"

"What?" He jerked himself back, panicking for a moment as he searched for the thread of the conversation. "There isn't enough time to plan properly."

How could he plan when he could barely think? Sweat had begun to trickle cold down his back. They were all looking at him, all staring at him. Wondering.

"The answer is no." The statement whipped out as he sprang to his feet. He wanted them to leave, all of them, couldn't bear to have their pity and curiosity staring him in the face. "That's an end to it."

"But—"

"An end." He shouted it, causing Roxanne to blink and Lily to bite her bottom lip. "I'm still in charge here, young lady. When I want your suggestions and advice, I'll request them. Until then, do as you're told. Is that clear?"

"Very." Pride kept her head high, but there was shocked hurt in her eyes. He'd never shouted at her before. Never. They had argued, certainly, but always with an underlayment of love and respect. All she saw in her father's face was fury. "If you'll excuse me, I'm going to take a walk before the show."

Luke rose slowly as the door slammed behind Roxanne. "I have to go along with your reasons for rejecting the job, Max, but don't you think you were a little hard on her?"

Max rounded on him, his temper a wildly slashing sword. "I don't believe I need your opinion on how to deal with my own child. You may sleep with her, but I'm her father. My generosity to you over the years does not equal the right to interfere with family business."

307

"Max." Lily reached for his arm, but Luke was already shaking his head.

"It's all right, Lily. I believe I'll take a walk myself."

THE SEA WAS SPLATTERED with starlight. With her hands clasped tightly on the rail, Roxanne stared out at it. There was a vicious headache behind her eyes, the direct result of refusing the tears that burned them. She would not blubber like a child because her father had scolded her.

She heard the footsteps behind her and turned eagerly. But it wasn't Luke as she hoped. It was Sam.

"Charming," he said and caught the flying ends of her hair. "A beautiful woman in starlight with the sea behind her."

"Lose your wife?" She glanced deliberately behind him before arching a brow. "I don't believe I see her anywhere."

"Justine isn't the kind of woman who needs to be in a man's pocket." He shifted, caging her between his arms as he placed his hands on the rail. A quick bolt of lust twisted through him. She was beautiful, and belonged to someone else. He needed nothing else to covet her. "She's attractive, smart, rich and ambitious. In a few years, she'll be an excellent Washington hostess."

"How you must have charmed her with all those romantic compliments."

"Some women prefer the direct approach." He leaned toward her, stopping only when Roxanne's hand shot up and pushed against his chest.

"I'm not your wife, Sam, but the direct approach is fine with me, too. How's this? I find you revolting, pathetic and obvious. Sort of like a dead skunk on the side of the road." This was said in the most pleasant of tones, with the most pleasant of smiles. "Now, why don't you back off before I have to say something insulting."

"You're going to regret that." His voice was mild as well, for the

308

benefit of the few people strolling the deck. But his eyes had chilled to ice. "Very, very much."

"I don't see how, when I enjoyed it tremendously." Her eyes were as cold as his, but with a shimmer of inner heat that threatened to erupt. "Now, please get out of my way."

Anger veiled discretion so that he gripped her arms and pushed her back. "I'm not through with you."

"I think—" She broke off, shoving Sam aside so that she could scramble between him and Luke. "Don't." She curled fingers around Luke's lapel and spoke between clenched teeth.

"Go inside, Roxanne." He stared at Sam over her head. If eyes were weapons, Sam would already have died a painful death.

"No." She recognized murder in his eye. If she stepped aside she thought it was more than likely Sam would end up overboard. However much the image appealed, she couldn't allow Luke to be responsible. "We have a show in a few minutes. You won't be able to do what you need to do if you break your hand punching in his face." She tossed a furious look over her shoulder. "Get the hell out of here, or I swear, I'll let go of his coat."

"All right. It wouldn't do to cause a scene here. There'll be another time." He nodded at Luke. "Another place."

Roxanne continued to hold on until she saw Sam stroll inside. "Damn you," she hissed.

"Damn me?" His fury still churned like the water in their wake, but he could only stare at her and repeat. "Damn me?"

"Yes. Do you realize what a mess you almost caused?" All the fury and frustration she'd felt since slamming out of her father's cabin shot out and smacked Luke with a bull's-eye. "Just how were we going to explain to Jack, or the captain for that matter, why you beat up a passenger and dumped his unconscious body overboard?"

"He was touching you. Goddammit, when I walked out he had you trapped against the rail. Do you think I could stand by and watch someone treat you that way?"

"So, what are you, Sir Callahan? My white knight? Let me tell you something, pal." She shoved a finger hard against his chest. "I can slay my own dragons. I'm not some weak, wimpy female who needs rescuing." She poked him again, her nail almost piercing flesh. "I can handle myself. Got it?"

"Yeah. I got it." Because he thought he did, he yanked her against him and kissed her hard until her muffled protest died and her arms came tight around him.

"I'm sorry." Turning her head, she buried her face in his shoulder. "It has nothing to do with that idiot, nothing to do with you."

"I know." He kissed her hair. He'd felt the sting of Max's whip as well, a burn infinitely more painful than any belt Cobb had lifted.

"He hurt me." Because her voice had sounded too small, she pressed her lips together and tried to strengthen it. "He's never hurt me like that before. It wasn't the job, Luke. It wasn't—"

"I know," he said again. "I can't explain it, Rox, except that maybe he's got something else on his mind, maybe he isn't feeling well, maybe a dozen things. He's never come down on you like that before. Don't hold one slip against him."

"You're right." She sighed, drew back. "I'm overreacting." Gently, she lifted a hand to his cheek. "And I took it out on you when you were being such a macho guy. Would you have beat him up for me, baby?"

He grinned, relieved she'd recovered enough to tease. "You bet, doll face. I'd've cremated him."

She gave a quick shiver and lifted her mouth. "Oooh, I just love being kissed by a tough guy."

"Then you're going to get a real charge out of this."

IT WAS ONE OF THE MOST difficult paths Max had ever walked, that narrow carpeted passageway from his cabin to Luke's. He knew his daughter was in there, along with the man he'd considered his son. He lifted his hand to knock, lowered it again. There was pain in his fingers tonight, bone-deep pain. He rapped them hard against the cabin door as if to punish himself.

Luke answered the door. He instantly felt that stiffnecked embarrassment that displayed itself in numbing politeness. "Max? Is there something you need?"

"I'd like to come in for a moment, if you don't mind."

Luke hesitated. At least he could be grateful both he and Roxanne were still fully dressed. "Sure. Would you like a drink?"

"No, nothing. Thank you." He stood miserably just inside the door, his eyes on his daughter. "Roxanne."

"Daddy."

They stood another moment, frozen in a triangle. Three people who had shared so many intimacies. Max found all the speeches he'd prepared had vanished from his brain like smoke. "I'm sorry, Roxy," was all he could think of to say. "I have no excuse."

The stiffness went out of her shoulders. "It's okay." For him, she could set even pride aside. She did so now as she held out her hands and crossed to him. "I guess I was nagging."

"No." Humbled by her easy forgiveness, he brought both her hands to his lips. "You were stating your case, as I've always expected you to do. I wasn't fair or kind." His smile wobbled a bit as he looked up at her. "If it's any consolation, it's the first time in nearly twenty years that Lily's shouted at me and reverted to name calling."

"Oh? Which ones did she use?"

"Jerk was one, I believe."

Roxanne shook her head. "I'll have to teach her some better ones." She kissed him and smiled again. "You'll make it up with her?"

"I think I'll have a better shot if I've made it up with you, first."

"Well, you have."

"Both of you," Max murmured and looked toward Luke.

"I see." Though she wasn't sure she did, Roxanne understood what was needed. "All right then, why don't I go clear your path with Lily?" She touched Luke's arm as she passed, then left them alone.

"There are things I need to say." Max lifted his hands in a rare helpless gesture. "I believe I'll take that drink after all."

"Sure." Luke slid the bottom drawer of the dresser open and pulled out a small bottle of brandy. "No snifters, I'm afraid."

"I can rough it if you can."

Nodding, Luke poured three fingers of brandy into water glasses. "You have some things to say about me and Roxanne," Luke began. "I've wondered why you haven't brought it up before."

"It's hard to admit, but I didn't know how. What I said this afternoon—"

"You were out of line with Rox," Luke interrupted. "Not with me."

"Luke." Max laid a hand on Luke's arm. His eyes were filled with appeal and regret. "Don't close the door on me. I was angry, but anger, contrary to the popular belief, does not always carve out the truth. I sliced to hurt, because I was hurting. I'm ashamed of that."

"Forget it." Uneasy, Luke set the brandy aside and rose. "It was a moment of temper, that's all."

"And do you believe what I said in temper above what I've said and shown you all these years?"

Luke looked back, and his eyes were those of that wild, reckless boy again. "You've given me all I've ever had. You don't owe me anything else."

"A pity people don't realize what power words wield. They'd have more respect for the use of them. It's easier for Roxanne to forgive because she's never doubted my love. I'd hoped that you wouldn't have cause to doubt it either." Max set his brandy, untouched, beside Luke's. "You're the son Lily and I could never make together. Can you understand that there have been entire blocks of time that I've forgotten you hadn't been born to me? And that if I thought of it, it didn't matter."

For a moment Luke said nothing, could say nothing.

Then he sat on the edge of the bed. "Yes. Because there were times I nearly forgot myself."

"And perhaps because the lines were blurred in my heart, I found it hard, very hard, to accept what's between you and my daughter."

Luke gave a half laugh. "It gave me some bad moments, so much so that I nearly sent her away." He lifted his head. "I couldn't send her away, Max, not even for you."

"She wouldn't have gone." He understood both of his children. He laid a hand on Luke's shoulder, squeezing though his fingers wept with pain. "Free lesson," he murmured and watched Luke smile. "Love and magic have a great deal in common. They enrich the soul, delight the heart. And they both take unrelenting and unabating practice."

"I'll remember."

"See that you do." Max started toward the door, but stopped when a thought ran through his head. "I would like grandchildren," he said, and Luke's mouth dropped open. "I would like them very much."

Chapter Twenty-one

Sam was quite satisfied with the progress of his plans. He was a highly respected member of the community, a recognizable force in Washington. As the senator's right-hand man, he had his own office, a modestly decorated bastion of masculinity with leather chairs and neutral colors. He had his own secretary, a sharp-minded political veteran who knew exactly what number to call to ferret out information.

Though he would have preferred a zippy foreign make, Sam was forward-thinking and drove a Chrysler. The grassroots grumbling about buying American was growing. He had plans to be America's favorite son.

According to his timetable, he would slip seamlessly into the senator's position within six years. All the groundwork was there. The years of dedicated public service, the contacts in Washington, in the corporate world and on the streets.

Factoring in his advantages, Sam had nearly tossed his hat into the ring for the most recent election. But patience had won out. He knew his youth would be an initial strike against him, and a good number of bleeding hearts would have interpreted the move as disloyalty to the old fart Bushfield.

So, he bided his time and took his next steps with a cool-eyed look at the nineties. He courted and married Justine Spring, a wealthy department-store heiress with polished looks and impeccable lineage. She championed the correct charities, could plan a dinner party for fifty without turning a hair and had the extra advantage of photographing like a dream.

When Sam had slipped the ring on her finger, he'd known he'd taken another important step. The American people preferred their leaders to be married. With the proper timing, he would campaign for the Senate seat as the devoted father of one, and Justine would be rosily pregnant with their second, and last, child.

He fancied himself a latter-day Kennedy—not the politics, naturally. These were the Reagan years. But the youth, the good looks, the pretty wife and the young, charming family.

It would work because he knew how to play the game. He was climbing the ladder toward the Oval Office with slow, calculated steps, and was already halfway up the rungs.

There was only one niggling sense of failure in Sam's world. The Nouvelles. They were loose ends untied, dangling questions unanswered. He wanted revenge on them for personal reasons, but he needed it for what he considered sharp professional motives. It was important that they be weakened, crushed, so that any vicious truths they might shout about his character would be laughed aside.

He'd had ample time to observe them up close on his honeymoon cruise. Now, cozied into the sumptuous Helmsley Palace in New York, awaiting the parties and celebrations for the Statue of Liberty's one hundredth birthday, he had time to shuffle through his impressions.

The old man looked tired. Sam remembered the lightning-quick movements of those hands a decade before and judged that Max was slowing down. It was interesting as well that the aging magician was spending so much time looking for some mystical rock.

Sam wrote *the philosophers' stone* on Leona's elegant hotel stationery and idly circled it. Maybe he'd have some of his men do some digging into the rock.

There was Lily, as tacky and top-heavy as ever. And as naive, Sam thought, with a smile that curled his lips back from his teeth. He'd made a point of joining her on deck one day, and by the time he'd strolled away, she'd been patting his hand and telling him how glad she was he'd made something good out of his life.

And Roxanne. Ah, Roxanne. If magic existed at all, it existed there. What spell had conjured the skinny, wildhaired girl into a stunning woman? A pity he hadn't had the opportunity to make a few moves in that direction before Justine. He'd have enjoyed seducing her, using her in a way that would shock and disgust his pretty, lukewarm wife.

But no matter how alluring the prospect, he'd had to move carefully there. The incident on ship had very nearly created a scene a public figure—a married public figure—could ill afford.

Which brought him to Luke. Always to Luke. There was the key to the Nouvelles. Sam could dismiss Mouse and LeClerc as callously as he would dismiss servants. They were nothing. But Luke was the linchpin. Destroying him would put a crack in the wall of the Nouvelles that might never be shored up. It would also be such a sweet, personal triumph.

The business with Cobb wasn't progressing as Sam had hoped. It had taken him years after leaving New Orleans to reach the position where he could afford to hire detectives to investigate Luke's background.

It had cost, and cost dearly, but Sam considered it an investment in the future, and payment for the past. Locating the junkie whore who'd been Luke's mother had been a stroke of luck. But Cobb, Cobb had been icing on the cake.

Sam closed his eyes and drifted out of the elegant suite in the Helmsley, transporting himself to a dank waterfront bar.

The air smelled of fish and urine, and the cheap whiskey and tobacco consumed by the patrons. Pool balls smacked angrily together across the room, and the men who played cast surly glances at the table as they chalked cues.

A single whore sat at the end of the bar with mean eyes and a preference for Four Roses while she waited to ply her trade. Her eyes skimmed over Sam as he sat in the corner, lingering a moment in consideration, then passed on.

He'd chosen the shadows. A hat was pulled low on his head, and a bulky coat disguised his frame. It was chill enough in the bar with a late-winter wind battering sleet against the windows. But the light sweat of anticipation greased Sam's skin.

He watched Cobb walk in. Saw him hitch up his heavily buck-led belt before scanning the room. Once he spotted the figure in the corner, he nodded, strolled with what Sam assumed was meant to be nonchalance to the bar. He brought a glass of whiskey to the table.

"You got business with me?" It was a tough tone, delivered before his first sip of whiskey.

"I have a business offer."

Cobb shrugged his massive shoulders and attempted to look bored. "So?"

"I believe you know an acquaintance of mine." Sam left his own drink untouched on the table. He'd noted, with mild disgust, that the glass was none too clean. "Luke Callahan."

Surprise flickered before Cobb narrowed his eyes. "Can't say as I do."

"Let's not complicate a simple matter. You've been fucking Callahan's mother on and off for years. You lived with them when he was a boy—a kind of unofficial stepfather. At that time, you were doing some unimaginative pimping and dipping your toe into pornography—with an emphasis on children and adoles-cents."

Cobb's face suffused with color so that the network of broken capillaries flared like torches. "I don't know what that ungrateful shit told you, but I treated him good. Kept food in his belly, didn't I? Showed him what was what."

"You left your mark on him, Cobb. I've seen that for myself." Sam smiled, and Cobb caught a flash of white teeth.

"The boy needed discipline." Whiskey was curdling in Cobb's nervous belly. He sent more down to join it. "I seen him on TV. Big shot now. Don't see him paying me or his old lady back for all the years we did for him."

Sam heard exactly what he'd hoped to hear: resentment, bitterness and envy. "You figure he owes you?"

"Goddamn class A right he does." Cobb leaned forward, but gleaned no more than a vague impression of Sam's face through the smoke and dingy shadows. "If he sent you here to rattle my chain—"

"No one sends me. Callahan owes me, as well. You can be of use to me." Sam reached into his pocket and took out an envelope. After a quick glance around the room, Cobb picked it up. His wide thumb flipped through five hundred in well-used twenties.

"What do you want for it?"

"Satisfaction. This is what I want you to do."

So Sam had sent his dog to New Orleans.

The blackmail wasn't as effective as he'd hoped, Sam mused. The thirty or forty thousand a year was paid without comment. Since Sam had made it his business to know precisely what income Luke reported each year, he would up the ante. There would be a plain white postcard waiting for Luke when he returned to New Orleans. This time the figure on it would be ten thousand.

Sam calculated that a few months of these slim postcards would slide neatly under Luke's foundations. Before long, they would crumble.

IT INFURIATED HIM. Luke crushed the white square in his fist and hurled it across the room. It terrified him.

Ten thousand dollars. It wasn't the money itself. He had enough of that, and could easily get more. It was the realization that Cobb was not only never going away, but that he was growing greedy.

The next time it could be twenty thousand, or thirty.

Let the fucker go to the press, he thought. The tabloids could have a field day with it.

MASTER MAGICIAN'S SECRET CHILDHOOD

So what?

ESCAPE ARTIST'S LIFE AS A WHORE

Who gave a shit?

THE NOUVELLES' UGLY TRIANGLE
Magician's affair with mentor, and his master's daughter

Oh, God. Luke scrubbed his hands over his face and tried to think. He was entitled to his life, damn it. The one he'd put together piece by piece since he'd run away from that gin-soaked apartment with his back screaming with pain and the terror of not knowing what they might have done to him after he'd lapsed into unconsciousness.

He would not, could not stand to have what he'd run from dug up and smeared into his face. He wouldn't see the stink of that mud flung at the only people he'd ever loved. And yet. And yet he was losing something of himself every time he answered one of those postcards like a well-trained monkey.

There was one alternative he hadn't yet considered. Luke picked up a teacup, intently studying the delicate design of violets against the cream-colored china. One he'd dreamed about, certainly, but had never put on the floor for a vote.

He could fly up to Maine and lure Cobb out of his hole. Then he could do what he'd yearned to do every time the belt had slashed his flesh. He could kill him.

The cup shattered in his hand, but Luke didn't jolt. He continued to stare down while the image formed more truly in his mind, and the blood welled like a thin smile across his palm.

He could kill.

The pounding on the door jerked him back. The thought was still wheeling like dazzling colored lights in his head as he yanked it open.

"Hi!" Roxanne's hair dripped into her eyes. Her T-shirt clung wetly to her torso. She lifted her lips to Luke's and brought him the scent of rain and summer meadows. "I thought you'd like a picnic."

"Picnic?" He fought hard to bank the violence and smile at her. He glanced toward the torrent falling outside the window as he shut the door behind her. "I guess this kind of weather should cut down on ants."

"Barbecued chicken wings," she said, holding out a cardboard box.

"Oh yeah?"

"The really sloppy kind, and a big bowl of LeClerc's potato salad that I swiped from the fridge, and a very nice white Bordeaux."

"Seems you've thought of everything. Except dessert."

She sent him a long sideways glance as she knelt on the rug. "Oh, I thought of that, too. Why don't you get us a couple of glasses—what's this?" She picked up a shard of broken china.

"I—broke a cup."

When he bent down to pick up the pieces, she spotted the blood on his hand. "Oh, what have you done?" She snatched his hand, clucking over it while she daubed at blood with the hem of her shirt.

"It's just a scratch, doc."

"Don't joke." But she saw with relief that it was, and shallow at that. "Your hands are worth quite a bit, you know. Professionally."

He skimmed a finger down the slope of her breast. "Professionally?"

"Yes. And I do have a personal interest in them, as well." After nibbling on his lips, she sat back on her heels in strategic retreat. "How about those glasses—and a corkscrew?"

Ready to oblige, he rose and started toward the kitchen. "Why don't you dig out a dry shirt? You'll drip on the potato salad."

"No, I won't." The sopping shirt landed a step behind him, splatting on the linoleum. Luke glanced down at it, then at her. It should be an interesting picnic, he mused. Chicken, potato salad and a wet, half-naked woman. The lingering tension dissolved in a grin. "I love practical women."

It was dark. The shadows were suffocating and stank of sweat. The walls were close on all four sides, and overhead the ceiling dropped low like the lid of a coffin.

There was no door. No latch. No light.

He knew he was naked, for the heat pressed down on his exposed skin like an anvil that throbbed and throbbed under a relentless hammer. Something was crawling over him. For a horrible minute he feared it was spiders. But it was only the creep of his own perspiration.

He tried to be quiet, very, very quiet, but the sound of his labored breathing rattled and whooped with a hollow echo despite the cramped space.

They'd come if he wasn't quiet.

He couldn't stop it. He couldn't stop his panicked heart from booming in his chest or the small animal-like sounds of terror that kept bubbling up in his throat.

His hands were tied. The rope bit into his thin wrists as he twisted and struggled for freedom. He smelled blood and tasted tears and the sweat stung his abraded wrists like a torch.

He had to get out. Had to. There had to be a way to escape. But there was no trap door, no clever mechanism, no slick panel waiting to slide away at his touch.

He was only a boy, after all. And it was so hard to think. So hard to be strong. The sweat froze like tiny balls of ice when he realized he wasn't alone in the box. He could hear the heavy, excited breathing close, could smell the sour stink of gin.

He howled like a wolf when the hands gripped him, his body jerking, bucking, drawing up tight.

"You'll do what you're told to do. You'll do what you're told, you little bastard."

The slash of the belt sliced white-hot pain through flesh, through blood and into bone. And he screamed, and he screamed, and bolted upright. For a moment his dazed eyes saw only the dark. His skin was still shivering against the bite of the belt as hands reached for him.

He jerked away, fists clenched, teeth bared. And saw Roxanne's stunned face.

"You had a nightmare," she said calmly, though her heart was tripping at double time. He didn't look quite sane. "It was a nightmare, Luke. You're awake now."

The madness faded from his eyes before he closed them on a groan. His skin was still quivering when she risked touching a hand to his shoulder. "You were thrashing around. I couldn't bring you out of it."

"I'm sorry." He rubbed his hands over his face, willing the nausea away.

"You don't have to be sorry." Gently, she brushed the sweat-dampened hair from his brow. "Must have been a lulu."

"Yeah." He reached for the bottle and upended a swallow of warm wine into his mouth.

"Tell me?"

He could only shake his head. There were things he could never tell, not even to her. "It's over." But there was a tic in his jaw. Roxanne smoothed her fingers over the movement to soothe.

"Why don't I get you some water?"

"No." He grabbed her hand before she could rise, clinging tight as if he couldn't bear her to be even as far away as the next room. "Just be here. Okay?"

"Okay." She slipped her arms around him.

He'd forgotten they were naked. But oh, the feel of her skin against his was magic, vanquishing those last tattered remnants of the nightmare. Needy, he buried his face into the soft curve of her shoulder.

"It's still raining," he murmured.

"Umm-hmm." Instinctively, she stroked his back, her fingers gliding coolly over the ridges of old scars. "I like the way it sounds, the way it makes the light so soft and the air so heavy."

He watched it fall, still hard and heavy though the thunder had danced on to the west. Beyond the terrace doors his tangle of geraniums stood triumphant against the gloom. "I always liked red flowers best. I could never figure out why. Then one day I realized they made me think of your hair. That's when I knew I loved you."

Her fingers paused, lying still against his back. Her heart broke a little, but sweetly, as it must with joy. "I didn't think you'd ever tell me." On an unsteady laugh she pressed her lips to his throat. "I was considering going to Madame and asking her for a potion."

"You're all the magic I need." He tipped her face back to his. "I was afraid to say it. Those three words are an incantation that releases all kinds of complications."

"Too late." Her lips curved against his. "The spell's already cast. Here." She lifted her hands, palms out, waiting until he placed his against them. "I love you, too. Nothing can change it. No sorcery, no enchantment, no trick of the eye."

Very slowly he slid his fingers between hers so that their spread palms became sturdy, joined fists. "In all the illusions, you're the only truth I need."

He knew then that he would pay Cobb, would dance with the devil himself to keep her safe, to keep what they had unspoiled.

She saw the flash in his eyes, like lightning against a churning sky. His fingers tensed on hers. "I need you, Roxanne." He released her hands to pull her close and press her back onto the rug. "Now. God, now."

Like brushfire, the force of that need burned from him into her, scorching the blood. His desperation tumbled with them over the rug, igniting the spark of hers, fanning the flames higher, brighter, until it was a roar of heat.

His hands were everywhere, streaks of lightning over her flesh that sent hundreds of pulse points thudding. Their playful, good-hearted loving of the afternoon paled like the moon against the sun.

He clasped her hands in his again, holding her arms out to the side as he raced his mouth over her. His teeth scraped, nipped, satisfying an urgent hunger for the taste of flesh. Her hands flexed once, twice, under his grip even as her body greedily absorbed the sensation of being taken, possessed. Devoured.

To want and be wanted like this. She could never explain it, never describe it. Could only thank God for it. When he dragged her higher, into that blinding heat, the pleasure was so intense she felt her soul quake.

More, was all she could think.

She tore her hands free to take them over him, all speed and eagerness. Agile and quick and more than half mad, she rolled on top of him, flesh sliding hot and wet over flesh, mouth meeting ravenous mouth like the clash of bright, dangerous swords.

The power built inside her, sang in her blood, seemed to spark from her fingertips as she felt his muscles bunch and quiver beneath her touch. He'd taught her the magic, tutored her in its varieties. Now, for this moment, the student had become the master.

He groaned, dazed by the suddenness and strength of her assault. Her answer was a laugh, low and breathless and devastating. He would have sworn he smelled hell smoke mixed with that taunting perfume of wildflowers.

"Roxanne." Her name shuddered through his lips between heaving breaths. "Now. For God's sake."

"No." She laughed again, dipping her head. "Not yet, Callahan. I'm not finished with you yet." She teased his nipple, then slid down, over his rib cage, down his taut belly until an oath exploded from him.

His need was like a wild beast, snapping and clawing for freedom. And she held the whip, tormenting, promising, preventing him from that final burst that would lead to escape.

"You're killing me," he managed.

She trailed her tongue over him. "I know."

And the knowledge made her giddy. Drunk with power, she took him to the thin, quivering edge of relief, then retreated. Witchlike, she slid up his body.

"Tell me again." Her eyes were open and glowing. "Tell me now, when you want me so much it feels like it's ripping you apart. Tell me now."

"I love you." He gripped her hips with unsteady hands when she straddled him.

"Magic words," she murmured and shifted her body up to take him inside her.

When he filled her, when her throbbing muscles contracted to welcome him, she threw her head back with the sheer stunning pleasure of it. For the space of a dozen heartbeats she held him tight inside her, her body angled back and still as a statue.

He'd never forget how she looked, her skin the palest gold and gleaming with damp, her lips full and parted, her eyes closed, her hair tumbling fire down her back.

Then her body shuddered, wracked by a fast, hard orgasm. A slow, sinuous moan slipped from her, but still she didn't move. Then her lips curved, her lids fluttered up to reveal eyes deeper, more beautiful than any emerald he could covet.

She groped for his hands, locked fingers tight and rode him like a woman possessed.

When at last there was no more to take, no more to give, her body flowed like water down to his. The rain had stopped. Watery sunlight crept mystically into the room. He stroked a hand down her hair.

"Move in with me," he said.

She used what was left of her strength to lift her head and arch a brow. "My bags are already packed."

He grinned and gave her pretty butt a light pinch. "Pretty sure of yourself."

"Damn right." She gave him a smacking kiss. "I only have one question."

"What's that?"

"Who's going to do the cooking?"

"Ah." He trailed a finger down her ribs, searching for a foolproof escape. "I burn everything."

Roxanne hadn't been born yesterday. "Me too."

There was an easy way out, he decided. "The Quarter's lousy with restaurants."

"Yeah." Her grin spread. "Aren't we lucky?"

She settled back into his arm. As they lay close in the thin sunlight it seemed possible that the biggest problem they would face would be their appetites.

Chapter Twenty-two

IT WAS AS EASY AS PULLING A RABBIT OUT OF A HAT. THEY had, after all, lived with each other for years. They knew each other's habits, flaws, eccentricities.

She got up at dawn; he pulled the covers over his head. He took endless showers that used up all the hot water; she took paperback novels into the bathtub and stayed submerged in plot and bubbles until the water turned cold.

He worked out with weights on the living room floor; she preferred the structure of a thrice-weekly exercise class.

The stereo blared with rock when Luke had the controls and ached from the blues when Roxanne had her way.

They did have plenty in common. Neither would have thought of complaining about the need to practice a single routine over and over and over. They both adored Cajun food, movies of the forties and long, meandering walks through the Quarter.

And they both shouted when they argued.

They did plenty of shouting over the next few weeks. They thrived on it. Friction was as much a part of their relationship as breathing, and both would have regretted its loss.

As August steamed through New Orleans, passing toward the blessed relief of fall, they squabbled and made up, snarled and snapped and pushed each other with regularity into frustration and laughter.

For her birthday he gave her a crystal wand, a long, slim staff of amethyst wrapped with thin silver wires and crusted with cabochons of ruby, citrine and deep blue topaz. She set it on a table by the window so that the sun would strike it every day and pulse its magic through the air.

They were wildly in love and shared everything. Everything but the secret Luke paid for every month with a cashier's check for ten thousand dollars.

MAX HAD CALLED A MEETING, but he was in no hurry to start. He sipped LeClerc's hot, chicory-flavored coffee and bided his time. It felt good to have his family gathered around him again. He hadn't realized what a blow it would be to have both Roxanne and Luke out from under his roof. Even though they lived only a short walk away, the loss had staggered him.

He felt he was losing so much in such a short span of time. His children, who were no longer children, his hands, with their stiff fingers that so often seemed to belong to a stranger.

Even his thoughts, and that frightened him the most. So often they seemed to float away from him, to hang just out of reach so that he would stop, desperately trying to capture them again.

He told himself it was because he had so much on his mind. That was why he'd taken a wrong turn on his way to the French Market and had ended up lost and disoriented in a city he'd known most of his life. That was why he was forgetting things. Like the name of his stockbroker. Or the cupboard where LeClerc had stored the coffee mugs for years.

But today, having them all around him, he felt more strong,

more sure. His voice reflected none of his doubts as he called the meeting to order.

"I believe I have something of interest," he began when the room quieted. "A particular collection of jewelry—" He noted that Roxanne's eyes cut to Luke's. "I've taken a more specific interest in the sapphire portion of this collection. The lady appears to have an affection for this stone, and her jewelry wardrobe—which is extensive—reflects it. There is also a rather elegant pearl and diamond choker that is not to be scoffed at. Naturally, this is only part of the collection, but enough, I believe, for our needs."

"How many pieces?" Roxanne pulled a notebook out of her purse and prepared to scribble information in her own complex code. Max beamed his pride toward his precise and practical daughter.

"Of the sapphires, ten." Max steepled his hands. Odd, now that the game had begun, he no longer felt the ache in them. "Two necklaces, three pairs of earrings, a bracelet, two rings, a pin and an enhancer. Insured for half a million. The choker is valued at ninety thousand, but I believe that to be slightly excessive. Eighty thousand is a more reasonable estimate."

Luke accepted a cookie from the plate Lily passed him. "We got any visuals?"

"Naturally. Jean?"

LeClerc picked up the remote, aimed it toward the television. The set clicked on, then the VCR below it hummed into life. "I have transferred photographs to videotape." As the first picture flashed on, he struck a match and, holding it over the bowl of his pipe, began to suck. "I enjoy these new toys. This necklace," he continued, "is of a conservative design, perhaps lacking in imagination. But the stones themselves are good. There are ten fancy-cut sapphires of a cornflower blue. Total weight, twenty-five carats. The diamonds are very good quality baguettes of a total weight approximately eight point two carats."

But it was the next picture, the enhancer, that caught Roxanne's attention. With a quick sound of surprise she stared at the screen, then at her father.

"Justine Wyatt. If that's not the same piece I saw her wearing on the ship last summer, I'm brain-dead."

"You were never that, my sweet," Max said. "It's precisely the same piece."

The smile started first, spread into a grin, then bubbled out in a laugh of sheer good humor. "We're going to do it after all. Why didn't you tell me?"

"I wanted it to be a surprise." He preened, delighted with her reaction. "Consider it a kind of early Christmas gift, though it will be closer to Easter by the time we have everything in place." He gestured toward the set. "Skip ahead, will you, Jean? We can come back to this. The photos are copied from the insurance file. Our own contribution should be more entertaining."

The pictures zigzagged through fast forward then settled into live-action videos aboard the *Yankee Princess*.

"Home movies." Mouse grinned over a mouthful of cookies. "I took these ones."

"And a budding Spielberg in our midst," Max congratulated.

Indeed, the video was clear as crystal, the picture steady as a rock, the sound perfect. The slow pans, zooms and wide shots flowed together without any of the jerks and jolts of the amateur.

"Oh, look. There's that nice Mrs. Woolburger. Remember, Max. She was in the front row at every show."

"And there's Dori." Roxanne leaned forward, propping her elbows on her thighs. "And . . . oh." She flushed a bit when Mouse's lens zoomed in on the portside rail, capturing her and Luke in a long kiss.

It was odd and exciting to watch herself skim her fingers up into Luke's hair, to see the way his head tilted so that his mouth could cover hers more truly.

"That's the love interest," Mouse said with a wide grin. "Every good movie's got one."

"Run that part back again." Luke kneaded his fingers over Roxanne's shoulder.

Roxanne snatched the remote before LeClerc could oblige. "Ah, the plot thickens," she murmured as Sam and Justine strolled out on deck. Roxanne inched forward even as the picture focused in on a close-up of the bracelet they'd just studied in the still. The camera followed their progress over the deck, where they chose chairs side by side.

There were none of the secret smiles and lingering touches of newlyweds. Without exchanging a word, they settled back, she with a glossy magazine, he with a Tom Clancy techno-thriller.

"Romantic devils, aren't they?" Roxanne considered as she studied Sam. The breeze was ruffling his hair. He had the light tan of a man used to being outdoors. "The camera's good to him. I suppose that's a political asset."

"Barbie and Ken," Luke commented behind her. "The amazing plastic people."

Mouse thought Sam had shark's eyes, but he didn't say so because he thought the family would chuckle, and he didn't mean it to be funny. In his heart he wished Max had stood by his original decision so that they would all give Sam, his wife and her pretty stones a wide berth. But to Mouse, Max was the smartest person in the world, and it would never occur to him to question or doubt.

As the screen faded to gray, then bled to color again, Roxanne let out a low whistle.

"So that's the choker."

"Superb, isn't it? Freeze it there, darling." When Roxanne complied, Max began to lecture like a dedicated professor.

"The choker was a gift from her parents on her twenty-first birthday, four years ago this coming April. It was purchased at Cartier's, New York, for a sum of ninety-two thousand, five hundred and ninety-nine dollars—plus all the accompanying taxes."

"They hose you on that in New York," Luke murmured and received an acknowledging nod from Max.

"I can't believe I missed seeing a piece like that," Roxanne commented.

"She wore it on farewell night." Lily remembered it very well. "I think you and Luke were—occupied—until the show."

"Oh." Roxanne remembered, too, and slid a glance at Luke over her shoulder. "I guess we were."

Luke wrapped an arm around her waist and pulled her back off of the hassock and into his lap. "It's one of a kind, isn't it?"

Max beamed. He'd taught his children well. "Yes, as it happens. That will make it more difficult, though not impossible, to dispose of. I believe that should be enough, Roxanne." The set switched off. He settled back. Max's mind was so clear he wondered if he'd imagined the fog that so often settled over it. "We're awaiting blueprints of the house in Tennessee, as well as the New York pied-à-terre. The security systems on both residences will take some time."

"That'll give us time to enjoy Christmas first." It wasn't a question. For Lily, taking time to enjoy every aspect of the holiday was a sacred trust. "Since we're all here, we can trim the tree tonight." She shot a sly glance at Roxanne and Luke. "Jean's got a roast in the oven."

"With those little potatoes that get all crusty, and the carrots?" Luke felt his stomach, which had made do for two weeks with take-out and one disastrous attempt at fried chicken, give a yearning sigh.

Roxanne elbowed him in the ribs. After all, it had been she who'd fried the chicken. "The man's a walking appetite. We don't need to be bribed to stay."

"It doesn't hurt." Luke sent a beseeching look at LeClerc. "Biscuits?"

"You bet. And maybe enough left over for a doggie bag for a young wolf."

THE DAYS TO CHRISTMAS and the new year passed quickly. There were presents to buy and wrap, cookies to bake. In the case of the

Nouvelle/Callahan apartment, there were cookies to burn. The annual magic show to benefit the pediatric wing raised five thousand much-needed dollars. But it was Luke who carried on Max's tradition of entertaining the children who would spend the most magical night of the year confined to bed or wheelchair.

In the hour it took to pluck a coin out of a small ear, or cause magic flowers to spring up out of an empty pot, Luke discovered why Max devoted so much of his time to these children.

They were the most satisfying of audiences. They knew pain, and their reality was often unforgiving. But they believed. For an hour, that was all that mattered.

He dreamed again that night, after leaving those small faces behind. He dreamed, and awakened with his heart pounding and a scream burning his throat.

Roxanne shifted, murmuring in her sleep. He closed his cold fingers over hers and lay, for a long time, staring at the ceiling.

A LONG, RAINY WINTER clung stubbornly to March. Those entertainers who plied their trade on street corners suffered. In the house on Chartres, LeClerc kept his kitchen cozily warm. Though it stung the pride, he stayed indoors, rarely venturing out even to market. When he did, he felt each gust of wind sneak through his thinning skin and whip straight into the marrow of his bones.

Old age, he thought when he allowed himself to address the issue, was a motherfucker.

When the door opened on a blast of cold wind and chilling rain, he pounced.

"Close the goddamn door. This ain't no cave."

"Sorry."

Luke's apology earned a scowl. He was hatless and gloveless, and wore only a denim jacket as protection from the elements. LeClerc felt bitter envy swirl into his heart.

"You come here for a handout?"

Luke sniffed the air and caught the unmistakable aroma of baked apples. "If I can get one."

"Why don't you learn to cook for yourself? You think you can waltz in here and waltz back out again with a full belly anytime you please? I don't run no soup kitchen."

"It's like this." Since Luke was too used to the rough side of the Cajun's tongue to cower, he poured himself a cup of the coffee warming on the stove. "I figure a man can only be good, really good, at a limited number of things."

LeClerc sniffed, "What you so good at, *mon ami*, you can't boil an egg?"

"Magic." Luke took a teaspoon of sugar, made a fist and poured a rain of white grains into the funnel of his thumb and forefinger. He waited a beat then opened his hands wide to show it empty. LeClerc gave a snort that might have been a laugh. "Stealing." He handed LeClerc back the tattered wallet he'd lifted out of the old man's back pocket when he'd passed to the stove. "And making love to a woman." He picked up his cup and sipped. "But you'll have to take my word on that one, 'cause you ain't getting no demonstration."

LeClerc's leathery face split with a grin. "So, you think you do those things good, eh?"

"I do those things great. Now, how about one of those baked apples?"

"Sit and eat at the table like you been taught." No longer displeased with the company, he went back to kneading his dough. His hands were competent with the homey chore; the snakes twining up his arms slithered. "Where's Roxanne?"

"At that exercise class. She said she might have some lunch with a couple of the other women after."

"So, you're on the prowl, *oui?*"

"I was working out the kinks on this escape, needed a break." He didn't want to admit the apartment seemed empty without her in it. "It'll be ready for Mardi Gras."

"You have only two weeks."

"It's enough. Dangling over Lake Pontchartrain from a burning rope ought to draw a hell of a crowd. Challenger's betting fifty K I don't get out of the cuffs and make it back onto the bridge before the rope burns through."

"And if you don't?"

"Then I lose fifty thousand and get wet."

LeClerc put the dough into a big bowl, covered it. "It's a long drop."

"I know how to fall." He forked warm, spicy apple into his mouth. "I wanted to check over a couple of details with Max. He around?"

"He's sleeping."

"Now?" Luke lifted a brow. "It's eleven o'clock."

"He don't sleep so good at night." Worry creased his brow as he washed clinging dough from his hands, but his back was to Luke. "A man's entitled to sleep late now and again in his own house."

"I didn't mean—he never used to." Luke glanced toward the hallway, realized for the first time how quiet the house was. "He's okay, isn't he?"

Luke stared at LeClerc's rigid back. In his mind he could see Max, working his hands, working his fingers, flexing them, spreading them, manipulating them again and again like a pianist before a performance.

"How bad are his hands?" Luke saw by the slight stiffening of LeClerc's shoulders that he'd hit the mark. The homey scent of spice and apples and bread dough made him vaguely ill as he waited for the answer.

"Don't know what you mean." LeClerc kept his back turned as he shut off the water in the sink and reached for a dish towel.

"Jean. Don't con me. Give me credit for caring as much as you do."

"Goddamn." But there was no strength behind the oath, and Luke had his answer.

"Has he seen a doctor?" Luke's stomach churned. The fork rattled against his saucer as he pushed it away.

"Lily nagged him to one." LeClerc turned then, his small, dark eyes reflecting all the frustration and emotion he'd suppressed. "They give him pills to ease the pain. The pain in his fingers, *comprends?* Not the pain here." He tapped a fist to his heart. "It doesn't bring the magic back. Nothing will."

"There's got to be something—"

"*Rien,*" LeClerc interrupted. "Nothing. Inside each man is a timetable. And it says this is when his eyes will dim, or his ears clog up. This is the day he will get out of bed with his bones stiff and his joints aching. And today is the day his bladder will fail him or his lungs will go weak, or his heart will burst. The doctors will say do this, take that, but the *bon Dieu* has set the time, and when He says *c'est assez*, nothing can stop it."

"I don't believe that." Didn't want to. Luke scraped his chair back as he rose. "You're saying we've got nothing to do with it, no control."

"You think we do?" LeClerc gave a short bark of a laugh. "That is the arrogance of the young. Do you think it was an accident that you came to the carnival that night, that you found Max, that he found you?"

Luke remembered all too clearly the powerful draw of the poster, the way the painted eyes had seduced him into the tent. "It was good luck."

"Luck, *oui.* It's just another name for fate."

Luke had had enough of LeClerc's fatalistic philosophy. It dug too close to his own deeply buried beliefs. "None of this has anything to do with Max. We should get him to a specialist."

"*Pourquoi?* So he can have tests that break his heart? He has arthritis. It can be eased, but it can't be cured. You're his hands now, you and Roxanne."

Luke sat again, brooding into the black pool of his cooling coffee. "Does she know?"

"Maybe not in her head, but in her heart, she knows. Just as you." LeClerc hesitated. Following instinct, and his own fate, he sat across from Luke. "There is more," he said quietly.

Luke lifted his gaze. The look on LeClerc's face had fear skittering up his spine. "What?"

"He spends hours with his books, with his maps."

"The philosophers' stone?"

"*Oui*, the stone. He talks to scientists, to professors, even to mediums."

"It's caught his imagination," Luke said. "What's the harm of it?"

"Perhaps nothing of itself. This is his Holy Grail. I think if he finds it, he'll have peace. But for now ... I've seen him stare at the single page in a book, and an hour later, he has yet to turn the page. At breakfast he might ask Mouse to move the parlor sofa under the window. And at lunch he asks why the furniture has been rearranged. He says to Lily we must rehearse this new trick today, and after she waits for him in the workroom, after she goes to find him huddled with his books in the library, he remembers nothing of a rehearsal."

The fear dug in with tiny teeth and claws. "He has a lot on his mind."

"It's his mind that concerns me." LeClerc sighed. He thought his eyes too old for tears, but they prickled hot and had to be fought back. "Yesterday, I found him standing in the courtyard. He was in costume, with no coat against the wind. 'Jean,' he says. 'Where is the van?' "

"The van? But—"

"We have no van." LeClerc kept his eyes level with Luke's. "Not for nearly ten years, but he asks if Mouse has taken it to wash before the show. So, I tell him there is no show today, and he must come inside, out of the cold." LeClerc lifted his cup and swallowed deeply. "Then he looks around him, lost, and I can see fear in his eyes. So I take him inside, up to bed. He asks if Roxanne is home from school, and I tell him no, not yet. But soon. He says Luke must bring his pretty girlfriend back to dinner, and I say *bien*, I will make *étouffée*. Then he sleeps, and when he wakes I think he remembers none of it."

337

Luke uncurled the hand he'd fisted in his lap. "Jesus."

"A man's body betrays him, he moves slower. But what does he do when it's his mind?"

"He needs to see a doctor."

"Ah, *oui*, and this will be done because Lily will insist. But there's something you must do."

"What can I do?"

"You must see that he doesn't go with you when you fly to Tennessee." Before Luke could speak, LeClerc waved the words back. "He must be a part of the planning, but not the execution. What if he forgets where he is, what he's doing? Can you risk it? Can you risk him?"

"No," Luke answered after a long pause. "I won't risk him. But I won't hurt him, either." He debated for a moment, then nodded. "I think we should—"

"Jean, what is that marvelous bouquet?" Max strolled in, looking so fit and alert that Luke almost dismissed LeClerc's story. "Ah, Luke, so you followed your nose as well. Where's Roxanne?"

"Out with some friends. Want some coffee?" Luke was already up and moving toward the stove. Max sat, stretching out his legs with a sigh. His fingers were moving, moving, moving, like a man playing an invisible piano.

"I hope she doesn't dawdle too long. I know Lily wanted to take her out for new shoes. The child can't seem to keep them on her feet."

Luke's hand jerked. Coffee splashed on the counter. Max was discussing Roxanne as if she were twelve again.

"She'll be along." His heart felt like an anvil in his chest as he carried the coffee back to the kitchen table.

"Have you worked out the bugs in the Water Torture escape?"

Luke wanted to scream at Max to stop, to leap off whatever time machine was holding his mind prisoner. Instead he spoke calmly. "Actually, I'm working on the Burning Rope. Remember?" he prodded gently. "It's set for Shrove Tuesday. Next week."

"Burning Rope?" Max's hand paused. The coffee cup that was halfway to his lips trembled. It was painful to watch his fight to return to the present. His mouth drooped open and hung slack, his eyes darted wildly. Then they focused again. His hand continued to bring the cup to his lips. "You'll draw a good crowd," he said. "The early press is excellent."

"I know. And I couldn't ask for a better cover for the Wyatt job. I want to move on it that night."

Max frowned. "There are a number of small details yet to be worked out."

"There's time." Despising himself, Luke leaned back. He hooked an arm casually over the back of his chair. "I want to ask you for a favor, Max."

"All right."

"I want to pull the job myself." Luke saw the shock on Max's face, the disappointment. "It's important to me," he plowed on. "I know the rules about no job being personal, but this one's the exception. There's a lot of baggage between Sam and me."

"All the more reason not to let emotions cloud the issue."

"They are the issue." At least this much was true. "I owe him. This would go a long way toward paying off old debts." Then he pulled out his trump card, hating himself. "If you don't trust me to carry it off, if you don't think I'm good enough, just say so."

"Of course I trust you. But the point is . . ." He didn't know what the point was, except that his son was taking yet another step away. "You're right. It's past time for you to try something on your own. You're as good as they get."

"Thanks." He wanted to take those restless hands in his, but only lifted his coffee cup in salute. "I was taught by the best."

"WHAT DO YOU MEAN you're doing it on your own?" Roxanne demanded. With her gym bag tossed over her shoulder she'd followed Luke from the living room, where he'd dropped his bombshell, into the bedroom.

"Just what I said. It's my show."

"Like hell. We all work together." Despite annoyance, her ingrained tidiness had her unzipping the bag to remove towels and workout clothes. "Daddy wouldn't agree to it."

"He did agree to it." Luke peeled off his denim jacket and tossed it in the vicinity of a chair. It slid off the arm and hit the floor. "It's no big deal."

"It is, too." Roxanne rezipped her bag and set it in its proper place on the closet shelf. She kicked aside a jumble of Luke's shoes. "If we've all been in on the planning stages from the get-go, why do you think you're the only one who gets to have the fun?"

"Because." He dropped down on the bed and tucked his arms behind his head. "That's the way I want it."

"Look, Callahan—"

"You look, Nouvelle." His use of her last name usually made her chuckle. Though her lips twitched, the stubborn chin was still up. "Max and I talked it over. It's cool with him, so let it go."

"Maybe it's cool with him, but not with me." She stuck her hands on her hips. "I'm in, pal. That's that."

His eyes glittered. "I want to do it myself."

"Tough. I want to have straight blond hair but you don't see me whining about it, do you?"

"I like your hair," he said, hoping to distract her. "It looks like a bunch of corkscrews that caught on fire."

"That's poetic."

"I especially like it when you're naked. Want to get naked, Rox?"

"Put a sock in your hormones, Callahan. You're not shaking me loose. I'm going."

"Suit yourself." It didn't matter if she went along or not. But arguing with her about it had taken her mind off Max. "But I run the show."

"In your dreams." She planted her hands on either side of his legs at the foot of the bed. "Full partners all the way."

"I've had more experience."

"That's what you said about sex, but I caught on, didn't I?"

"Now that you mention it." He reared up and made a grab for her. She danced easily out of reach.

"Come here," he demanded.

She tilted her head, sending him a long, seductive smile over her shoulder. "You look strong enough to get up and walk, Callahan. Why don't you come get me?"

He knew how to play the game. After a negligent movement of his shoulders, he gazed at the ceiling. "No thanks. Not that interested."

"Okay. You want to go eat early, avoid the Mardi Gras rush?"

"Sure." Without moving an inch he shifted his eyes down, watched her slowly peel off her shirt. Beneath she wore a thin white cotton athletic bra that should have been as alluring as cold gumbo. The blood drained out of his head and into his loins.

"I feel like something hot." She folded the shirt neatly, laid it on top of the dresser. With deliberate movements she unsnapped her jeans. He heard the quiet rasp of the zipper and concentrated on not swallowing his tongue. "And spicy."

She pulled the denim down, revealing practical cotton briefs in the same snowy white as the bra. Her skin was winter pale and flawless. The jeans went through the same meticulous routine as the shirt.

Idly she picked up her brush, tapping it against her palm. "What are you in the mood for, Callahan?" She strolled just close enough to the bed that when his hand shot out it could grip her arm. She was laughing as she hit the mattress.

"I won," he claimed, rolling on top of her.

"Uh-uh. Tie score." She lifted her head to meet his descending lips with hers. "We're partners. Don't you forget it."

Chapter Twenty-three

FAT TUESDAY STARTED OFF WITH PANCAKES. FOR ALL LeClerc's talk about luck and fate, he believed in hedging his bets. He'd served pancakes on the last day before Lent as long as she could remember, and Roxanne was practical enough not to thumb her nose at superstition. Her only alteration was to buy a mix rather than slog through LeClerc's complicated recipe.

Her pancakes might have been thin and singed around the edges, but they fulfilled the basic requirements. She managed to chew her way through one of the rubbery disks, but as Luke plowed contentedly through half a dozen, she assumed their luck for the year was set.

And perhaps it was.

The streets and sidewalks of the Quarter were packed with celebrants on this last day of Mardi Gras. The sounds of music and laughter swung up to her balcony as they had for the week of constant partying. Tonight, she knew the volume and the frenzy would increase. Parades, costumes, dancing—that last hurrah before the forty days of sobriety to usher in Easter. But there would also be stumbling drunks, muggers, vicious fighting and a few murders.

Behind its beautiful and seductive mask, Mardi Gras could wear a surly face.

Had the evening been free for her, she and Luke might have gone over to the house on Chartres and watched the goings-on from the balcony. As it was, they would be spending most of the night of revelry in Tennessee relieving Mr. and Mrs. Samuel Wyatt of approximately a half of a million in jewels.

Fair trade, Roxanne thought with a smile. The Wyatts would collect on their obscene insurance premiums, balancing that with the sting of having possessions snapped up from under their noses. The Nouvelles would keep the links in an old food chain secure. It wasn't only the Nouvelles who profited, after all.

Roxanne pressed a hand to her queasy stomach. The pancake, she thought, hadn't settled well. She hoped Luke's cast-iron stomach was holding up. The last thing he needed was nausea while he hung upside down above Lake Pontchartrain.

She needed to start over there herself. The escape was due to begin in just over an hour, and Luke would want her close by. The Burning Rope made her uneasy, but she'd grown accustomed to being nervy and tense before one of his escapes.

She picked up her purse, then dropped it again with a moan.

Damn those pancakes! she thought and made a dash for the bathroom.

"SHE SHOULD BE HERE." Torn between concern and annoyance, Luke tried to prepare his mind for the job to come. His body was ready. "Why didn't she just come with me?"

"Because she'd have nothing to do during the setup except worry!" Lily kept an eagle eye on Max, who was granting an interview to one of the television reporters. She had worries of her own. "You concentrate on you," she ordered Luke. "Roxanne'll be along."

"Christ knows how she'd get through now." He scanned the

bridge. Behind the barricades people swarmed and jockeyed for a better view. The local authorities had cooperated by closing the bridge to vehicular traffic for the hour Luke required from setup to completion. But that hadn't stopped the crowds. They'd streamed onto the bridge from both sides to press up against the barricades.

Luke wondered idly how many pockets would be picked over the lake that afternoon. He was always willing to lend a hand to an associate.

Where the hell was Roxanne?

He shaded his eyes against the brilliant glare of sun and gave the New Orleans side of the bridge one last look.

Lily was right, he told himself. He had to concentrate on the job at hand. Roxanne would get there when she got there.

At this height over the water, the wind was stiff. He'd factored that in, but he accepted that nature could often play capricious tricks with calculations. That wind was going to batter the living hell out of him.

"Let's do it."

He stepped to his mark. Instantly the crowd began to clap and call out encouragements. The cameras focused. After some delicate diplomacy, it had been decided that Lily would hype the escape rather than Max. She took her mike and, looking splashy in a red jumpsuit, held up a hand for silence.

"Good afternoon, ladies and gentlemen. Today, you're privileged to witness one of the most daring escapes ever attempted. The Burning Rope."

She continued, explaining exactly what would happen and introducing the two police officers, one from New Orleans, one from Lafayette, who examined the shackles and straitjacket Luke would use.

Once Luke's arms were in position, Lafayette cuffed one wrist, looped the chain through and secured the other. The key was held by Miss Louisiana, who'd come to the event decked out in full evening gear and tiara. New Orleans fit the restraint in place.

The rope was tied around Luke's ankles by the current calf-roping champion of the National Rodeo. There was a drumroll, courtesy of the Drum and Bugle Corps of a local high school.

Luke was lowered face first toward the waters of Lake Pontchartrain. Someone in the crowd screamed. Luke blessed them for their timing. There was nothing like a touch of hysteria or a couple of good faints to add to the drama.

A sharp gust of wind slapped his face hard enough to make his eyes water. His body twisted and swayed. He was already working on the cuffs.

He felt the tug when the rope played out. He had five seconds before a volunteer torched the end of the rope and sent the fire crawling toward him. He had to fight a surprising flood of vertigo when the wind cupped him in a playful hand and sent him spinning.

Fucking physics, he thought. A body in motion remains in motion, and he was trapped in a wide pendulum swing that thrilled and delighted the crowd, but made his job that much more difficult.

His satisfaction on freeing his hands was short-lived. He could smell the smoke. Slippery as a snake, he wormed his body inside the straitjacket, felt a bright flash of pain in his abused joints. His fingers went busily to work.

His mind was cold with control. Only one thought intruded, punching through the mechanics of the work like a relentless fist.

He would not stay trapped.

He heard the roar from above when the straitjacket plunged toward the water, empty. The rescue boat bobbing on the lake gave a congratulatory blast of its horn. Though he appreciated the sentiment, Luke was aware it was too early to open the champagne.

On a grunt of effort, he folded at the waist, stomach muscles straining as he levered himself up to fight the cowboy's knots from his legs. He didn't look at the fire, but he could smell it. It was inches away and sneaking closer.

He didn't think he'd die from singed feet, but he figured it would be damn uncomfortable. The clock in his mind warned him that he had minutes only before the fire ate through the rope and sent him diving headlong into the lake.

The cowboy had some tricky moves, Luke discovered. He wished he'd taken LeClerc's advice to slip a knife into his boot. But it was too late for regrets now. He'd manage the knots, or he'd take a swim to cool his hot foot.

He felt the rope give. This final stage took intricate timing. If he released himself too quickly, he'd take a dive. If he waited too long to set up, he'd end his escape with a trip to the burn ward. Neither appealed.

He hooked his hand around the second rope. Misdirection, and the fact that it was thin as wire, had kept the crowd from seeing it. Luke felt the heat from the burning rope smoke his knuckles as he secured his handhold.

He kicked his feet free and began to monkey his way up. From atop the bridge it appeared as though he was climbing on a thin column of fire. Indeed he would require some generous use of LeClerc's salve for singes and burns.

The crowd held its breath, let it out on a gasp each time the wind caught him. When he reached the top, he felt Mouse's good, solid grip on his arms. LeClerc bent down, ostensibly to offer a word of congratulations.

"Got him?" he muttered to Mouse.

"Yep."

"*Bien.*" LeClerc flicked a knife from his sleeve and severed both ropes.

There were shrieks and shudders when the rope of fire fell into the lake.

"Want to pull me the rest of the way up?" Luke nearly had his breath back. He knew the moment the rush of adrenaline faded, he was going to hurt like a mother. With Mouse's assistance he gained his feet. The cameras were already closing in, but Luke was scanning the crowd.

346

"Roxanne?"

"Must've gotten tied up," Mouse said and thumped Luke hard enough on the back to make him stagger. "Your shirt was smoking," he said mildly and grinned. "That was a neat one, Luke. Maybe we could go to San Francisco and do it on the Golden Gate? Wouldn't that be great?"

"Sure." He passed a hand casually through his hair, just to make sure it wasn't on fire. "Why not?"

MAYBE IT WAS STUPID, and overly possessive. Maybe it was a lot of unattractive things, but Luke knew only one pertinent fact when he walked into the bedroom, smelling of smoke and triumph, and found Roxanne stretched out on the bed. He was pissed.

"Well, that's really nice." He tossed his keys onto the dresser with a clatter that had Roxanne moaning and opening her eyes. "I figured you had to have been in some sort of a life-threatening accident, and here you are, taking a nap."

She took what she thought was a dreadful risk and opened her mouth to speak. "Luke—"

"I guess it wasn't any big deal to you, the fact that I've been working on this bit for months, that it was probably the biggest thing I've ever done or that you promised you'd be there when I got back up." He stalked to the foot of the bed, scowled briefly, then stalked away. "Just because I needed to concentrate, expected a little support from my woman—"

"Your woman?" That was enough to have her rearing up. "Don't you toss that phrase at me as though I was tucked somewhere between your silk suit and your record collection."

"You're a little higher than my record collection, but obviously my place is a few notches lower."

"Don't be such a jerk."

"Damn it, Rox, you knew this was important to me."

"I was going to come, but I—" She broke off as her stomach

roiled. "Oh, shit." She scrambled up and dove into the bath-room.

By the time she'd finished retching, Luke was there with a cool, damp cloth and a repentant attitude. "Come on, baby, back to bed." It seemed her weakened body poured out of his arms and onto the sheets. "I'm sorry, Rox." Gently he bathed her clammy face. "I came in swinging and didn't even take a good look at you."

"How bad do I look?"

"Don't ask." He kissed her forehead. "What happened?"

"I thought it was the pancakes." She kept her eyes closed and her head very still and only opened her mouth wide enough to let the words whisper out. "I was hoping you'd come home green so I'd know it was food poisoning."

"Sorry." He smiled and brushed his lips across her brow again. She was clammy, but he didn't think there was a fever. "I'd say you have one of those twenty-four-hour things."

If she hadn't been so weak, she'd have been insulted. "I never get those."

"You never get anything," he pointed out. "But when something snags you, it snags big time." He remembered her chicken pox, the only childhood illness she'd ever succumbed to. That and the bout of seasickness aboard the *Yankee Princess* were the only times he remembered seeing her down. Until now.

"I just need to rest a little while more. I'll be fine."

"Roxanne." Luke set the cloth aside to take her face in his hands. "You're not going."

Her eyes shot open. She tried to sit up, but he held her in place with only the slightest pressure. "Of course I'm going. This whole gig was my idea in the first place. I'm not missing out on the payoff because I ate a bad pancake."

"It wasn't the pancakes," he corrected. "But it doesn't matter what caused it, you're sick as a dog."

"I'm not. I'm a little queasy."

"You're in no shape to pull a job."

"I'm in perfect shape."

"Fine, we make a deal." He sat back, eyeing her. "You get up now, walk to the living room and back without falling on your face, and we move forward as planned. You don't make it, I go alone."

Because it was a dare, it was irresistible. "All right. Move."

When he rose, she gritted her teeth and swung her legs out of bed. Her head spun, and fresh, nasty sweat popped out on the back of her neck, but she gained her feet.

"No holding on," Luke added when she braced a hand against the wall.

That stiffened her spine. She straightened, walked briskly into the living room. And sank into a chair. "I just need a minute."

"No deal." He crouched in front of her. "Rox, you know you can't do it."

"We could postpone—" She broke off, shaking her head. "No, that would be stupid. I'm being stupid." Weak, frustrated, she let her head fall back. "I hate missing this one, Callahan."

"I know." He picked her up to carry her back to bed. "I guess sometimes things don't work out exactly the way you want." He didn't think it was the time to mention his plans had taken a beating as well. Turning their flush of shared triumph into an evening of romance by asking her to marry him had seemed inspired. Now it would have to wait.

"You don't know the security system as well as I do."

"We've gone over it a dozen times," he reminded her, insulted. "It won't be my first night on the job."

"It'll take you longer."

"Sam and Justine are in Washington. I'll have the time."

"Take Mouse." Sudden panic had her grabbing for his hand. "Don't go alone."

"Rox, relax. I could do this in my sleep. You know that."

"It doesn't feel right."

"You don't feel right," he corrected. "I want you to get some rest. I'll call Lily and have her come by to look in on you. Keep a light burning, babe." He kissed her then, lightly. "I'll be back before sunrise."

"Callahan." She tightened her grip as he eased back. It was foolish, she thought, this awful reluctance to let him go. "I love you."

He smiled and leaned down to kiss her again, the light, friendly kiss of a man who knew he'd have time for more soon. "I love you, too."

"Break a leg." She sighed, and let him go.

LUKE LOVED TO FLY. From the very first time he'd strapped into the cockpit to take his initial lesson from Mouse, he'd been hooked. It had no longer been a matter of learning a practical skill that could add convenience to both of his careers. It had been, from that soaring beginning, pure delight.

The plane he piloted was registered to a John Carroll Brakeman, a nonexistent insurance executive. To complete the alias, Luke had added a short, trim beard, a three-piece pin-striped suit—with several successful inches of padding beneath it. His black hair was sprinkled with silver at the temples.

When he landed in Tennessee, he logged in, checked his return flight plan and carried his monogrammed briefcase to the spiffy Mercedes 450 he'd rented. He drove it to the Hilton, checked into his reserved suite and left orders not to be disturbed.

Fifteen minutes later, minus the beard, the padding and the silver temples, he hurried down the stairwell to the parking lot. The dark sedan he'd ordered under another alias was waiting. Because it was safer than picking up the keys at the desk, Luke popped the lock, hot-wired the engine and drove serenely away.

Once the job was completed, he would return the sedan to the parking lot and slip back into his room. He would re-don his disguise and check out. Richer by approximately one and a half million dollars, he'd fly back to New Orleans. Nothing would connect him with either the alias or the burglary.

A roundabout route, perhaps, but as Max was wont to say, a roundabout route still gets you where you want to go.

Two blocks from Sam's house, Luke parked the dark, nondescript sedan on a tree-lined street. In this suburban paradise, all the lawns were trimmed, the dogs well behaved and the houses respectably dark at one A.M.

Streetlamps pooled light he easily avoided. Clad in black from head to foot, he slipped between shadows. There was a trace of fog that might give him some problems at the airport. But he felt the mist had been custom-made for him. There was a half-moon, but its light was trapped behind shifting clouds and the air was sweet with hints of spring.

He circled the Wyatt estate, a sprawling two-story brick with white columns that resembled slender bones in the half-light. There was no car in the drive. The security lights beamed like swords over the lawn and picked up pretty banks of golden daffodils and the tender furled leaves of trees still greening. He was almost sorry that Sam was in Washington. It would have added spice to the sweetness of satisfaction to have stolen in and taken what he wanted while his old enemy snored.

A tall privacy fence guarded the house on three sides, and old leafy trees shielded the front. Luke used both as shelter as he approached.

He missed Roxanne severely when he started on the security. The new computerized systems annoyed him, insulted his creativity. He supposed the numbers and complex sequences appealed to Roxanne's logical mind, but to Luke they took the art of thievery into the ennui of accounting.

Even with her instructions playing in his head, it took him twice as long as it would have taken her to access the code. Still, she didn't have to know.

Satisfied, he chose the rear entrance and handily picked the lock. He preferred the method to jimmying, which any second-rate B&E man could accomplish, and certainly held it above smashing a pane of glass, which took no skill whatsoever.

Luke stepped into a neat sitting room that smelled of lemon oil and wisteria. The old excitement crept up his spine. There was something indescribably arousing about standing in a dark, empty house, surrounded by the shapes and shadows of another person's possessions. It was like being told their secrets.

Luke walked silently from the sitting room, turning left in the corridor toward Sam's office. His fingers were already itching inside the thin surgical gloves to turn the dial of the safe.

He needed no light. His eyes had had time to adjust, and he knew the square footage of the Wyatt home a great deal better than its owners.

There was a quality of silence to an empty house Luke had always enjoyed. It was a whispering, a humming, an eerily pleasant kind of music the air took on when there was no one inside to breathe it.

He had turned into Sam's office before it struck him that the music was absent. Then the light flashed on, blinding him.

"Well, Luke, come right on in." Sam leaned back in his desk chair, causing the leather to creak. "I've been expecting you. Please." He gestured, and the light glinted off the chrome of the .32 he held. "Join me for a drink."

Luke studied Sam's smile, scanned the smooth surface of the desk where two brandies rested. He imagined it was Napoleon, but doubted its flavor would wash the oily taste of a setup out of his mouth.

"How long have you known?"

"Oh, several months now." With the gun aimed at Luke's chest, he leaned forward to cup his snifter. "I'm ashamed to say I didn't suspect earlier. All this time, I put the Nouvelles' extravagant lifestyle down to a little blackmail or some short cons. Sit," he invited. "I'm so terribly sorry you came alone."

"I work alone," Luke said, hoping to salvage at least that much.

"You were always pathetically gallant. Sit," he repeated, and his voice was as cold as the chrome of the handgun. Gauging his best chance was to play the scene out, Luke sat. "The brandy's excellent." Sam set aside his snifter to lift the phone. "Don't worry," he said when he noticed the flash in Luke's narrowed eyes. "I'm not phoning the police. I don't believe we'll need them." He punched a series of buttons, waited. "He's here. Yes. Use the back door." He was smiling when he replaced the receiver. "A little surprise. Now what shall we talk about while we wait?"

"You might be able to make breaking and entering stick," Luke said calmly. "There's a possibility of attempted burglary. All of which I can probably finesse into a joke. Poor judgment, I could say, trying to pull a fast one on a childhood rival."

Sam paused a moment as if considering. "I doubt that would work, particularly after I pointed out the pattern. One I admit I didn't catch on to until recently. You son of a bitch," he said with the smile still spread over his face. "You sanctimonious bastards—all of you. Acting outraged because I knocked over a couple of shops while you were nothing but petty thieves and grifters yourselves."

"Not petty," Luke corrected and decided to try the brandy after all. "And never grifters. What do you want?"

"What I've wanted all along. To make you pay. I hated you, right from the start. Keep your hands where I can see them," he warned. Luke shrugged and sipped brandy. "I didn't know precisely why, only that I did. But I believe it was because we were so alike."

Now Luke smiled. "You've got a gun on me, Wyatt. You can kill me or send me to prison. But don't insult me."

"Always cool, and still reckless. It was a combination I might have admired if you hadn't been so disgustingly superior. You held the Nouvelles in the palm of your hand. Oh, I saw the potential even then, but you were in the way."

"Face it, pal." Maybe, just maybe, he could anger him enough to force him into a mistake. "You fucked up."

Sam's eyes glittered, but the gun didn't waver. "What I fucked was your girl. And I seduced Roxanne away from you. Believe me,

353

if I'd realized the potential there, I'd have fucked her rather than—what was her name? Annabelle."

The fury bounded up. Luke had to curl his hand around the arm of the chair to stay seated. "I should have broken more than your nose."

"There, for the first time, you're correct. You should have destroyed me, Callahan, because now, I'll destroy you. Come in, Mr. Cobb."

Now Luke did jerk to his feet. Brandy splashed over his gloved hand. There, in the doorway, was his oldest nightmare.

"I believe you two know each other," Sam continued. Oh, this was rich, he thought. Magnificent. What more could he ask for than to see Luke's face go white? A great deal more, he decided, chuckling to himself. A great deal more. "You might not be aware that Mr. Cobb has been working for me for quite some time now. Help yourself to the bar while I explain a few salient points to our mutual friend."

"Don't mind if I do." Cobb strutted over to the whiskey decanter and poured a double. He liked the idea of sharing a drink with a man of Wyatt's caliber, being invited—after all this time—into his home. "Looks like he's got you by the short hairs, Luke."

"Succinctly put. Now that we're all together, I'll outline the deal." It was perfect, so perfect, Sam could barely keep his voice from shivering with excitement. "It was my idea to have Mr. Cobb contact you and squeeze you for a few thousand a month. Imagine my surprise when you paid quietly and with ease, even when I gave him permission to increase the amounts. Now, how, I asked myself, does a man—even one with a certain amount of financial success—pay off blackmail demands in excess of a hundred thousand a year without altering his lifestyle by even the smallest degree?" Waiting a beat, Sam tapped a finger against his curved lips. "He can't, of course, unless he has another source of income. So, I began tracking you. I still have contacts of my own, you know. Then I laid the bait and watched you nibble. My

354

insurance company, my security system, my schedule. It wasn't difficult to make it seem as though I planned to be in Washington this week."

The first wave of sickness had sweat springing cold to the back of Luke's neck. "You opened the cage door," he managed. "That doesn't mean I'll let it lock behind me."

"I'm aware of that. You see with a clever lawyer you might just wriggle out of the charges. Since you came alone, it would be difficult if not impossible to spread the blame to the Nouvelles. I could simply kill you." Lips pursed, he lifted the gun, sighting in on Luke's forehead. "But then, you'd only be dead."

"Don't kill the golden goose," Cobb said and chuckled at his own wit.

"Certainly not, particularly if you can make him roast slowly."

"And he'll keep paying, too." Cobb poured more whiskey.

"Yes, though not in the way you mean." Sam smiled at Cobb, then pulled the trigger.

The sound of the bullet exploded in the small room. Luke felt it echo through him as if he were a hollow tunnel. Dazed, he watched Cobb stagger, saw the look of surprise on his face, and the blood flow through the neat black hole that had suddenly appeared in his forehead.

The glass of whiskey hit the rug first, rolled unbroken across the bright Turkish carpet. And Cobb fell like a tree.

"That was easier than I imagined." Sam's hand shook once, but it was excitement rather than nerves. "Much easier."

"Jesus." Luke tried to spring to his feet but found his limbs heavy. He rose slowly, like a man fighting his way up through water. The room spun like a carousel and the bright, bloody carpet flew up to meet him.

WHEN HE AWAKENED, his head felt clogged. The drummers banging inside it were muffled with wads of cotton wool.

"Obviously you have good stamina." Sam's voice seemed to drift through the mists. "I thought you'd be out longer."

"What?" Wobbly, Luke managed to crawl up on his hands and knees. He had to fight a powerful wave of nausea before he dared lift his head. When he did, he saw Cobb's dead-white face. "Oh, God." Lifting a hand, he wiped the sweat from his face. He was light-headed and sick, but still aware enough to realize he no longer wore his gloves.

"No gratitude?" Sam demanded. He sat behind the desk again, but when Luke focused in, he saw he held a different gun. "After all, the man made your life hell, didn't he? Now he's dead."

"You didn't even flinch." Sam, the gun, the room wavered as Luke fought to clear his head. "You shot him in cold blood and didn't even flinch."

"Thank you. Remember, I can do the same with you—or Max or Lily. Or Roxanne."

He wasn't going to beg, not on his hands and knees. Painfully, Luke pulled himself to his feet. His legs wobbled, adding humiliation to terror. "What do you want?"

"Exactly what I'm going to get. I can call the police now, tell them you and Cobb broke in while I was working late in my office. I surprised you, you pulled a gun. Then you argued between yourselves, and you shot him. During the confusion, I managed to get my gun. This is my gun by the way."

He gestured with a trim .25. He wanted to pull the trigger, wanted badly to pull it and feel that jolt of power again. But that would be too quick. Too quick, too final.

"The other is unregistered, and untraceable—except for the fact that it now has your fingerprints on it. You'll be charged with murder, and with your connection to Cobb, I doubt you'd wiggle out."

He smiled then, hugely. A man dazzled by his own brilliance.

"That's our first scenario," he went on. "Which would play nicely, I believe. I don't like it as much as the second, because it involves me. The second is that you take the body and dispose of it. Then you go."

"Go?" Struggling to remain lucid, Luke dragged a hand through his hair. "Just like that?"

"Exactly. Only you don't go back to New Orleans. You don't contact the Nouvelles. You, quite literally, disappear." The grin on Sam's face spread, erupted into a fast, wild giggle. "Abracadabra." The sound had cold fingers squeezing Luke's spine.

"You're out of your mind."

"You'd like to think so, wouldn't you?" Sam asked, and his eyes glittered. "You'd like to think so because I've beaten you, beaten you at last."

"All of this?" Luke's voice was still slurred from the drug. He spoke slowly, carefully, as if to be certain he understood the words himself. "You planned all this, you murdered Cobb, just to get back at me?"

"Does that seem unreasonable?" Sam leaned back in his chair, swiveled it side to side. "Perhaps I'd think so if I were in your position." He jerked forward again, and had the pleasure of seeing Luke jolt and brace. "But you see, I'm not. I'm in charge. And you'll do exactly as I say. If you don't, I'll have you arrested for murder, and I'll see that Maximillian Nouvelle is investigated for grand larceny—unless I find it more enjoyable to kill him."

"He took you in off the street."

"And kicked me back onto it." The smile on Sam's face twisted into a sneer of disgust. "Don't expect loyalty from me, Callahan, especially if you're not willing to put your own on the line."

"Why don't you just kill me?"

"I prefer the idea of you grubbing for a living in some godforsaken town, having sweaty dreams about Roxanne and the men she'll fill her life with, losing that star you've held on to so tightly over the years. Escape this, Callahan. You go, or the Nouvelles pay, for the rest of their lives. And don't think you can leave now, then reappear in a few weeks. You may slip the noose, but I'll pull it taut around Max's neck, that I promise. I have all the evidence I need to hang him, right in the safe you never had the opportunity to open."

"No one would believe you."

"No? A dedicated public servant with a pristine record? A man who brought himself out of the hell of the streets? Who, though he felt a certain loyalty to the old man, could no longer conceal the facts? And who, recognizing the signs of senility, would plead for confinement in a mental health facility rather than prison?"

That turned fear to ice, a sharp, ragged spear of ice that threatened to draw blood. "No one's going to put Max away."

"That's up to you. Your call, Callahan."

"You've got the hammer." He felt his life slipping through his fingers like sand. "I'll disappear, Wyatt. But you'll never be entirely sure when I'll be back. One night I'll just be there."

"Take your old friend with you, Callahan." He gestured toward Cobb. "And think of me, every day, when you're in hell."

Chapter Twenty-four

LUKE KNEW IT WAS FOOLISHLY RISKY, BUT RISKS NO LONGER seemed to matter. He left the second rental car in the hotel parking lot and, using the main elevators in the lobby, rode up to his room. Once inside he pulled a bottle of Jack Daniel's out of a paper sack, set it on the dresser and stared at it.

He stared for a long time before breaking the seal. He tipped the bottle back, taking three long swallows to let the fire burn through the worst of the misery.

It didn't work. He'd already learned from the harsh example of his youth that liquor didn't negate miseries, it only compounded them. But it had been worth a shot.

He could still smell Cobb. The sweat and blood and stench of death clung to his skin. It had been a hideous job, weighing down the body and sinking it into the river.

He'd wanted him dead. God knew he wanted the man dead. But he hadn't known what sudden, violent and pitiless death could do.

Luke couldn't forget how Sam had fired the gun—so casually, as if taking a life was as simple an event as an evening of cards. He hadn't done it out of hate, or for gain or in blind passion. He'd done it thoughtlessly, like a young child might tumble a building of blocks. All because Cobb had been marginally more of use to him dead than alive.

Control, Luke thought, easing down on the bed like an old man. All these years he'd thought he'd been in control. But that had been a lie. All along there had been someone behind the scenes, pulling the strings and making a mockery out of what he'd thought he'd made and could make out of his life.

All because of some twisted sense of jealousy, and an overheated grudge due to a broken nose. Anyone standing in that leather and oak office that evening would have seen that Sam was more than ambitious, he was more than cold-blooded. He was crazy. But there was only one person still alive who had seen it.

What could he do? Luke rubbed the heels of his hands over his eyes as if to wipe away the image of what had been so that he could clearly see what had to be.

He'd broken into a private home. If the police knew where to look they would find the trail, and that trail would lead directly back to the Nouvelles. If Luke went to the police with a tangled story of blackmail and murder, whom would they believe? The thief, or the sober citizen?

He could risk that. Though he wasn't certain he could face prison without going mad, he could risk that. But there was a chance Sam would make good on his other threats. Max in a mental ward, Lily devastated, Roxanne ruined. Or perhaps Sam would find murder more to his liking and kill them—kill them with the gun that carried Luke's fingerprints.

That thought brought panic bubbling up so that he grabbed the phone and punched in numbers. His fingers grabbed hard on the receiver. She answered on the first ring, as if she'd been waiting for him.

"Hello . . . Hello? Is anyone there?"

He could see her, as clearly as if he'd conjured her into the room. Sitting up in bed, the phone to her ear and an open book in her lap, an old black-and-white movie flickering on the television.

Then the image was gone, vanished like smoke, because he knew he would never see her that way again.

"Hello? Luke, is that you? Is something—"

He set the phone down, slowly, quietly.

He'd made his choice. To answer her, to tell her would be to keep her and watch her suffer. To leave her, without a word, without a sign, would mean she would grow to hate him, safely.

Like a man already drunk, he rose and brought the bottle back to bed. It wouldn't ease his miseries, but it might bring him sleep.

IN THE MORNING, freshly showered, the disguise in place, he checked out of the hotel and headed for the airport. He wanted to live. Perhaps only to make certain, from a distance, that Sam left the Nouvelles undisturbed. And perhaps to bide his time, to wait, to watch and to plan a suitable revenge.

Yet he had no flight plan, no destination. Though he loved to fly, his life was now as empty as the bottle he'd left behind him.

"HE SHOULD HAVE BEEN BACK hours ago." Rubbing her damp palms together, Roxanne paced her father's workroom. "Something went wrong. He should never have gone alone."

"It's not his first job, my dear." Max lifted a brightly painted box from a waist-high bench and revealed Mouse's grinning severed head. "He knows what he's doing."

"He hasn't checked in."

"This isn't a weigh station." At a press of a button of the remote concealed in Max's sleeve the head gave a long, echoing moan. Another switch and the eyes rolled left and right, the mouth moved. "Excellent, excellent. Lifelike, don't you think?"

"Daddy." To gain his full attention, Roxanne shoved the box back down over the head. "Luke's in trouble. I know it."

"How do you know it?" He switched off the remote.

"Because no one's heard from him since he left here last night. Because he was due back by six A.M., and it's nearly noon. Because when I called the airport to ask about John Carroll Brakeman, they said he'd filed his flight plan but he'd never shown up."

"Obvious reasons. Just as it's obvious the head is still inside this box." With a show of his old flair, Max plucked the box off the table. The head was gone, replaced by a thriving geranium. "I raised you better than to accept the obvious."

"This isn't a magic trick, damn it." She spun away. How could he play games when Luke was missing? Max laid a hand on her shoulder, and she stiffened.

"He's a bright, resourceful boy, Roxy. I knew the first time I saw him. He'll be back soon."

She hurled his own words back at him. "How do *you* know?"

"It's in the cards." To distract and amuse her, Max pulled a deck from his pocket, whipped them into a fan. But his stiffened fingers couldn't make the flourish. To Max, it seemed as though the cards had come alive to jump gleefully from his hands and scatter. He watched with eyes dulled with horror as they flew out of his grip.

Roxanne felt his heart break as keenly as she felt her own. She crouched to gather the deck and hurried to fill the awful silence.

"I know Luke sometimes breaks routine, but not like this." She cursed the cards, cursed age, cursed her own inadequacy to fill the gap. "Do you think I should go look for him?"

He continued to stare at the floor, though the cards were gone, hidden behind Roxanne's back. Now you see them, now you don't. But Max had a better magic formula. He simply stopped fighting to keep his mind on what was. When he brought his eyes back to his daughter's there was a smile in them, a mild, pleasant, utterly heart-wrenching smile. "If we look hard enough, long enough, we always find what we need. Do you know many people believe

362

there's more than one philosophers' stone? But they've fallen into the trap of the obvious."

"Daddy." Roxanne reached out with her free hand, but Max shook his head, miles away from the daughter who stood watching him with tears in her eyes.

Abruptly, he slammed a book with enough force to make Roxanne jump. There was no smile in his eyes now, but there was passion, and there was desperation. "I've nearly tracked it down now." He held up a ream of notes, shaking them. "When I do, when I finally have it . . . " Gently, he set the papers down, smoothing his aching fingers over them. "Well, the magic will be there, won't it?"

"Yes, it'll be there." She crossed to him to drape her arms around him, press her cheek to his. "Why don't you come upstairs with me, Daddy?"

"No, no, you run along. I have work to do." He sat to pore greedily through ancient books with ancient secrets. "Tell Luke to call Lester," he said absently. "I want to make certain that new lighting equipment's in place."

She opened her mouth to remind Max that the old Magic Door manager had retired to Las Vegas three years earlier. Instead she pressed her lips together hard and nodded. "All right, Daddy."

She climbed the stairs and went to search out Lily.

Roxanne found her in the courtyard, throwing bread crumbs to pigeons.

"LeClerc gets mad at me for doing this." Lily tossed a handful of shredded bread into the air and laughed when the pigeons bumped and squabbled for it. "They get doo all over the bricks. But they're so sweet, the way they bob their heads and watch you with those little black eyes."

"Lily, what's wrong with Daddy?"

"Wrong?" Lily's hand froze inside the plastic bag. "Did he hurt himself?" She turned and would have dashed inside if Roxanne hadn't stopped her.

"He isn't hurt. He's down in the workroom going through his books."

"Oh." Relief was so palpable Lily pressed a hand to her heart. She doubted a pigeon's could beat much faster. "You scared me."

"I'm scared," Roxanne said quietly and caused Lily's tentative smile to falter. "He's ill, isn't he?"

For a moment she said nothing. Then the pale blue eyes lost their helpless faraway look. They steadied. "I think we should talk." Lily slipped an arm around Roxanne's waist. "Let's sit down."

Taking charge, she steered Roxanne toward an iron bench beneath the still tender shade of a live oak. The waters of the little fountain tinkled gaily, like a brook over pebbles.

"Give me a minute, honey." She sat, keeping one of Roxanne's hands tight in hers while continuing to throw treats for the birds with her other. "I love this time of year," she murmured. "Not that the heat's ever bothered me like it does some, but spring, early spring is magic. The daffodils and hyacinths are blooming, the tulip stems are poking out. There's a nest in this tree." She glanced up, but her smile was wistful, a little lost. "It's the same every year. They always come back. The birds, the flowers. I can come sit out here and watch, and know some things are forever."

Pigeons cooed and clucked around their feet. From beyond the courtyard gates there was a steady whoosh of traffic. The sun was kind today, softened by a breeze that whispered through tender leaves. From somewhere close by in the Quarter, a flutist played an old Irish tune, "Danny Boy." Roxanne recognized it and shivered, knowing it was a song of death and loss.

"I made him go to the doctor." Lily kneaded Roxanne's hand, soothing as she was soothed. "Max could never hold out against good old-fashioned nagging. They ran tests. Then I had to make him go back so they could run more tests. He wouldn't check into the hospital so they could do everything at once. And I . . . well, I didn't push for that. I didn't want him to go in either."

A pulse began to beat hard behind Roxanne's eyes. Her voice sounded detached, and not at all her own. "What kind of tests?"

"All kinds. So many I lost track. They hooked him up to machines, and they studied graphs. They took samples of blood and made him pee in a cup. They took X rays." She lifted her shoulders, let them fall. "Maybe it was wrong, Roxy, but I asked them to tell me when they found out. I didn't want them telling Max if it was something bad. I know you're his daughter, you're his blood, but I—"

"You didn't do wrong." Roxanne rested her head on Lily's shoulder. "You did exactly right." It took a minute to bolster her courage. "It is something bad, isn't it? You have to tell me, Lily."

"He's going to keep forgetting things," Lily said, and her voice trembled. "Some days he might be just fine, and others, he won't be able to keep his mind focused, even with the medication. It's kind of like a train that jumps off the track. They said it might move real slow, but we should be prepared for times when he won't remember us." Tears slid silently down her cheek and plopped on their joined hands. "He might get angry, accuse us of trying to hurt him, or he might just do what he's told without questioning. He could walk to the corner for a quart of milk and forget how to get home. He could forget who he is, and if they can't stop it, one day he could just go away inside his mind where none of us could reach."

It was worse, Roxanne realized. Much worse than death. "We'll—we'll find a specialist."

"The doctor recommended one. I called him. We can take Max to Atlanta next month to see him." Lily took out one of her useless lace hankies to wipe her eyes. "Meantime he's going to study all Max's tests. They called it Alzheimer's, Roxy, and they don't have a cure."

"Then we'll find one. We're not going to let this happen to Max." She sprang up and would have swayed to her knees if Lily hadn't caught her.

"Honey, oh, honey, what is it? I shouldn't have told you like this."

"No, I just got up too fast." But the dizziness still swam in her head. Nausea clenched in her stomach.

"You're so pale. Let's go in and get you some tea or something."

"I'm all right," she insisted as Lily pulled her toward the house. "It's just some stupid virus." The minute they hit the kitchen door, the scent of the hearty soup LeClerc had simmering on the stove turned her pale skin green. "Damn it," she said through clenched teeth. "I don't have time for this."

She dashed to the bathroom with Lily fluttering behind her.

After she'd finished being sick, she was weak enough not to protest when Lily led her up to bed and insisted she lie down.

"All this worry," Lily diagnosed.

"It's a bug." Roxanne closed her eyes and prayed there was nothing left for her stomach to reject. "I thought it had run its course. Same thing happened yesterday afternoon. By last night I was fine. This morning, too."

"Well." Lily patted her hand. "If you told me you'd gotten sick two mornings in a row, I'd wonder if you were pregnant."

"Pregnant!" Roxanne's eyes popped open again. She wanted to laugh, but it didn't seem particularly funny. "You don't get afternoon sickness when you're pregnant."

"I guess not." But Lily's mind was working. "You haven't missed a period, have you?"

"I haven't missed one, exactly." Roxanne felt the first skip of panic, and something else. Something that wasn't fear of any kind but simple, subtle pleasure. "I'm a little late, that's all."

"How late?"

Roxanne plucked the bedspread with her fingers. "Couple of weeks. Maybe three."

"Oh, honey!" Lily's voice held pure delight. Visions of booties and baby powder danced in her head. "A baby."

"Don't get ahead of yourself." Cautious, Roxanne pressed a

hand to her stomach. If there was a baby in there, it was a mean one. That made her lips curve. She wouldn't expect Luke's baby to be sweet-natured, would she?

"They've got those home pregnancy tests now. You could find out right away. This'll knock Luke right off his feet."

"We never talked about it." The fear crept back. "Lily, we never even talked about children. He might not want—"

"Don't be silly, of course he wants. He loves you. Now you stay right here. I'm going down and get you some milk."

"Tea," Roxanne corrected. "I think my system might be able to hold down some tea—a couple of crackers."

"No strawberries and pickle relish?" She giggled when Roxanne groaned. "Sorry, sweetie. I'm just so excited. Be right back."

A baby, Roxanne thought. Why hadn't she considered she might be pregnant? Or had she? She sighed and turned cautiously to her side. She wasn't really surprised by the possibility. And though she thought she'd taken the pill faithfully, she wasn't sorry either.

Luke's baby and hers. What would he say? How would he feel?

The only way to know was to find him.

Reaching over, she pulled the phone onto the bed and dialed.

When Lily came back later with tea, dry toast and a pretty pink rosebud, Roxanne was lying on her back again, staring dully at the ceiling.

"He's gone, Lily."

"Hmmm? Who?"

"Luke's gone." She pushed herself up. Nausea had no chance against the emotions rioting inside her. "I called the airport. He took off from Tennessee at nine thirty-five this morning."

"Nine-thirty?" Lily set the tray on the dresser. "Why, it's after twelve now. It only takes an hour or so to fly back to New Orleans."

"He wasn't headed to New Orleans. I had to do a lot of wrangling to get his flight plan, but I managed it."

"What do you mean he wasn't headed for New Orleans? Of course he was."

"Mexico," Roxanne whispered. "He's going to Mexico."

BY THE NEXT MORNING, Roxanne was certain of two things. She was pregnant, and it was possible for a man to vanish from the face of the earth. But what could vanish could be conjured again. She wasn't a second-generation magician for nothing.

She was just zipping her traveling case when she heard the knock. Her first thought, like a flash of lightning, was Luke! She made it from the bedroom to the front door in a dash.

"Where have you—oh, Mouse."

"Sorry, Roxy." His big shoulders slumped.

"It's all right." She mustered up a smile. "Listen, I'm practically on my way out the door."

"I know. Lily said how you were going to Mexico to look for Luke. I'm going with you."

"That's a nice thought, Mouse, but I've already made my plans."

"I'm going with you." He might have been slow, he might have been sweet, but he could also be stubborn. "You're not going all that way alone in your ... in your condition," he finished on a burst. His face burned beet red.

"Lily's knitting booties already?" But she softened the sarcasm by patting his arm. "Mouse, there's nothing to worry about. I know what I'm doing, and I don't think carrying something the size of a pinprick's going to slow me down."

"I'm going to take care of you. Luke would want me to."

"If Luke was so damn concerned, he wouldn't be in Mexico," she snapped, and was immediately sorry as Mouse's face crumpled and fell. "Sorry. I guess being pregnant messes up your hormones and makes you cranky. I've already got my flight reservations, Mouse."

He wasn't going to budge. "You can cancel them. I'll fly you."

She started to protest, then shrugged. Maybe the company would do her good.

SHE MADE IT TO THE LADIES' room at the Cancún airport. It occurred to her as she retched that she could almost clock her nausea with a stopwatch. Perhaps the baby had inherited her sense of timing.

When she felt she could stand again, she rejoined a worried Mouse in the tiny, sunwashed terminal. "It's okay," she told him. "Just one of the benefits of expectant motherhood."

"You going to have to do that for nine whole months?"

"Thanks, Mouse," she said weakly. "I needed that."

They spent nearly an hour trying to get information on Luke's plane from the flight tower. Yes, he had been scheduled to land at that airport. No, he had never arrived. He had never come into radio contact or requested permission to divert. He had simply veered off somewhere over the Gulf.

Or, as the cheerful flight dispatcher suggested, into the Gulf.

"He didn't crash, damn it." Roxanne stormed back to the plane. "No way did he crash."

"He's a good pilot." Mouse hustled behind her, patting her shoulder, her head. "And I checked out the plane myself before he left."

"He didn't crash," she repeated. Unrolling one of Mouse's charts, she began to study the lay of the land on the Mexican side of the Gulf. "Where would he go, Mouse? If he'd decided to avoid Cancún."

"I'd make a better guess if I knew why."

"We don't know why." She rubbed the cold bottle of Coke Mouse had bought her against her sweaty brow. "We can speculate—maybe he wanted to cover a trail. We can't call Sam and ask him if his wife's sapphires are missing. There's been no announcement on the news of a burglary, but they often keep the wraps on for a while. If he ran into trouble in Tennessee, he might have decided, for his own idiotic reasons, to head west, let John Carroll Brakeman disappear."

"But why didn't he check in?"

"I don't know." She wanted to scream it, but kept her tone level. "These islands here. Some of them have to have airstrips. Official ones, and not-so-official ones. For smuggling."

"Yeah, sure."

"Okay." She handed the chart to Mouse. "Let's check it out."

THEY SPENT THREE DAYS searching the Yucatan Peninsula. They spread Luke's description up and down the coast, slipping money into eager hands and following false leads.

Roxanne's bouts of nausea left Mouse wringing his hands and wishing for Lily. If he tried to fuss or pamper, Roxanne snapped like a terrier. Conversely, her flashes of temper reassured him. He was well aware that given the chance, she would tramp off into the jungle alone, armed with no more than a canteen and a driving need. Until they located Luke, Mouse considered Roxanne his responsibility. When she looked too pale or too flushed, he forced her to stop and rest, bearing her tantrums like an oak bears the tapping of a woodpecker—with silence and grave dignity.

The routine became so set, both of them began to feel they would spend the rest of their lives at it.

Then they found the plane.

It cost Roxanne a thousand American dollars for a ten-minute conversation with a one-eyed Mexican entrepreneur who ran his business out of a sod hut in the Mayan jungle near Mérida.

He pared his nails with a pocketknife while a wary-eyed woman with dusty feet fried tortillas.

"He says he wants to sell, do I want to buy." Juarez tipped tequila into a tin cup, then generously offered Roxanne the bottle.

"No, thanks. When did you buy the plane?"

370

"Two days ago. I give him good price." He'd all but stolen it, and the satisfaction of that made Juarez expansive to the pretty senorita. "He needs money, I give him money."

"Where did he go?"

"I don't ask questions."

She wanted to swear, but noting the skittishness of the woman by the stove, opted for tact. Her smile was laced with admiration. "But you'd know if he was still in the area. A man like you, with your contacts, you'd know."

"Sí." He appreciated the fact she showed respect. "He's gone. He camps one night in the jungle, then poof." Juarez snapped his fingers. "Gone. He moves softly, and fast. If he knows such a beautiful lady wants him, maybe he moves slower."

Roxanne pushed away from the table. Luke knew she wanted him, she thought wearily. And still, he was running. "Would you mind if I looked at the plane?"

"Look." Juarez gestured, and something in her eyes stopped him from demanding a separate payment for the privilege. "But you won't find him."

She found nothing of him, not even ashes from one of his cigars. There was no sign that Luke had ever sat in the cockpit or held the wheel or studied the stars through the glass.

"We can try north," Mouse said as Roxanne sat in the pilot's seat and stared out at nothing. "Or inland." He was groping, uneasy with the blank, dazed look on her face. "Could be he went farther inland."

"No." She only shook her head. Despite the heat hammering down on the roof of the plane, she was too cold for tears. "He left his message right here."

Confused, Mouse glanced around the cockpit. "But, Roxy, there's nothing here."

"I know." She closed her eyes, let the grief tear through her so hope could drain free. When she opened them again, they were clear, and they were hard. "There's nothing here, Mouse. He doesn't want to be found. Let's go home."

PART THREE

This rough magic I here abjure.

—William Shakespeare

Chapter Twenty-five

Now he was back. His five-year vanishing act was over, and like the veteran performer he was, Luke had posed his return engagement with a sense of drama and panache. His audience of one was captivated.

For a moment.

The man pressed against her cleverly assaulting her mouth, her mind, wasn't an illusion. He was flesh and blood. It was all so achingly familiar, the good solid weight of him, the taste of his skin, the trip-hammer of her own pulse as those strong, clever fingers crept up to cup her cheek.

He was real.

He was home.

He was the lowest form of life that had ever slunk through the mud.

Her hands tightened in his hair, then yanked with enough strength to make him yelp.

"Jesus, Roxanne—"

But that was all the misdirection she needed. She twisted, shoving her elbow hard into his ribs, popping her knee up between his legs. He managed to block the crippling knee, but she used that same stiffened elbow to catch him hard on the chin.

He saw stars. The next thing he knew, he was on his back with Roxanne straddling him and snarling as her carefully manicured nails shot toward his face.

He gripped her wrists, clamping down before those curled fingers could peel back his skin. They remained in that position, one that brought each uncomfortably sensual memories, breathing hard and eyeing each other with mutual dislike.

"Let me go, Callahan."

"I want to keep my face in the same condition it was when I walked in."

She tried to twist free, but the five years he'd spent doing God knew what hadn't weakened him. He was still strong as a bull. Biting would have been satisfying, but undignified. She settled on disdain.

"Keep your face. It doesn't interest me."

Though he loosened his hold, he remained braced until she stood, with as much grace and arrogance as a goddess rising out of a pool.

He got up quickly, with that eerie speed and economy of movement she remembered too well, and stood on the balls of his feet. Saying nothing, she turned her back on him and poured a glass of champagne. Even as the bubbles exploded on her tongue, they tasted flat and dry. But it gave her a moment, a much needed moment, to lock the last latch on her heart.

"Still here?" she asked as she turned back.

"We have a lot to talk about."

"Do we?" She sipped again. "Odd, I can't think of a thing."

"Then I'll do the talking." He stepped over pooling water and crushed roses to top off his own glass of wine. "You can try something new, like listening." His hand whipped out to snag her wrist before she could toss her wine into his face. "Want to fight some more, Rox?" His voice was low and dangerous and, Lord help her, sent a thrill racing up her spine. "You'll lose. Figure the odds."

They would be against. Temper might urge her to fly biting and scratching into his face, but she'd only end up on her butt again. Still, she had other weapons. And she'd use them all to pay him back for the years he'd left her alone.

"I won't waste good wine on you." When his fingers relaxed, she brought the glass back to her lips. "And my time's even more valuable. I have an engagement, Luke. You'll have to excuse me."

"Your calendar's free until the press conference tomorrow." He lifted his glass in toast. "I already checked with Mouse. Why don't we have a late supper? We can hash things out."

Fury simmered just below flash point. Carefully, Roxanne turned to her dressing table and sat. "No, thanks just the same." Setting her glass aside, she began to cream off her stage makeup. "I'd just as soon dine with a rabid bat."

"Then we'll talk here."

"Luke, time passes." She tossed used tissues aside. He could see that beneath the glamour she'd painted on for the stage, she was only more beautiful. None of the pictures he'd managed to find and hoard over the years came close to what she was in the flesh. None of the longings he'd suffered could equal what speared through him now.

"When it does," she continued, patting moisturizer over her skin, "events either become larger than they were or smaller. You could say that whatever we had has become so small, it's next to invisible. So let's not hash, all right?"

"I know I hurt you." Whatever else he had been prepared to say froze in his throat as her eyes flashed to his in the glass. They were green smoke, and in them the emotions which swirled were painful to watch.

"You have no idea what you did to me." The words were hardly more than a whisper and left him battered. "No idea," she repeated. "I loved you with all my heart, with everything I was or could be, and you shattered it. Shattered me. No, don't." She sucked in her breath, going stiff and still as his hand reached for her hair. "Don't touch me again."

He let his hand hang a bare inch away before dropping it to his side. "You have every right to hate me. I'm only asking you to let me explain."

"Then you ask too much. Do you really think anything you could say would make up for it?" She turned on her seat and rose. She'd always been strong, he remembered. But she was stronger now, and distant as the moon. "That whatever explanation you could conjure up would put things right so I'd welcome you back with open arms and a turned-down bed?"

She stopped herself, realizing she was preciously close to shouting and losing whatever small handhold she had on dignity. "I do have a right to hate you," she said with more calm. "I could tell you that you broke my heart, and I put it back together with a lot of sweat and effort. And that would be true. I can also offer you a more pertinent truth. I simply have no heart where you're concerned. You're smoke and mirrors, Luke, and who knows better how deceiving they are than I?"

He waited until he could be sure his voice would be as even as hers. "You want me to believe you feel nothing?"

"It only matters to me what I believe."

He turned away, amazed that he'd wanted to be close to her for so long and now desperately needed distance. She was right. Time passes. No matter how much magic was left in him, he couldn't wink away the years.

Still, he wasn't going to let the past continue to dictate his future. And he wanted that cool, succulent taste of revenge. For all of those things, he needed her.

"If you're telling me the truth about your feelings, then doing business with me shouldn't be a problem."

"I handle my own business."

"And very well, too." Changing tactics, he took out a cigar and sat. "As I said earlier, I have a proposition for you. A business offer I think you'll be very interested in."

She shrugged and removed the silver stars at her ears. "I doubt it."

"The philosophers' stone" was all he said. The earrings clattered on the dressing table.

"Don't push the wrong button, Callahan."

"I know who has it. I know where it is, and I have some ideas on how to get it." He smiled. "Those buttons suit you?"

"How do you know?"

Perhaps it was the flare of his lighter as he lit the cigar, but Roxanne thought she saw something hot and vicious flash into his eyes. "Let's just say I've made it my business to know. Are you interested?"

She shrugged, picked up her brush and began to pull it slowly through her hair. "I might be. Where do you think it is?"

He couldn't speak. Not when the memories and all the longings that ran through them were flooding him. Roxanne brushing her hair, all rose and gold, laughing over her shoulder. So slender, so lovely.

Their eyes met in the mirror again. The shock of the mutual memory snapped like lightning in the air. Her hand trembled once as she set the brush aside.

"I asked where you thought it was."

"I said I know." He took a long, quiet breath. "It's in a vault in a library of a house in Maryland. It's owned by an old friend of ours." Luke drew in smoke, expelled it in a thin blue cloud. "Sam Wyatt."

Roxanne's eyes narrowed. Luke knew that look, and knew he had her. "You're telling me Sam has the philosophers' stone. The stone Max spent years looking for."

"That's right. It seems to be genuine. Sam certainly believes it to be."

"Why would he want it?"

"Because Max did," Luke said simply. "And because he's convinced it represents power. I doubt he sees anything mystical about it." He shrugged and crossed his legs at the ankles. "It's more a symbol of conquest. Max wanted it, Sam has it. Has had it for the last six months."

It seemed wise to sit again, to get her bearings. She hadn't really believed in the stone. There had been times when she had hated even the legend of it for drawing her father further and further away from his narrowing pinpoint on reality. Yet if it existed . . .

"How do you know about it, about Sam?"

He could have told her. There were so many things he could have told her reaching back over that five-year gulf. But to tell some was to tell all. He, too, had pride.

"It's my business how. I'm asking you if you're interested in acquiring the stone."

"If I were interested, there's nothing stopping me from acquiring it on my own."

"I'd stop you." He didn't move from his relaxed slouch on the chair, but she sensed the challenge, and the barrier. "I've put a lot of time and effort into tracing that stone, Roxanne. I won't let you slip it out from under me. But . . . " He turned the cigar to study the tip. "I'm offering you a kind of partnership."

"Why? Why should you offer, why should I accept?"

"For Max." He looked back at her. "Whatever is between us, or not between us, I love him, too."

That hurt. As she absorbed the pain, she gripped her hands together on her lap. "You've certainly shown your devotion over the last five years, haven't you?"

"I offered to explain." He shrugged, reached out for his champagne. "Now you'll have to wait. You can work with me and have the stone, or I'll get it alone."

She hesitated. Her mind was already mulling over the possibilities. It wouldn't be difficult to locate Sam's home in Maryland—not since he was the front-runner in the upcoming senatorial elections. The security would be a little more difficult for precisely the same reason, but not impossible.

"I'll need to think about it."

He knew her too well. "Yes or no, Rox. Now. It would take you months to gather the information I already have. By the time you did, I'd have the stone."

"Then why do you need me?"

"We'll get to that. Yes or no."

She stared at him, at the face she'd known so well. There had been a time when she would have known what he was thinking, and certainly what he was feeling. But the years had made a stranger of him.

That was for the best, she decided. If he remained a stranger she could cope.

"Yes."

The wave of relief was like a flood of fresh air. He could breathe again. His only outward reaction was a slight smile and nod. "Good. There are certain conditions."

Her eyes frosted. "Of course there are."

"I think you can live with them. There's an auction to be held this fall in Washington."

"The Clideburg estate, I know."

"You should also know that the jewelry alone is valued in excess of six million."

"Six point eight, conservatively."

"Conservatively," he agreed and downed the last of his champagne. "I want to hit it."

For an instant she couldn't speak at all. "You're out of your mind." But the excitement in her eyes betrayed her. "You might as well stroll into the Smithsonian and try to cop the Hope Diamond."

"Bad luck." Oh yes, he knew he had her. Rising, he reached for the bottle to pour them both more wine. "I've done quite a bit of the initial research. There are a few bugs to iron out."

"Atomic-sized, I imagine."

"A job is a job," he said, quoting Max. "The bigger the complications, the grander the illusion."

"The auction's in October. That doesn't give us much time."

"Time enough. Particularly if you announce at your press conference tomorrow that you'll be working with a partner again."

"Why in hell would I do that?"

"Because we will, Roxy, onstage and off." He took her hand and, ignoring her resistance, drew her to her feet. "Strictly business, babe. I'm a mystery come back. Put that together with the act we'll create, and we'll be a sensation. And have a tidy diversion in October—in our performance at the gala before the auction."

"You got us booked already?"

He didn't mind the sarcasm, not when he played to win. "You leave that to me. It's all a hook, Rox, the performance, the auction, the stone. When it's all over, we'll both have what we want."

"I know what I want." He still held her hand. She would have sworn she felt the power leaping from his fingers. It was a sensation that both frightened and aroused. "I'm not sure about you."

"You should be." His eyes locked on hers. "You always were. I want you back, Roxanne." He brought her rigid fingers to his lips. "And I've had a long time to figure out how to get the things I want. If you're afraid of that, back out now."

"I'm not afraid of anything." She yanked her hand free of his, tossed up her chin. "I'm in, Callahan. When the job's done, I'll snap my fingers." She did so, in front of his nose. "And you'll be gone. That's what I want."

He only laughed and, taking her by the shoulders, yanked her to him for one short, hard kiss. "God, it's good to be back. Knock them dead at the press conference, Roxy. Tell them you're working on something new. Whet their appetites. Afterward, I'll come to your suite. We can start working out the details."

"No." She pressed both hands on his chest to shove him away.

"I'll handle the press, then I'll come to you. Make sure you have enough to keep me interested."

"That I can promise. I'm at the same hotel as you, one floor down."

Some of the color washed out of her cheeks. "How long have you been there?"

"I only checked in an hour before the show." Curious about her reaction, he tilted his head. "Why does that bother you?"

"It just means I'll have to check my locks more carefully."

The smile died out of his eyes. "No lock would keep me out if I decided to come in, Rox. A no from you would. Make it around noon," he said and started toward the door. "I'll buy you lunch."

"Luke." She didn't move toward him. That was something she couldn't give. "Have you seen Lily yet?" When he only shook his head, the heart she thought was so barricaded against him broke a little. "I'll get her for you if you like."

"I can't." In his entire life he'd only loved two women. Facing both on the same night was more than he thought he could handle. "I'll talk to her tomorrow."

Then he was gone, quickly and without another word. Roxanne wasn't certain how long she stood staring at the door he'd closed behind him. She couldn't be sure what she was feeling. Her life had been turned upside down when he'd left her. She didn't think it had righted again by his return. If anything, he'd skewed it in an entirely different manner. This time, it would be up to her to control the angle and degree.

But she was tired. Bone tired. Even the act of changing from her costume to street clothes seemed almost more than she could bear. Her fingers froze on the snap of her jeans when she heard the knock on her door.

If he'd come back, she—but no, she thought with a sneer. Luke wouldn't bother to knock.

"Yes, who is it?"

"It's me, honey." Eyes bright, Lily poked her head in the door.

Some of the gleam faded when she scanned the room and found it empty but for Roxanne. "Mouse told me—I waited as long as I could." She stepped in, spotted the mess of water and flowers on the floor. "He *is* here!" The smile was back and brilliant. "I could hardly believe it. Where's he been? Is he okay? Where is he now?"

"I don't know where he's been." Roxanne picked up her purse, checking the contents to give her something to do with her hands. "He seems fine, and I have no idea where he is."

"But—but—he didn't just leave again?"

"Not the way you mean. He's staying in town, at our hotel. We may have some business to discuss."

"Business?" With a laugh, Lily threw her arms around Roxanne and squeezed. "I guess that's the last thing you two would have to talk about. I can't wait to see him. It's like a miracle."

"More like one of the seven plagues," Roxanne muttered.

"Now, Roxy, I'm sure he must've explained everything."

"I didn't want to hear it." She pulled away, fighting not to resent Lily's easy acceptance. "I don't care why he left or where he was. That part of my life's over."

"Roxy—"

"I mean it, Lily. If you want to kill the fatted calf, go right ahead. Just don't expect me to join the feast." She crouched to toss mangled roses in the trash. "It seems we might be working together, temporarily. But that's all. There's nothing personal between us anymore. That's the way I want it."

"It may be what you say you want," Lily said quietly. "It may even be the way you feel right now. But that isn't the way it is, or ever can be." Lily knelt down to lay a hand on Roxanne's shoulder. "You didn't tell him about Nathaniel."

"No." She tossed a rose aside and stared dully down at the spot of blood where a thorn had pierced her thumb. "I was afraid at first when he said he was at the hotel that he already knew. But he doesn't."

"Honey, you have to tell him."

"Why?" Her eyes burned fierce and furious.

"Luke has a right—"

"His rights ended five years ago. All the rights are mine now. Nathaniel's mine. Damn it, Lily, don't look at me that way." She sprang to her feet to escape the soft, pitying gaze. "What should I have said? Oh, by the way, Callahan, a few months after you took a hike, I gave birth to your son. Looks just like you, too. He's a great kid. Why don't I introduce you to him sometime?" She pressed her hand over her mouth to hold back a sob.

"Don't, Roxy."

"I'm not going to." She shook her head when Lily's arms came around her. "I never cried over him. Not once. I'm not going to start now." But she let herself be comforted, turning her cheek to Lily's shoulder. "What would I tell Nate, Lily? Here's the father I told you had to go away. He's back now, but don't get used to it because he might play now-you-see-him-now-you-don't."

"He wouldn't turn his back on his son. He couldn't."

"I won't risk it." She took a deep breath and stepped back, steadier. "If and when I decide to tell Luke about Nathaniel, it'll be at a time and place of my choosing. I call the shots on this." She gripped Lily's shoulders and held firm. "I want your promise that you'll say nothing."

"I won't tell him, if you promise to do the right thing."

"I'm trying to. Let's get going, okay? It's been a long day."

HOURS LATER, ROXANNE STOOD in the doorway of the room where her son slept. Shadows were just beginning to fade, going pale and pearly in the early dawn. She listened to Nathaniel breathing. Her child, her miracle, her most potent magic. And she thought about the man who slept in a room below, the man who had helped her create a life.

And she remembered how frightened she'd been when she'd sat down to tell her father that she was pregnant. How tightly Max had held her. Unflagging support from him, from Mouse and LeClerc. The booties Lily knitted that had looked like mutant mittens, the wallpaper Mouse had surprised her with for the nursery, the milk LeClerc had forced her to drink.

The day she had felt the baby quicken for the first time. She'd nearly given in and wept then, but she'd held the tears off. Maternity clothes, swollen ankles. That first solid kick that had awakened her out of a sound sleep. Lamaze classes with Lily as her coach. And always that tiny seed of hope that remained planted deep that Luke would come back before their child was born.

But he hadn't. She'd gone through eighteen sweaty hours of labor, at turns terrified and exhilarated. She'd watched their son fight his way from her womb, she'd listened to his first indignant cry.

And every day she'd looked at him and loved him and had seen Luke mirrored in his face.

She'd watched her son grow, and had seen her father swallowed up by the illness no one could fight. She'd been alone. No matter how much love she'd felt in her home, there had been no one to turn to in the night. No arms to come around her and offer her comfort when she wept because her father no longer recognized her.

There was no one to stand with her now, and keep watch over her son as the dawn came up.

Chapter Twenty-six

LILY FLUFFED HER HAIR, CHECKED HER MAKEUP IN THE mirror of her rhinestone-studded compact, fixed a bright, friendly smile on her face. She rolled back her shoulders, making sure her tummy—which she hated to admit was becoming the teeniest bit of a problem—was sucked in. Only then was she satisfied enough with her appearance to knock on the door of Luke's suite.

It wasn't a matter of being disloyal to Roxanne, she told herself, fidgeting. All she was doing was saying hello—and maybe she'd give the boy a piece of her mind while she was at it. But it wasn't being disloyal, even if her heart was nearly bursting with the sheer joy of seeing him again.

Besides, she'd waited until Roxanne had gone down to her press conference.

By the time she heard the bolt turn, she'd chewed off most of her lipstick. She held her breath, bumped her smile up a few degrees, then stared blankly at the short, dark-haired man who stood on the other side of the threshold. He stared back at her through silver-framed lenses as thick as her thumb. However much Luke might have changed, Lily thought, he couldn't have lost six inches in height.

"I'm sorry. I must have the wrong room."

"Lily Bates!" The voice screamed the Bronx and was as friendly as a pastrami on rye. Lily found her hand clasped and pumped enthusiastically. "I'd recognize you anywhere. *Any*-where! You're even prettier than you are onstage."

"Thank you." Habit had her fluttering her mink eyelashes even as she levered her weight back to prevent him from pulling her into the room. Any woman with a killer body had best have killer instincts as well. "I'm afraid I got the door numbers mixed up."

He kept her hand captured in his and used his other to push up the glasses that were sliding down his prominent hooked nose. "I'm Jake. Jake Finestein."

"Nice to meet you." They continued the little tug-of-war. Lily glanced uneasily over her shoulder, wondering if anyone would come to her aid if she shouted for help. "I'm sorry I bothered you, Mr. Finestein."

"Jake. Jake." He grinned and flashed an amazing set of large white teeth, so straight they might have been surveyed by the Corps of Engineers. "No need for formalities between us, Lily. Wonderful show last night." His black bean eyes, magnified by the thick lenses, beamed up at her. "*Won*-der-ful."

"Thank you." She was bigger than he was, she told herself. And certainly outweighed him. His short-sleeved shirt showed puny, toothpick arms and bony wrists. Worse came to worst, she could take him. "I really can't chat now. I'm running late."

"Oh, but you've got time for a cup of coffee." He swung his free hand back to indicate the table laden with pots and cups and covered plates. "And breakfast. I bet you haven't eaten a thing yet this morning. I ordered up some nice bagels. You eat a little bit, have a nice cup of coffee, you relax. Me, I got to eat a little something in the mornings or my system suffers all day. How about some orange juice?" He tugged her in another inch. "They squeeze it fresh."

"Really, I can't. I was just—"

"Jake, will you quit talking to yourself? It makes me crazy." Hair still dripping from the shower, Luke strode out from the bedroom buttoning his shirt. He stopped dead, the annoyance on his face shuddering into blank shock.

"Who needs to talk to himself when he's got a beautiful woman?" Jake's grin twisted into a wince as Lily's fingers tightened on his. "And I mean *bee*-u-ti-ful. We've been having a nice chat. I was just telling Lily she should sit down, have some coffee, maybe a bagel."

"I—I could use some coffee," Lily managed.

"Good, good. I'm going to pour you some. You want cream? Sugar? Sweet'n Low?"

"Yes, fine." She didn't care if Jake poured heavy-weight motor oil out of the pot, she had eyes only for Luke. "You look wonderful." She heard the tears in her voice and cleared her throat to disguise them. "I'm sorry. I'm interrupting your breakfast."

"It's all right. It's good to see you." It was so awful, so hideously polite. He just wanted to stand and stare and absorb everything about her. The pretty, ridiculously youthful face, the silly enameled parrots that swung at her ears, the scent of Chanel that was already filling the room.

"So, sit, sit." Jake made grand gestures toward the table. "You'll talk, you'll eat."

Luke cut his eyes toward the table. "Take off, Jake."

"I'm going, I'm going." Jake fussed with cups and saucers. "You think I'm hanging around to spoil the big reunion? Mrs. Finestein didn't raise any fools. I'm going to get my camera and go take pictures like I was a tourist. Madam Lily." He grasped her hand again, squeezed. "A pleasure, a sincere pleasure."

"Thank you."

Jake sent Luke a last telling look, then walked to the second bedroom and shut the door discreetly behind him. If he pressed his ear to the crack for a few minutes, what harm did it do?

"He's—ah—a very nice man."

"He's a pain in the ass." Luke worked up what nearly passed as a grin. "But I'm used to him." Nervous as a boy on his first date, he shoved his hands in his pockets. "So sit. We'll talk, we'll eat."

Luke's killingly accurate mimicking of Jake had Lily's lips trembling up. "I don't want to take up your time."

He would have preferred being stabbed in the heart. "Lily, please."

"Maybe just some coffee." She made herself sit, keeping the smile planted. But the cup rattled in the saucer when she lifted it. "I don't know what to say to you. I guess I want to know if you're okay."

"I'm all in one piece." He sat as well, but for once his appetite had deserted him. He made do with black coffee. "How about you? Roxanne—well, she wasn't much in the mood to fill me in on everyone last night."

"I'm older," Lily said in a weak attempt at gaiety.

"You don't look it." He searched her face, fighting against emotions that threatened to swamp him. "Not a day."

"You always knew just what to say to a woman. Must be the Irish." She took an unsteady breath and began to pick apart a bagel. "LeClerc's fine. Crankier than he used to be. He doesn't come on the road often now. Mouse is married. Did you know?"

"Mouse? Married?" Luke gave a quick spontaneous laugh that had tears swimming in Lily's eyes. "No shit? How did that happen?"

"Alice came to—to work for us," Lily said carefully. It wouldn't do to say that Roxanne had hired her as Nathaniel's nanny. "She's bright and sweet, and she fell head over heels for Mouse. It took her two years to wear him down. I don't know how many hours she spent helping him tinker with engines."

"I'm going to have to meet her." Silence fell, taunting him. "Can you tell me about Max?"

"He won't get better." Lily lifted her coffee again. "He's gone someplace none of us can reach him. We didn't—we couldn't put him in a hospital so we've arranged for home care. He can't do anything for himself. That's the worst, to see him so helpless. It's hard on Roxanne."

"What about you?"

Lily pressed her lips together. When she spoke, her voice was strong and steady. "Max is gone. I can look into his eyes, and there's no Max there. Oh, I still sit with his body, and feed it or clean it, but everything he was has already died. His body's just waiting to catch up. So it's easier for me. I've done my grieving."

"I need to see him, Lily." He wanted to reach out. His fingers were inches from touching hers before he curled them away. "I know Roxanne might object, but I need to see him."

"He asked for you, dozens of times." There was accusation mixed with the hurt. She couldn't prevent either. "He'd forget that you weren't there, and he'd ask for you."

"I'm sorry." It seemed a pitiful response.

"How could you do it, Luke? How could you leave without a word and break so many hearts?" When he only shook his head, she looked away. "Now I'm sorry," she said stiffly. "I don't have any right to question you. You were always free to come and go as you pleased."

"Direct hit," he murmured. "Much more accurate than anything Rox threw at me last night."

"You devastated her." Lily hadn't known the hot anger was trapped inside until it burst free. "She loved you, since she was a little girl. She trusted you. We all did. We thought something terrible had happened to you. Until Roxanne came back from Mexico we were sure of it."

"Wait." He gripped her hand, holding tight. "She went to Mexico?"

"She tracked you there. Mouse went with her. You have no idea what shape she was in." Frightened, pregnant, heartsick. Lily shook her hand free and rose. Her temper, always so even, was all the more effective when it spiked. "She looked for you, afraid you were dead or sick or God knows. Then she found your plane and the man you'd sold it to. And she knew you didn't want her to find you. Damn you, I didn't think she'd ever get over it." She shoved the chair against the table hard enough to make china rattle. "Tell me you had amnesia. Tell me you got hit on the head and forgot us, forgot everything. Can you tell me that?"

"No."

She was crying now, big silent tears coursing down her face while he looked on miserably.

"I can't tell you that, and I can't ask you to forgive me. I can only tell you that I did what I thought was best for everyone. I didn't see a choice."

"You didn't see a choice? You couldn't see your way clear to letting us know you were alive?"

"No." He picked up a napkin and stood to dab at her tears. "I thought about you every day. In the first year I'd wake up at night thinking I was home, then it would hit me. I'd reach for a bottle instead of Roxanne. I might as well have been dead. I wish I could have forgotten, that I could have stopped needing my family." He balled the napkin in his fist as his voice thickened. "I was twelve before I found my mother. I don't want to spend the rest of my life without her. Tell me what I need to do to convince you to give me another chance."

For Lily love was a fluid thing. No matter how strong the dam, it would always flow free. She did the only thing she could do. She opened her arms and took him into them, rocking and stroking when he buried his face in her hair.

"You're home now," she murmured. "That's what matters."

And it was all there, just where he had left it. The softness, the sweetness, the strength. Emotions rose up in him like a river at flood point. He could only cling. "I missed you. God, I missed you."

"I know." She lowered into a chair and let him lay his head in her lap. "I didn't mean to yell at you, sweetie."

"I didn't think you'd want to see me." He straightened so that he could touch a hand to her cheek, feel that creamy skin. "I never deserved you."

"That's silly. Most people would say we deserved each other." She gave a watery chuckle and hugged him hard. "You'll tell me about it sometime soon, won't you?"

"Whenever you want."

"Later. I just want to spend some time looking at you." Sniffling, she held him at arm's length, studying his face with a mother's eagle eye. "Well, you don't look any the worse for wear." She smoothed the faint lines at the corner of his eyes with her fingertips. "You look a little thinner maybe, a little tougher." With a sigh, she pressed a kiss to his cheek, then fussed the imprint of her lipstick away with her thumb. "You were the most beautiful little boy I'd ever seen." When he winced, she laughed. "Do you still have magic?"

"It kept me alive." He took both of her hands and pressed them to his lips. Shame and simple gratitude ran riot through him. He'd tried to prepare for her anger, for the chill of her resentment, even her disinterest. But he had no defense against the constancy of her love. "You were beautiful last night. Watching you and Rox onstage, it was like the years between never happened."

"But they did."

"Yes, they did." He stood then, but kept her hand in his. "I don't have an incantation to make them disappear. But there are things I can do that might set it right."

"You still love her."

When he only shrugged, she smiled, rose and cupped his face in her hands. "You still love her," she repeated. "But you'll have to have more than a pocketful of tricks to win her back. She's not a pushover like me."

His mouth grimmed. "I can push hard."

With a sigh, Lily shook her head. "Then she'll just push back. Max would say you catch more flies with honey than with a rolled

393

up newspaper. Take it from me, a woman—even a stubborn one—likes to be wooed." He only snorted, but Lily pressed on. "I don't just mean flowers and music, honey. It's a kind of attitude. Roxy needs to be challenged, but she also needs to be courted."

"If I got down on one knee, she'd plant a foot in my face."

Absolutely, Lily thought, but thought it politic not to agree. "I didn't say it would be easy. Don't give up on her, Luke. She needs you more than you could possibly understand."

"What do you mean?"

"Just don't give up."

Thoughtfully, he drew Lily back into his arms. "That's not the kind of mistake I'd make twice. I'll do what needs to be done, Lily." His eyes darkened as he stared at something hateful only he could see. "There are scores to settle."

"AND THERE WAS A BIG DOG in the park. A gold one. He peed on all the trees."

Roxanne cuddled Nate in her lap, laughing as he recounted his adventures of the morning. "All of them?"

"Maybe a hundred." He looked soulfully into his mother's face with his father's eyes. "Can I have a dog? I'd teach him to sit and shake hands and play dead."

"And pee on trees?"

"Uh-huh." He grinned, turning in her lap to wrap his arms around her neck. Oh, he knew how to charm, she thought. He'd been his father's child since his first toothless grin. "I want a big one. A big boy one. His name's gonna be Mike."

"Since he's already got a name, I suppose we'll have to look into it." She twirled one of Nate's glossy curls around her finger. Much like, she thought wryly, her son twirled her heart around his. "How much ice cream did you eat?"

His eyes widened. "How come you know I had ice cream?"

There was a telltale smear of chocolate on his shirt and a

suspicious stickiness on his fingers. But Roxanne knew better than to use such pedestrian clues. "Because mothers know all and see all, especially when they're magicians too."

His lip poked out as he considered. "How come I can never see the eyes in back of your head?"

"Nate, Nate, Nate," she sighed lustily. "Haven't I told you they're invisible eyes?"

Abruptly she dragged him up into her arms, holding him tight with her eyes squeezed shut against tears. She couldn't say why she felt like weeping, didn't want to consider the reasons. All that mattered was that she had her child safe in her arms.

"Better go wash your hands, Nate the Great." Her voice was shaky, but muffled against his neck. "I've got to get to my appointment."

"You said we were going to the zoo."

"And we will." She kissed him, set him on his short, sturdy legs. "I'll be back in an hour, then we'll go see how many monkeys look just like you."

He raced off, laughing. Roxanne stooped to gather the miniature cars, plastic men and picture books that were scattered over the rug. "Alice? I'm heading out. Be back in an hour."

"Take your time," Alice sang back and made Roxanne smile.

Soft-voiced, reliable, unshakable Alice, she thought. Lord knew she would never have been able to continue her work without the steady support of the ethereal Alice.

And to think she'd nearly turned Alice aside because of her frail appearance and whispery voice. Yet out of the legion of prospective nannies she'd interviewed, it had been Alice who had convinced Roxanne that Nathaniel would be safe and happy in her care.

There had been something about her eyes, Roxanne thought now as she walked into the hallway. That pale, almost translucent gray and the quiet kindness in them. Her practical nature had nearly swayed her toward the more prim and experienced applicants, but Nate had smiled at Alice from his crib, and that had been that.

Roxanne still wondered who had done the hiring. Now Alice was family. That single smile from a six-month-old infant had added one more link to the Nouvelle chain.

Roxanne chose the stairs and walked one flight down to face another link. The missing link, she thought nastily and had her shoulders braced when she rapped on Luke's door.

"Prompt as always," Luke commented when he opened the door.

"I only have an hour, so let's get down to business." She sailed past him, leaving a faint trace of wildflowers to torment his system.

"Hot date?"

She thought of her son and smiled. "Yes, and I don't like to keep him waiting." She chose a chair, sat and crossed her legs. "Let's hear the setup, Callahan."

"Whatever you say, Nouvelle." He saw her lips twitch, but she conquered the smile quickly. "Want some wine before lunch?"

"No wine, no lunch." She gestured, a regal flick of the wrist. "Talk."

"Tell me how you played the press conference."

"Where you're concerned?" Arching a brow, she sat back. "I told them I was bringing someone into the act who would dazzle them. A sorcerer who'd been traveling the world learning the secrets of the Mayans, the mysteries of the Aztecs and the magic of the Druids." She smiled faintly. "I hope you're up to the hype."

"I can handle it." He picked up a pair of steel handcuffs from the coffee table and toyed with them as he spoke. "You weren't all that far off. I learned a number of things."

"Such as?" she asked when he handed her the cuffs for inspection.

"How to walk through walls, vanish an elephant, climb a pillar of smoke. In Bangkok I escaped from a trunk studded with nails. And walked off with a ruby as big as your thumb. In Cairo it was a glass box dropped into the Nile—and emeralds almost as green as your eyes."

"Fascinating," she said and yawned deliberately as she passed him the cuffs. She'd found no secret catch.

"I spent nearly a year in Ireland, in haunted castles and smoky pubs. I found something there I'd never found anywhere else."

"Which was?"

"You could call it my soul." He watched her as he snapped the cuffs to his wrists. "I recognized Ireland, the hills, the towns, even the air. The only other place I've been that pulled me that way was New Orleans." He tugged his wrists apart so that the metal snapped. "But that might have been because you were there. I'd take you to Ireland, Rox." His voice had softened, like silk just stroked. "I imagined you there, imagined making love to you in one of those cool, green fields with the mist rising all around like witch smoke and the sound of harp strings sobbing on the air."

She couldn't take her eyes off his, or the image he so skillfully invoked. His magic was such that she could see them, tumbled on the grass, blanketed in fog. She could all but feel his hands on her skin, warming it, softening it as those old needs crackled like dried wood to a hot flame.

She dug her nails hard into her palms, then tore her eyes away. "It's a good line, Callahan. Very smooth." Steadier, she stared back at him. "Try it on someone who doesn't know you."

"You're a hard woman, Roxy." He held the cuffs up by one end and dropped them into her lap. There was a small sense of satisfaction when she smiled.

"You haven't lost your touch here, either, I see. Odd though. If you've been plying your trade so successfully all these years, why didn't I hear about you?"

"I imagine you did." He rose to answer the knock on the door and spoke casually back to her. "You'd have heard of the Phantom."

"The—" She bit her tongue as the room-service waiter wheeled in a tray. Rubbing her palms together she waited while lunch was

397

set up and Luke signed the check. Naturally, she'd heard of the Phantom, the strange, publicity-shy magician who appeared in all corners of the world, then disappeared again.

"I ordered for you," Luke said as he took a seat at the table. "I think I remembered what you like."

"I told you I don't have time for lunch." But curiosity had her wandering over. Barbecued chicken wings. Her lips thinned even as her heartbeat thickened. She wondered how he'd managed it when she knew very well it wasn't on the hotel's menu. "I lost my taste for them," she said and would have turned away but he grabbed her hand.

"Let's be civilized, Rox." He flicked a rose out of the air, offered it.

She took the bud, but refused to be charmed. "This is as good as it gets."

"If you won't eat with me, I'm going to think it's because the menu reminds you of us. And I'm going to think you're still in love with me."

She wrenched away, tossing the rosebud onto the table. Without bothering to sit, she snatched up a piece of chicken and bit in. "Satisfied?"

"That was never a problem with us." Grinning, he handed her a napkin. "You'll make less of a mess if you sit." He lifted his hands. "Relax. Nothing up my sleeve."

She sat and began to wipe sauce from her fingers. "So, you worked as the Phantom. I wasn't sure he really existed."

"That was the beauty." Luke settled back, cocking one foot on his knee. "I wore a mask, did the gig, took a bit extra if something appealed and moved on."

"In other words . . ." The sauce was damn good. She licked a bit from her thumb. "You went on the grift."

That put the fire in his eyes and, she hoped, in his gut. He shot her a look that could have smelted iron. "It wasn't grifting." Though he had made a few dollars early on with Three Card Monte and the Cups and Balls. "It was touring."

She gave an unladylike snort and went back to her chicken. "Right. Now you've decided you're ready for the big time again."

"I've always been ready for the big time." His only outward sign of annoyance was the tapping of his fingers on his ankles. But she knew him, knew him well, and was delighted to have scored a hit. "You don't want any explanations on where I went or why, so let's just say I was on sabbatical."

"Great word, sabbatical. Covers so much ground. Okay, Callahan, your sabbatical's over. What's the deal?"

"The three gigs hinge together." He poured the golden wine for himself and left her glass empty. "The performance, the auction and the hit. All the same weekend."

She raised her brows. It was the only reaction she chose to give him. "Ambitious, aren't we?"

"Good is what I am, Rox." The smile was a dare, the sort Lucifer might have aimed toward heaven. "As good as ever, maybe better."

"And as self-effacing."

"Modesty's like tact. It's for wimps. The performance is the diversion for the auction." He showed his empty palm, then turned his hand and danced a Russian ruble along his fingers. "The auction draws the eye from the job at Wyatt's." The ruble vanished. After snapping his fingers, he poured three coins into her glass.

"An old trick, Callahan." Willing to play, she dumped the coins into her hand. "As cheap as talk." With a flourish, she turned her palm up to show that the coins had turned into small silver balls. "This doesn't impress."

Damn it, he hadn't realized that disinterest could stimulate. "Try this. You join the luminaries for the auction after our performance. You're an honored guest, anxious to bid on a few baubles."

"And you are?"

"Attending to a few details at the theater, but I'll be joining you. You bid spiritedly against a certain gentleman on an emerald ring, but he outreaches you."

"And what if other attendees covet that ring?"

"Whatever the bid, he'll top it. He's French and rich and romantic and desires that ring for his fiancée. *Mais alors*." Luke slipped into French so smoothly, Roxanne blinked. "When he examines the ring, as a practical Frenchman might, he discovers it to be paste."

"The ring's a fake?"

"That and a number of other items." He linked his hands together, resting his chin on them. Over them, his eyes glowed with that old amused excitement that nearly tricked a grin out of her. "Because, my only love, we will have switched the take in those soft, dark hours before dawn. And while Washington and its very fine police force are abuzz with the daring theft of several million in jewels, we will quietly slip over to Maryland and relieve the aspiring senator of the philosophers' stone."

There was more, a very important more, but he would time the telling as carefully as his staging.

"Interesting," she said in a voice like a yawn, though she was fascinated. "There's just one little detail I don't understand."

"Which is?"

She funneled her hands and poured his coins next to his plate. "How the hell do we break into a heavily secured art gallery in the first place?"

"The same way we break into a house in the 'burbs, Roxy. Expertly. It also helps that I have what we could call a secret weapon."

"Secret weapon?"

"Top secret." He took her hand before she could avoid it and raised it to his lips. "I've always been a sucker for the taste of barbecue sauce on a woman's skin." Watching her, he traced his tongue over her knuckles. "Especially if it's your skin. Do you remember the day we had that picnic? We lay on the rug and listened to the rain? I think I started nibbling on your toes and worked my way up." He turned her hand over to scrape his teeth along her wrist. "I could never get enough of you."

"I can't recall." Her pulse jumped and scrabbled. "I've been on a number of picnics."

"Then I'll refresh your memory. We shared this same meal." He rose, drawing her slowly to her feet. "There was rain running over the windows, the light was gloomy. When I touched you, you trembled, just as you're trembling now."

"I'm not." But she was.

"And I kissed you. Here." He brushed his lips over her temple. "And here." Along her jaw. "And then—" He broke off with an oath as a key turned in the lock.

"What a town!" Jake barreled in, laden with shopping bags. "I could spend a week."

"Try another hour," Luke muttered.

"Ooops. I'm interrupting." Grinning, he set his bags down and crossed the room to take Roxanne's limp hand and pump it. "I've been looking forward to meeting you. Would've popped into your dressing room last night, but it would have cost me my life. I'm Jake Finestein, Luke's partner."

"Partner?" Roxanne echoed.

"Roxanne, our secret weapon." Disgusted, Luke sat and poured more wine.

"I see." She didn't have a clue. "Just what's your secret, Mr. Finestein?"

"Jake." He reached around her to cop one of the chicken wings. "Luke didn't fill you in yet? You could say I'm a wunderkind."

"Idiot savant," Luke corrected and made Jake laugh heartily in the peculiar hiccuping rasps that were his own.

"He's pissed, that's all. Thought you'd fall right into his arms. Guy's a pretty good thief, but he doesn't know squat about women."

Roxanne's lips curved in a genuine smile. "I think I like your friend, Callahan."

"I didn't say he was a friend. A thorn in my side, sand in my shoe."

"A fly in his soup." Jake winked and punched at his glasses. "Guess he didn't mention how I saved his life in Nice."

"He didn't mention it."

"You nearly got me killed," Luke pointed out.

"You know how things get twisted up after a few years." Always ready to socialize, Jake poured himself some wine. "Anyway, there was a little disagreement in a club."

"It was a fucking bar fight." Luke gestured with his glass. "Which you started."

"Details, details. There was a matter of an attractive young woman—I mean *a*-ttrac-tive—and a rather overbearing gentle-man."

"A hooker and a john," Luke muttered.

"Didn't I offer to beat his price? Business is business, isn't it? It's not like they'd signed a legal contract." Though it still offended his sense of free enterprise, with a sigh and a shrug, Jake continued. "In any case, one thing led to another, and when Luke got in the way—"

"When I stepped in to keep you from getting a shiv under the rib."

"Whatever. There was an altercation. It was me who bashed the big bastard with a whiskey bottle before he slit your throat, and what thanks do I get? I dragged him outside—rapped my shin on a chair, too, and didn't walk right for days. The bruise." He tossed up a hand. "Oiy! It was big as a baseball." He scowled at the memory, sipped, then sighed it away. "But I'm rambling."

"What else is new?"

To show there were no hard feelings, Jake patted Luke's shoul-der. "I find out Luke here's a magician, and he finds out I'm to computers what Joe DiMaggio was to baseball. A heavy hitter. No system I can't crack. It's a gift." He flashed his militarily aligned teeth and reminded Roxanne of a bespectacled beaver. "God knows where it comes from. My father ran a kosher bakery in the Bronx and had trouble with a cash register. Me, give me a keyboard and I'm in heaven. So one thing leads to another, and we hook up."

"Jake was in Europe running from a forgery rap."

"A slight miscalculation," Jake said mildly, but color rose up his skinny neck. "Computers are my passion, Miss Roxanne, but forgery is my art. Unfortunately, I became overanxious and rushed."

"It happens to the best of us," Roxanne assured him and earned his undying gratitude.

"A woman of understanding is more precious than rubies."

"She's passed precious little my way."

Roxanne arched a brow at Luke. "But you see, Callahan, I *like* Jake. I'm assuming that your skill with computers will get us past the security."

"There hasn't been a system invented that can stop me. I'll get you in, Miss Roxanne, and out again. As for the rest—"

"Let's take it one step at a time," Luke interrupted. "We have a lot of work to do, Rox. Are you up for it?"

"I can hold my own, Callahan. I always have." She turned to Jake with a smile. "Have you ever been to New Orleans?"

"It's a pleasure I'm anticipating."

"We're flying out tomorrow. I'd like you to come to dinner when it's convenient for you." She spared a brief glance for Luke. "I suppose you can bring him along."

"I'll keep him under control."

"I'm sure you will." Taking Luke's glass she clinked it against Jake's and made his beady eyes shine. "I think this is the start of a beautiful relationship." She took one sip before setting the glass aside. "You'll have to excuse me, I have a date. I'll wait to hear from you."

Jake pressed a hand to his heart as Roxanne closed the door behind him. "Oiy! What a woman."

"Make one move in that direction, pal, and you'll be eating all your meals through a straw."

403

"I think she liked me." Stars glittered behind the thick lenses. "I think she was definitely smitten."

"Check your glands, Finestein, and go get your tools. Let's see how close you can come to Wyatt's signature."

"Even his broker won't know the difference, Luke. Trust me."

"I have to," Luke muttered. "That's the problem."

Chapter Twenty-seven

IT WAS PERHAPS THE MOST DIFFICULT ROLE HE'D EVER played. Certainly it was the most important. Taking a detour on his way from D.C. to New Orleans, Luke arrived at the Wyatt estate in Tennessee with his hat in his hand, and revenge in his heart.

He knew it had to be done, the pleading, the humility, the face of fear. It might have rankled the pride, but keeping the Nouvelles safe well outdistanced the ego. So he would wear a mask—not the literal mask he'd worn off and on over the last five years—but one that would convince Sam Wyatt to accept Luke's return. At least temporarily.

He needed only a few months. At the end of it he would have everything he wanted. Or he would have nothing.

He knocked, and waited. When the uniformed maid answered, Luke ducked his head and swallowed audibly. "I, ah, Mr. Wyatt's expecting me. I'm Callahan. Luke Callahan."

After a brisk nod, she led him down the hallway he remembered and into the office where he had once witnessed a murder, and suffered his own small death.

As he had five years before, Sam sat behind his desk. This time, as well as the elegant furnishings there was an oversized campaign poster on an easel. The photographed smile flashed with sincerity and charm. In bold letters outlined in red and blue the caption read:

SAM WYATT FOR TENNESSEE
SAM WYATT FOR AMERICA

In a cloisonné bowl at the edge of the desk was a pile of buttons featuring the same face, the same sentiment.

As for the candidate himself, Sam had changed little.

Luke noted that a few silvery hairs had been allowed to glint at his temples, faint lines crinkled beside his eyes as he smiled. And he did smile, hugely. Very much, Luke thought, as a spider might when he spotted a fly struggling feebly in the web.

"Well, well, the prodigal returns. That will be all," he said to the maid, then leaned back, still grinning, when the door shut behind her. "Callahan—you look remarkably well."

"You look . . . successful."

"Yes." In an old habit, Sam turned his wrist so he could admire the gold cuff links winking at his cuffs. "I must say your call yesterday surprised me a great deal. I didn't think you had the nerve."

Luke straightened his shoulders in what he knew would appear to be a pitiful attempt at bravado. "I have a proposition for you."

"Oh, I'm all ears." Chuckling, Sam rose. "I suppose I should offer you a drink." He walked deliberately to the brandy decanter, and his eyes gleamed as he turned back. "For old times' sake."

Luke merely stared at the offered snifter while his breath came quick and loud. "I really don't—"

"What's the matter, Callahan? Lose your taste for brandy? Don't worry." Sam toasted, then drank deeply. "I don't have to doctor your drink to get what I want out of you this time. Sit." It was an order, master to dog. While the fire burned bright in his blood,

Luke let the brandy slosh in his glass as he meekly obeyed. "Now ..." Sam leaned against the corner of the desk, smiling. "What makes you think I'd let you come back?"

"I thought ..." Luke drank as if to bolster his courage. "I hoped that it had been long enough."

"Oh no." Reveling in the power, Sam shook his head. "Between you and me it can never be long enough. Perhaps I didn't make myself clear enough—what has it been? Five years ago. It was right here in this same room, wasn't it? Isn't that interesting?"

Idly he wandered to the spot where Cobb had sprawled, bleeding. The rug was new. An Italian antique he'd purchased with his wife's money.

"I don't suppose you've forgotten what happened here?"

"No." Luke pressed his lips together, averted his eyes. "No, I haven't forgotten."

"I believe I told you exactly what I would do if you came back. What would happen to you, and what would happen to the Nouvelles." As if struck with a notion, Sam lifted a finger, tapped it against his lips. "Or perhaps you've lost your enchantment with the Nouvelles after such a long separation. You might not care that I can send the old man to prison, send them all if it comes to that. Including the woman you once loved."

"I don't want anything to happen to them. There's no need for you to take any of this out on them." As if to steady his trembling voice, Luke took another sip. It was damn good brandy, he mused. A pity he couldn't relax enough to enjoy it. "I just want a chance to come home—only for a little while," he added quickly. "Sam, Max is really ill. He may not live long. I'm only asking you to let me spend a month or so with him."

"How touching." Sam moved behind the desk again. Opening a drawer he took out a cigarette. He allowed himself only five a day, and only in private. In today's political climate, smoking was a liability. He might have been well ahead in the polls, but he wasn't a man to take chances with his image. "So, you want to spend time with the old man while he dies." Sam lighted the cigarette, took one deep satisfying drag. "Why in hell should I care?"

"I know—I don't expect you to care. I hoped that since it would be for such a short time. A couple of months." Luke looked up again, his eyes full of pleas. "I don't see how it could matter to you."

"You're wrong. Everything about you, everything about the Nouvelles will always matter to me. Do you know why?" His fierce grin spread into a snarl. "You, none of you, recognized what I had, who I was. You took me in out of pity and tossed me out in disgust. And you thought you were better. You were nothing but common thieves, but you thought you were better than me."

The old anger reared up, nearly choking him. It was the hate that had ripened with it which kept his voice clear.

"But you weren't, were you?" he continued. "You're left without a home, even without a country, and the Nouvelles are saddled with a pathetic old man who can't remember his own name. But here I am, Callahan. Rich, successful, admired and on my way to the top."

Luke had to remind himself of the plan, the long term, the satisfaction of a clever sting. Otherwise he might have leaped up then and there and twisted Sam's neck. Because part of what Sam had said was true. Luke had no home. And Max had lost his identity.

"You have everything you want." Luke kept his shoulders slumped. "I'm only asking for a few weeks."

"You figure that's all the old man has left in him?" Sam sighed, and tipped back his brandy. "A pity. I actually hope he lives a long time yet, a long, long time with his mind vegetating, his body shriveling and the entire situation pulling the heart out of his family."

He smiled suddenly, the glossy politician's smile that lured voters. "I know all about Alzheimer's. More than you might imagine. As I was inspired by Max's predicament, part of my platform has been lending a sympathetic, even a compassionate ear to families dealing with the care and feeding of loved ones with minds like turnips. Ah!" He laughed at the sudden flash in Luke's eyes. "That offends you. Insults your sensibilities. Well, let me tell you something, Callahan, I don't give a damn about Maximillian Nouvelle or any of the others like him. Turnips don't vote. But don't worry, once I'm elected, we'll continue the ... illusion," he decided, enjoying the irony of the word. "We'll continue to make promises—even keep a few of them—about research and state funding, because I know how to plan for the long term."

He settled back and let himself project, opening himself to the one man Sam was certain could do nothing to harm him. "The Senate seat's only the next step—the next step toward the White House. Another decade, and I'll have won it all. Once I have control, complete control, things will be run my way. The bleeding hearts will be bled dry, and all those whining special-interest groups can whine themselves into oblivion. In the next century Americans will learn that they have a leader who understands control and power. A leader who knows how to use both and isn't afraid of taking some losses when he does."

His voice had risen, like an evangelist who is bent on saving souls. Luke watched in silence while Sam drew himself in. Sooner or later he would snap, Luke mused. God help us all if Wyatt had any buttons under his thumb when he did.

Sam drew on the cigarette again, then focused back on Luke as he tamped it out. "But I don't imagine you're interested in politics or the fate of a nation. Your interests are more personal."

"I made some money over the last few years." Wanting Sam to see nerves, Luke moistened his lips. "I'll pay you, give you whatever you want for a few weeks with Max and the Nouvelles."

"Money?" Delighted, Sam threw back his head and laughed. "Do I look like I need your money? Have you any idea how much I rake in every month in campaign contributions? That's over and above what I have from my lovely wife."

"But if you had more you—you could increase your television campaign, or whatever it took to make sure the election went your way."

"It's going my way," Sam snapped. His eyes went wide and bright. "Do you want to see the fucking numbers? The people of this state want me, Callahan. They want Sam Wyatt. After I'm finished with him, they wouldn't elect Curtis Gunner dog catcher. I'm winning." He slapped his hands on the desk, scattering ash. "I'm winning."

"A million dollars," Luke blurted out. "Surely you could use a million dollars to make sure. I only want a little time in exchange. Then I'll disappear again. Even if I wanted to stay, if I tried, Roxanne wouldn't have me." He bowed his head, a man defeated. "She's made that clear."

"Has she?" Sam drummed his fingers on the desk. He was calm again. He knew it was important to stay calm. Just as it was important to exploit whatever advantages came your way. "So you've seen her."

"In D.C. I went to her show." Fear radiated from him as he glanced up. "Only for a moment. I couldn't stop myself."

"And your course of true love hit another bump?" Nothing could have pleased him more. But he wondered, because he knew quite a bit about Roxanne, and a small boy named Nathaniel. "And did she catch you up on the highlights of her life during your absence?"

"She would barely speak to me," Luke whispered. "I hurt her, and since I can't explain why I left, she isn't about to forgive me."

Better and better, Sam thought. He didn't know about the child. How much would Roxanne suffer before—and if—she told him? And if she did, how much more would Luke bleed in having to leave again?

He considered it all for a moment. It seemed to him that Luke's return was more satisfying than his staying away altogether. It was, after all, more enjoyable to watch people suffer than to imagine it. And it appeared he could be paid for being entertained.

"A million dollars? Just how did you manage to accumulate so much?"

"I . . . " With a hand that shook, Luke set the brandy aside. "I performed."

"Haven't lost the magic touch? I imagine you continued to steal as well." Pleased by Luke's guilty start, he nodded. "Yes, I thought so. A million dollars," he repeated. "I'll have to think about it. Campaign funds are so carefully scrutinized these days. We wouldn't want any hint of graft or corruption to taint my image—especially when Gunner professes to be so squeaky clean. I'd like to . . . " He trailed off as a new idea dawned. It was so perfect, he realized, as if fate had handed him another tool.

"I believe we might be able to make a deal."

With eagerness in his eyes, in his voice, Luke leaned forward. "I'll have the money within a week. I can bring it to you wherever you say."

"The money will have to wait until after the election. I'll want my accountant to find a nice safe channel for it. In the meantime I have work for you. It'll buy you the time you want so badly."

It was a curve Luke hadn't expected. He'd counted on Sam's greed being enough. "Whatever you want."

"You might recall a little incident called Watergate. The burglars there were sloppy. You'd have to be very neat, very clever."

Luke changed gears and nodded. "You want me to steal documents?"

"I have no way of knowing if there are any documents worth stealing. But a man with your connections should be able to manufacture papers, photographs, that sort of thing. And if one can steal, one can also plant."

Folding his hands, Sam inched forward. It was so perfect. With his new tool he would not simply win the election, he would destroy his opponent, politically, personally, publicly.

"Curtis Gunner is the happily married father of two. His record in the State Senate is clean as a whistle. I want you to change all that."

"Change it? How?"

411

"Magic." Resting his chin on his folded hands, he grinned. "That's what you're best at, isn't it? I want photos of Gunner with other women—with whores. And with other men, yes, with other men." He had to press a hand to his side as giddy laughter shook him at the image. "That will be even more interesting. I want letters, papers documenting his involvement in illegal business deals, others, showing he siphoned off welfare money for personal use. That ought to kick his liberal ass. I want you to make them good, unimpeachable."

"I don't know how—"

"Then you'll find a way." Sam's eyes glittered. The power was here, all here, he realized. This time he hadn't even had to look for it. "You want to take your sentimental journey, Callahan, then you pay for it. You put together the faked photos, the papers, receipts, correspondence. I'll give you from now until, we'll say, ten days before the election. Yes, ten days," he murmured to himself. "When this leaks, I'll want it fresh in the voters' minds as they walk behind the curtain to pull the lever." Feeling generous, he inclined his head. "That gives you the same amount of time with the Nouvelles."

"I'll do whatever I can."

"You'll do exactly as I say, or when the time's up, you'll pay. They'll all pay."

"I don't know what you mean."

With a new smile playing around his mouth, Sam lifted his ivory-handled letter opener, testing the tip with his thumb. "You satisfy me with the job I'm giving you. Completely satisfy me. Or everything I threatened you with five years ago will come true."

"You said if I left, you wouldn't do anything to them."

With one vicious stroke he stabbed the tip of the letter opener into the padded corner of his blotter. "And you put it all back on the line by coming here. You've tossed the dice again, Callahan. What happens to the Nouvelles depends on just how well you play. Understood?"

"Yeah. Yeah, I understand."

He was going to play, Luke thought. And this time, he was going to win.

"So, so?" Dancing with impatience, Jake trailed Luke to the Cessna.

"So, are my things on board?"

"Yeah, yeah. What happened with Wyatt? Me, I'm just a peon, sure. Just a lowly soldier behind the front lines, just a—"

"An asshole," Luke finished for him. He climbed into the cockpit and began to check gauges. "It went fine," he said when Jake lapsed into offended silence. "If you consider the fact that I had to lower myself to playing the babbling beggar when what I wanted to do was cut out his heart."

"From what I hear, this dude don't have a heart anyway." Jake strapped in, shoved his glasses back up his nose. It was obvious that Luke was in a dangerous mood—which meant the short flight to New Orleans would be an eventful one. As a precaution Jake downed Dramamine and Valium with what was left of his warming orange soda. "Anyway, you got the time you need, right?"

"I got it." Luke broke off to check in with the tower and get the go-ahead for takeoff. As he began his taxi, he glanced at Jake, who was already pale, glassy-eyed and white-knuckled. "I've also got another job for you."

"Oh, good. Yeah, great." In self-defense, Jake closed his eyes when the plane's nose lifted. As he'd told Luke time and time again, he hated flying. Always had, always would. Which was why, he was certain, Luke crammed him into a cockpit on the average of once a week.

"Wyatt's deal included some creative mudslinging." As the plane continued its climb, Luke felt most of his tension draining away. He loved flying. Always had, always would. "It's right up your alley."

"Slinging mud." Cautious, Jake opened one eye. "So what do I know about slinging mud?"

"He wants doctored photographs, papers, business correspondence, putting this Curtis Gunner in a bad light. Illegal, unethical and immoral documents—the kind that lose elections and break up families, destroy lives."

"Shit, Luke, we got nothing against this Gunner guy, right? I know you had to dance with the devil to buy the time you need to put the screws to Wyatt. But, hell, it doesn't seem quite kosher."

After leveling off, Luke drew out a cigar. "Life sucks, Finestein, if you haven't noticed. You do the job, and do it good—with just one small adjustment."

Jake sighed. "I said I was in for the deal, so I'm in. You'll get the stuff—and it'll be hot enough to burn."

"I'm counting on it."

"So, what's the adjustment?"

Luke clamped the cigar between his teeth and grinned. "You don't do it on Gunner, you do it on Wyatt."

"On Wyatt? But you said . . . " Jake's pale face cleared into a dreamy smile. The Valium was taking hold. "Now I get it. Now I get it. A double cross."

"Christ, you're a quick study, Finestein." His grin was still widening as Luke banked the plane and headed for home.

Chapter Twenty-eight

THE BEDROOM LILY AND MAX HAD ONCE SHARED WAS FULLY equipped for the care of a patient with severe cognitive impairment. Roxanne had worked closely with hospital staff and an interior decorator to be certain that her father's environment was safe and practical without having the atmosphere of a hospital room.

Monitors and medicines were necessary, but so, in her opinion, were the bright colors and soft materials Max had always loved. A team of three nurses had eight-hour shifts, a physical therapist and a counselor made regular visits. But there were also fresh flowers, plumped pillows and a wide selection of Max's favorite classical music.

A special lock had been installed on the terrace doors to prevent him from wandering out alone. Roxanne had coldly dismissed one doctor's advice to have the windows fixed with bars and had hung new lace curtains instead.

Her father might be a prisoner of his illness, but she wouldn't make him one in his own home.

It pleased her to see the sunlight streaming through the lace at the windows, to hear the muted strains of Chopin as she stepped into her father's room. It no longer ripped so viciously at her heart when he didn't recognize her. She'd come to accept that there would be good days, and there would be bad ones. Now, seeing him sitting at his desk, patiently shifting sponge balls between his fingers, she could feel some small seed of relief.

Today, he was content.

"Good morning, Miss Nouvelle." The first-shift R.N. sat by the window reading. She set the book aside and smiled at Roxanne. "Mr. Nouvelle's taking some practice time before his therapy."

"Thank you, Mrs. Fleck. If you'd like to take a break for ten or fifteen minutes, LeClerc has fresh coffee on."

"I could probably force some down." Mrs. Fleck had twenty years as a nurse, and kind eyes. It had been the eyes more than the experience that had prompted Roxanne to hire her. She hefted her sturdy bulk out of the chair and touched Roxanne's arm briefly as she left the room.

"Hello, Daddy." Roxanne crossed to the desk, bent to kiss her father's cheek. It was too thin, so thin she often wondered how the fragile skin withheld the pressure of bone. "It's a pretty day. Have you looked outside? All of LeClerc's flowers are blooming, and Mouse fixed the fountain in the courtyard. Maybe you'd like to sit down there later and listen to it."

"I have to practice."

"I know." She stood with a hand light on his shoulder, watching his twisted fingers struggle to manipulate the balls. Once he could have snapped his fingers and made fire, but it was best not to think of that. "The performance went well. The finale was especially smooth. Oscar's gotten to be quite a ham, and such a trooper even Lily isn't nervous around him anymore."

She continued to talk, not expecting a response. It was a rare day when Max would stop whatever he was doing to look at her, much less engage in a real conversation. "We took Nate to the zoo. He just loved it. I didn't think I'd ever get him out of the snake house. He's getting so big, Daddy. Sometimes I look at him and can hardly believe he's mine. Did you ever feel that way, when I was growing up? Did you ever just look and feel sort of dazed all over and wonder how that person came from you?"

One of the balls bounced onto the floor. Roxanne bent to retrieve it, then crouched so that her eyes were on a level with Max's as she passed it back to him.

Max's gaze skittered away from hers, like a spider seeking a corner to spin a web. But she was patient and waited until he looked at her again.

"Did you worry all the time?" she asked softly. "In the back of your mind, under and over all the day-to-day business of living? Were you always afraid you'd do the wrong thing, say the wrong thing, make the wrong choice? It never gets easier, does it? Having a child is so wonderful, and it's so scary."

Max's smile bloomed slowly. For Roxanne it was like watching the sun come up over the desert. "You're very pretty," he said, stroking her hair. "I have to practice now. Would you like to come to the performance and watch me saw a woman in half?"

"Yes." She watched him work the balls with his fingers. "That would be nice." She waited a moment. "Luke's back, Daddy."

He continued to work the balls, his smile turning into a frown of concentration. "Luke," he said after a long pause. And again. "Luke."

"Yes. He'd like to see you. Is it all right if I let him visit?"

"Did he get out of that box?" Max's facial muscles began to twitch. The balls scattered, bouncing. His voice rose, petulant and demanding. "Did he get out?"

"Yes." Roxanne took her father's restless hands. "He's just fine. I'm going to see him in a little while. Would you want me to bring him to you?"

"Not when I'm practicing." Max's voice pitched higher, cracked. "I need to practice. How can I get it right if I don't practice?"

"All right, Daddy." To calm him, Roxanne gathered up the balls and set them within reach on the desk.

"I want to see him," Max muttered. "I want to see him when he's out of the box."

"I'll bring him." She kissed the thin cheek again, but Max was already involved with squeezing the sponge balls into his palms.

WHEN ROXANNE WALKED downstairs, she had her strategy mapped out. Luke was back; she couldn't ignore that. Nor would she ignore his tie to Max. But that didn't mean she wouldn't watch him like a hawk when she allowed a visit.

Just as there were certain steps to take toward a job, there were steps to take with Luke. She would work with him because it suited her, because his proposition intrigued her and because unless he'd changed dramatically in the last five years, he was the best. On stage, or opening the securest safe.

So she would use him for her own ends, take her share of the profits and walk away.

Except there was Nathaniel.

Stooping on the second to the last step, Roxanne picked up a tot-sized Ferrari. She slipped it into her pocket, but kept her fingers over it, thinking of the child whose fingers guided it on races across the rug or long rides over the brick courtyard. The child who was even now in his preschool class enjoying the morning with his current best friends. Could she ignore Luke's tie to the child he didn't know existed? Was this an illusion she should maintain for the rest of her life?

More time, she assured herself as she headed back to the kitchen. She needed more time.

It didn't help her peace of mind to find Luke there, sitting at the table as he had so often throughout his life, looking right at home with a cup of coffee in one hand and the last powdery bite of a beignet in the other.

LeClerc was laughing, so obviously pleased to have the prodigal home, so obviously ready to forgive and forget that Roxanne became only more determined to do neither.

"Quite a trick, Callahan, the way you slip through the cracks."

He acknowledged her and the job with an easy smile. "One of the five things I missed most while I was away was LeClerc's cooking."

"This boy was a walking appetite always. Sit, little girl. I fix your coffee."

"No, thank you." She knew her voice was cold, and felt a slight pang when LeClerc's eyes shifted from hers. Damn it, did they expect her to hire a brass band? "If you've finished your *petite déjeuner*, we might get to work."

"Ready when you are." He rose, snatching another pastry from the basket on the table. "I'll just take one for the road." He winked at LeClerc before strolling out the door Roxanne held open. "Does he still do all the gardening himself?" Luke asked as they crossed the flower-decked courtyard.

"Occasionally he lets—" Nate. "One of us help," she finished. "But he's still a tyrant about his roses."

"He hardly looks older. I was afraid." He paused, covering Roxanne's hand as she reached for the doorknob of the workroom. "I don't suppose you could understand, but I was afraid they would have changed. But when I was sitting in the kitchen just now, it was the way it always was. The smells, the sounds, the feel of it, just the same."

"And that makes it easy for you."

He wished he could blame her for twisting the knife so expertly. "Not entirely. You've changed, Rox."

"Have I?" She turned. He was closer than she would have liked, but she wouldn't cringe away, or yearn forward. Instead she stood straight and smiled coolly.

"There was a time I could read everything on your face," he murmured. "But you've pulled a switch. You look the same, you smell the same, sound the same. I imagine if I could take you into bed, you'd feel the same, but you've clicked that one little switch." With his eyes on hers he passed a hand over her face. "Now there's another woman superimposed over the one I remember. Which one are you, Roxy?"

"I'm exactly who I want to be." She twisted the knob and pushed the door open. "I'm who I made myself." She hit the lights and flooded the big workroom with its colored trunks, long tables and clusters of magic. "So, you saw the show. You should have a good idea how I work now. The basic style is elegance, touches of flash, but always with grace and fluidity."

"Yeah, real pretty." Luke bit into the beignet, scattering powdered sugar. "Maybe a little strong on the feminine side."

"Really?" Her brow arched. She picked up a silver dagger with a jeweled hilt she used as a prop. "I suppose you'd prefer strutting across the stage beating your chest and flexing your muscles."

"I think we can come to a happy medium."

Leaning a hip against the table, Roxanne tapped the blade against her palm. "I think we have a miscommunication here, Callahan. I'm the show. I'm perfectly willing to let you stage your comeback as part of the diversion, but I am and will remain in charge of the staging."

"My comeback." He ran his tongue across his teeth. "You're right about one thing, babe. There is a miscommunication. Has-beens have comebacks. I've been bugging their eyes out in Europe."

"Isn't it sweet how so many of those tiny villages still flock to sideshows?"

His eyes narrowed, glinted. "You want to put down that knife and say that?"

She only smiled, running a fingertip along the tip. "Now as I see it, we're doing a one-night-only. The prepublicity should give us enough for a sellout. 'One Night of Magic with Roxanne Nouvelle.' " She tossed her head so that her hair swung out and back. "With a special appearance by Callahan."

"At least your ego hasn't changed. Partners, Roxanne." He stepped closer. "You want top billing, I'll be a gentleman about it. But the sign reads 'Nouvelle and Callahan.' "

She moved a shoulder. "We'll negotiate."

"Look, I'm not wasting time with your petty bullshit."

"Petty? You want to talk petty?" She swung toward him and drove the knife into his heart. The look of stupefaction on his face had her falling back against the table, doubled over with laughter.

"God, what a sucker."

"Cute." He rubbed his chest where the trick knife had thudded. The heart beneath it had stopped dead. "Real cute. Now do you want to get down to business, or do you want to play?"

"Sure, we'll get down to business." She set the knife aside then propped herself up on the table. "It's my show, and it runs an hour forty-five. I'm willing to give you fifteen of it."

"I'll have fifty—including ten minutes for the finale, which we do together."

"You're taking Oscar's place?" When he gave her a blank look, she smiled. "The cat, Callahan. I do a finale with the cat."

"We'll shift that to the last act before intermission."

"Who the hell put you in charge?"

"It's my gig, Roxanne." Leaving it at that, he walked over to one of the brightly painted trunks. It was as tall as he and sectioned into three equal parts. "I want to work in an escape, a multiplication bit I've been working on, one large-scale illusion and a transportation."

To give her hands something to do, she picked up three balls to juggle. "Is that all?"

"No, the finale's separate." He turned back, picked up another ball. Gauging her rhythm, he tossed it in among the three. She picked up the fourth ball without blinking an eye. "I want to do a variation on the broomstick illusion we did on the cruise. I've got most of the kinks worked out already. I'd like to start rehearsing as soon as possible."

"You'd like a lot of things."

"Yeah." He stepped forward and, quick as a snake, slipped his hands under hers to take the balls. "The trick's figuring out when to move and when to wait." He grinned at her through the circling balls. "We can rehearse here, or we can use the house I just bought."

"Oh?" She hated the fact that she was interested. "I figured you'd bunk at a hotel."

"I like my own space. It's a good-sized house in the Garden District. Since I haven't bothered much with furniture yet, we'd have plenty of room."

"Yet?"

"I'm back, Rox." He sailed the balls toward her, but she batted them aside. "Get used to it."

"I don't give a damn where you live. This is business, and a one-shot deal at that. Don't get it into your head that you're coming back on the team."

"I'm already on it," he said. "That's what pisses you off." He held up a hand for peace. "Why don't we see how we manage this? Mouse and Jake already have their heads together over the security angle, and—"

"Hold it." Fired up, she shoved off the table. "What do you mean they have their heads together?"

"I mean, Jake came over with me. He and Mouse went off to talk electronics."

"I'm not having this." She shoved him aside so that she had a clear field to pace. "All right? I'm not having it. No way you're waltzing back here and taking over. I've been running things for over three years. Ever since Max—ever since he couldn't anymore. Mouse is mine."

"I didn't realize he'd become property since I'd left."

Furious, she swung back. "You know very well what I mean. He's *my* family. He's *my* team. You gave that up."

He nodded. "I gave a lot up. You want to make it personal. Fine. I spent five years doing without everything that mattered to me. Because it mattered to me. Now I'm taking it back, Roxy. All of it." The hell with caution, with courtship, with control, he thought as he grabbed her by the shoulders. "Every last bit of it. Nothing's going to stop me."

She could have pulled away. She could have scratched and bit and fought her way free. But she didn't. Something in his eyes, something wild and desperately unhappy kept her rooted to the spot even when he crushed his mouth to hers.

She tasted the fury and the frustration and something more, a longing too deep for words, too wide for tears. Those old, carefully buried needs fought their way up so that she answered greed with greed.

Oh, how she wanted him still. How she wanted to blank out time and space and simply be again. It was so much as it had been: his taste, the way his mouth slanted over hers, that whip-quick, pulsing excitement that left her body straining urgently toward fulfillment.

But it was not the same. Even as her arms clamped around him she could feel that he was leaner. As if he'd taken a blade and ruthlessly hacked himself down to muscle and bone. Beneath the physical she could sense other changes. This Luke wouldn't laugh as quickly, rest as easily or love as sweetly.

But, oh, how she wanted him still.

He could take her there, on the table where magic had been conjured for a generation. On the floor where enchanter's dust lay scattered. Here and now. And if he did, if he took back what had been lost to him, he might find his salvation. He might find his peace. But even if it brought him hell and chaos, he'd thank God for it. He let his mind wallow in the thought while his hands molded the body that melted so perfectly against his.

She was the only one. The always one. There was nothing and no one to stop him from claiming her again.

Except himself.

"It's the same." He tore his mouth from hers to bury it against her throat. "Damn it, Roxanne, it's the same between us. You know it."

423

"No, it's not." Yet she clung to him still, wishing.

"Tell me you don't feel it." Furious and frantic, he dragged her back to study her face. He saw what he needed to see there—the heavy eyes, the pale skin, the swollen mouth. "Tell me you don't feel what we do to each other."

"It doesn't matter what I feel." Her voice rose, as if by shouting she could convince herself. "What matters is what is. I'll trust you onstage. I'll even trust you on the job. But nowhere else, Luke. With nothing else ever again."

"Then I'll do without trust." He dipped his fingers in her hair, combing them through. "I'll take what's left."

"You're waiting for me to say I want you." She pulled away, giving herself time for two steadying breaths. "All right, I want you, and maybe I'll decide to act on it. No strings, no promises, no baggage."

He felt like someone was kneading the muscles in his gut as if they were bread dough. "Decide now."

She nearly laughed. There was so much of the old Luke in the command. "Sex is something I'm cautious about." She sent him a level look. "And that's all it would be."

"You're cautious," he murmured, stepping to her again, "because you're afraid it would be a whole lot more." He tilted his head down to kiss her again, but this time she slapped a hand on his chest.

"Is this your answer for everything?"

Because whether she knew it or not, they'd made progress, he smiled. "Depends on the question."

"The question is, can we pull off a complicated series of jobs while our hormones are humming?" She smiled back, daring him. "I can if you can."

"Deal." He took her hand. "But I'm going to get you into bed along the way. So, why don't you come to my place? We can . . . rehearse."

"I take rehearsals seriously, Callahan."

"Me too."

With a laugh, she rocked back on her heels, and dipped her hands in her pockets. Her fingers brushed the little car, and she remembered. Too much. The smile died out of her eyes.

"We'll make it tomorrow."

"What is it?" Frustrated that the shutter had dropped between them again, he took her chin in his hand. "Where did you go?"

"I just don't have time to work it in today."

"You know that's not what I meant."

"I have a right to my privacy, Luke. Give me the address, and I'll be there tomorrow morning. To rehearse."

"Fine." He dropped his hand. "We'll play it your way. For now. There's one more thing before I go."

"What?"

"Let me see Max." His temper tripped when she hesitated. "Goddammit, scrape and claw at me all you want. But don't punish me that way."

"You don't know me at all, do you?" she said wearily. She turned away, walked to the door. "I'll take you up to him."

HE'D KNOWN IT WOULD BE BAD. Luke had gathered all the snippets from the press on Max's condition, had read everything he could find on Alzheimer's. He'd been sure he'd been prepared for the physical changes, and the emotional ones.

But he hadn't known how badly it would hurt to see the man, that larger-than-life figure from his boyhood, so shrunken, so old and so lost.

He stayed for an hour, in the sunny room with Mozart playing. He talked endlessly, even when there was no response, and he searched Max's face for signs of recognition.

He left only when Lily came in and gently told him that it was time for Max's exercise.

"I'll come back." Luke put his hand over Max's and felt the

thready pulse in the narrow wrist. "I've got a couple of new bits you might like to see."

"Have to practice," Max said, staring down at Luke's strong, lean hand. "Good hands. Have to practice." He grinned suddenly. "You have potential."

"I'll be back," Luke said again and walked blindly toward the door. He found Roxanne down in the front parlor, watching the street through the window.

"I'm sorry, Roxy." When he stepped behind her, wrapping his arm around her waist, she didn't object, but gave for a moment, leaning into him.

"There's no one to blame. I tried that route at first. Doctors, fate, God. Even you, just because you weren't here." When he pressed a kiss to the top of her head she squeezed her eyes tightly shut. But they were dry when she opened them. "He's gone somewhere he has to be. That's how I deal with it. He isn't in pain, though sometimes I'm so afraid there's a deeper kind of pain I can't see. But I know how lucky we are to be able to keep him home, and close until he's ready to go away completely."

"I don't want to lose him."

"I know." Understanding was too deep for her to prevent a reaching out. She lifted a hand to the one on her shoulder and linked fingers. Where Max was concerned, she could give without limitation. "Luke, I need to set the rules, and it's not to punish you. I'd like you to see Max as much as possible. I know it's difficult, and it's painful, but I have to believe it's good for him. You were— are—a big part of his life."

"I don't have to tell you how I feel about him, what I'd do for him if I could."

"No. No, you don't." She let out a long breath. "I'll need you to let me know when you'd like to come. Dropping in unannounced disrupts his routine."

"For chrissake, Roxanne."

"There are reasons." She turned, standing firm. "I'm not going to explain myself, I'm just going to set the boundaries. You're welcome here. Max would want that. But on my terms."

"So I make appointments?"

"That's right. Mornings are usually best, like today. Sometime between nine and eleven." When Nathaniel was safely in preschool. "That way we can set rehearsals for the afternoon."

"Fine." He strode toward the door. "Draw me up a goddamn schedule."

Roxanne heard the front door slam. The familiar echo of it nearly made her smile.

Chapter Twenty-nine

FOR THE FIRST TIME IN HER LIFE, ROXANNE SUFFERED FROM the disapproval of her family. They didn't say she was wrong. There were no lectures, no unsolicited advice, no withholding of smiles or conversation.

She might have preferred that to the murmurs she heard before she walked into a room, the long sorrowful stares she felt behind her back. They didn't understand. She could tell herself that and forgive them—or nearly. None of them had ever found themselves pregnant and deserted and alone. Well, perhaps not really alone, she amended as she propped her chin on her hand and watched Nathaniel play cars in the courtyard. She'd had family, a home and unquestioning support.

But none of it made up for what Luke had done. She'd be damned if she'd reward him by sharing her perfectly beautiful child and risking the steady balance of Nate's happiness.

Why couldn't they see that?

She glanced up when the kitchen door opened, and smiled at Alice as the woman crossed the courtyard. An ally, Roxanne thought, smug. Alice didn't know Luke, had no emotional investment in him. She of all people would agree that a mother had the right to protect her child. And herself.

"There was an awful wreck," Nathaniel told Alice.

Interested, she bent down, her wispy blond hair swung out, her full-skirted cotton dress nearly brushing the bricks. "Looks grim," she agreed in her quiet voice. "Better call nine-one-one."

"Nine-one-one!" Nathaniel agreed, delighted, and began to make siren noises.

"That's the third wreck in fifteen minutes." Roxanne scooted over on the iron bench so Alice could sit. "The fatalities are mounting."

"Those roads are treacherous." Alice smiled her pretty, ethereal smile. "I've tried to educate him on the advantages of car pools, but he prefers traffic jams."

"He prefers traffic accidents. I hope it's not warping his mind."

"Oh, I think we're safe there." Alice took a deep breath to bring in the scent of roses and sweet peas and freshly watered mulch. The courtyard was her favorite spot, a shady summery place designed for sitting and thinking. So typically Southern. As a transplanted Yankee, she embraced all that was South with the same fervor a converted Catholic embraces the Church. "I thought I'd take Nate to Jackson Square after preschool. Let him run around a little."

"I wish I could go with you. I never feel as though I'm spending enough time with him when I'm prepping for a job."

Alice had accepted all sides of the Nouvelles' professions with philosophical ease. To her they weren't stealing so much as spreading excess profits around. "You're a wonderful mother, Roxanne. I've never seen you let work interfere with Nate's needs."

"I hope not. His needs are the most important thing to me." She laughed as he bashed two cars together and made crashing noises. "Homicidal?"

"Healthy aggression."

"You're good for me, Alice." With a sigh, Roxanne sat back. But she was rubbing her hands together, a sure sign of nerves.

"Everything seemed so balanced, so right, so easy. I like routine, you know? I suppose it comes from the discipline of magic."

Alice studied Roxanne with calm eyes. "I wouldn't say you were a woman who disliked surprise."

"Some surprises. I won't have Nate's life disrupted. Or mine either, if it comes to that. I know what's best for him. Damn it, I want to know what's best for him. And I certainly know what's best for me."

Alice was silent a moment. She wasn't a woman to speak without thinking. She gathered those thoughts as carefully and as selectively as she would pick wildflowers. "You want me to tell you that keeping Nate a secret from his father is the right thing to do."

"It is." Roxanne glanced at Nate, cautiously lowering her voice. "At least until I feel it's time. He has no rights to Nate, Alice. He gave them up when he walked away from us."

"He didn't know there was an us."

"That's beside the point."

"It may be beside, or it may be the point. I'm not in a position to know."

"So." Roxanne's lips thinned at the new betrayal. "You're lining up with the rest of them."

"It's not like choosing sides for kickball, Roxanne." Because friendship came first with Alice, she closed a hand over Roxanne's rigid fingers. "Whatever you do or don't do, we're all behind you. Whether we agree or not."

"And you don't."

With a sigh, Alice shook her head. "I don't know what I would do in your position. And only you can know what you really feel in your heart. I can say that in the week since I met Luke, I like him. I like his intensity, his recklessness, his single-minded focus on a goal. Those are some of the same reasons I like you."

"So you're saying I should let him in, trust him with Nate."

It was so hard to give advice, Alice thought. She wondered why so many people thrived on it. "I'm saying you should do what you feel is right. Whatever that is, it won't change one simple fact. Luke is Nathaniel's father."

LUKE, LUKE, LUKE. Roxanne fumed as she watched him run through his Woman in the Glass Box routine with Lily. Mouse and Jake stood off to the side, drawn away from the electronic jammer they'd been tinkering with to watch.

Why was it Luke came back and he was suddenly the sun with all of them revolving like planets around him? She hated it.

It was all wrong. They were rehearsing here, in his barn-like living room with its lofty ceilings and fancy plasterwork. Suddenly they were on his turf, with him calling the shots.

There was rock music on the stereo. He was timing his bit to Springsteen's *Born to Run*. They always worked with classical, Roxanne thought, shoving her hands into the pockets of her sweatpants. Always. It infuriated her further that it suited him, and the illusion.

It was fast, exciting, sexy. Everything he did fit those three words. She knew damn well the audience would love it. That only soured her mood.

"Good." Luke turned to Lily and kissed her flushed cheek. "Time, Jake?"

"Three minutes, forty." He'd already clicked off the stopwatch.

"I think we can shave ten more seconds." Despite the air-conditioning, he was sweating. Still, he liked keeping that particular illusion at a frantic pace, and was revved for more. "Can you handle another run, Lily?"

"Sure."

Sure, Roxanne thought, sneering. Anything you want, Luke. Anytime you want it. Disgusted, she turned away to retreat to the far corner of the room. She'd work through the Spinning Crystal routine she hadn't had time to perfect before the last performance.

There, beside the massive stone fireplace, was a long folding table. A number of props were set up there, ready for practicing.

She was particularly pleased with the diamond-shaped crystal, its rainbow facets. It was a good, solid weight in her hands. She imagined the strains of Tchaikovsky, envisioned the shadowy stage, the crisscrossed spotlights softened with blue gel, and herself sheathed from head to foot in pure glistening white.

And swore when Springsteen's primal yell shattered her concentration.

Luke caught the bitter snarl she tossed at him, and grinned. "Mouse, how about setting up for the levitation? I think we've got this one."

"Sure." Mouse lumbered off to oblige.

"Pulling everyone's string, aren't you?" Roxanne said when Luke joined her at the table.

"It's called teamwork."

"I've got another name for it. Worming. Slithering."

"That's two words." He covered her hands over the crystal. "Think of it this way, Rox. Once we pull this off, you'll never have to come within ten feet of me again. Unless you want to."

"I am thinking of that." It was better than thinking of how just the touch of his hands on hers made her blood thicken. "I need to know more about the Wyatt job. You're holding back, and I don't like it."

"So are you," he said evenly. "And neither do I."

"I don't know what you're talking about."

But she'd broken eye contact. "Yes, you do. There's something you're not telling me. Something everyone's holding their breath over. Once you come clean, we'll deal with the situation."

"Come clean?" She cut her eyes back to his, and they were hot and lethal. "Something I'm not telling you? What could it be? Let's see . . . could it be that I detest you?"

"No." He outmaneuvered her by running his hands up her arms while hers were trapped around the crystal. "You've been busy letting me know that for more than a week. And you only detest me when you make yourself think about it."

"But it comes so naturally." She smiled, sweet as a honeyed stiletto.

"Only because you're still crazy about me." He kissed the tip of her nose when she hissed at him. "This is business, right?"

"Yes."

"So let's get down to it." His smile was slow and dangerous. "Then we'll see what comes naturally."

"I want more information."

"And you'll get it. Just like you'll get the stone when it's finished."

"Wait." She grabbed his arm when he started to turn. Unsteady, she set the crystal down again. "What are you saying?"

"That the stone's yours when it's finished. One hundred percent."

She searched his face looking for the truth, wishing she could see him clearly as she once had. "Why?"

"Because I love him, too."

There was nothing for her to say, because that was the truth, and that she could see clearly. Her chest tightened, restricting air as well as words. "I want to hate you, Callahan," she managed. "I really want to hate you."

"Tough, isn't it?" He skimmed a finger down her cheek. "I know, because I wanted to forget you. I really wanted to forget you."

She lifted her eyes to his, and for the first time since his return he saw the opening. He'd wormed his way in all right, he thought with some disgust. Through her love for Max. It wasn't the route he would have chosen.

"Why?" She hadn't wanted to ask, was afraid of the answer.

"Because loving you, remembering loving you was killing me."

That shook her knees and loosened her heart. "You're not going to get to me, Callahan."

"Oh, yeah." He took her hand to lead her to the center of the room. "I am."

"Nearly set." Mouse whistled through his teeth. It was great to have the two of them together again, he thought. Even if they weren't smiling. It embarrassed him to feel the sparks fly from them. It seemed to Mouse that was something that should happen in the dark, when two people were alone. That kind of intimacy was rough on witnesses.

Roxanne lifted her arms so that Mouse could fix his wires. But she never took her eyes from Luke. She hated to admit she liked this particular illusion. It sizzled, and it flowed; it had drama and it had poetry.

Besides, she'd had fun squabbling with him over each and every detail.

"Are we using the music?" she asked.

"Yeah. My pick."

"Why—"

"Because you chose the lighting."

She frowned, but it was tough to argue with quid pro quo. "So what is it?"

" 'Smoke Gets in Your Eyes.' " He grinned when she rolled hers. "The Platters, Rox. It's not classical, but it is a classic."

"If you knew anything about creating a theme, you'd know that the music should be consistent throughout the show."

"If you knew anything about flair, you'd know that the change of pace adds pizzazz."

"Pizzazz." She sniffed, tossed back her hair. "Let's just do it."

"Fine. Cue the music."

She brought her hands up, swayed. He held his out, curling his fingers toward him in invitation. Or in command. Resisting, refusing, she lifted her arm over her face, her palm toward him and turned fluidly to the side. Not a retreat. An allurement. Focused on her, only on her, he mirrored her move, step for step, as if they were bound by invisible threads. Their fingers brushed, lingered, drew away.

Roxanne felt the power ripple through her like wine.

She didn't need her memory of the script to keep her eyes on his. She couldn't have looked away. The concentration on his face pierced her, so it was easy to allow her head to roll loosely, dreamily on her shoulders.

Perhaps she could have won the duel. Or perhaps, in surrender, she already had.

Luke threw up his hands, a dramatic demand which Roxanne resisted by gliding away. Only to stop, poised, when his arms lowered and reached out for her. Slowly, as if caught in a trance, she turned back.

She didn't move when he stepped close. His hand passed in front of her face. Her eyes shuddered closed. Never more than a whisper away from bodies brushing, he circled her. His gestures were long, slow, exaggerated as her feet tipped off the floor, as her hair rained back, as her body lifted.

While the music built, his hands traced her, still that whisper away from contact. Her body quivered, beyond the control of her concentration. She watched him through her lashes, unable to help herself, certain she would scream with need and frustration if those hands continued to skim over her without touching.

He thought he could hear her heart pounding. Barely, he resisted the urge to press his hand over her breast to feel that thud of life. His mouth was dry, and he knew he was breathing too quickly. But he was beyond illusion now.

He'd meant the segment to be romantic, sexual, and had known he would be treading deep water. But he hadn't known how quickly he could drown.

He bent his head toward hers, his lips hovering, so close to tasting. The quiet sound she made as she struggled not to moan roared in his head.

He took her hand, running his fingers over the palm, down the back. When their fingers were linked he, too, began to rise. His eyes were riveted on her face as they lay suspended together. As the music began to fade, he turned his body, cupped a hand under her head and brought his mouth to hers.

Locked together, they tilted toward vertical, bodies revolving. When their feet touched the ground, his arms were still around her and her mouth was still a captive.

Jake clicked off the stopwatch and cleared his throat. "Don't guess anybody cares about time," he murmured and stuck the watch in his pocket. "Radio Shack," he said, inspired. "Come on, Mouse. We gotta get to the mall."

"Huh?"

"The mall, the mall. We need those parts."

Mouse blinked in confusion. "What parts?"

"*Those* parts." Jake rolled his eyes and jerked his head toward Roxanne and Luke. They'd drawn apart now, but only far enough to stare at each other.

"Oh, I need some things, too." Teary-eyed, Lily grabbed Mouse and pulled. "I need lots of things. Let's get going."

"But rehearsal—"

"I think they've got it cold," Jake said and was grinning as they pulled Mouse out of the house.

The silence spun in Roxanne's already dizzy head. "It—it ran long."

"You're telling me." He'd been ready to explode. Now he ran his hands gently up and down her back before freeing her from the levitation harness. "But it's going to be a hell of a finale."

"Needs work."

"I'm not talking about that finale." He released himself. "I'm talking about you and me." Watching her, he skimmed his hands under her sweatshirt and let them roam over the warm, smooth skin of her back. "And this." He kissed her again, softly.

She had no choice but to grip his shoulders for balance. "You're not going to seduce me."

He traced his lips over her jaw, knowing just where to nip to make her shiver. "Want to bet?"

"I can walk away from you anytime." But her body was pressed against his, and her mouth was racing over his face. "I don't need you."

"Me either." He scooped her up and started toward the stairs.

If her body would stop shivering she was sure she'd regain her bearings. For now it seemed best to hold on tight.

She knew what she was doing. God, she hoped she knew. This terrible ragged yearning made everything else seem so small and pitiful. This was all there was, all there needed to be. On a moan, she pressed her face against his neck.

"Hurry," was all she said.

He'd have flown up the stairs if he'd been able. It felt as though he had the way his muscles were quivering and his breath heaving. Once he'd kicked the bedroom door closed behind them, he sought her lips again. He could only thank whatever powers there were that he'd had the foresight to buy a bed.

And a hell of a bed it was. The huge, cushy four-poster gave like a cloud when they fell onto it. He paused for a moment, only a moment, to look down at her and remember—to force her to remember all they had been to each other, what they had done for each other, and to each other, beyond that gulf of five years.

He saw the struggle for denial in her eyes and battered it with a greedy kiss. She wouldn't hold back from him now, he wouldn't permit it. Cuffing her wrists in his hands he drew her arms high over her head. If she touched him he'd ignite like a stick of dynamite. First he wanted to make sure she felt everything he wanted her to feel.

She twisted against his hold, her heart leaping to her throat to bang like a drum in the hollow. He only lowered his lips to it as a prelude to an exploitation of every secret he remembered.

He'd dreamed of this countless times, in countless rooms in countless places. Only this was more potent than any fantasy. The taste of her, rioting through him, was like a feast after years of fasting. He wouldn't deny himself now, or ever again.

She didn't struggle against the flood of sensation. Couldn't bear to. He was giving her back everything he'd taken away, and more. She'd nearly forgotten what it was to crave, and had never really understood what it meant to abandon all will. After so long an abstinence it was so simple, so right, to only feel. Every time his lips found hers, there was a shock of recognition and a shiver of the unknown.

His blood burned when he heard his name tumble from her lips. Each sigh, each moan was a hammer thrust in his gut. Frantic for more, he released her hands to tug at her clothes. He groaned in violent pleasure when he found her gloriously naked beneath.

"Hurry," she said again, tearing his shirt in her rush to be flesh against flesh. The furnace building inside her was nearing flash point. She wanted him in her when it exploded. She wanted him stoking that fire inside her.

He wanted to savor. He needed to devour. Gasping for air, he fought the snap of his jeans while her hands tortured him and her mouth seared like lightning over his shoulders and chest.

He plunged. At the first urgent stroke she came in a geyser of dark, nameless delights. Her body arched, vibrated like a harp string. Air tore from her lungs in a cry that was both pain and triumph.

Then she locked around him, her legs soft as silk, strong as steel. Half mad, he drove himself into her, again and again, until he found his own release, and perhaps his salvation.

HE STAYED WHERE HE WAS, spread over her, intimately joined. He knew she'd been silent for too long. If things had been as they once were, she would have lifted a hand to lazily stroke his back. She would have sighed and nuzzled or whispered something to make him laugh.

But there was nothing but that long empty silence. It frightened him enough to kindle temper.

"You're not sorry this happened." He curled a hand possessively in her hair to keep her still when he leaned back to look at her. "You might be able to convince yourself of that, but not me."

"I didn't say I was sorry." How difficult it was to be calm when your life had just shifted on its foundations. "I knew it would happen. The minute I walked into my dressing room and saw you again, I knew." She managed what passed for a shrug. "I often make mistakes without being sorry for them."

His eyes glinted before he rolled away from her. "You know just where to hit, don't you? You always did."

"It's not a matter of striking back." She was going to be practical about this. If it killed her. "I enjoyed making love with you again. We were always good in bed."

He snatched her arm before she could reach her knotted sweatshirt. "We were good everywhere."

"Were," she agreed, carefully. "I'll be honest, Callahan. I haven't made much time for this sort of thing in my life since you left."

He couldn't stop it. His ego inflated as helplessly as a balloon swells with helium. "Oh, yeah?"

She couldn't understand how one man could infuriate, arouse and amuse a woman simultaneously. "Don't look so smug. It was my choice. I was busy."

"Admit it." He traced a lazy finger down her breast. "I spoiled you for anybody else."

"My point is." She slapped his hand away before the touch dissolved what was left of pride. "You happened to catch me at a . . . " Vulnerable wasn't quite the word she wanted. "An incendiary time. I imagine anyone who held the match in the right spot would have set me off."

"If that's the case, you should be pretty well burned out now."

He'd always been quick. She shouldn't have been surprised to find herself on her back again with his hands proving that fires could be kindled out of embers.

"It's just sex," she managed to gasp.

"Sure it is." He laved the damp flesh between her breasts. "And a redwood's just a tree." He used his teeth to torment her nipples until her nails dug crescents into his back. "A diamond's just a rock."

She wanted to laugh. She needed to scream. "Shut up, Callahan."

"Glad to." He lifted her hips and slid gloriously into her.

SHE DIDN'T THINK she was burned out. Hollowed out was closer. There didn't seem to be a nerve left in her body. When she managed to open her eyes again, the light had gone rose with twilight. To give her mind a chance to settle, she took note of the room for the first time.

There was nothing in it but the bed where they sprawled and a single enormous chest of drawers in gleaming cherry. Unless you counted the clothes that were tossed over the rugless floor, draped over the doorknob or piled in corners.

How like him, she thought. Just as it was like him to have shifted his body so that hers could curl naturally against it.

How many times had they lain just like this, night after night? There had been a time when she would have drifted right off to sleep, safe, secure, satisfied.

But they were different people now.

She started to sit up. His arm merely tightened around her.

"Luke, this doesn't change anything."

He opened one eye. "Babe, if you want me to prove my point again, I'd be more than happy. You'll just have to give me a couple of minutes."

"The only point we've proved is that we still know how to scratch one another's itch." Most of her anger had died, leaving a gulf of sorrow that was only more potent. "There's no need to— What the hell is this?" She twisted to get a better look at the back of his shoulder.

"It's a tattoo. Haven't you ever seen a damn tattoo?"

"A few in my time." She pursed her lips, studying it in the dimming light. Just above where the scars of his youth began their crisscross on his back was the painted image of a snarling wolf. She didn't know whether to laugh or cry and opted for the former. "Jesus, Callahan, did you go crazy or what?"

It embarrassed the hell out of him. "Tattoos are in."

"Oh, right, and you're Mr. Trendy. Why the hell did you let somebody scar you—" She broke off, appalled. "I'm sorry."

"It's okay." He shrugged and dragged the hair out of his eyes as he sat up. "I was feeling mean one night, a little drunk, a lot dangerous. I decided to get a tattoo instead of looking for a convenient head to bash in. Besides, it reminded me of where I'd come from."

She studied him, the arrogant tilt of the head, the hard gleam of his eyes that warred with the encroaching gloom. "You know, I can almost believe in Lily's amnesia theory."

"Let me know when you want the truth. You'll get every bit of it."

She looked away. It was easy, much too easy for him to pull her in. "It wouldn't make any difference. There's nothing you can say that can wipe away five years."

"Not unless you're willing to let me." He caught her face in his hands, brushing her hair back so that only his fingers framed her. The gentleness he'd forgotten, that she had been certain had burned out of him, was back. Such things were harder to resist than passion. "I need to talk to you, Rox. There's so much I need to say."

"Things aren't what they were, Luke. I can't begin to tell you how much they've changed." And if she stayed, she would say more than was wise before she thought it through. "We can't go back, and I need to consider where we might go from here."

"We can go anyplace. We always could."

"I've gotten used to going on my own." She took a deep breath before shifting away to dress. "It's getting late. I have to go home."

"Stay here." He touched his fingertips to her hair, and tempted her beyond measure.

"I can't."

His fingers curled, tightened. "Won't."

"Won't then." She smoothed down her shirt, rose. It was easier to be strong when she was standing on her feet again. "I run my life now. You can stay or you can go, and I'll deal with the consequences of either. If I owe you anything, it's gratitude for making me tough enough to handle whatever comes." She tilted her head, wishing her heart felt as courageous as the words. "So thanks, Callahan."

Her easy dismissal sliced him open and left him bleeding. "Don't mention it."

"See you tomorrow." She walked from the room, but was running by the time she hit the landing.

Chapter Thirty

THE HOUSE WAS IN AN UPROAR WHEN ROXANNE RETURNED. She'd no more than stepped across the threshold when she was caught up in the chaos. While everyone talked at once, she swung Nathaniel up in her arms and kissed him firmly on his pursed and waiting lips, partly in greeting and partly in apology for not being the one to give him his bath and help him into his favored Ninja Turtles pj's.

"Hold on." She settled Nate on her hip, holding up a hand in a futile hope to stem the tide.

Delighted with the confusion, Nate bounced and began to sing a sea chantey about drunken sailors at the top of his voice.

She caught snatches about the telephone, caviar, Clark Gable, San Francisco and Aces High. Her mind, already muddled from her afternoon with Luke, struggled to decipher the code.

"What? Clark Gable called from San Francisco and came over to eat caviar and do card tricks?"

Because Alice laughed, Nate decided it must be a grand joke. Giggling, he tugged on his mother's hair. "Who's Clark Gable, Mama? Who is he?"

"He's a dead man, baby, like certain other people around here are going to be if they don't *shut up!*" Her voice had risen admirably on the last two words. There was a gratifying stunned silence. Before anyone could draw in the breath to start again, she pointed at Alice. Roxanne knew if she couldn't count on Alice for a calm, reasonable explanation, all was lost.

"It really started because of *San Francisco,*" Alice began. "The movie—you know, Clark Gable, Spencer Tracy. You know how the evening nurse likes to watch old movies on the television in your father's room?"

"Yes, yes."

"Well, she had it on while Lily was helping your father eat dinner—"

Lily interrupted by putting her hands over her face and sobbing. Roxanne clicked into panic mode.

"Daddy?" Still gripping Nate, she turned and would have bolted up the stairs if Alice hadn't stopped her.

"No, Roxanne, he's fine. Just fine." For a small, fragile-looking woman, she had a strong grip. She clamped her fingers over Roxanne's arm and held on. "Let me tell you the rest before you go up."

"He started talking," Lily said behind her hands. "About— about San Francisco. Oh, Roxy, he remembered me. He remembered everything."

Nate was so touched by her tears he reached out. Lily gathered him close, rocking and sniffling while Nate patted her cheek. "He kissed my hand—just like he used to. And he talked about a week we'd spent in San Francisco and how we had champagne and caviar on the terrace of our hotel room and watched the fog roll in on the bay. And how—how he tried to teach me card tricks."

"Oh." Roxanne pressed a hand to her lips. She knew he could have moments of clarity but she couldn't quite tamp out that stubborn spark of hope that this one would last. "I should have been here."

"You couldn't know." LeClerc took her hand. He could only think of how it hurt and healed to have sat for a moment with his old friend. "Alice had just gotten off the phone to Luke when you walked in."

"I'll go up." She leaned over to where Nate had tucked his head on Lily's shoulder to comfort. "I'll be in to kiss you good night, knucklehead."

"Can I have a story?"

"Yes."

"A *really* long one, with monsters in it."

"An epic one, with horrible monsters in it." She kissed him and watched his smile bloom.

"Grandpa said I grew a foot. But I only have two."

Tears swam in her eyes as she lowered her brow to her son's. "The third's invisible."

"How come he could see it then?"

"Because he's a magician." She kissed the tip of his nose, then turned to go to her father.

He was wearing a silk robe of royal purple. His hair, a glinting steel gray, was freshly combed. He sat at his desk, much as he had day after day when she visited him. But this time he was writing, using the long, flourishing strokes she remembered.

Roxanne glanced at the nurse who was standing at the foot of the bed filling out the chart. They exchanged nods before the nurse carried the chart out of the room and left them alone.

There were so many things racing through Max's mind. They crashed and boomed together like music. He had to rush to keep up with the notes, to write them down before they faded and were lost to him.

He knew they would fade, and that was his hell. The effort it cost him to fight off the fog, to hold the pen in fingers that cramped with the movement would have exhausted a younger man. But there was a burning in him, bright and hot, that seared beyond the physical. If it hulled out his body, so be it. His mind was his own again. If it lasted for an hour or a day, he wouldn't waste a moment.

Roxanne stepped closer. She was afraid to speak. Afraid that he would look up and that his eyes would pass over her as if she were a stranger. Or worse, as if she were a shade, some transparent illusion that meant nothing more to him than a trick of the eye.

When he did look up, alarm came first. He looked exhausted, so pale and drawn, so horribly thin. His eyes were bright, perhaps overbright, but in them she saw something beyond beauty. She saw recognition.

"Daddy." She tumbled the last few feet to him to fall on her knees with her head pressed to the thin wall of his chest. She hadn't known, hadn't allowed herself to know how much she'd needed to feel his arms around her again. How much she'd missed the feel of his hands stroking through her hair.

Her chest heaved once in an attempt to throw off the pressure building there with a sob. But she wouldn't greet him with tears. "Talk to me, please. Talk to me. Tell me how you feel?"

"Sorry." He bent his head to brush a cheek against her hair. His little girl. It was hard, much too hard to try to remember all the years that had passed between his child and the woman who held him now. They were a mist, a maze, and so he contented himself with accepting her as his little girl.

"So sorry, Roxy."

"No. No." Her eyes were fierce as she sat back on her heels. Her hands squeezed his until they ached, but the pain was sweet. "I don't want you to feel sorry."

She was so unbelievably lovely, he thought. His child, his daughter, her face flushed with determination, tears trembling in her eyes. The strength of her love, the sheer demand of it nearly felled him.

"Grateful, too." His moustache twitched as his lips curved up. "For you. For all of you. Now." He kissed her hands, sighed. He

446

couldn't talk. There was really so little he could talk about. But he could listen. "Tell me what new magic you've conjured."

She curled up at his feet, keeping her fingers linked with his. "I'm doing a variation on the Indian Rope Trick. Very moody and dramatic. It plays well. We set up a videotape so I could review it myself." She laughed up at him. "I amaze myself."

"I'd like to see it." He shifted, tucking a hand under her chin so he could watch her eyes. "Lily tells me you're working on a broomstick illusion."

It took all her will to hold her gaze steady. "You know he's back then."

"I dreamed he was—" And the dream and reality swirled together so that he couldn't be sure. Simply couldn't be sure. "Right here, sitting beside me."

"He comes to see you, almost every day." She wanted to get up, to pace, but couldn't bear to separate her hand from her father's. "We're working together again, temporarily. It was too intriguing a job to pass on. There's to be an auction in D.C.—"

"Roxanne," he interrupted. "What does it mean to you—Luke's coming back?"

"I don't know. I want it to mean nothing."

"Nothing's a poor thing to wish for," he murmured, smiled again. "Has he told you why he left?"

"No. I haven't let him." Restless, she did rise, but couldn't bring herself to move away. "What difference could it make? He left me. He left all of us. Once this job is done, he'll leave again. It won't matter this time, because I won't let it."

"There isn't a magic trick in the book that can shield a heart, Roxy. You have a child between you this time. My grandchild." It pained Max more than he could say that he only had dim memories of the boy.

"I haven't told him." At her father's silence, she whirled around, surprised how ready she was to battle. "You disapprove?"

He only sighed. "You've always made your own decisions. Right

447

or wrong, it's your choice. But nothing you can do will alter the fact that Luke is Nathaniel's father." He lifted a hand to her. "There's nothing you'd want to do to change that."

The muscles in her stomach loosened. The sharp fingers squeezing the base of her neck vanished. Magic, she thought, letting out a long clear breath. Say the magic words. "No, there's nothing I would do to change that." *Oh, I've missed you, Daddy.* She didn't say it, afraid it would hurt him. "It's so hard to be in charge, Max. So bloody hard."

"Easy's boring, Roxy. Who wants to spend their life with easy?"

"Well, maybe just a passing acquaintance."

He was smiling again, shaking his head. "Roxy, Roxy, you can't con me. You thrive on being in charge. The plum doesn't roll far from the tree."

She chuckled, kneeling beside him again. "Okay, maybe. But I wouldn't mind being told what to do—now and again."

"You'd still do what you want."

"Sure." Swamped with love, she threw her arms around him. "But it's more satisfying if someone tries to tell me what to do first."

"Then I'll tell you this. Grudges are bridges with faulty spans. Falling off one is a lot more rewarding then getting stuck on the other side."

"Free lesson?" she murmured and, with a sigh, pressed her cheek to his.

ROXANNE WAS A LITTLE WOBBLY when she left her father sleeping and started back downstairs. He'd been so tired, and with his encroaching fatigue she'd all but been able to see the clouds rolling in again. When she'd tucked him into bed much as she would do for her son, he'd called her Lily.

She had to accept that he might remember nothing in the morning when he awakened. The hour she'd had with him would have to be enough.

Weary and weepy, she paused at the base of the stairs to straighten her shoulders. She owed her family a solid front, a show of strength. As she walked toward the kitchen, she fixed an easy smile on her face.

"I could smell the coffee all the way . . . " She fumbled to a halt as her tumbling emotions took one more roll. There, gathered with her family, was Luke, leaning back against the kitchen counter with his hands tucked in his pockets.

Once again, everyone spoke at once. Roxanne only shook her head and marched to the stove to pour coffee. "He's sleeping. Talking all this time tired him out."

"Maybe he'll be fine now." Lily twisted the beads she wore around and around her fingers. "Maybe it's all going to go away." The look in Roxanne's eyes had her glancing away. It was so hard to bury hope, then unearth it again only to feel it die. "It was so good to talk to him again."

"I know." Roxanne cradled the coffee cup in both hands but didn't drink. "We can schedule more tests."

Lily made a tiny sound of distress and immediately began to fiddle with the cow-shaped creamer on the kitchen table. They all knew how difficult and disorienting the tests were for Max. How wrenching they were for those who loved him. "We can hope that the new medication is helping," Roxanne continued. "Or we can leave things as they are."

It was LeClerc who spoke, laying his spindly hand on Roxanne's shoulder to knead out some of the tension. "What do you want to do, *chère*?"

"Nothing," she said on a half sigh. "What I want to do is nothing. But what I think we should do is agree to whatever tests the doctors recommend." She took a deep breath, scanning faces. "Whatever the outcome, we had this evening. We'll have to be grateful for that."

"Can I go sit with him?" Mouse stared down at the toes of his shoes. "I won't wake him up."

"Of course you can." Roxanne waited until Mouse and Alice had left before she turned to Luke. "Why are you here?"

"Why do you think?"

"We agreed you wouldn't drop by for casual visits," she began, only to have the fury in his eyes stop her cold.

"This isn't casual. If you'd like to discuss why, here and now, I'd be glad to." She could still blush, he noted. It was fascinating to watch the color rise, blooming high on her cheeks while her eyes showed temper that had nothing to do with embarrassment. "Added to that," he continued blandly, "when Lily called about Max I wasn't about to sit home marking cards."

"Honey." Lily reached out a tentative hand. "I think Max would want Luke here."

"Max is asleep," she snapped back. "There's no need for you to stay. If he's up to it in the morning, you can have all the time you want with him."

"Damn generous of you, Roxanne."

The weakness showed through only briefly when she pressed her fingers to the thudding in her left temple. "I have to think of Max first. No matter what's between us you have to know I wouldn't keep you from him."

"Just what is between us?"

"I'm hardly going to discuss that now."

Whistling quietly between his teeth, LeClerc began to wipe the stove. He knew he should leave, give them privacy. But it was much too interesting. Lily didn't bother with a diversion. She clasped her hands and watched avidly.

"You climbed out of bed with me and walked away." He pushed away from the counter. "There's no way I'm leaving this unresolved."

"Unresolved?" The irony of it was so sharp she was amazed it didn't slice him into little pieces. But that was fine. She'd do the cutting herself. "You have the nerve to talk to me about leaving something—anything—unresolved? You walked out to do a job one night and never came back. A real clever variation on the old going-out-to-buy-a-pack-of-cigarettes, Callahan. But damn if I can claim to be impressed."

"I had reasons," he tossed out while Lily shifted her eyes from face to face with the eagerness of a tennis buff at Wimbledon.

"I don't give a shit about reasons."

"No, all you care about is making me crawl." He advanced another step and gave serious consideration to strangling her. "Well, I won't."

"I'm not interested in seeing you crawl. Unless it's naked, over broken glass. I went to bed with you, okay?" She pinwheeled her arms to make her point. "It was a mistake, abject stupidity, a moment of mindless lust."

He took a fistful of her sweatshirt. "It may have been stupid and it may have been lust, on both parts, babe. But it wasn't a mistake." His voice had risen to a boom that made her aching head reel. "And we're going to settle this, once and for all, if I have to gag you and cuff you to get you to listen."

"Just try it, Callahan, and all that'll be left of those hands you're so proud of is bloody stumps. So take your threats, and your piti-ful ..."

But he wasn't listening to her anymore. Fascinated, Roxanne watched the color drain out of his face until it was as white and lax as melted wax. The eyes that were staring over her shoulder dark-ened to cobalt. "Oh, God," was all he said, and the hand gripping her shirt went limp.

"Mama."

Roxanne's heart stopped, simply stopped at the sound of her son's voice. She turned, certain she heard her bones creak like rusty hinges with the slow, dreamlike movement. Nate was standing in the kitchen doorway, knuckling sleepy eyes with one hand and dragging his battered stuffed basset hound with the other.

"You didn't come kiss me good night."

"Oh, Nate." Cold, she was suddenly so cold, even as she bent to scoop her child into her arms. "I'm sorry. I would have come up soon."

"I didn't hear the end of the story Alice read, either," he complained, yawning and tucking his head in the familiar curve of her shoulder. "I fell asleep before the dog party."

Go Dog Go, Roxanne thought, dazed. Nathaniel did love his bedtime stories. "It's late, baby," she murmured.

"Can I have ice cream?"

She wanted to laugh, but it came out perilously close to a sob. "Not a chance."

Luke could only stare, stare at the small boy through eyes that were dazzled and hot and gritty. His heart had dropped to his knees and trembled there, leaving a raw, ragged hole in his chest. The child had his face. *His* face. It was like looking into a telescope lens, and seeing himself at a distance. In the past. In the past he'd never been given.

Mine, was all he could think. Oh, sweet Jesus. Mine.

After another wide yawn, Nate stared back, all curiosity and sleepy confidence. "Who's that?" he wanted to know.

In all the scenarios that had twisted through Roxanne's mind, introducing her son to his father had never been quite like this. "Ah—he's . . . " A friend? she wondered.

"This is Luke," Lily piped up, rubbing a hand up and down Luke's rigid arm. "He was kind of like my little boy when he was growing up."

"Okay." Nate smiled. All sweetness, no guile. What he saw was a tall man with black hair pulled back in a stubby ponytail and a face as pretty as a prince in one of his storybooks. "Hi."

"Hi." It amazed Luke how calm his voice sounded when his heart had vaulted back from his feet to lie lodged and swollen in his throat. He needed to touch, was afraid if he tried his hand might pass through the curve of the boy's cheek as in a dream. "You like dogs?" he said and felt incredibly stupid.

"This is Waldo." Always friendly, Nate held out the stuffed toy for Luke's inspection. "When I get a real dog I'm going to name him Mike."

"That's a pretty good name." Luke did touch, just the tips of his fingers to Nate's cheek. The boy's flesh was warm and soft against his.

More sly than shy, Nate cuddled his head against his mother's shoulder and beamed at Luke. "Maybe you'd like some ice cream now."

Roxanne couldn't bear any more—not the pain or the wonder in Luke's eyes or her own terrified guilt. "Kitchen's closed, smart guy." She tightened her grip possessively on her son. The urge to turn and run with what was hers was so cowardly it shamed her. "Lights out, Nate. You have to go to bed before you turn into a frog."

He giggled at that and made respectable frog noises.

"I'll take him up." Lily held out her arms for Nate before Roxanne could protest.

Nate twisted one of Lily's curls around his finger and poured on the charm. "Will you read me a story? I like it best when you read them."

"You bet. Jean?" Lily cocked a brow, amused to note that LeClerc was still wiping the sparkling surface of the stove. "Why don't you come with us?"

"As soon as I finish tidying up." He sighed when Lily narrowed her eyes at him. Too often discretion was a bitter pill to swallow. "I'll come along now."

Never one to let an opportunity pass, Nate began to negotiate as they trooped down the hall. "Can I have two stories? One from you and one from you?"

As Nate's voice faded away, Roxanne stood facing Luke, trapped in the silence.

"I think . . ." She cleared the tremor out of her voice and tried again. "I think I want something stronger than coffee." She started to turn, but Luke's hand whipped out snake-quick and gripped her arm. She felt his fingers press down to the bone.

"He's mine." His voice was low, deadly, terrifying. "Good Christ, Roxanne, that boy is my son. Mine." The force of it struck him so viciously that he shook her. Her head snapped back so that she had no choice but to stare into his ice-pale face. "We have a child, and you kept it from me. Goddamn you, how could you not tell me I had a son?"

"You weren't here!" she shouted, swinging out. The crack of her hand against his cheek stunned them both. Appalled, she pressed her fingers to her lips, then let her arm fall stiffly to her side. "You weren't here," she said again.

"I'm here now." He shoved her away before he did something he'd never forgive himself for. "I've been here for two weeks. 'Don't come by for casual visits, Callahan,'" he ground out, and there was more than fury in his eyes now, there was torment. "You weren't doing that for Max. You were setting up rules so I wouldn't see our son. You weren't going to tell me about him."

"I was going to tell you." She couldn't catch her breath. Never in her life had she feared him, physically. Until now. He looked capable of anything. Of everything. Unconsciously she rubbed the heel of her hand between her breasts as if to force the air in and out again. "I needed time."

"Time." He lifted her off her feet with that quick, baffling strength that both frightened and aroused. "I lost five goddamn years, and you needed time?"

"You lost? You lost? What did you expect me to do, Luke, when you came back into my life? Oh, hello, nice to see you again. By the way, you're a daddy. Have a fucking cigar."

He stared at her for one long frozen moment. Violence leaped through him, a deep, dark need to destroy, to inflict pain, to scream for revenge. He dropped her back on her feet, watched the fear jump into her eyes though she didn't flinch. On a vicious oath, he turned and yanked the door open.

Outside, he dragged in hot, thick air. The scent of flowers spun in his head, seemed to cling to his skin like sticky pollen though he rubbed his hands hard over his face. The pain was so sharp, so sudden, a rapier thrust through the heart that left him shocked and disbelieving while the blood drained.

His son. Luke pressed the heels of his hands against his eyes and uttered a sound that was raw with grief and rage. His son had looked at him, smiled at him and thought him a stranger.

She followed him out. Odd, she was calm now. It wouldn't have surprised her to have him turn on her, strike out at her. There had been that kind of danger in his eyes. She would defend herself if the need arose, but the time for fear had passed.

"I won't apologize for keeping it from you, Luke. I did what I thought best. Right or wrong, I'd do it again."

He didn't turn to look at her, but continued to stare out across the courtyard toward the fountain that played its quiet, liquid song.

They'd made that miracle together, he thought. Conceived the boy in love and laughter and lust. Was that why he'd been so beautiful, so perfect, so incredibly lovely? "Did you know you were pregnant when I left?"

"No." She caught herself rubbing her hands together and made herself drop her arms to her sides. "Right after, though. I was sick that afternoon, remember? It turns out that I was having my morning sickness a little late in the day."

"Trust you not to do the conventional." He jammed his hands in his pockets, struggling, struggling to be calm, to be reasonable. "Was it difficult?"

"What?"

"The pregnancy," he said between his teeth. But he didn't turn to look at her yet. Couldn't. "Was it difficult? You were sick?"

Of all the things she'd expected him to ask, this was the last. "No." Off balance, she pushed a hand through her hair. "I had the nausea, for a couple of months, then I breezed through the rest. I've probably never felt better."

In his pockets, his hands curled to fists. "And when he was born?"

"It wasn't a walk on the beach, but I don't feel as though I strolled through the valley of the shadow of death either. Little over eighteen hours, and out popped Nathaniel."

"Nathaniel." He repeated the name in a whisper.

"I didn't want to name him after anyone. I wanted him to have his own."

"He's healthy." Luke continued to stare at the fountain. He could almost see the individual drops as they rose, fell and rose again. "He looks . . . healthy."

"He's fine. He's never sick."

"Like his mother." But he has my face, Luke thought. *He has my face.* "He likes dogs."

"Nate likes most everything. Except lima beans." She let out a shaky breath and took a chance. "Luke," she murmured, touching a hand to his shoulder. He whirled on her so quickly she fell back a step. But when he grabbed her, it wasn't to punish.

His arms simply came around her, bringing her close. His body shuddered once as it enfolded hers. Unable to deny either of them this, she stroked a hand through his hair and returned the embrace.

"We have a son," he whispered.

"Yes." She felt a tear sneak past her defenses, and sighed. "We have a terrific son."

"I can't let you keep him from me, Roxanne. No matter what you think of me, what you feel for me, I can't let you keep me from him."

"I know. But I won't let you hurt him." She drew away. "I won't let you become so important to him that you leave a hole when you go away."

"I want my son. I want you. I want my life back. By God, Roxanne, I'm taking what I want. You're going to listen to me."

"Not tonight." But he already had her by the hand. She swore ripely when he dragged her across the courtyard toward the workroom. "I'm not going through any more emotional wringers tonight. Now let me go."

"I've lived in an emotional wringer for five years." To simplify matters he hauled her off her feet. "You'll just have to tough it out for another hour." Yanking open the door he carried a struggling Roxanne inside.

"How can you do this? How can you behave this way?" She let out a grunt when he dumped her, butt first, onto a workbench. "You just found out about your son, and instead of sitting down and having a calm, adult conversation, you're tossing me around."

"We're not going to have a conversation, calm, adult or otherwise." He snatched up handcuffs and snapped one end over her wrist. "A conversation means two or more people are talking." Quick thinking had him dodging her fist the first time, but it was only a feint. She landed the second and bloodied his lip. "What you're going to do," he said, trapping her hands in front of her and locking them, "is listen."

"You haven't changed." She would have rolled off the table despite the obvious result of smashing her nose on the floor if he hadn't caught her and secured the loop of the cuffs in a vise. "You're still a bastard, and a bully."

"And you're still a stubborn know-it-all. Now shut up." Satisfied she had no choice but to stay put, he stepped back. Roxanne hissed at him, then fell into an icy silence.

He wanted to talk, she thought. She'd let him talk until his tongue fell out. That didn't mean she had to listen. All of her concentration focused on freeing her wrists from the cuffs. He wasn't the only one with tricks up his sleeve.

"I left you," he began. "I can't deny it. I won't deny it. I left you and Max and Lily and everything that mattered and flew to Mexico with fifty-two dollars in my wallet and the burglar's tools Max had given me for my twenty-first birthday."

Concentration or not, she sniffed at that. "You're forgetting several hundred thousand in jewels."

"I didn't have any jewels. I never got into the safe." Though she turned her head and tried to bite, he caught her chin in his hand and forced her head back until their eyes met. "It was a setup. Are you listening to me? It was a fucking setup right from the start. God knows what might have happened to you if you'd been with me. As bad as it was, I've always been grateful you were sick that day and stayed home."

"Setup, my ass." She twisted away and cursed the fact that she had never been, and would never be, as good as Luke at escapes.

"He knew." The old rage began to burn through him again. With his eyes on middle distance, Luke wiped the blood from his lip. "He knew about the job. He knew about us." He brought his gaze back to Roxanne's face. "He knew all about us."

Something fluttered into her stomach and was ignored. "What are you saying? Are you trying to make me believe that Sam knew we were planning to steal from him?"

"He knew that—he wanted us to."

Her lips thinned and curved without humor. "Just how gullible do you think I am, Callahan? He hinted to me about knowing something years ago, that time we ran into him in D.C. But if he'd known about us, he'd have used it. He'd hardly have wanted us to break into his house and relieve him of his wife's jewelry."

"He never intended for us to take the jewelry. And he used it all right, Rox. He used it to make me pay for being in his way all those years ago. For breaking his goddamn nose. For humiliating him. He used it to hurt the rest of you for having the gall to take him in, trying to help him out, and for rejecting him."

A new sensation was eroding her disdain. And it was cold, very cold. "If he knew for certain we were thieves, why hasn't he pointed his pillar-of-the-community finger at us?"

"You want me to tell you how his mind works? I can't." Fighting for the control to speak calmly, Luke turned away. On the table were three pewter cups and colored balls. He began to work the old routine as he continued. "I can offer an educated guess. If he turned you in, and you didn't manage to beat the rap, all he'd have was the satisfaction of seeing you in prison. With the Nouvelle reputation and celebrity, you'd very likely get a lot of press, maybe a movie-of-the-week." She snorted, but he didn't even glance over. His hands were moving faster, faster. "What he wanted was to see you miserable. And me the most miserable of all. He'd known for a long time. Months at least."

"How? We've never had a whiff of suspicion in our direction. How did some two-bit politician figure it all out?"

"Through me." Luke's hands faltered. He stepped back, flexed his fingers, then began again. "He set Cobb on me."

"Who?"

"Cobb. The guy my mother was living with when I took off." He looked at Roxanne then, his expression carefully blank. "The guy who got off beating me until I passed out. Or locking me up, or cuffing me to the pipes in the bathroom. The one who sold me for twenty bucks to a drunken pervert."

Her face went white and stiff. What he was saying was horrid enough, but hearing it recited in that flat, empty voice froze her blood. "Luke." She would have reached out, but the steel only rattled against the teeth of the vise. "Luke, let me go."

"Not until you hear it. Hear all of it." He picked up a cup again, vaguely surprised to see the faint outline of his fingers against the pewter where he'd squeezed. So the shame was still there, he realized. And it would always be there, like the slight distortion on the carved pewter. "That night—do you remember that night in the rain, Rox? You'd told me about that four-eyed son of a bitch manhandling you. I went crazy because I knew what it was like—to be forced. And I couldn't stand the idea of you . . . of anyone hurting you that way. Then I was holding you. And I kissed you. I tried not to, but I wanted you so bad. I wanted everything about you. And for just a minute, one incredible minute, I thought maybe it would be all right."

"It was all right," she whispered. It felt as though the vise was around her heart, squeezing, squeezing. "It was wonderful."

"Then I saw him." Luke set the cups down again. There was a time for illusion, and a time for truth. "He walked right by us, and he looked at me. I knew it wasn't all right. It might never be. So I sent you away, and went after him."

"What—" She bit her lip, remembering how drunk Luke had been when he'd come home that night. "You didn't . . ."

"Kill him?" He tossed his head up and the smile on his face chilled her. "It would have been simpler all around if I had. What was I, twenty-two, twenty-three? Christ, I might as well have been twelve again, that's how much he scared me. He wanted money— so I gave him money."

She felt a quick twist of relief. "You paid him? Why?"

"So he'd keep what he knew to himself. So he wouldn't go to the press and tell them I'd sold myself."

"But you didn't—"

"What difference did it make what the truth was? I'd been sold. I'd been used. I was ashamed." He looked over again, but his eyes were no longer blank. The swirl of emotion in them battered her heart. "I still am."

"You did nothing."

"I was a victim. Sometimes that's enough." He shrugged it away, but the gesture was jerky. "So I paid him. Whenever he'd send me a postcard, I sent back the amount he'd written on it. When you moved in with me, I always made sure I got the mail. Just in case."

Sympathy dried up into shock. "Wait a minute. Just a minute. You're saying he was still blackmailing you after we were together? All that time, and you didn't tell me?" Pure reflex had her kicking out in his direction. "You didn't trust me enough to share that with me?"

"Goddammit! I was ashamed, ashamed of what had happened to me, ashamed that I didn't have the balls to tell him to get fucked. I was terrified he'd get tired of yanking my chain and make good on his threat to tell the press that Max had—" He broke off, swearing. He hadn't meant to go quite that far.

Both the shame and the anger clenched in his gut as he waited.

Chapter Thirty-one

ROXANNE DREW IN A LONG, QUIET BREATH. SHE WAS AFRAID she knew, very much afraid she knew, what was coming next. But she had to be sure. "That Max had what, Luke?"

All right, he thought, he'd give her all. There'd be no more question of trust. "That Max had used me sexually."

The angry flush died away until her face was pale as glass. But her eyes glittered, dark as a storm, and as dangerous. "He would have said that? He would have lied that way about you and Daddy?"

"I don't know. I couldn't take the chance, so I paid. And by paying I set myself up for worse."

She closed her eyes. "What could be worse?"

"I said Wyatt set Cobb on me, and Wyatt was calling the shots. I didn't know it, though I should have figured that Cobb wasn't smart enough to pull off something as smooth as the blackmail scam. Whenever they raised the ante, I paid. No questions. That didn't sit well with Wyatt. So he did a little more digging to figure out how I managed to pay upwards of a hundred thousand a year without whining."

"A hundred—" Even the thought choked her.

"I'd have paid twice as much to keep you." When she looked up at him again, he realized that was only half the answer. "And to keep you from seeing I'd been a coward. That someone had forged a chain I couldn't wiggle free from." He turned away and spoke slowly. "I'd been used. I never knew whether Cobb's client got his money's worth out of me, but I'd been used just the same."

"I knew. I told you I'd always known."

"You didn't know what it did to me. Inside. The scars on my back." He shrugged and turned back. "Hell, they're like the tattoo, Roxy. Just a reminder of where I'd come from. But I didn't want you to see past them. I wanted to be invincible for you—for me. It was pride, and Christ knows I paid for it."

She sat quietly now. The cuffs on her wrists were a transient restraint, easily opened with a key. The chains on Luke's pride were made of sterner stuff. "Do you really believe it would have changed anything I felt for you?"

"It changed what I felt *about* me. Wyatt understood that. He used it. And because he was studying every move I made, he saw the pattern. He had months to work out the setup. I guess that's why it was so fucking smooth."

She was no longer struggling, no longer angry. She was simply numb. "He knew you were coming that night."

"He knew. He was waiting for me in his office. He had a gun. I figured he'd kill me and that would be that. Sam didn't want that to be that. He offered me a brandy. The coldhearted bastard offered me a drink, and he told me what he knew. He painted some pictures of what it would be like if you and Max were sent to prison. He knew Max wasn't so stable, and he taunted me about a lot of things." His mouth grimmed. "I was feeling sick. I guess I thought it was the situation, but it was the brandy."

"He'd drugged you? God."

"While I was sitting there, trying to calculate the odds, Cobb came in. That's when I learned about their partnership. Rox, he told Cobb to pour himself a drink. And then ... then he killed him. He pointed the gun, he pulled the trigger and he killed him."

"He—" She shut her eyes again, but her vision was clear. She'd begun to see perfectly. "He was going to let you take the fall for murder."

"It was perfect. I passed out, and when I came to, he was holding a different gun." Steadier than he'd expected to be, Luke sat on the bench and lit a cigar as he told her the rest.

"So, I left. I disappeared," he finished. "And I spent five years trying to forget you. And failing miserably. I went all over the world, Rox. Asia, South America, Ireland. I tried drinking myself to death, but I never did like the aftermath of a good drunk. I tried work. I tried women." He slanted her a look. "They worked some better than the bottle."

"I bet."

The chilly annoyance in her tone cheered him. "About six months ago, a couple of things happened. I found out about Max's condition. You'd done a pretty good job of keeping that under wraps."

"My personal life is mine. I don't discuss it with the press."

He studied the tip of his cigar. "I guess that's why I never read anything about Nate."

"I don't share my child with the public."

"Our child," he corrected, looking back at her. He let that simmer while he continued. "The other thing I found out was that Wyatt was running for the Senate in the coming election. Maybe I got jaded over the last five years, Rox. Maybe I just got smart. But I started to think, and I started to wonder. And I started to plan. Running into Jake was handy. Up till then I'd been living on what I could make as the Phantom. I couldn't touch my Swiss accounts because I didn't have the numbers, and there was no way to get them." He grinned. "Until Jake. He went to work on it, and life got easier. Money smooths the way, Rox. And it's going to get me what I want."

"Which is?"

"Besides you." He tapped out his cigar. "Let's call it justice. Our old friend is going to pay."

"This isn't just about the stone, is it?"

"No. I want it, for Max, but no. I've got a way to get him. It's taken me a long time to work it out, and I need you to make it work. Are you still with me?"

"He stole five years from me. Took away my son's father. And you have to ask?"

He grinned, leaning over to kiss her, but she turned her head away. "I want to ask you something, Callahan, so back off."

He eased back an inch. "This far enough?"

"Are you here because I'm a necessary part of the plan?"

"What you are, Roxanne, is necessary." He slipped off the table and turned to run his hands up her outer thighs. "Vital." Because her head was still turned away, he contented himself with nibbling on her earlobe. "I told you there were other women."

"I'm hardly surprised," she said, her voice dry as the Sahara.

"But I didn't tell you that they were poor, pale illusions. Smoke and mirrors, Rox. There was never one day when I didn't want you." He slid his hands to her waist, coaxing her face toward his by running kisses along her jaw. "I've loved you as long as I can remember."

He could feel her softening, warming as he slipped his hands under the sweatshirt to skim fingers along her ribs. "When I left, it was for you. Coming back was for you. There's nothing you can say, nothing you can do that would make me leave you again."

His thumbs just brushed the undersides of her breasts. "I'll kill you if you try this time, Callahan." Desperate, she turned her mouth to his. "I swear it. I won't let you make me love you again unless I'm sure you're staying."

"You never stopped loving me." The excitement was building, unbearably. He cupped her breasts, using his thumbs to tease the nipples into aching points. "Say it."

"I wanted to." Her head fell back with a moan as he pressed his lips to her neck. "I wanted to stop."

"Say the magic words," he demanded again.

"I love you." She would have wept, but the sob turned to a gasp. "Damn you, I've always loved you. I never stopped. Now unlock these stupid cuffs."

"Maybe." He tugged on her hair until her eyes opened and locked on his. The expression on his face had a thrill of panicked excitement ripping up her spine. "Maybe later."

And his mouth came down on hers, smothering any protest and turning shock into churning arousal.

It had gone so quickly the first time, all flash and fire and need. He wanted to do more than savor now. He wanted to take her step by trembling step, inch by aching inch toward madness. And he wanted to shock her, stun her, so that this moment when all the secrets were revealed would be seared into her mind, never to be forgotten.

He skimmed his tongue up the long line of her throat while his hands traced over her, lazily possessive. "If you don't like it, I'll stop," he murmured, nipping at her lips. "Should I stop?"

"I don't know." How could he expect her to think rationally when her head was reeling? "How much time do I have to make up my mind?"

"I'll give you plenty of time."

The marvelous truth was she had no mind, no will, no reason. If this was a matter of power, then she was totally in his. And glorying in it. She would never have believed that helplessness could be erotic. The knowledge that her body was his, utterly, touched off little fires in her blood that burned like a drug. She wanted to be taken, exploited for their mutual pleasure, and in this single private moment, conquered.

A long, throaty moan vibrated from her when he tore her shirt down the center. She braced for the onslaught, craved it, but his hands, his mouth, were torturously gentle.

Sensation crashed into emotion, each rising dangerously. Each time, every time she strained toward that final, airless peak, he pulled her back, leaving her gasping and crazed.

It was stunning to watch her, to see everything she felt reflected on her face, to feel every thrill that rocked her body, to hear her murmur his name again and again as the pleasure swamped her.

Her power was all the more potent because she was too dazed to realize she held it. Her surrender made him as much her prisoner as she was his—the completeness of it, and the fearlessness. That she would melt for him made him feel strong as a god, and humble as a beggar.

Slowly, he slid the loose pants down her hips, exploring each newly exposed inch of flesh, pleasuring her with teeth and tongue and clever fingertips until she shuddered violently over the first peak.

"I love you, Roxanne." He pressed her back against the bench. "Always you," he murmured as the hands he'd freed came tight around him. "Only you."

He filled, she surrounded. And they took each other.

IT ANNOYED HIM THAT SHE wouldn't let him spend his nights with her, nor would she spend hers with him. He needed more than the intimacy of sex. He needed to be able to turn to her in the night, to watch her wake in the morning.

But she stood firm, and kept her reasons to herself.

She no longer put any restrictions on his visits to the house on Chartres. There were reasons for that as well. It hurt them all that Max had slipped away again, and each day he was hospitalized for tests was unbearably long. Roxanne knew that having Luke around boosted morale—her own included. And she wanted to give Nate a chance to know him as a man before the boy had to accept him as a father.

Rational or not, any decision she made on allowing Luke back into her life would be focused on her son. Their son.

They worked together. As one week passed into two the act they'd created between them grew slick and flashy. They crafted their job at the auction as meticulously. Roxanne had to admit Luke had entwined all the details as craftily as the Chinese Linking Rings. She was suitably impressed with the first of the forged pieces that arrived from the source he'd commissioned in Bogotá.

"Nice work," she'd told him, deliberately downplaying the craftsmanship in the tiered diamond and ruby necklace. She'd stood at the mirror in his bedroom, draping it around her own neck. "A bit ornate for my taste, of course, but quite good. What did it cost us?"

She was naked, as was he. Luke had tucked his arms behind his head as he'd stretched on the bed and watched her in the glow of the lowering sun. "Five thousand."

"Five." Her brows rose as her practical nature absorbed that shock. "That's very steep."

"The man's an artist." He grinned as she frowned and toyed with the faux stones. "The real one's worth upwards of a hundred and fifty, Rox. We'll cover our overhead nicely."

"I suppose." She had to admit, to herself anyway, that without testing equipment she would have been fooled. Not only did the stones look genuine but the setting was deceptively antique. "When can we expect the rest?"

"In time."

In time, she thought now as she carried two bags of groceries into the kitchen. It was beginning to irk her that Luke continued to be vague. He was testing her, she decided and dumped the bags on the counter. She didn't care for it.

"You got eggs in those bags?" LeClerc demanded, glowering.

She winced, grateful her back was to him, then shrugged. "So, make an omelette."

"Make an omelette, make an omelette. Always the smart talk.

Get—out of my kitchen." He waved her off. "I got supper to make for an army."

Which meant only one thing. "Luke's here?"

"You surprised?" He snorted and began to take groceries out of the bag. "Everybody's always here. You call this a ripe melon?" Accusation in every cell, LeClerc held out a cantaloupe.

"How the hell am I supposed to know if it's ripe?" Marketing never put her in a sunny mood. "They all look the same."

"How many times I tell you, smell, listen." He tapped the melon, holding it close to his ear. "Still green."

Roxanne planted her hands on her hips. "Why do you always send me out for fruits and vegetables then complain about what I bring home?"

"You got to learn, don't you?"

Roxanne thought about that a moment. "No." Turning on her heel, she marched out, muttering. The man was never satisfied. Here she'd gone straight from rehearsal to the market, and he didn't even say thanks.

And she hated cantaloupe.

She would have stalked straight upstairs if she hadn't heard the voices from the parlor. Luke's voice. Nate's belly giggles. Moving quietly, she walked to the door and looked in.

They were on the floor together, dark heads bent close, knees brushing. Toys were scattered on the rug, a testament to what her men had been doing while she slaved over melons. Now, Luke was patiently explaining some little pocket trick he'd brought along. The Vanishing Pen, if Roxanne wasn't mistaken. Amused, she leaned against the doorway and watched father attempting to teach son.

"Right under the nose, Nate." To illustrate, Luke tweaked Nate's and made him giggle again. "Right before your eyes. Now, here, let's try it. Can you print your name?"

"Sure I can. N-A-T-E." He took the pen and paper Luke offered, his face screwed in intense concentration. "I'm learning to write Nathaniel, too. Then Nouvelle, 'cause that's my last name."

"Yeah." A shadow passed over Luke's eyes as he watched Nate struggle with the *A*. "I guess it is." He waited until Nate had completed a very slanted *E*. "Okay. Now watch carefully." Keeping his movements slow, Luke rolled the pen inside the paper and twisted both ends. "Now, pick a magic word."

"Umm—"

"Nope, umm's not good enough," Luke said and sent Nate off in a fit of fresh giggles.

"Boogers!" Nate decided, delighted to use a word he'd picked up from a sophisticated pal at preschool.

"Disgusting, but it may work." Luke tore the paper in two and had the pleasure of seeing Nate's eyes widen.

"It disappeared! The pen's been disappeared."

"Absolutely." Unable to resist the flourish, Luke held up his hands, turning them, back to front and back again. His son's bug-eyed belief made him feel like a king. "Want to learn how to do it?"

"Can I?"

"You have to take the magician's oath."

"I did that already," Nate said, jaded. "When Mama showed me how to make the quarter go through the table."

"Does she teach you stuff about magic?" He was greedy for anything he could learn about his son's thoughts, feelings, desires.

"Sure. But you have to promise not to tell anybody, even your best friends, 'cause it's secret."

"That's right. Are you going to be a magician one day?"

"Yeah." Unable to keep still for long, Nate bounced his rump on the rug. "I'm going to be a magician, and a racecar driver and a policeman."

A cop, Luke thought, amused. Well, well, where did they go wrong? "All that, huh? Let's see if you can learn this trick before you go win the Indianapolis 500 and chase bad guys."

He was pleased that Nate was interested rather than disappointed when he saw the workings of the trick. It seemed to Luke that he could all but hear the child's mind working it through, exploring the possibilities.

He had good hands, Luke thought as he posed them with his own. A quick mind. And a smile that broke his father's heart.

"This is neat."

"Amazing," Luke said, solemn-eyed, and turned Nate's smile into a grin.

"Amazing neat."

He couldn't help it. Luke leaned down to kiss the grin. "Try it again, slick. Let's see if you can do this with distractions. Sometimes there are hecklers in the audience."

"What's that?"

"Oh, people who yell things or talk too loud. Or ... tickle you."

Nate gave a squeal of delight when Luke snatched him. After a short, furious battle, Luke let himself be pinned. He grunted with exaggerated bursts as Nate bounced on his stomach.

"You're too tough for me, kid. Uncle."

"Uncle who?"

"Just uncle." Chuckling, Luke ruffled Nate's dark hair. "It means I give up."

"Can you show me another trick?"

"Maybe. What's it worth to you?"

Nate bartered what always worked with his mother and scooted down to give Luke a smacking kiss on the mouth. Dazed by the easy affection, moved unbearably, Luke lifted an unsteady hand to Nate's hair.

"Do you want a hug to go with it?"

"Sure." Luke opened his arms and experienced the unspeakable pleasure of cradling his son. With his eyes closed, he rubbed his cheek to Nate's. "You weigh a ton."

"I'm a walking appetite." Nate leaned back to grin down at Luke. "Mama says so. I eat everything 'less it's nailed down."

"Except lima beans," Luke murmured, remembering.

471

"Yuck. I wish I could make all the lima beans in the whole world disappear."

"We'll work on it."

"I gotta pee," Nate stated, with the carefree childhood habit of announcing bodily functions.

"Don't do it here, okay?"

Nate giggled and held himself uninhibitedly to prolong the inevitable another moment. He liked being with Luke, liked the smell of him that was different from anyone else in his family. Though he'd never had to do without male influence or companionship, there was something different about *this* man. Maybe it was magic.

"Do you have a penis?"

Luke strangled back a laugh because the child was eyeing him owlishly. "I certainly do."

"Me too. Girls don't. Mama neither."

Cautious, Luke tucked his tongue in his cheek. "I believe you're right about that."

"I like having one, 'cause you can stand up to pee."

"It does have its advantages."

"I gotta go." Nate scrambled up, dancing a bit. "You want to go ask LeClerc for some cookies?"

From penises to cookies, Luke thought. Childhood was fascinating. "Go ahead. I'll catch up with you."

Nate turned and spotted his mother, but his bladder was straining. "Hi. I gotta pee."

"Hi yourself. Go be my guest."

Nate trotted off, one hand on his crotch.

"An interesting conversation," Roxanne managed after she heard the powder room door slam.

"Man talk." Luke sat up, grinning. "He's so—" He broke off when Roxanne pressed a hand to her mouth. "What is it?" Alarmed, he rose, trampling a plastic truck as he started toward her.

"Nothing." She wouldn't be able to hold it off this time. Simply wouldn't. "It's nothing." Turning, she bolted up the stairs.

She would have locked herself in her room, but Luke was at the door before she could shove it to. Furious with herself, she whirled away and tossed open the French doors to her terrace.

"What the hell's wrong with you?" he demanded.

"There's nothing wrong with me." The ache was so fierce, so complete she could only combat it with sharp words. "Go away, will you? I'm tired. I want to be alone."

"One of your tantrums, Rox?" His own feelings were brittle as he turned her to face him. Music drifted up from the Quarter, hot driving jazz. It seemed to fit the moment. "Seeing me with Nate get your back up?"

"No. Yes." She jerked away to drag her hands through her hair. Oh God, oh God, she was losing.

The closer she came to the edge, the calmer Luke became.

"I'm going to see him, Roxanne. I'm going to be a part of his life. I have to, and by Christ, I have a right to."

"Don't talk to me about rights," she threw back, humiliated by the catch in her voice.

"He's mine, too. However much you'd like to block that out, it's a fact. I'm trying to understand why you won't tell him I'm his father, I'm trying not to resent that, but I won't stay away because you want to keep him to yourself."

"That's not it. Damn it, that's not it." She rapped a fist against his chest. "Do you know how it makes me feel to see you together? To see the way you look at him?" Tears spilled over, but she fought back the sobs.

"I'm sorry it hurts you," Luke said stiffly. "And maybe I can't blame you too much for wanting to punish me by not letting me be his father."

"I'm not trying to punish you." Desperate to get it all out, she pressed her lips together. "Maybe I am, I'm not sure, and that's the hardest part. Trying to know what to do, what's right, what's best,

473

and then seeing you with him, knowing all that time that was lost. Yes, it hurts me to see you with him, but not the way you mean. It hurts the way it hurts to watch a sunrise, or to hear music. He holds his head the way you do." She dashed furiously at tears. "He always did, and it broke my heart. He has your smile, and your eyes, and your hands. So much smaller, but yours. I used to look at them while he was sleeping, count his fingers and look at his hands. And I'd ache for you."

"Rox." He'd thought, he'd hoped, they had passed through the worst of this the night he'd told her everything. "I'm sorry." He reached out, but she pivoted away.

"I never cried over you. Not once in five years did I allow myself a tear for you. That was pride." Pressing the back of her hand to her mouth, she rocked. "It helped me get through the worst of it. I didn't cry when you came back. And when you told me what had happened, I hurt for you, and I tried to understand what you must have felt. But damn you. Damn you, you were wrong." She spun back, clasping an arm around her middle to hold back the worst of the pressure. "You should have come home. You should have come to me and told me then. I would have gone with you. I'd have gone anywhere with you."

"I know." He couldn't touch her now, no matter how much he needed to. She seemed suddenly so fragile that to touch might be to break. He could only stand back and let the storm rage over both of them. "I knew it then, and I nearly did come back. I could have taken you away, away from your family, away from your father. It didn't have to matter that he was ill, that I owed him, all of you, whatever good things I had. I might have risked the fact that Wyatt could have set the cops on me at any time so that they'd hunt me down as a murderer. But I didn't. I couldn't."

"I needed you." Tears blinded her until she covered her face with her hands and let them come freely. "I needed you."

It hurt, oh, it hurt to let go almost as much as it had to hold back. Crying wracked the body, burned the throat, battered the heart. She lost herself in the violence of grief, going limp when his arms came around her, sobbing shamelessly when he lifted her to carry her to bed and cradle her.

He could only hold her as five years of suppressed mourning flooded out. There were no words to comfort. He had known her nearly twenty years and could count on one hand the number of times she'd wept in front of him.

And never like this, he thought, rocking her. Never like this.

She couldn't stop, was afraid she never would. She didn't hear the door open. Didn't feel Luke turn his head, shake it in silent denial as Lily looked in.

Gradually, the wracking sobs turned to dry gasps, and the violent shudders softened to quivers. The hands fisted at his back relaxed.

"I need to be alone," she whispered through a throat dry as dust.

"No. Not again. Never again, Roxanne."

She was too weak to argue. After one shaky sigh, she let her head rest against his shoulder. "I hate this."

"I know you do." He pressed a kiss to her hot, aching temple. "Do you remember that time after you found out Sam had used you? You cried then, and I didn't know quite how to handle it."

"You held me." She sniffled. "Then you broke his nose."

"Yeah. I'll do more this time." Over her head his gaze sharpened like a blade. "That's a promise."

She couldn't think about that now. She felt drained and, oddly, free. "It was easier to give you my body than to give you this." She let her swollen eyes close, soothed by the stroke of his hand over her hair. "I could tell myself it was lust, and if there was still love tangled up with it, I could still be in control. But I was afraid to let you be my friend again." Steadier, she let out a long breath. "Let me get up, wash my face. Leave me alone for a while."

"Rox—"

"No, please." She eased back. It was a point of trust, deeper than any other she'd offered that she let him see the ravage the tears had caused. "There's something I need to do. Take a walk, Callahan. Give me a half an hour."

She kissed him, softly, before he could think of an argument. "I'll be back."

This time she smiled. "I'm counting on it."

HE BROUGHT HER FLOWERS. He'd realized, a bit guiltily, that he hadn't given Roxanne what Lily would consider a proper wooing either time around. The first time he'd been overwhelmed by her, the second he'd been too tense.

It might have been a little late in the day for the hearts-and-flowers routine seeing as they were lovers, partners and shared a child, but as Max might have said, better late than too soon.

He even went to the front door rather than wandering in through the kitchen. Like a suitor coming to call, he fingercombed his hair and rang the bell.

"Callahan." Roxanne opened the door with a baffled laugh. "What are you doing out here?"

"Asking a beautiful woman out to dinner." He offered the roses, then with a sweeping bow, produced a bouquet of paper flowers that bloomed from the secret pool beneath his shirt cuff.

"Oh." It threw her off—the charming smile, the formal greeting, the armful of fragrant rosebuds and the silly trick. The change in routine automatically triggered suspicion. "What are you up to?"

"I told you. I'm asking you out on a date."

"You—" The laugh snorted out unladylike through her nose. "Right. In twenty years you've never asked me out on a date. What do you want?"

It wasn't easy to court a woman who was glaring at you out of red-rimmed and narrowed eyes. "To take you to dinner," he said between his teeth. "Maybe for a drive afterward—somewhere we can park on the side of the road and neck."

"There a gas leak in your house, or what?"

"Goddammit, Rox, will you come out with me?"

"I can't really. I have plans." She did lower her head to draw in the scent of roses. Before she could fully appreciate them, she snapped her head back again. "You didn't bring these to me because I cried, did you?"

Jesus, she was a tough nut. "You'd think I never brought you flowers before."

"No, no, you did." She held back a smile, though she was beginning to enjoy the picture emerging. "Twice. Once when you were two hours late for dinner—a dinner I'd gone to the trouble to cook."

"And you threw them at me."

"Of course. And the second time ... Oh yes, that was when you'd broken the little porcelain box Lily had given me for Christmas. So, Callahan, what have you done this time?"

"Nothing, unless it's trying to be nice to an exasperating woman."

"Well, I'm not throwing them at you, am I?" She smiled then, and took his hand. "Come on in. We're having dinner here."

"Rox, I want to be alone with you, not in a houseful of people."

"The houseful of people is out for the evening, and God help you, Callahan, I'm cooking."

"Oh." The depth of his love was proven then and there as he summoned up a smile. "Terrific."

"Yeah, I bet. Let's go into the parlor, I have something for you."

He nearly asked if it was a dose of bicarb, but restrained himself. "If you don't want to go to the hassle of cooking, babe, we could send out." He followed her into the parlor, saw the boy sitting on the edge of the couch. "Hey, slick."

"Hi." Nate studied him for a long moment with a kind of absorbed intensity that made Luke want to squirm. "How come you don't live here if you're my daddy?"

"I—" Rocked straight to the soul, Luke could only stare.

"Mama said you had to go away for a long time 'cause a bad guy was after you. Did you shoot him dead?"

"No." He had to swallow, but couldn't. Both his son and the woman he loved waited patiently. "I thought I might trick him instead. I don't think I'd like shooting anybody." Desperately out of his element, he looked at Roxanne. "Rox." Though his eyes pleaded for help, she shook her head.

"Sometimes stepping out cold's the only way," she murmured. "No rehearsal, Callahan. No script, no props."

"Okay." On watery legs he walked to the couch and crouched down in front of his son. For a moment he was tossed back to his debut performance in a stuffy carnival tent. Flop sweat pooled at the base of his spine. "I'm sorry I wasn't here for you, or for your mother, Nate."

Nate's gaze faltered. His stomach had felt funny ever since his mother had sat him down and told him he had a daddy. He didn't know if it was good funny—the way it felt after Mouse had swung him in circles, or bad, like when he'd eaten too much candy on Halloween.

"Maybe you couldn't help it," Nate murmured, pulling at the threads in the hole worn into the knee of his jeans.

"Whether I could or not, I'm still sorry. I don't guess you need me much, you're pretty grown up and all. We—ah—get along okay, don't we?"

"Sure." Nate poked out his bottom lip. "I guess."

And he'd thought Roxanne was a tough nut, Luke mused. "We could be friends if that's okay with you. You don't have to think of me as your father."

Tears swam in Nate's eyes when he looked up again. His lips quivered and ripped right through Luke's heart. "Don't you want me to?"

"Yeah." His throat ached. His heart healed. "Yeah, I do. A lot. I mean, hey, you're short and ugly now, but I think you've got potential."

"What's potential?"

"Possibilities, Nathaniel." Gently, Luke cupped his son's face in his hands. "Lots and lots of possibilities."

"Potential," Nate repeated, and in an echo of his mother's childhood, savored the word. His smile spread sweetly. "Bobby's father built him a tree house. A *big* one."

"Oh-oh." Amazed and delighted, Luke glanced back to where Roxanne still stood, holding her flowers. "The kid catches on fast."

"It's that sly Irish blood. A Nouvelle is much too proud to wheedle."

"Wheedle, hell, it's a smart boy who knows when to press his advantage. Right, Nate?"

"Right." He shrieked with pleasure when Luke swung him up. Deciding to go for the gold, he leaned close to Luke's ear and whispered, "Can you tell Mama I should have a dog? A really big dog?"

Luke tilted a finger under Nate's chin so that they grinned identical grins. "I'll work on it. How about a hug?"

"Okay." Nate squeezed his arms hard around Luke's neck. His stomach still felt funny, and the sensation had spread to his chest. But he thought it was a good feeling after all. On a sigh, he settled his head on his father's shoulder, and accepted.

Chapter Thirty-two

"I'm trying to concentrate." Roxanne waved a hand over her shoulder to brush Luke back. He was breathing down her neck.

"I'm trying to ask you out on a date."

"You're certainly hung up on dates these days." She hunched forward, adjusting the light on her father's desk. Spread before her were the blueprints for the art gallery. They had yet to agree on a point of entry. "From the top down, Callahan. It just makes sense. The exhibit's on the third floor, why come in on ground level and climb up?"

"Because that way we can walk up stairs instead of dangling fifteen feet from a rope."

She slanted a look over her shoulder. "You're getting old."

"I beg your pardon. It so happens I'm a parent now. I have to take certain precautions."

"The roof, Daddy Warbucks."

He knew it was the cleanest way, but enjoyed the debate. "We'd have to get Jake up there, too. He doesn't like heights."

"So, you'll blindfold him." She tapped a pencil against the

drawing. "Here, east window, third floor. I'm already in, twiddling my thumbs in that storeroom until deadline. I go into the surveillance room at exactly eleven seventeen, which gives me one minute, thirty seconds, and one minute, thirty seconds only, to doctor camera six before the alarm kicks in."

"I don't like the idea of you handling the inside work."

"Don't be such a man, Luke. You know damn well I'm better with electronics. Then I switch the surveillance tapes." Pulling her hair back in one hand, she grinned. "I wish I could see the guard's face when he gets a look at Mouse's video work."

"Only amateurs think they have to be in on the punch line, babe."

"Get bent, Callahan," she said mildly. "To continue, as long as Jake and Mouse have taken care of business, I can deal with the window from inside. In you come, my hero." She fluttered her lashes.

"And we have six and a half minutes to open the display, take the proper loot and replace it with our fakes."

"Then, presto! We're out, leaving not a trace." She ran her tongue over her top lip. "You and I will go back to our hotel room, and fuck like minks."

"God, I love it when you're crude." He rested his chin on the top of her head. "We still need to refine the timing."

"We have a few weeks." She stretched her arms out, then up, to link them around his neck. "And just think of all those lovely, lovely glitters. All ours, Callahan."

He winced, let a quiet breath out between his teeth and straightened. "That's something I've been meaning to talk to you about, Rox." He couldn't predict how she'd react, and took the coward's way by stalling. "Want a brandy?"

"Sure." She stretched again. It was nearly one in the morning. The house was quiet, the hall beyond the office dark with shadows. She thought briefly about seducing Luke on the cushy leather couch, and smiled slowly when he handed her a snifter.

"Sure you want to talk?"

He knew that look, that tone, and nearly escaped into it to avoid the issue. "No, but I think we have to. About the take from the auction."

"Mmmm."

"We're not going to keep it."

She choked on the brandy. Luke thumped her on the back and hoped for the best. "Christ, don't make bad jokes while I'm drinking."

"It's not a joke, Rox. We're not going to keep it."

She, too, knew that look, that tone. It meant Luke had made up his mind about something and was ready to battle. "What the hell are you talking about? What's the point in taking it if we're not going to keep it?"

"I explained that the heist was a diversion for the Wyatt job."

"Of course, and a very profitable one, despite an outrageous overhead."

"Yes, but not monetarily. Not for us."

She drank more brandy, but it did little to relieve the sudden chill in her midsection. "Just what are we going to do with over two million in jewels, Callahan, jewels that are costing us approximately eighty thousand to heist?"

"We're going to plant them. They're very important props for a sting I've been dreaming about for nearly a year."

"A sting." Roxanne rose so that she could walk off her agitation and think. "Sam. You're going to plant them on Sam. This is your justice, isn't it?" Her eyes were hot when she turned back to him. "This is what you'd planned all along."

"I've worked on every angle of this for months. Every piece hinges on the whole of it."

"You've worked on?" A flood of betrayal threatened to swamp her. She fought it back, unsure if she could survive that kind of loss again. "That's why you came back. To hit on Sam."

"You're why I came back." He didn't like the chill in her voice, or the vulnerability he sensed beneath it. And he hated, really hated, explaining himself again. "I told you why I left, Rox, and I can't take those years back. But I'm not losing you again, and I'm not taking any chances with my family." He hesitated. She was likely to slice him into thin, jagged ribbons, but he had to tell her everything. "That's why I went to see Wyatt before I came to New Orleans."

"You've seen him?" Baffled, she dragged a hand through her hair. "You went to see him, and you don't consider that taking chances?"

"I made a deal with him. I'd figured on bribing him with money. A million dollars for a few months' time."

"A million—"

"But he didn't go for it," Luke interrupted. "Or he didn't go for that alone. So we made a deal." Picking up his snifter, he swirled brandy, sniffed, sipped. He enjoyed this part, the way a man enjoyed contemplating a long, stimulating evening with a beautiful woman. "He agreed to give me time, until right before the election, if I came up with compromising photographs of Curtis Gunner. They'd have to be faked, of course, seeing as Gunner's straight as an arrow. Wyatt wants papers, too, implicating Gunner in unethical business deals, and illicit relationships. All I have to do is create them, and plant them right before the voters head off to pull the lever of their choice."

Letting out a long breath, Roxanne lowered to the arm of the sofa. She needed the brandy now, she realized, and tilted back the snifter for a long sip. "That's what it cost you to come back?"

"If I didn't agree, I can't be sure what he might do to you, to Max, Lily, everyone I care about." Luke's eyes locked on hers. "And now there's Nathaniel. There's nothing I wouldn't do to keep him safe. Nothing."

Icy fear rippled down her spine. "He wouldn't hurt Nate. He . . . Of course he would." Roxanne pressed her fingers to her eyes, struggling to justify her conscience with necessity. "I know we have to do whatever needs to be done, but we've never hurt innocent people before. I can't rationalize starting now. We'll find another way." She dropped her hands into her lap. Her face was composed again, and cold. "I know we can find another way."

Luke was certain he'd never loved her more than he did at this moment. She was a woman who would protect what was hers, always, and never would she compromise her own code of ethics.

"Jake's already forging documents that I'll plant, along with the take, in Wyatt's safe. They won't be quite what he's expecting," he added before she could protest. "The initial photos Jake's come up with are pretty good, just need a little refining. But all in all, Wyatt looks great. There's one in particular of him in this black leather G-string and boots that I'm real fond of."

"Sam? You're doing the photographs using Sam?" Her lips started to curve, but she stopped the smile, stemmed the admiration. Damn Luke, she thought, she wasn't through yet. "You're double-crossing him, using his own plot to ruin him politically."

"Hey, I've got nothing against Gunner, and plenty against Wyatt. It seemed like solid gold justice to me. In addition to the photos and the documents—some of which will implicate Wyatt in a number of robberies you'll be very familiar with—I've been filtering money into two accounts in Switzerland. Accounts in his name."

"Very clever," she murmured. "You worked it all out. But you didn't bother to fill me in."

"No, I didn't. I wanted to make sure you were in for the long run, Roxanne. I figured the initial plan would challenge you, intrigue you. And I'd hoped by the time I told you all of it, you'd trust me. You want to be pissed because I held back on you, you're entitled. Just as long as you're in for that long haul."

She considered and realized that first hot spurt of anger had eased. Good God, she thought, she hoped she wasn't mellowing. The problem was, she could see it from Luke's side as well as from her own. Not only could she see it, but the simple beauty of the sting enchanted her. She couldn't have planned it better herself.

"From tonight, Callahan, we're in this fifty-fifty, or there's no deal."

"Aren't you going to swear at me, call me at least one name?"

"I'm saving it." She lifted her glass in toast. "To Nouvelle and Callahan."

He tapped his glass to hers and their eyes remained on each other's as they sipped. "Weren't you about to seduce me before I interrupted it?"

"As a matter of fact . . ." She set her brandy aside. "I was."

LUKE STOOD BESIDE Max's chair, looking out of the French doors, wondering what the man saw through the glass. Was it the buildings of the Quarter, the flower-strewn balcony across Chartres, the pieces of gray sky that promised rain? Or was it something else, some long-ago memory of place and time?

Since his relapse, Max's mind had sunk deeper into whatever world it inhabited. He rarely spoke at all now, though he sometimes wept silently. His body was sinking as well, fading away pound by precious pound.

The doctors spoke of plaques and tangles, those primary structural changes found in the brains of Alzheimer patients. Abnormal forms of proteins—tau proteins, B-amyloid, substance P. They meant nothing to Luke, and he'd thought plaques and tangles had sounded like some sort of complex magic trick.

He knew Roxanne had been in to say good-bye and was now down the hall with Nate, overseeing his packing for their week in D.C. Now that he had this moment alone with Max, he didn't know what to do with it.

"I wish you were coming with us." Luke continued to look out the glass. It was so difficult to look at Max, at that blank expression, at the clawed fingers that worked and worked and worked as if manipulating coins. "I'd feel a lot better if I could have gone over the whole plan with you. I think you'd like the act. Drama, emotion, flair. It has it all. I've gone over every detail." Hearing the echo of his mentor's voice in his head, Luke allowed himself a smile. "I know, I know, calculate the odds, then prepare for surprises. I'm going to pay that bastard back for the five years he took from me, Max, from all of us. And I'm going to get you the stone. I'm going to put it right into your hands. If there's any magic in it, you'll find it."

Luke didn't expect a response, but made himself crouch down. Made himself look into the eyes that had once commanded him to come inside a sideshow tent, demanded he take a chance, take a risk. They were as dark as ever, but the power in them was gone.

"I want you to know I'm going to take care of Roxanne and Nate. And Lily and Mouse and LeClerc. Rox would get her back up if she heard me say that; she's been doing a good job of taking care of everything. But she's not going to have to do it alone anymore. Nate calls me Dad. I didn't know that could mean so much." Gently, he covered the gnarled, restless hands with his own. "Dad. I never called you that. But you're my father." Luke leaned forward and kissed the papery cheek. "I love you, Dad."

There was no response. Luke rose and walked out to find his own son.

Max continued to stare through the glass, to stare and stare, even when a tear slipped out of his eye and ran slowly down the cheek that Luke had kissed.

JAKE TAPPED ANOTHER sequence into his portable computer and let out a crow of delight. "What'd I tell you? What'd I tell you, Mouse? There's always a back door."

"You're in? You're really in?" Filled with admiration, Mouse leaned over Jake's stooped shoulder. "Holy cow."

"The Bank of fucking England." He sniggered, linking his fingers and stretching his hands out to crack his knuckles. "Betcha Charles and Di have an account. Man, oh man, all those pretty pounds sterling."

"Wow." Mouse read the celebrity magazines faithfully, and the Princess of Wales was a favorite. "Can you see how much they have, Jake? You oughta transfer some from his into hers. I don't think he's nice enough to her."

"Sure. Why not?" Jake's fingers poised over the keys, stopping when Alice gently cleared her throat.

"I thought you promised Luke you wouldn't use the computers to poke into anyone's business." She didn't look up, only continued to knit serenely on the sofa at the other end of the suite.

"Well, yeah." Jake's fingers itched. "I'm just practicing is all." He rolled his eyes at Mouse. "Ah, showing Mouse some of the tricks this baby can do since we adjusted her."

"That's very nice. Mouse, I don't think Diana would appreciate your invading her privacy this way."

"You don't?" He glanced over at his wife, who only lifted her head and smiled. "No, I guess not." Defeated, he let out a windy sigh. "We're supposed to be checking the Swiss account," he reminded Jake.

"All right, all right." The keyboard clattered, the modem hummed. "But it just makes me sick, I gotta say. My stomach, I tell you, it feels like I ate some bad whitefish. He wants ten thousand more transferred into that creep's account. I tried to tell him, didn't I try to tell him that I could sneak the money out of some crooked CEO's account instead of bleeding his? But no, oh no. Luke wants to pay for the whole sting. That man is stubborn. *Stubborn.*"

"It's a matter of pride," Alice murmured.

"It's a matter of ten fucking thousand." Jake winced and sent her a quick glance. "Excuse my French. It's just that we're not making a dime on this. Not a dime! Don't you think we ought to clear something—cover our overhead, realize a reasonable profit?"

"We're getting satisfaction," Mouse stated and made his wife's heart swell with pride. "That's better than money."

"Satisfaction won't buy you any Italian shoes," Jake grumbled, but accepted that he was outnumbered. Besides, he could always access another account later.

Alice gathered her knitting and rose. It was barely ten, but she was outrageously tired. "I think I'll leave you two to your toys and go on to bed."

Mouse bent to kiss her, stroking a hand down her pale hair. It never failed to amaze him that someone so tiny, so pretty could belong to him. "You want me to order up some tea, or anything?"

"No." What a sweet man he was, she mused. And how thick-headed. She'd all but dangled her knitting under his nose. Deciding it was worth one more shot, she took the bootie she'd completed out of her basket. "I think I'll try to finish the other one of these tonight. It's a nice color, don't you think? Such a pale, pretty green."

"It's real nice." He smiled and ducked his head to kiss her again. "Nate sure likes finger puppets."

"It's not a puppet." As angry as she had ever been with him, Alice set her teeth. "It's a bootie, damn it." With that she swept into the adjoining bedroom and shut the door.

"Alice never swears," Mouse said half to himself. "Never. Maybe I should go see . . . " The revelation hit like a bare-knuckled punch to the jaw. "A bootie."

"A bootie?" Jake's face cracked with a grin. "Well, ain't that some shit? Congratulations, Mouse old man." He jumped up to thump his friend on the back. "Looks like there's a bun in the oven."

Mouse went pale, turned a color similar to the famous bootie, then paled again. "Oh boy." It was the best he could manage as he staggered toward the bedroom. By the time he got the door open and closed again, his palms were dripping sweat.

Alice stood with her back to him, calmly belting her robe. "So, the light dawns," she muttered and walked to the dresser, began to brush her hair.

"Alice." Mouse swallowed so hard his throat clicked. "Are you . . . are we . . . "

It wasn't in her nature to stay angry for long. She loved him too much to try. Her lips curved as she met his eyes in the mirror. "Yes."

"For sure?"

"For absolutely sure. Two home pregnancy tests and an obstetrician don't lie. We're expecting, Mouse." Her voice broke as she dropped her gaze to her hands. "It's okay, isn't it?"

He couldn't answer. His throat was too full of his heart. Instead he crossed to her in three jerky steps. Gently, very gently he wrapped his arms around her, spreading his big hand over her still flat belly.

It was much better than words.

ACROSS THE DISTRICT LINE in the lush suburbs of Maryland, Sam Wyatt sat at his antique rosewood desk with a snifter of Napoleon brandy. His wife was upstairs in their big Chippendale bed, nursing one of her infamous migraines.

Justine hardly needed the excuse of a headache, he thought as he swirled and sipped the dark amber liquor. He'd long ago lost interest in making love to an icy stick who disguised herself as a woman in designer clothes.

There were other ways to find sexual release, if one was cautious, and paid enough. He didn't keep a mistress. Mistresses had a habit of growing disenchanted and greedy. Sam had no intention of living with the backlash of a tell-all book after he was in the White House.

And he would be living in the White House, he thought. In the dawn of the twenty-first century, he would be sitting in the Oval Office, sleeping in Lincoln's bed. It was inevitable.

His senatorial campaign was proceeding brilliantly. Every new poll showed him further and further in the lead. It would take a miracle for his opponent to close the gap, and Sam had never believed in miracles.

In any case, he had an ace named Luke Callahan up his sleeve.

When he chose to play that ace, a week before the election, Gunner would be crushed.

There were only weeks left until that moment of truth, which meant many long days and nights ahead. He'd kissed babies, cut ribbons, roused the common man with speeches glinting with promises, wooed the corporate structure with his stance on private enterprise, charmed women with his easy smiles and lanky body.

Sam considered his rise in political power and prestige a stupendously structured long con.

As he told Luke, he'd deliver on some of the promises, for the con was far from over. He would continue to woo and charm and glad-hand. His image as a self-made man striving to achieve the American dream would hold him in good stead. And his hand-picked staff of advisers would keep him apprised of the proper foreign and domestic policies.

He had only one policy, and that was power.

He had everything he wanted—until he wanted more.

He thought of the stone locked away in his safe. If he had believed in magic he might have considered how so much had fallen into place for him after he'd acquired it. But for Sam, it was simply another victory over an old enemy.

It was true enough that once it had been in his possession the pace of his success had increased. Sam attributed that to luck, timing and his own personal and political skill.

He'd learned a lot from the down-home and popular senator from Tennessee. He'd sucked up knowledge greedily while playing the man-behind-the-man with the flair of an accomplished thespian—until the opportunity to become *the* man had presented itself.

No one knew that Sam had watched Bushfield die. He had grieved publicly, delivering a moving, tear-choked eulogy, comforting the widow like a son, taking charge of the loose strings of the senator's duties as the devoted heir.

And he had stood and watched as the senator had gasped and

choked, as his face had burned to purple, as he'd flopped like a landed trout on the floor of his private office. Sam had held the little enameled box containing the nitroglycerin tablets in his hand, saying nothing as his mentor had reached out, his eyes bulging with pain, glazed with confusion.

Only when he'd been sure it was too late had Sam knelt and slipped one of the tablets under the dead man's tongue. He'd made a frantic call to 911, and when the paramedics arrived, they were moved by the urgent way Sam had been performing CPR.

So he had killed Bushfield and had garnered several staunch backers in the medical community.

It hadn't been as thrilling as putting a bullet in Cobb's heart, Sam thought now. But even the passive act of murder had brought its own kind of rush.

Leaning back, he plotted the next round, a spider content to spin his web and wait for the unwary fly.

The arrogance of Callahan's return to the Nouvelle troupe continued to intrigue him. Did the fool actually believe that five years would suffice? Or that money would pay for the insubordination of returning to the stage without permission? Sam hoped so, he dearly hoped so. He hadn't struck out yet because it amused him to lull Luke into complacency. Let him put on his show, Sam mused. Let him try to seduce Roxanne's heart away a second time. Let him try to be a father to his son. Sam enjoyed the idea of the man falling into the bosom of his family, temporarily picking up his career and his life. It would be only sweeter to snatch it all away again.

And he would, Sam thought. Yes, he would.

He'd kept close track of the Nouvelles. He was forced to admit an admiration for Roxanne's style, her flair for larceny. There were carefully documented accounts of her activities in a ledger locked in his safe. They had cost him, but his wife's inheritance allowed for such indulgences.

The time was coming when he would use them. The payment

for Luke taking a step into the spotlight without consent would be a high one. And all the Nouvelles would pay for it. And if, as Sam imagined, they believed they could pull off one more heist for old times' sake, they would play directly into his hands.

Because he could wait, he could watch, and he could arrange for the authorities to scoop up all of the Nouvelles after their next job.

That was a very sweet alternative.

He wondered if they would tamper with the auction. It seemed to him that sort of heist held the glamour which appealed to them. He might even let them get away with it. Briefly, very briefly. Then he would snap the jaws of the trap shut, and watch them bleed.

Oh yes, Sam thought, chuckling to himself as he leaned back. It was just that kind of clear thinking that was going to make him an excellent commander-in-chief.

Chapter Thirty-three

SAM ARRANGED FOR TICKETS TO THE NOUVELLES' MUCH-touted Kennedy Center performance. Front row center. Justine sat beside him, draped in silk and sapphires and smiles—the devoted wife and partner.

No one would have guessed they'd come to detest each other.

As the magic unfolded, Sam applauded enthusiastically. He threw back his head and laughed, leaned forward with eyes wide and shook his head in disbelief. His reactions, caught often by the panning television cameras, were as carefully staged as the evening of illusion.

Beneath it, the old jealousy ate at him. Luke was once again the center of attention, the shining star, the holder of power.

Sam hated him for it, as blindly and unreasonably as he'd hated Luke at first sight. He detested and envied the ease with which Luke drew the audience in, the obvious sexual spark between him and Roxanne, the smoothness with which he could take what could not be and make it so.

But he was the first to rise to his feet when the applause rolled out over the finale. He brought his hands together to join the thunder, and he smiled.

Roxanne looked down at him as she took her bows. Though she lowered her lashes, the venom shot through them. Their gazes held, and for her, for just an instant, they were completely alone. The rage heaved up, volatile as lava, so that she took a step forward, a step toward him, stopping only when Luke's hand linked firmly with hers.

"Just smile, babe." He spoke clearly under the cover of applause and gave her fingers a quick squeeze. "Just keep on smiling."

She did, until at last they walked off the stage together. "I didn't know it would be so hard." Her body trembled from the effort of suppressing the urge to attack. "Seeing him sitting there, looking so pompous and prosperous. I wanted to jump offstage and claw at him."

"You did fine." He rubbed the small of her back, steering her through the wings toward her dressing room. "Phase one, Roxy, and on to the next."

She nodded, then paused with her hand on the knob of her door. "We steal things, Luke. I understand most people wouldn't find that acceptable. But still, what we take are things, easily replaced. He stole time. And love, and trust. None of those can be replaced." She looked back at him over her shoulder, her eyes glinting not with tears or even regret, but with purpose. "Let's get the son of a bitch."

He grinned and patted her butt. Jake was right, he mused. She was a hell of a woman. "Change. We've got work to do."

THEY ATTENDED THE POST-PERFORMANCE reception, clinking glasses with Washington dignitaries. Luke bided his time, then slipped away from Roxanne. This was a part he had to play alone. As he'd expected, it took Sam only moments to seek him out.

"That was quite a show."

Luke took a champagne flute from a passing tray, letting his fingers shake ever so slightly. "I'm glad you enjoyed it."

"Oh, I did. And I admire your nerve, performing without checking with me first."

"I didn't think—It's been five years." Luke scanned the crowd with nervous eyes, lowered his voice. As if in plea, he clamped a hand over Sam's wrist. "For God's sake, what harm did it do?"

Delighted to have his quarry on the ropes, Sam considered, sipping champagne. "That's yet to be tallied. Tell me, Callahan, what do you think of young Nathaniel?"

This time Luke didn't have to fake the tremor in his hand. It was pure rage. "You know about Nate?"

"I know everything there is to know about the Nouvelles. I thought I made that clear." Absently, he set his empty glass on a tray. "Tell me, have you finished the project I assigned you?"

"Except for some finishing touches." Luke tugged at his tie. "I explained to you every time I checked in that to handle a job like this, to make sure it all holds up to any investigation takes time."

"Time I've been generous with," Sam reminded him, and added a hearty clasp on Luke's shoulder. "And time that's rapidly running out."

"You gave me a deadline. I'll meet it." He glanced around the room again. "I know what's depending on it."

"I hope you do." He held up a hand, warding off Luke's answer. "Two days, Callahan. Bring everything to me in two days, and I might just forget the impertinence you took tonight. Enjoy your evening," he added as he walked away. "Since it's one of the few you have left with your family."

"You were right, pal." Jake, natty in his waiter's uniform, shifted his tray. "He's slime."

"Just don't screw it up," Luke said under his breath. Quick as a flash, he dropped Sam's monogrammed gold cuff link into Jake's plastic-lined pocket.

"Hey, trust me."

"And stop grinning, for Christ's sake. You're a servant."

"So, I'm a happy servant." But Jake did his best to look properly solemn as he strolled away.

AN HOUR LATER, Jake handed Luke a plastic bag containing the cuff link and a single sandy blond hair.

"Mind how you use them, sport. Don't want it to look too obvious."

"Hell, let's be obvious." There was a grinding in his gut as he held the bag up to study the elegant example of men's jewelry. It was discreet, button-shaped, with the SW swirled fluidly into the gold. If all went well, Luke mused, this little trinket would send Sam Wyatt to hell.

"Have you checked the equipment?" he asked Jake.

"Checked, rechecked. We're online. Watch this." He picked up a device no bigger than his palm. "Mouse," he whispered. "You read?"

There was a moment's pause, then Mouse's voice boomed out of the transmitter. "Right here, Jake. Clear as a bell."

With a grin, Jake offered the transmitter to Luke. "Better'n *Star Trek*, huh?"

The grinding eased to a pleasant, excited flutter. "I hate to admit it, Finestein, but you're good. We've got fifteen minutes, so keep your butt in gear."

"My butt's always in gear." He grinned and swiveled his skinny hips. "This one's going to be fabulous, Luke. Fab-*u*-lous."

"Don't count your chickens before they cackle," Luke murmured, quoting Max. He checked his watch. "Roxanne's waiting. Let's move out."

"Saddle up. Wagons ho! Get the lead out." Jake chuckled to himself as they headed for the door.

"Amateur," Luke muttered, but found himself grinning. It was going to be a hell of a night.

*

496

THE HAMPSTEAD GALLERY was a three-story, neo-Gothic building tucked behind graceful oaks. On this crisp fall night so near Halloween, the leaves fluttered burnt gold in a breeze that cackled with coming winter, and wisps of ragged fog danced over the concrete and asphalt. Above, the moon was sliced neatly in half, its outline so sharp and keen, it seemed that some passing god might have taken his ax to cleave it. Without clouds to hamper it, the moonglow showered down, white and sweet, to silver the trees. But the leaves clung yet to the branches, and provided sheltering shadows.

It was all a matter of timing.

The gallery fronted on Wisconsin Avenue. Washington was not a city that boogied with nightlife. Politics ruled, and politics preferred a patina of discretion—particularly in an election year. At one A.M. the traffic was light and sporadic. Most of the bars were closed.

There was an underbelly of nocturnal activity, the crack houses, the corner drug deals, the hookers who worked the stroll on Fourteenth and those who were addicted to bartering for those temporary pleasures. Nightly murders were as common in this cradle of democracy as campaign promises.

But here in this little corner of the city, all was quiet.

Luke stood in the shadows behind the building, under the grinning gargoyles and lofty pilasters. "This better work, Mouse."

The transmitter around his neck picked up every breath. "It'll work." Mouse's voice was quiet and clear through the mini-speaker. "It's got a range of a hundred feet."

"It better work," Luke said again. He held what looked like a crossbow in his hands.

It was—or had been—just that before Mouse had modified it. It was now a gas-propelled grappling hook. Luke's finger hovered over the trigger while he thought of Roxanne, already curled up inside the third-floor storeroom. He hit the release then watched with boyish pleasure as the five-clawed hook shot up trailing rope. The tiny engine hummed under his hands, vibrating like a cat.

He heard the clink as the spiked metal hit the roof. He switched off the engine before gently, slowly pulling the rope toward him. It went taut when the spikes dug into the weathered brick of the ledge.

Luke tested it, tugging hard, then reached up high enough to swing his legs free of the ground.

"She'll hold. Nice work, Mouse."

"Thanks."

"Okay, Finestein, you go first."

"Me?" Jake's voice piped out in a squeak. His eyes rolled white in a face he'd rubbed liberally with blacking. He looked, pathetically, like a second-rate banjo player in a minstrel show. "Why me?"

"Because if I'm not behind you, poking you in the ass, you won't make it up."

"I'll fall," Jake claimed, stalling.

"Well, try not to scream if you do. You'll rouse the guards."

"All heart. I always said you're all heart."

"Up." Luke held the rope out with one hand and jerked his thumb skyward.

Though his feet were still on the ground, Jake clutched the rope like a drowning man. He squeezed his eyes shut and rose to his toes.

"I'll puke."

"Then I'll have to kill you."

"I hate this part." One last gulp and Jake was shimmying up like a monkey on a vine. "I really, really hate this part."

"Keep going. The faster you climb, the quicker you're on top."

"Hate it," Jake continued to mutter and climbed with his eyes stubbornly shut.

Luke waited until Jake had reached the second story before he began his own ascent. Jake froze like an icicle in a blizzard. "The rope." His voice was a keening whisper. "Luke, the rope's moving."

"Of course it's moving, you jerk. It's not a staircase. Keep going."

Luke bullied Jake up another twelve feet. "Grab hold of the ledge, haul yourself over."

"Can't." Jake was praying in the Hebrew he'd learned for his bar mitzvah. "Can't let go of the rope."

"Shit for brains." But this wasn't something unexpected. "Put your foot on my shoulder. There, come on. Feel it?"

"That you?"

"No, it's Batman, asshole."

"I don't want to be Robin anymore. Okay?" Jake put enough weight on Luke's shoulder to make Luke wince.

"Fine. Just get your balance. Keep your weight centered on me and take hold of the ledge. If you don't," Luke continued in the same, calm, unhurried tone, "I'm going to start swinging the rope. Know what it feels like to be hanging three stories up on a rope that keeps swinging so that you bash your face into the bricks?"

"I'm doing it. I'm doing it." With his eyes still shut, Jake uncurled frozen fingers from the rope. His hand scraped brick twice before he got a grip. Indulging in another of those muffled screams, he rolled himself over and landed with a thud.

"Graceful as a cat." Luke swung soundlessly over. "We're up, Mouse." He checked his watch, noting that Roxanne had another ninety seconds before leaving her hiding place. "Do it."

INSIDE THE STORAGE CLOSET that smelled of Mr. Clean and Murphy's oil soap, Roxanne checked the luminous dial of her watch. Rising, working out the kinks that came from sitting for over two hours, she counted down the seconds.

She held her breath as she eased the door open, stepped into the corridor. The darkness here was shades paler than it had been inside. There was a light at the end of the corridor that sent out a pool of pee-yellow to aid the guards on their rounds.

She walked toward it, counting.

Five, four, three, two, one. . . . Yes. A small sigh of satisfaction escaped as the light flickered, died.

Mouse had come through. Moving fast now, Roxanne raced in the dark, past the now blind security cameras toward the surveillance room.

"GODDAMMIT!" THE GUARD WHO'D been beating the hell out of his partner at gin swore in the dark and snatched his flashlight out of his belt. "Fucking generator should—ah." He sighed with relief at the electrical hum. The lights flickered back on, the monitors blinked back to life, computers buzzed on. "Better check," he said, but his partner was already dialing the phone.

Lily picked up on the second ring. "Washington Gas and Light, good evening."

"This is the Hampstead Gallery, we've lost power."

"I'm sorry, sir. We have reports of a line down. A crew is being dispatched."

"Line down." The guard broke the connection and shrugged. "Assholes probably won't have it fixed before morning. Fucking electric company, bleeds you dry."

"Generator's handling it." Both turned to survey the monitors. "Figure I'll make my sweep now."

"Right." The guard plopped down in front of the bank of monitors to pour coffee from his thermos. "Watch out for any big, bad burglars."

"Just keep your eyes open, McNulty."

The monitors continued to run their sequences, flipping every few seconds from display to display, shadowy corridor to shadowy corridor. It was enough, to McNulty's thinking, to bore a hole in your head so your brains drained out. He spotted his partner, working the third floor, and flipped him the bird.

It eased the boredom a little.

He started to hum, thought about trying to stack the deck for the next hand of gin. Something on monitor six caught his eye. He blinked, snorted at his own imagination, then made small, strangled sounds in his throat.

It was a woman. But it wasn't. A pale, beautiful woman in a flowing white dress with long silver hair. She faded in and out on the screen. And he could see—Jesus, he could see the paintings right through her. She smiled at him, smiled and held out a beckoning hand.

"Carson." McNulty fumbled with his two-way, but all he got in response to his call was a mechanical buzz. "Carson, you son of a bitch, come in."

She was still there, swaying inches from the floor. He saw his partner as well, starting his sweep of the second floor.

"Carson, goddammit!"

In disgust, he shoved the two-way back in his belt pouch. His mouth was dry, his heart hammering, but he knew it would be his ass if he didn't investigate.

ROXANNE SHUT OFF the projector and the hologram of Alice winked off. Once her equipment was back in her bag of tricks, she raced toward the surveillance room. The minutes were ticking away.

Her blood was cool, her hands rock steady as she went to work. She ejected the tape from camera four, replaced it with her own. Following Jake's instructions, she reprogrammed the computer. The camera was now inoperable, but the monitor would continue to show the required sequence. The only difference was, the guards would be watching a doctored tape. It took precious moments to redo camera six and erase the hologram. Even with Jake's expertise there had been no foolproof solution to the time lapse. Those damning thirty seconds where Alice's image had appeared could be fudged somewhat by turning back all the cameras and resetting them. Once the burglary was discovered, and the tapes were examined carefully, the lapse would show.

By then, if all went well, it wouldn't be their problem.

"SHE SHOULD BE FINISHED." Luke watched the final second tick away then nodded to Jake. "Jam it."

"My pleasure." Secure now that he had something solid under his feet, Jake withdrew what appeared to be a complex remote control—one of those daunting pieces of home equipment that operated TV, VCR, stereo. He could have adapted it for just that purpose.

On closer look it might have been mistaken for a pocket calculator. Jake's fingers played along the tiny keyboard. Somewhere in the distance a dog began to howl.

"High-pitched frequency," Jake explained. "Going to drive any mutt within a half mile nutso. The security's garbage for fifteen minutes—seventeen at the outside. That's all this baby will last."

"It's enough. Stay up here."

"You bet." He gave Luke a happy salute. "Break a leg, pal."

With a dashing smile, Luke slipped over the side. His feet had no more than touched the window ledge when the pane shot up.

"Christ, what's more romantic than a man swinging in a window on a rope?" Roxanne stepped back to give Luke room to land.

"I'll show you when we get back to the hotel." He stole a moment to kiss her thoroughly. He could feel the excitement drumming, from him to her, from her to him. It had been a long time since they'd worked in the dark together. "Any hitches?"

"Not a one."

"Then let's rock and roll."

"I'M TELLING YOU, I saw someone," McNulty insisted.

"Yeah, yeah." Carson gestured toward the bank of monitors. "A floating woman—a *transparent* floating woman. I guess that's why she didn't set off any alarms. Where is she now, McNulty?"

"She was there, damn it."

"Waving to you, right? Well, let's see." Carson tapped a finger on his chin. "Maybe she walked through a wall somewhere. That could be why I didn't see her when I made my sweep. That could be why you didn't see her when you left your post to go ghost-busting, *McNutty*."

"Play back the tape." Seized with inspiration, McNulty punched in rewind on tape six himself. "Prepare to eat your words."

McNulty reran and played back the tape twice, and was going for a third when his partner stopped him.

"You need a vacation. Try St. Elizabeth's. I hear it's real quiet there."

"I saw—"

"I'll tell you what I see. I see an asshole. If the asshole wants to report a floating babe, he's on his own." Carson sat down and dealt himself a hand of solitaire.

Determined, McNulty planted himself in front of the monitors. A tic began to jerk under his left eye as he stared, waiting for the illusion to reappear.

LUKE SLIPPED HIS PRIZED burglar's tools out of his pocket. With the rest of the security conquered, the lock on the display case was a joke. And the laugh would be on Sam.

He chose a pick. His fingers were already itching as he bent to the lock. Abruptly, he straightened, turned to Roxanne and offered the tool.

"Here. You do it. Ladies first."

She started to take the pick, then drew back her hand. "No, no, you go ahead. It's your gig."

"Are you sure?"

"Positive." Then, touching the tip of her tongue to her top lip,

503

she leaned toward him. "Besides," she murmured, voice smoky, "watching you work gets me hot."

"Oh yeah?"

She chuckled, gave him a kiss. "Christ, men are so easy. Lift the lock, Callahan."

She stood behind him while he worked, one hand resting lightly on his shoulder. But she wasn't watching the delicate way he probed and jiggled. Her eyes were on the jewels beyond the glass, glittering brilliantly against the draped blue velvet.

"Oh my. My, oh my, they do shine." She felt the tug, the pull, the unabashed arousal. "I love those pretty stones. All that color, all that flash. Those rubies there. Did you know they've nearly mined all the rubies there are—at least that we know about. That's why they're worth more carat to carat than diamonds."

"Fascinating, Rox." The lock gave. Carefully, silently, Luke slid the glass doors open.

"Oh." Roxanne drew in a deep breath. "Now you can almost smell them. Hot, sweet. Summer candy. Can't we keep—"

"No." He took her backpack from her.

"Just one, Luke. Just that one ruby necklace. We could pop the rocks. I could keep them in a bag and just look at them now and again."

"No," he repeated. "Now get to work. You're wasting time."

"Oh, well. It was worth a shot."

They filled her bag, piece by glittery piece. She was a pro, but she was also a woman, and a connoisseur of gems. If her fingers lingered to caress an emerald here, a sapphire there, she was only human.

"I always figured tiaras were for beauty queens from Texas with two first names," she murmured, but she sighed as she slipped the sparkling circlet in the pack. "Time?"

"Seven minutes, on the outside."

"Good." She took out the Polaroid she'd shot of the display that evening. Working with it, they arranged the faux jewels in their proper place.

"They look good," Luke decided. "Perfect."

"They should, they cost enough."

"I love it when you're greedy. Now, for my favorite part." Taking the Baggie and a pair of tweezers from his pocket, Luke delicately removed the hair he'd picked from the shoulder of Sam's tux. After he'd placed it at the rear on a glass shelf, he poured the cuff link into his palm.

"Pretty fancy duds for a heist," Roxanne commented.

"Let him explain it." Luke wedged it in the thin space between the wall of the case and the bottom shelf, allowing only the faintest glint of gold to show. "Yeah, let him explain it," he said again. "Let's go."

Hands linked, they made the dash from display to window. Roxanne climbed up, swung her legs out, then shot him a smoldering look over her shoulder. "Nice working with you again, Callahan."

ROXANNE JAMMED A LOOSE PIN back in her hair. The French twist went with her subtly elegant gray suit in raw silk. She'd put the look together, adding discreet diamond studs, a jeweled lapel pin in the shape of an elongated five-pointed star and black Italian pumps. She considered it suitable for an afternoon at the auction.

Beside her, Lily bubbled over with excitement in a snug hot-pink dress and purple bolero jacket. "I just love stuff like this. All these snooty people with their little numbered cards on a stick. I wish we were really going to buy something."

"They'll be auctioning artwork as well." Roxanne took out her compact, ostensibly to powder her nose. She angled the mirror back, searching for Luke in the rear of the room. "You bid on whatever you like."

"I have such bad taste."

"No, you have your taste. And it's perfect." Trying not to be concerned that she couldn't spot Luke, Roxanne snapped the compact closed. "There's no reason we can't have fun while we're here. As long as we get the job done."

"I've got my part cold." Lily crossed her legs and drew some admiring glances from the men down their line of seats.

There was a lot of murmuring going on as people continued to file in and take their chairs. At the front of the high-ceilinged room stood the auctioneer's pedestal, a long, linen-draped display table and two uniformed guards. Armed guards. Along the side sat a Louis XIV desk with a telephone, a computer and stacks of ledgers and notepads. Phone-in bids were encouraged.

Roxanne paged through the thick, glossy catalogue, and like others around her, made notations, circling and checking off items.

"Oh, just look at this lamp!" Lily's enthusiasm was as genuine as the stones in Roxanne's ears, and only made the pretense all the more believable. Several heads turned at her exclamation. "Wouldn't it look perfect in the front parlor?"

Roxanne studied the photo of an Art Nouveau monstrosity and smiled. Only Lily. "Absolutely."

The auctioneer, a short, rotund man who bulged against the gray flannel of his pin-striped suit, took his place.

Curtain, Roxanne thought and sat back, waiting for her cue.

Artwork and antiques took up the opening lots. The bidding was quick if not sprightly, with someone occasionally bold enough to call out his offer rather than lifting the numbered card.

Roxanne began to enjoy the show.

Some shot their cards into the air, others waved them languidly as if the effort of bidding several thousand bored them beyond measure. Some grunted, some barked, some tapped a finger at the air. Adept at interpreting the signals, the auctioneer moved smoothly from lot to lot.

"Oh, look!" Lily gave a squeal of delight as an ornately carved highboy, circa 1815, was trundled out between two burly men. "Isn't it beautiful, honey? It'd be just perfect for Mouse and Alice's nursery."

Roxanne was still trying to become accustomed to the idea of Mouse's impending fatherhood. "Ah . . . " The highboy belonged in a castle—or a bordello. But Lily's eyes were shining. "They'll love it," Roxanne stated positively, and hoped to be forgiven.

Lily waved her card in the air before the description was complete, and earned several chuckles.

Indulgent, the auctioneer nodded toward her. "Madam opens the bid for one thousand. Do I hear twelve hundred?"

Lily punctuated each bid with a gasp or a giggle, waving her card like a bayonet. She gripped the arm of the man beside her, squirmed and overbid herself twice. All in all she gained the attention of everyone in attendance.

"Sold, to number eight, for three thousand, one hundred dollars."

"Number eight." Lily turned her card around, squealed when she read the number, then lustily applauded herself. "Oh, that was exciting."

To show her interest, and because the piece caught her eye, Roxanne bid on a Deco sculpture. She found herself flushed with pride when she acquired it for twenty-seven fifty.

"Auction fever," she murmured to Lily, faintly abashed. "It's catching."

"We have to do this more often."

As the afternoon wore on, those interested only in lots already sold drifted out. Others came in. The first lot of jewelry was displayed, a collar of sapphires, citrine and emeralds, accented with full-cut diamonds. Beneath the raw silk jacket, Roxanne's heart began to thud.

"Oh, isn't it elegant?" Lily said in a stage whisper. "Isn't it dreamy?" ·

"Hmm. The sapphires are indigo." Roxanne gave a little shrug. "Too dark for my taste." She knew they were glass, with a little cobalt oxide added to the strass.

She watched the lots come and go, diamond bracelets that were no more than glittery zircons, rubies that were more glass with gold salts fused with the strass, agate masquerading as lapis lazuli.

She hated to admit it, and would never do so to Luke, but the money had been well spent. Each new piece brought a rustle of excitement from the crowd, and the bidding soared.

She bid on several lots, always careful to gauge the enthusiasm of those who bid against her. Lily commiserated with her each time she dropped out.

And at last, the ring. Roxanne folded out the catalogue where she had darkly circled the photograph. She allowed herself a strangled gasp as the description began and murmured to Lily.

"From Bogotá," she said, excitement vibrating in her voice. "Grass green, absolutely perfect in color and transparency. Twelve and a half carats, mounted à jour."

"It matches your eyes, honey."

Roxanne laughed, and leaned forward in her seat like a runner on the mark.

The bidding started at fifty thousand, which separated the mice from the men. After the third offer, Roxanne raised her card and joined in.

When the bidding reached seventy thousand, she spotted him. He wasn't sitting where he'd told her to look for him, which was probably deliberate, to keep her on her guard. He looked artistic and distinguished and nothing at all like Luke. Long brown hair was slicked back into a queue, and a matching moustache adorned his upper lip. He wore rounded spectacles with gold rims and a tailored suit of royal blue set off by a fuchsia shirt.

He bid laconically and steadily, by lifting a finger and ticking it back and forth like a metronome. He didn't glance back even when Lily muffled gasps behind her hands or bounced enthusiastically on her seat. Roxanne pushed, perhaps further than was wise, topping his bid long after it was only the two of them. Caught up in the game, in the challenge, she shot up her card when the offer struck one hundred and twenty thousand.

It was the absolute silence that reigned after her bid that brought her back to reality. That, and the viselike pressure of Lily's fingers over hers.

"Oh, my." Roxanne pressed her hand to her mouth, grateful for once that her coloring brought on blushes. "I lost my head."

"One hundred and twenty-five thousand," Luke stated in a cool, French voice. When the gavel came down he rose. Turning to Roxanne, he bowed smoothly from the waist. "My pardon, *mademoiselle*, for disappointing such a beautiful woman." He strode to the Louis XIV desk, took off his spectacles and began to polish them with a snowy square of white linen. "I will inspect."

"Monsieur Fordener, the auction is still in progress."

"*Oui*, but I always inspect what I acquire, *n'est-ce pas?* The ring, if you please."

As Luke stood behind the desk, holding the ring up to the light, the auctioneer cleared his throat and began the next lot.

"One moment!" Luke's voice snapped like a whip. His eyes behind the clear lenses were cold blue ice. "This is a fraud. This is . . . an insult!"

"Monsieur." The auctioneer tugged at the knot of his tie as people shifted in their seats and muttered. "The Clideburg collection is one of the finest in the world. I'm sure you—"

"I am sure." Luke nodded stiffly. In his hand he held a jeweler's loupe. "This . . . " He held up the ring, pausing dramatically. "Is glass. *Voilà*." He strode onto the stage, sticking the ring under the auctioneer's nose. "Look, look. See for yourself," he demanded, holding out the loupe. "Bubbles, streaks, banding."

"But—but—"

"And this." With a flourish, Luke pulled out an aluminum pencil. Those attending who knew gems recognized it as a method for distinguishing genuine stones from imitations. Luke drew the point of the pencil over the stone, then held it up, showing the shining, silvery line.

"I will have you arrested. I will have you in prison before the day is out. Do you think you can cheat Fordener?"

"No. No, monsieur. I don't understand."

"Fordener understands." He tossed up his head, gesturing to the room. "*Nous sommes trompés!* We are duped!"

In the resulting chaos, Roxanne took the risk of catching Luke's eye. Take your bow, she thought. The curtain was about to go up on the last act.

Chapter Thirty-four

"THE PAPERS ARE FULL OF IT." ROXANNE NIBBLED ON A croissant as she scanned the headlines. "It's the biggest thing to happen in D.C. since Ollie North."

"Bigger," Luke claimed, pouring more coffee. "People are used to subterfuge and lies in the government. This is a jewel heist. A magnificent one, if I say so myself, and that equals romance, magic. And greed."

"The authorities are baffled," Roxanne read and grinned up at Luke. "They're testing every stone, called in one of the top mineralogists. Of course, all the standard tests were used when the gallery purchased the collection. Polariscopes, dichroscopes, the methylene iodide and benzene bath, roentgen X ray."

"Show off."

"Well, I did spend four years studying." Setting the paper aside, she stretched her arms high. She was still in her robe, and naked under it. It felt wonderful to be lazy, to have this little island of calm before the next bout of excitement.

Over the rim of his cup, Luke watched the robe shift, gape and reveal a tantalizing glimpse of ivory skin. "Why don't we finish breakfast, in bed?"

With her arms still extended, Roxanne smiled. "That sounds—"

"Mama!" Like a rocket out of his adjoining room, Nate shot across the carpet. "I did it. I tied my shoe." Balancing one hand on the table, he plopped his sneakered foot on her lap. "By myself."

"Incredible. The boy's a prodigy." She studied the loose bow that was already becoming undone. "This is certainly a red-letter day."

"Let me see that." Luke nipped Nate at the waist and hauled him onto his knee. "Okay, come clean. Who helped you?"

"Nobody." Eyes wide, Nate stared up into his father's face. While his son was distracted, Luke quickly secured the bow so that it would stay put. "I swear to God."

"I guess you're all grown up then. Want some coffee?"

Nate screwed up his face. "Nah. It tastes yucky."

"Let's see then, what else?" Luke bounced the boy on his knee as he considered. "You know, Rox, it seems to me any kid who can tie his own shoes should be able to take care of a dog."

"Callahan," Roxanne muttered under Nate's enthusiastic cheer. "You'd feed it, wouldn't you, slick?"

"Sure I would." Eyes solemn, glowing with sincerity and good intentions, Nate nodded. "Every single day. And I'd teach him to sit, too. And to shake hands. And . . ." Inspiration struck. "To fetch your slippers, Mama."

"After he'd chewed them, no doubt." It would take a harder woman than she to resist two pairs of laughing blue eyes and two crooked smiles. "I'm not sharing the house with some yappy little purebred."

"We want a big, ugly mutt, don't we, Nate?"

"Yeah. A big, ugly mutt." He wound his arm around Luke's neck and looked imploringly at his mother. This was his cue, and performing was, after all, in his blood. "Daddy says they have lots of poor, homeless puppies at the animal shelter. It's like being in jail."

"Low, Callahan, really low," Roxanne said under her breath. "I suppose you think we should go spring one."

"It's the humanitarian thing to do, Rox. Right, Nate?"

"Right."

"I suppose we could look," she began, but Nate was already hooting and leaping off Luke's lap to catch her in a fierce hug. "You two ganged up on me." Over Nate's head she smiled mistily at Luke. "I suppose I'll have to get used to it."

"I'm going to go tell Alice right now!" Nate streaked away, skidded to a halt. "Thanks, Dad." He grinned over his shoulder. "Thanks a lot."

Luke couldn't do much about the grin splitting his face, but he thought it politic to pretend a sudden interest in his breakfast.

"You're going to spoil him."

He moved his shoulders. "So? You're only four years old once. Besides, it feels good."

She rose to walk over and curl on his lap. "Yes, it does. It feels very good." With a little murmur of pleasure she cuddled against him. "I guess we have to get dressed. There's work to do yet."

"I wish we could spend the day with Nate. Just the three of us."

"There'll be other days. Lots of days when this is all over." She smiled, and with her arms linked around his neck, leaned back. "I'd love to see how Tannenbaum's doing right now."

"He's a veteran." Luke kissed her nose. "We should be getting a call within the hour."

"I just hate missing his performance. It should be a once-in-a-lifetime."

HARVEY TANNENBAUM was indeed a veteran. For more than two-thirds of his sixty-eight years he'd been a successful fence, dealing with only the cream of the crop. To Harvey, Maximillian Nouvelle had been the cream of the cream.

Roxanne's proposition that he come out of his four-year

retirement and play a small but pivotal role in an elaborate con had initially thrown him off balance. Then it had intrigued him.

In the end, Harvey had graciously agreed to participate, and to show his sentiments toward Max and the Nouvelles, had taken the job gratis.

He was even looking forward to it.

Certainly it was a new twist for Harvey. It was the first time in his long life he had voluntarily walked into a police station. Certainly the first time he had ever confessed—without duress—a transgression to the authorities.

Since it was the first, and by all likelihood the last, Harvey was playing it for all he was worth.

"I come here as a concerned citizen," he insisted, staring up at the two plainclothes officers to whom he'd been passed by an over-worked sergeant. His eyes were sunken, red-rimmed and shadowed, thanks to a dusk-to-dawn movie marathon on cable. He looked, in his baggy suit and wide-striped tie, like a desperate man who'd spent a sleepless night in his clothes.

Only the desperation was an illusion.

"You look worn out, Harvey." Sapperstein, the senior detective, took the compassionate route. "Why don't you let us drive you home?"

"Are you listening to me?" Harvey let his indignation rise. "Hell's fire, boys, I come in here—and it ain't something I do lightly—to give you the tip of a lifetime. All you can do is tell me to go on home. Like I was senile or something. I didn't sleep a wink all night worrying if I had the nerve to do this, and all you want to do is pass me off."

Impatient by nature, irritable by circumstance, the second detective, a basset-eyed Italian named Lorenzo, drummed his fingers on his overburdened desk. "Look, Tannenbaum, we're kind of busy around here today. You know how it is when there's a major jewel heist, don't you?"

"Indeed I do." He sighed, remembering the good old days. "We used to know how to keep the fun in our work. Today, these young guys; it's just business. No flair, no creativity. No, you know, magic."

"Sure." Sapperstein summoned up a smile. "You were the best, Harvey."

"Well, you sure as hell never tagged me, did you? Not that I'm admitting anything, mind, but there are some that might say I handled more ice than a trio of Eskimos."

"Those were the days," the second detective said between his teeth. "Now, we'd just love to sit around and go back down memory lane with you, but we've got work to do."

"I come here to help you fellas out." Harvey folded his arms and kept his wide butt planted. "I'm doing my goddamn civic duty. And before I do it, I want immunity."

"Christ," Lorenzo muttered. "Call the D.A. Harvey wants immunity. Let's get the paperwork moving."

"No need to be sarcastic," Harvey muttered. "Could be I shouldn't be dealing with underlings. Maybe I'll just go to the commissioner."

"Yeah, you do that," Lorenzo invited.

"Put a lid on it," Sapperstein advised. "You got something to say, Harvey, spill it. You look tired, we're tired, and we are pressed for time."

"Maybe you're too busy to hear what I know about the art gallery heist then." Harvey started to heave himself up. "I'll just run along. Wouldn't want to hold you up."

Both detectives' ears perked up. Sapperstein kept his persuasive smile in place. He knew it was probable that Harvey was just blowing hot air. After all, word was that he'd been out of business for a couple years, and he could have been feeling a tug of nostalgia.

Then again . . .

"Wait." Sapperstein patted Harvey's shoulder to ease him back down. "You know something about that, do you?"

"I know who did it." Harvey's smile was smug. He waited one

dramatic beat, deciding he owed Roxanne for offering him the job. "Sam Wyatt."

Lorenzo swore and broke a pencil in half. "How come I get the crazies?" he asked a higher power. "Why is it always me?"

"Crazy? Why, you snot-nosed punk. I was passing rocks under cops' noses while you were still pissing your diapers. You can't show more respect than that, I'm out of here."

"Take it easy, Harvey. So you saw senatorial candidate Sam Wyatt steal the Clideburg collection?" This was asked with studied patience by Sapperstein.

"Shit! How could I see him lift them?" Righteous frustration had Harvey tossing up his hands. "What? You figure I stand on street corners and look for thieves? You're not going to hang any accessory bullshit on me. I was home sleeping like a baby when the job went down. And since I wasn't sleeping alone," he added with a wicked grin, "I got me an alibi."

"Then why do you claim that Mr. Wyatt stole the Clideburg collection?"

"Because he told me!" Agitation and excellent projection had Harvey's voice ringing out in the noisy station house. "For Christ's sake, put two and two together, will you? Maybe somebody—just for hypothetical purposes we'll say that somebody was me—used to turn over a few rocks for him now and then."

Lorenzo snorted. "You're trying to tell us that you fenced for Sam Wyatt?"

"I said no such thing." Harvey blustered, turned red. "I said hypothetically. If you think you're going to trick me into incriminating myself, you've got another think coming. I came in here of my own free will, and I'm walking out the same way. I ain't going to jail."

"Take it easy. Want some water? Lorenzo, get us a cup of water here."

"Sure? Why the hell not?" In disgust, Lorenzo stomped off.

"Now, Harvey." In his best cop-as-diplomat voice, Sapperstein continued. "We're here to listen. That's a fact. But if you're going to make up stories like this about a respected member of the government, you're just going to get yourself in trouble. Maybe you don't like the guy's politics, and you're entitled."

"Politics, balls." Harvey let out his own snort of disgust. "I don't give a flaming shit about his politics. But I'm telling you—hypothetically, got it?"

"Sure, I got it."

"Hypothetically, I've known Sam for a long time. Since he was a teenager. Never cared for him personally, but business is business. Right? Anyway, he used to use me pretty regular. Before he got into politics it was mostly small time, but after, he started hitting bigger targets."

"So you've known Sam Wyatt since he was a kid?" Even Sapperstein's patience could be strained. He took the cup Lorenzo brought back and held it out to Harvey. "Look, you're not doing anyone any good this way—"

"I don't like being pressured," Harvey interrupted. "And that's just what the son of a bitch is trying. Look, I'm retired—hypothetically. And if I want to turn down a job, I turn it down."

"Okay, you turned him down." Sapperstein rolled his eyes. "You're not involved. What do you know?"

"I know plenty. I get a call, right? He tells me he's going to hit the gallery, and I tell him good luck, what's it to me? So he wants me to start working on liquidating the rocks. I give it a pass, and he gets nasty. Starts talking about making it rough for me. You know, I had a kid by my second wife, Florence. He's a dentist on Long Island. Well, Wyatt knows about him and says he'll make things tough. While he's threatening me, he's complimenting me. Telling me how I'm the best and he can't trust any second-rate fence with this kind of merchandise. Reminds me how we worked together before, and how this score's going to set us both up for good."

Harvey drank the rest of his water and sighed. "I gotta say, I've been losing some sleep over this. Wyatt had me worried, and I have to admit, he had me interested. A job like this doesn't come along every day. The commission would set me up good. I've been thinking about moving to Jamaica. It's warm there all the time. Half-naked women everywhere you look."

"Stay focused, Harvey," Sapperstein advised. "What did you do about the job?"

"I played along. First I thought I might do it, then I started thinking how much heat was going to blow when it went down. I'm not as young as I used to be, and I don't need the aggravation. So I figured I'd do the right thing—turn him in, you know? There must be like a reward or finder's fee for that haul. I can do a good deed and make a couple bucks out of it."

"So he passed you the stuff?" Lorenzo spread his hands. "Let's see it."

"Give me a break. I met him yesterday, at the zoo. By the ape house."

"Fine," Sapperstein said, cutting his partner off. "Keep going."

"He tells me he'd pulled it off. He was really high about it, bragging, you know? Never smart to get that emotionally involved with a job. He told me how he'd done it, and how he had planted fakes to buy more time. And he told me he wanted them fenced right after the election."

"That's reaching, Harvey."

"Maybe you think so, but I can tell you something else. The guy's not right. Here." Harvey tapped his head.

Sighing, Sapperstein took up a pad. "What cab company did you use to get to the zoo?" He scribbled the information down as Harvey related it. "What time did you get picked up? How'd you get back?" All this could be easily verified. "Just for argument's sake, how did he tell you he pulled it off?"

Harvey's heart swelled, as it would if he had a fat fish on the line, or a sparkling gem in his hand. In concise phrases he described a break-in so similar to the genuine heist that it would fall beautifully into place during the investigation.

"Pretty slick—and high-tech. Holograms, electronic jammers." It could have worked, Sapperstein thought as his cop's blood began to heat.

"He learned something of magic from these performers out of New Orleans. Lived with them awhile, he told me. They're like famous or something now. Anyway, he used to try to do card tricks."

"You know, even if some of this checks out, it's not enough for us to question Sam Wyatt."

"I know the ropes, kid. I got more." With a flourish worthy of a master, he reached inside his shirt pocket and whipped out a paper folded once. As a force of habit, Sapperstein took it by the edges.

Written on it were descriptions of the Clideburg collection.

"He gave that to me, to help me arrange for the fencing. But he made a big mistake. I don't like threats, and by Christ, I'm retired." He wagged his eyebrows. "Hypothetically."

"Don't get cocky." Lorenzo scowled at the paper Sapperstein was slipping into an evidence bag. "I guess you want me to send that to the lab."

"You get enough pieces, Lorenzo, you've just got to start putting them together. Have them check it for prints. Find out if Wyatt's are on file. While you're at it, see if we can come up with a hand-writing sample."

Lorenzo heaved a gusty sigh. "I just heard they lifted a piece from the display at the gallery. Cuff link, gold. Engraved with the initials SW."

Sapperstein's nose all but twitched. "Okay, Harvey, why don't you come over and sit here?" Sapperstein led him away to a bench near the door of the station. "We'll take it from here."

"I get immunity." Harvey clutched Sapperstein's jacket sleeve. "I won't do time for this crap."

"I don't think that's something you have to worry about." With a last pat on the shoulder, the detective walked away. His bland smile vanished when he reached his partner. "I'm going to get all I can on the cuff link. You tell the lab to put a rush on that paper. Bitch later, Lorenzo," he said and there was fire in his eyes. "That old man might just have made our careers."

The old man sat patiently, biding his time. They were wrong, he thought, when they said revenge was sweet. It had a tang. A delicious, lingering tang. And he was enjoying this one for his old pal Max.

"THEN IT'S THE LAST ACT." She gazed out the window as the wind tossed leaves along the curbs. "I wish Daddy could be here for this one." She shook off the mood, made herself smile. "I hope this doesn't delay our return to New Orleans by more than a day or so. I'd hate to miss Halloween at home."

"We'll make it." Lifting her hand, he kissed it. "That's a promise."

SAM'S BAGS WERE PACKED for his trip to Tennessee. He had ten days of campaigning on his schedule, all of which would be spent hand in glove with his staff, and his wife. Justine had already given him trouble over the amount of luggage she claimed to need. She was upstairs, pouting over the ruthless way he'd slashed her four suitcases to two.

She'd get over it, Sam mused. Once she could have Senator and Mrs. Samuel Wyatt printed on her Christmas cards, she'd get over a lot of things.

He was sorry the timing didn't allow him to dole out Luke's punishment immediately. He'd thought he would enjoy stringing out the tension, but it gnawed at him. He wanted to strike quickly, finally.

It should have pleased him that he'd been on target about the Clideburg collection. Sam had no doubt who had engineered the theft. It would be another weight on the scale if he decided to turn his documentation over to the police.

But that would have to wait until Luke had brought him the file on Gunner.

Then he would use these last ten days before the election to secure his place in history.

He ignored the doorbell, leaving that for the servants. His packing was being completed by his valet, but Sam always dealt with the contents of his briefcase personally. His papers, his speeches, the condoms he used religiously in all extramarital affairs, his schedule, pens, notepads, a weighty book on economics. He snapped the locks shut as a maid came to the doorway.

"Mr. Wyatt, the police are here. They'd like to speak with you."

"Police?" He caught the avid interest in the maid's eyes and decided to fire her at the first opportunity. "Show them in."

"Officers." Sam came around the desk to extend his hand to both Sapperstein and Lorenzo. It was a good politician's shake. Firm, dry and confident. "It's always a pleasure to entertain the boys on the force. What can I get you? Coffee?"

"No, thanks." Sapperstein answered for both of them. "We'll try not to take up too much of your time, Mr. Wyatt."

"I'd like to say take all you want, but I'm catching a plane in a couple hours. Hitting the campaign trail." He winked, quick and friendly. "Either of you have friends or relatives in Tennessee?"

"No, sir."

"Well, I had to give it a shot." He gestured toward a chair. "Have a seat, Officer . . . ?"

"Detective Sapperstein, and Detective Lorenzo."

"Detectives." For reasons that baffled him, Sam began to sweat around the collar of his monogrammed shirt. "Why don't you tell me what this is all about?"

"Mr. Wyatt, I have a court order." Sapperstein took it out and paused an extra moment to slip on his reading glasses. "We're authorized to search the premises. Detective Lorenzo and I will head the team that's waiting outside."

"A search warrant?" All of Sam's charm died. "What the hell are you talking about?"

"The Clideburg collection, which was stolen from the Hampstead Gallery on October twenty-third. We have evidence that you're involved in the theft and, by order of Judge Harold J. Lorring, are authorized to conduct a search."

"You're out of your mind." With palms that were suddenly wet, Sam snatched the order from Sapperstein. "This is a fraud. I don't know what game you're playing but . . . " He broke off, sneering. "Callahan sent you. He thought he could rig this whole business to shake me up. Well, he's wrong. You can go back and tell the bastard that he's dead fucking wrong, and I'll bury him for it."

"Mr. Wyatt," Sapperstein continued. "We are authorized to make this search, and will do so with or without your cooperation. We apologize for any inconvenience this causes you."

"Bullshit. Do you think I don't smell a con? You're meat." Triumphant, he jabbed a finger at them. "Both of you. Get out of my house, or I'll call the cops myself."

"You're free to do so, Mr. Wyatt." Sapperstein took the official paper back. "We'll wait."

He wouldn't fall for it. It was a pitiful ploy, Sam told himself as he called through for the office of Judge Harold J. Lorring. By the time he was told a search order had indeed been signed less than thirty minutes before, he was dragging at the knot of his silk tie. He punched the number for his lawyer.

"Windfield, this is Sam Wyatt. I've got a couple of jerks who say they're cops standing in my office with some trumped-up search warrant." He yanked the tie off, threw it. "Yes, that's what I said. Now get your fat ass over here and deal with it." Sam slammed down the receiver. "You don't touch a thing. Not one fucking thing until my lawyer gets here."

Sapperstein nodded. "We've got time." He couldn't help it,

something about Sam set him off. He glanced at his watch and smiled. "But I think you're going to miss that plane."

Before Sam could growl out a response, Justine hurried in. "Sam, what in the world is going on? There are two police cars parked in front of the house."

"Shut up!" He sprang at her like a tiger and shoved her toward the door. "Shut up and get out."

"Mr. Wyatt." The maid was nearly swooning with excitement. "You have guests in the foyer."

"Send them away," he said between his teeth. "Can't you see I'm busy?" He walked to the liquor cabinet and poured two fingers of whiskey. He'd lost his head for a moment, but that was all right. Anyone might react the same way under the circumstances. He downed the whiskey and waited for it to settle.

"Officers." With his poster smile back in place, he turned. "I apologize for losing my temper. It was such a shock. It isn't every day I'm accused of robbery."

"Burglary," Lorenzo corrected, for the hell of it.

"Yes, of course." He'd have the man's badge—if it wasn't a fake. "I do prefer to wait until my lawyer arrives, just to verify the procedure. I assure you, you're free to turn the house upside down. I have nothing to hide."

Voices in the corridor had everyone turning. When Luke shoved through the door past the maid, followed closely by Roxanne, Sam's newly regained composure teetered on the edge.

"What are you doing in my house?"

"You called, you demanded I come." Luke slipped a protective arm around Roxanne. "I don't know what you want, Wyatt, but I don't appreciate the tone of your invitation to visit. I . . . " He trailed off, as if spotting the detectives for the first time. "Who are these people?"

"Cops. Nice to see you." Enjoying himself, Lorenzo grinned.

"What is this about?" Roxanne tossed her head up, a lovely, valiant woman obviously running on nerves.

"I'm sorry," Sapperstein stated, "I'll have to ask you both to leave. This is official."

"I want to know what this is all about. You've done something horrible again, haven't you?" She whirled on Sam. "You won't hurt Luke." She gripped his lapels and shook. "You used me once, but never, never again."

"Darling, please." Luke moved to her. "Don't upset yourself. He isn't worth it. He never was."

"I brought you into my home." She shoved Sam back. Only the presence of witnesses kept him from striking her. "I trusted you and my family trusted you. Isn't it enough that you betrayed us all those years ago? Must you still harbor this cancerous hate for us?"

"Keep your hands off me." He grabbed her by the wrists, twisting. Roxanne's cry of pain had both detectives moving quickly to intervene.

"Take it easy, Wyatt."

"Sweetheart."

That was her cue. In a blind rush of tears, Roxanne stumbled toward Luke and knocked the briefcase from the desk. The locks sprang. An icy glimmer of diamonds spilled out, chased by the fire of rubies.

"Oh." Roxanne pressed her hands to her mouth. "My God, it's the Queen's lace necklace from the Clideburg collection. You." She lifted her arm, pointing an accusing finger. "You stole them. Just like you stole from Madame all those years ago."

"You're crazy. He planted them." Sam looked around wildly, unable to believe his carefully structured world could fall apart so quickly. "The bastard planted them. He set me up." He lunged. Luke braced. Even as Lorenzo moved to intercept, Roxanne shifted her body. It burned her that it would appear she was scrambling out of harm's way. But then, the end justifies everything. Her foot hooked nimbly under Sam's leg and sent him sprawling on the open briefcase.

"You didn't run far enough." Sam sat up, breath heaving. "You won't pull off this little magic trick, Callahan. I've still got you. In the safe." He wiped a hand across the back of his mouth as he rose. His eyes were too wide, his face gray, his lips peeled back in a mockery of a grin. "I have evidence in the safe against this man. He's a thief and a murderer. This woman's a thief as well. They all are. I can prove it. I can prove it." Limping toward the safe, he continued to mutter under his breath.

"Mr. Wyatt." Sapperstein put a restraining hand on his shoulder. "I advise you to wait for your attorney."

"I've waited long enough. I've waited years. You wanted to search, didn't you? Well, search this." He spun the dial on the safe, twisting it back and forward until the last number of the combination. He yanked it open and reached in. Then he stared, goggle-eyed, as a file folder spilled out, scattering garishly colored photographs.

"Interesting snapshots, Mr. Wyatt." Lorenzo scooped up a handful, pursing his lips as he shuffled through them. "You're real photogenic—and agile." He grinned, passing the photos to his partner.

"That's not me." Still staring, Sam wiped his mouth with the back of his hand. "It's Gunner. It's supposed to be Gunner. They're faked. Anyone can see that. I've never been with any of those people. I've never seen them before."

"None of them seem to consider you a stranger," Sapperstein murmured. He'd done a turn in Vice, but never seen anything quite so . . . creative. "You know, looks like these should come with a disclaimer. 'Don't try these tricks at home.' "

"Yeah." Getting into the spirit, Lorenzo tapped one snapshot depicting a particularly lewd and unusual position. "How do you suppose he twisted himself into that move? My wife would love it."

"Never mind." Sapperstein cleared his throat. There was, he remembered belatedly, a lady present. "Mr. Wyatt, if you would sit down until we—"

"They're faked!" Sam shouted. "He did it. He lied and cheated."

Breathing hard, he pointed at Luke. "But he'll pay. All of them will. I've got proof." He was chuckling as he reached into the safe. His nerve cracked completely when he pulled out a diamond tiara.

"It's a trick," he said—blubbered. "A trick." He backed up, staring at the jeweled crown in his hands while a giggle escaped through his terrible grin. "It'll disappear."

Sapperstein nodded to Lorenzo, who removed the tiara. "You have the right to remain silent," he began, slipping on the cuffs while Sapperstein emptied the safe of jewels.

"I'm going to be president." Spittle flew as Sam raged. "Eight more years, I only need eight more years."

"Oh, I think you're going to get more than that," Luke murmured. He snapped his fingers and offered Roxanne the rose that appeared between them. "Alacazam, Rox."

"Yeah." She pressed her face to his chest to hide a mile-wide grin. "But what are we going to do for an encore?"

Chapter Thirty-five

FALL IN NEW ORLEANS WAS WARM AND BRIGHT AND BLISSFULLY dry. The days grew shorter, but night after night the sunsets were a spectacular symphony of color and hue that seared the throat and dazzled the eye.

Max died during one of those brilliant light shows, in his own bed, with a ruby-red sun as his final curtain. His family was with him, and as LeClerc said over one of the innumerable cups of coffee consumed during that night, it was the best way to die.

Roxanne had to be content with that, and with the fact that Luke had placed the philosophers' stone in their father's frail hand so that he slipped from one world to the next holding it.

It wasn't a brilliant gem or a glittery jewel. The stone was a simple gray rock, worn smooth by time and questing fingers. In size, it had fit neatly into the cup of her palm, resting there as it had rested in other palms in other centuries.

If it had held power, she hadn't felt it. She hoped Max had.

They buried it with him on a bright November morning, with a blue sky overhead and a faint breeze rustling in the wild grass that sprang up between the raised tombs of the city he'd loved. There was perfume on the air, and the strains of Chopin stroked from a dozen violins.

Max would have detested black crape and organ music.

Hundreds had crowded into the cemetery, people he'd touched somehow during his life. Young magicians eager to make their marks, old ones whose hands and eyes were failing them even as Max's mind had failed him. Someone released a dozen white doves that fluttered and cooed overhead, giving the illusion of angels come to bear Max's soul away.

Roxanne found the gesture incredibly lovely.

Max's farewell performance, as he would have expected, was a class act.

Over the next few days, Roxanne drifted, never quite able to break free of the drag of grief. Her father had been the single most important influence in her life. While he had been ill, she'd had no choice but to take charge of the family. But as long as he'd been there in body, she'd had the illusion—again illusion—of having him.

She wished she could have shared their latest triumph with him. The headlines still shouted the scandal of Samuel Wyatt, former senatorial candidate, now indicted for grand larceny, among a variety of lesser charges.

They'd found other evidence in his Maryland home. A small device that resembled something between a remote control unit and a calculator, a fine set of burglar's tools in stainless steel polished to a gleam, a glass cutter, a motorized crossbow that propelled a grappling hook, a single gold cuff link, etched with the initials SW, and most damning, a diary, painstakingly detailing thefts committed over a span of fifteen years.

It had taken Jake a month to complete it, forging Sam's hand. But it had been a job well done.

Swiss accounts, in excess of a quarter of a million, had been unearthed. Luke considered it an investment that had already paid off—in spades.

Roxanne had been prepared to feel sympathy for Justine, but was amused when she read that Sam's devoted wife, cleared of all implication, had already filed for divorce and was living in a chalet in the Swiss Alps.

As for Sam, he no longer insisted he wanted to be president. He claimed he was president. The psychiatrists continued their deliberate tests while Sam ran his private government from a padded cell.

It was, Roxanne supposed, a kind of justice.

But that was behind her. The corner it had taken her five years to turn was at her back. A dozen long paths spread out before her, and she simply didn't know which she wanted to take.

"It's getting chilly out here." In the shadowy dusk, Lily crossed the courtyard to where Roxanne sat on the iron bench watching the fountain. "You should have a jacket."

"I'm fine." To show company was welcome, she held up a hand, slipping an arm around Lily's shoulder when the older woman joined her on the bench. "I love this spot. I can't remember a time when I haven't been able to feel better after sitting here."

"Some places are magic." Lily glanced up to the window of the room she'd shared with Max for so many years. "This one's always been magic for me."

They sat in silence for a few minutes, listening to the splash and tinkle of the fountain. The shadows lengthened and became the dark.

"Don't miss him too much, honey." Lily knew she'd put it badly, wished she had Max's flair for words. "He wouldn't want you to hurt for too long."

"I know. I was afraid at first if I let it stop hurting it meant I'd stopped loving him. But I know that's wrong. I was sitting here, remembering the day we all left for D.C." She tilted her head, resting it on Lily's shoulder. "He was in his chair, looking out of the French doors. Just looking out. He wanted to go, Lily. I knew it. I felt it. He needed to go."

She laughed, a low genuine sound Lily hadn't heard in too many days. "But he was stubborn," Roxanne continued. "Leave it to Max to die on Halloween. Like Houdini." Her arm tightened around Lily's shoulders. "I swear he must have planned it. And I was thinking now that if there's a heaven for magicians, he's there, doing pocket tricks with Robert-Houdin, trying to outdo the Herrmanns and conjuring with Harry Kellar. Oh, he'd like that, wouldn't he, Lily?"

"Yes." Damp-eyed but smiling, Lily shifted into a hug. "And he'd fight tooth and nail for top billing."

"Appearing tonight and for eternity, Maximillian Nouvelle, Conjurer Extraordinaire." Laughing again, she kissed both of Lily's cheeks. "I'm not hurting anymore. I'll always miss him, but it doesn't hurt."

"Then I'm going to say something else." She cupped Roxanne's face in her hands. "Make your own. You've always been good at that, Roxy, always bold and strong and smart. Don't stop now."

"I don't know what you mean."

Lily heard a door open and looked over her shoulder to see Luke under the pool of light by the kitchen door. "Make your own," Lily repeated and rose. "I'm going inside to put my two cents' worth in on those wallpaper samples Alice is mooning over. I swear that girl'll pick nothing but pastels and flowers if someone doesn't give her a goose."

"You're just the one to do it."

"You come in if you get cold," Lily ordered.

"I will."

Lily passed Luke on the courtyard. "And if you can't keep her warm," she said under her breath, "I wash my hands of you."

Luke sat on the bench, drew Roxanne close and kissed her until her bones went limp.

With her head tilted back on his arm she opened her eyes again. "What was that for?"

"Just following orders. But this one's for me." He kissed her again, lingering over it. With a satisfied sigh, he sat back, stretched out his long legs and crossed them at the ankles. "Nice night, huh?"

"Mmm. Moon's coming up. How many times did Nate con you into reading *Green Eggs and Ham*?"

"Enough so I can recite it by memory. Who the hell wants to eat green eggs anyway? It's disgusting."

"You miss the not so subtle metaphor, Callahan. It's about not judging things by their appearance, and testing new ground."

"Really? Funny, I've been thinking about testing new ground." But he wanted to be sure it was the time. The first silver fingers of moonlight slipped out of the sky as he turned his head to study her. "How are you, Rox?"

"I'm good." She felt his eyes on her, that old, familiar intensity. "I'm good, Luke," she repeated and smiled at him. "I know I couldn't keep him forever, no matter how much magic I tucked up my sleeve. It helps, knowing you loved him as much as I did. And maybe, in some strange way, the five years you were gone gave me the time to concentrate so closely on him when he needed me most. He hung on until you came back, and I could go on without him."

"Fate?"

"Life's a good enough word. Things are changing now." She huddled closer, not because she was cold. Because it felt right. "Mouse and Alice will be moving out before too long. And doesn't it fit neatly now that they're starting their own family you just happen to have a house that's perfect for them up for sale?"

"With a nice third-floor apartment, suitable for a bachelor. Now Jake can drive them crazy."

"You know you love him."

"Love's a strong word, Rox." But he smiled. "What I feel for Jake is more of a mild tolerance punctuated with periods of extreme annoyance."

"Lily's going to work on finding him a wife."

"She hides that sadistic streak so well. At least he's useful backstage." Because he enjoyed it, and it was a handy misdirection,

Luke picked up her hand to toy with her fingers. "You know, Rox, I've been thinking about the act."

She gave a sleepy sigh. "Think it's ready to take on the road?"

"Yeah, it's ready. But I was thinking about something closer to home."

"Such as."

"Such as this building for sale on the south edge of the Quarter. Good size. Needs a lot of work, but it has potential."

"Possibilities? What kind?"

"The magic kind. The Nouvelle Magic Shop, New Orleans. A theater to break in new acts, to amaze the masses. Maybe with a little magic store tucked in it to sell tricks. A first-class operation."

"A business." Intrigued but wary, she eased back so that she could see his face. In it she saw barely restrained excitement. "You want to start a business?"

"Not just a business. A possibility. You and me, partners. We'd perform there, draw some of the big names and give a few new ones a shot. A carnival, Rox, but this one would stay in one place. It could be just as magical."

"You've been giving this a lot of thought. Since when?"

"Since Nate. I want to be able to give him what Max gave me. A base." To give the idea a chance to simmer, he lifted her fingers to his lips, kissing them one by one. "We'd still go on the road. That's what we do. But we wouldn't be traveling nine out of twelve months. He'll be starting school full-time soon."

"I know. I've thought of that. I was planning to cut back once he did. Work around his schedule."

"If we did this, you wouldn't have to cut back, and you'd accomplish the same thing." He saw the interest light in her eyes and dove in for the kill. "There's just one hitch."

"There's always a trap door. What is it?"

"You have to marry me."

She couldn't say she was surprised. It was more like a quick, powerful electric shock. "Excuse me?"

"You're going to have to marry me. That's it."

"That's it?" She would have laughed, but she didn't think she had the strength for it. She did manage to gain her feet. "You're telling me I have to marry you. As in 'I do' and 'till death do us part'?"

"I'd ask you, but I figure you'd waste time weighing the odds. So I'm telling."

Her chin came up. "And I'm telling you—"

"Hold it." He held up a hand, standing so they'd be face to face. "I was going to ask you the night I came back from Sam's with my pockets full of sapphires."

That not only stopped her temper but muddled her head. "You were?"

"I had it pretty well planned. I was going to go for the romantic route. I even had a ring in my pocket. But I had to hock it in Brazil."

"In Brazil. I see."

"What would you have done if I had asked you then?"

"I don't know." That was the pure, sterling truth. "We'd never talked about it. I guess I thought things would keep going the way they were going."

"They didn't."

"No, they didn't." Baffled, she blew out a breath. "I would have thought about it. I would have thought about it hard."

"And if I ask you now you'll do the same thing. So I'm bypassing that. We're getting married or the rest of the deal's off."

"You can't bully me into marriage."

"If bullying doesn't work, I'll seduce you." He ran his hands up and down her arms, an old habit that still thrilled her. "And I'll start by telling you I love you. That you're the only woman I've ever loved. Ever will love." Smooth as silk, he drew her close to let his lips play over hers. "I want to make promises to you, and for you to make them to me. I want more children with you. I want to be here when they grow inside you."

533

"Oh, Luke." If she hadn't known better, she would have sworn she smelled orange blossoms. Marriage, she thought. It was so ordinary, so commonplace. So exciting. "Promise you'll never, ever call me the little woman."

"I'll swear it in blood."

"Okay." She pressed a hand to her mouth, as if shocked the word had escaped. Then she laughed and said it again. "Okay. You're on."

"No pulling back," he warned, lifting her up to spin her in a circle.

"I never welch."

"Then the next time we're onstage, it'll be introducing Callahan, and his beautiful wife, Roxanne Nouvelle."

"Not on your life." She punched his shoulder when he dropped her to the ground.

"All right. Just Callahan and Nouvelle." He arched a brow. "It's alphabetical, Rox."

"Nouvelle and Callahan. I'm the one who taught you your first card trick, remember?"

"You never let me forget. Deal." He shook her hand formally. "Nate's going to have himself two legally married parents and a dog. What more could a kid want?"

"It's so conventional, it's scary." She combed a hand through her hair. "And about that dog—"

"Jake's out walking him. Don't worry. Mike hasn't chewed up anything worth talking about for an hour. And don't bother with that hard-ass line, Roxy. I saw you feeding him chocolate chip cookies this morning."

"It was a plan. I figured if I fed him until he got fat, he wouldn't be able to waddle upstairs and pee on the bedroom rug."

"You scratched his ears, made kissy noises and let him lick your face."

"It was a moment of insanity. But I'm feeling much better now."

"Good, because there's just one more thing."

534

"Just one more."

"Yeah. We're giving up stealing."

"We're—" She really had no choice but to sit down. "Giving up?"

"Cold turkey." He sat beside her. "I've given this a lot of thought, too. We're parents now, and I'd like to make another baby as soon as possible. I don't think you should be doing second-story work with a baby on board."

"But—it's what we do."

"It's what we did," he corrected. "And we were the best. Let's go out on top, Roxy. With Max, it was the end of an era. We've got to start our own. And Christ, what do we do if Nate does grow up to be a cop?" He was kissing her fingers again, and laughing. "He might arrest us. What kind of guilt is that to lay on a kid, sending up his own parents?"

"You're being ridiculous. Children go through stages."

"What did you want to be when you were four?"

"A magician," she said on a sigh. "But to give it up, Callahan. Couldn't we just . . . cut back?"

"It's cleaner this way, Rox." He patted her hand. "You know it is."

"We'll only steal from really rich men with red hair."

"Bite the bullet, babe."

Letting out a groan she sat back. "Married, starting a business and going straight all at once. I don't know, Callahan. I may explode."

"We'll take it one day at a time."

She knew he had her. The image of Nate, all three feet of him, wearing a badge and tearfully locking her behind bars was too much. "The next thing you'll be telling me we should start doing kids' birthday parties." When he made no response, she sat bolt upright. "Oh God, Luke."

"It's not that bad. It's just . . . well, the other day when I took Nate to nursery school, I sort of got into this conversation with his teacher. I guess I promised we'd do this little act for the Christmas party."

There was silence for a full minute, then she began to laugh. She laughed until she had to hold her sides to keep her ribs intact. He was perfect, she realized. Absolutely perfect. And absolutely hers.

"I love you." She surprised him by throwing her arms around his neck and kissing him hard and long. "I love who you turned out to be."

"Same goes. Want to neck in the moonlight?"

"You bet I do." She pressed a finger to his lips before they met hers. "One warning, Callahan. If you go out and buy a station wagon, I'm turning you into a frog."

He kissed her finger, then her mouth, deciding he'd wait for a more opportune moment to mention the Buick he'd put a deposit on that morning.

As Max would have said, timing was everything.

NORA ROBERTS

For the latest news, exclusive extracts
and unmissable competitions, visit

f/NoraRobertsJDRobb
www.fallintothestory.com